The Edge of Time

By Rudy Scarfalloto

ISBN: 978-0-9826832-3-1
Library of Congress Control Number: 2010911648

Cover Design by Donna Overall

Serenity Press

Other Books by Rudy Scarfalloto

The Dance of Opposites
Cultivating Inner Harmony

CONTENTS

PART ONE
The Story of Smiley

–1–

Jason Mazarosky's red pickup truck sped along a narrow side street, splashing through a succession of puddles. His face contorted into a scowl. He hated having to run off and leave Katie alone at Mama Tang's Restaurant.

He temporarily forgot why he was in such a hurry, but quickly remembered, as he saw the traffic jam up ahead at the intersection of Forrest Park Road. "Oh, no," he said, craning his neck. He didn't have time to sit through that. Thinking quickly, he made a hard left turn into a driveway. "Yes," he said, smiling at his brilliance. He would kill two birds with one stone: bypass the traffic jam, so he could get to the Johnson house in time, and finally get his truck to the mechanic.

He glanced at his watch. Racing through the big vacant parking lot, he aimed his vehicle between two piles of used tires that stood against the back of the one-story building that housed Forrest Park Auto Service. He stopped quickly and smoothly about two feet from the brick wall. Jumping out, he slammed the door and jogged through the unpaved alleyway at the side of the building.

When he reached the front of the alleyway, his left hand grabbed a vertical pipe attached to the wall, swinging himself around the corner of the building and into the entrance of the spacious garage. No one in sight… "Hey, Raffi," he yelled, his voice reverberating off the high ceiling.

A pudgy little man with curly graying black hair stuck his head out from behind the raised hood of a car. He was startled by the loud voice, but smiled when he saw Jason's freckled face and shaggy brown hair.

"Hello, young man," said Raffi in a heavy Mid-Eastern accent, as he stepped away from the car. "You finally bring truck?"

"Yeah. Here, catch," he said, tossing his keys to the mechanic. "The truck's out back."

Raffi managed to catch the keys with both hands, even though he was already holding a ratchet in his left hand and a flashlight in his right.

"I have to run," said Jason, turning away. "I'll be working at the Johnson house, just down the street."

As he stepped off the curb and wove his way around the idling cars and trucks that filled all four lanes of Forrest Park Road, he felt another wave of dizziness. As usual, he ignored it.

On the other side of the street, he started to turn right to walk on the sidewalk. But, he stopped abruptly when he saw a familiar face just beyond the four-foot row of juniper hedges along the perimeter of Forrest Park.

"HEY, BRO!" Jason yelled. "WHAT ARE YOU DOING HERE?"

"Just hanging out," said the bearded young monk, with smile. He was sitting with his shoes off under a large oak tree.

"I MEAN, WHAT ARE YOU DOING *IN TOWN?*"

"I have a—" Brother Jerry's voice was drowned out by a honking car.

"I'LL CATCH YOU LATER," said Jason, walking on, "I'M IN A HURRY."
"Okay," said the monk with a wave and a smile.

Not too far from Brother Jerry, Jason passed by a bench occupied by a man in a business suit reading a newspaper. The man looked up to see who was making all the noise and then resumed reading. Jason often sat on that particular bench while his truck was being serviced across the street, because the bench was very secluded. It had the juniper hedges in front, a crescent-shaped row of rhododendrons behind, and was shaded by a large ginkgo tree.

When Jason came to the front gate of the huge two-story house just beyond the southeast corner of the park, he turned left and jogged on the unpaved driveway, kicking up dust.

Another wave of dizziness, stronger than the last. Why this dizziness, all of a sudden? It all started right after that weird dream, two days ago. He tried to remember the dream, but immediately put it out of his mind when he reached the house at the top of the driveway. Sticking his head into the window of the house, he looked around. "Hey, Sam!" he yelled.

A tall, heavy-set young man with a round baby-face and curly brown hair emerged from the kitchen carrying a sledgehammer in his massive right hand. "Yeah?" he asked, lifting his goggles.

"Is Rusty Hayes here yet?"

"No. Didn't you say you were meeting Katie for lunch?" "Yeah. I just left her at Mama Tang's Restaurant and ran over here when I remembered I had to talk to Rusty about the upstairs plumbing."

"You did what?" said Sam, putting his hands on his hips. "You left your fiancée, just so you could talk to that dodo?"

"You're right. I feel bad about it, but I couldn't call here because I forgot my cell phone, and I couldn't take a chance of Rusty Hayes leaving, because we absolutely have to start on the plumbing very soon, or we are in deep doodoo. And I couldn't just leave it up to you to talk to him because the last time you two met, you almost got into a fight—"

"Yeah, whatever. When is Hayes supposed to be here?"

"12:50."

Sam glanced at his watch. "Well, it's one o'clock right now, which means that he probably won't get here for another ten minutes or so. That's his style."

Jason ran his fingers though his hair, ignoring another wave of dizziness. He figured he was just fighting off a head cold, or maybe he was getting an inner ear infection. He sighed, wiping the beads of sweat from his forehead. "Say, what is it with you two guys, anyway?"

"Very simple. He's an uncivilized cretin."

"You two have been at it since middle school. Up until last week, it looked like things were easing up. And then, Boom! What's going on?"

"Ask him. He started it."

"Are you guys at least going to behave during the softball tournaments tomorrow?"

"That's up to him," said Sam, as he walked away. "Now leave me alone. I want to finish in the kitchen before I have to go to class."

Jason walked away from the window. He looked up at the slightly inclined roof, where two men had just dropped off the last of the two-by-fours.

Taking a deep breath, he sat with an audible grunt on a red milk crate, which buckled slightly under his weight. Another wave of dizziness. Strongest one yet. He rubbed his temples, and decided that if the dizziness didn't go away by tomorrow, he would see a doctor.

Reaching down into a nearby cardboard box, he pulled out a jumbo candy bar and a can of soda. The candy bar was gone in four bites. He then disposed of the soda in about ten seconds without stopping to breathe. Wiping his mouth on his sleeve, he came forth with a long and satisfying belch. Reaching into the cardboard box again, he pulled out a set of blueprints.

He was looking up to see if Rusty was in sight, when a huge wave of dizziness almost knocked him off the crate. "Whoa!" he said, extending his arms to the sides for balance.

Dropping the blueprints on the ground, he grabbed his temples. Numerous gold specks danced around in his field of vision. He felt an intense throbbing pressure between his eyebrows, followed by a whirling sensation inside his head.

His arms dropped straight down and his eyelids slowly descended. He did not hear the two-by-four as it tumbled off the roof. When the beam struck him on the head, he was already starting to topple over. He barely felt the blow on the head, though it did cause him to briefly see stars, specifically four stars, configured into the shape of a three-sided pyramid. And then, he passed out.

Immediately, he started dreaming that he was in a theater. The screen showed a close up of a dark-skinned young boy, with a round oriental face, looking very troubled. The screen became more panoramic and showed the boy standing on a large dome-shaped rock, wedged against the shore of a vast violet ocean.

–2–

Shoupang held his ground, as the strong wind pushed him back, almost knocking him off the rock. The salty spray from the surf stung his almond eyes, causing them to tear. He gazed all around, trying to see beyond the horizon. His six-year-old mind did not ask what he was searching for.

Without thinking, he opened his mouth yet again, projecting his voice as a long continuous "Ahhhhh" that seemed to disappear in the distance. And then, he just stood silently, waiting, without asking what he was waiting for.

But this time it was different. His call seemed to return from the horizon as a huge violet wave. It carried four luminous stars, configured into the shape of a three-sided pyramid. As the wave approached Shoupang, it slowed down and eventually stopped and settled down in front of the rock. The pyramid remained, hovering over its own inverted reflection in the water.

Up close, each star turned out to be a globe of iridescent light, bigger than Shoupang. He looked up at the sphere at the top of the pyramid. It glowed with a bright, silver light. The other three were red, green, and blue. Pulses of light traveled from one sphere to another.

The pyramid started giving off a beautiful soothing tone that embraced Shoupang, producing a happy feeling all over his body. He smiled. The glowing silver sphere on top of the pyramid was gentle and kind. The green sphere radiated peace. The red sphere made him feel safe. The blue sphere was playful and funny. Shoupang laughed.

When Shoupang awoke, the smile was still on his face. And he still felt the happy sensation in his body. Opening his eyes, he lifted his head from the pillow, looking for his mother and father. The room was still very dark. And then, he remembered. He wasn't living with his mother and father anymore. He was living with Uncle Macunda and Aunt Seva.

The happy feeling quickly faded. Recalling the scary men, the swords, the fire, and the blood, he almost screamed, just as he had done on previous mornings. But this time, he remembered his dream, still hearing the musical tone given off by the four stars. He relaxed. Closing his eyes, he went back to sleep, smiling.

–3–

Rusty Hayes sighed as he turned the steering wheel and eased his plumber's van into the driveway of the Johnson house, after the long traffic jam on Forrest Park Road. The first sight that caught his eye was the two-by-four striking Jason Mazarosky on top of the head.

"Jesus Christ," Rusty yelled, watching Jason fall to the ground.

Reaching the top of the driveway, he jammed on the brakes and jumped out.

"Jason," he said, kneeling down, "You okay?"

No response.

The commotion brought Sam running out of the front door. He kneeled next to Rusty and removed his goggles. "What happened?" he asked in a panic.

"The two-by-four fell from the roof and hit him on the head."

"Jesus Christ!" Sam gasped.

For a moment they just stared at their unconscious friend. Finally, Sam placed his fingertips gently on Jason's scalp. "No blood."

Rusty shook his head. "It hit him pretty hard. Look at his color. He doesn't look good at all."

Sam stood up quickly. "Where's your phone?"

"I'll get it," said Rusty bolting toward his truck.

"You call 911," said Sam, running into the house, "I'll call Max at the lumber yard."

–4–

The dream image of the young dark-skinned boy faded. Jason Mazarosky was now vaguely aware of being flat on his back on cold concrete. He had no idea where he was and what he had been doing prior to that dream. He tried to move his body, but it did not want to respond. Very strange. But for some reason, he was calm about the whole thing.

Suddenly, he was in the theater again. The screen now showed a dirt road meandering along a field of funny violet flowers, growing under a bright blue sky. An adolescent boy appeared on the road. He had dark skin and a round oriental face.

–5–

"Master, Master!" Shoupang yelled, kicking up dust as he ran along the dirt road, next to his uncle's field of growing indigo.

The old man chuckled as he kept a brisk pace; his blue robe waved behind him.

The boy stopped running when one of his sandals slipped off his foot. "Vishnu's nightmare," he muttered.

Spearing the sandal with his toes, he tried to put it on one-handed while walking quickly, but his arm got tangled in his robe, and his long jet-black hair fell over his eyes. He stopped and used both hands.

Reaching the old man, he turned and started walking backward and sideways. "Greetings, Venerable Sir," he said with a bow, bringing his palms together in front of his chest.

The old man stopped walking and returned the gesture. "Greetings, young friend. You have grown since the last time I saw you. How old are you now?"

"I am nearly thirteen and a half years," Shoupang said proudly.

"Time passes quickly," the old man chuckled, as he resumed walking.

"Heaven is smiling upon me today," Shoupang said rapidly. "I was helping the potters in one of my uncle's workshops and I went outside to draw water from the well at the very moment you were passing the north gate." He stopped talking to catch his breath. "Where are you going, Master?"

"To visit some friends," he said casually.

"Where are your friends?"

"In the mountains."

"The mountains! That is a long way from here. You have no provisions." The boy looked at the jagged peaks, blue and hazy in the distance. "You need food and warm clothing," he said in a loud voice, scaring a flock of birds that took flight from the indigo plants next to the road. "You should have a cart and a yak for such a journey. I will ask Uncle Macunda to provide them for you. He respects you."

"I am amply prepared," the old man smiled. "Thank you for your kind offer."

"Have you a guide to help you find your way through the foothills?"

"No."

"None of your students are accompanying you?"

"No."

"Are you meeting a caravan further along the road?"

"No."

"Surely, you are not traveling alone!"

"I am."

"But that is dangerous! Are you not afraid of wild animals and bandits?"

"I will be safe. Thank you for your concern."

Shoupang gazed at the mountain peaks. Remembering the vision he had that morning upon arising, he felt confident that the Master would not turn him down again. "Please let me join the hermitage," he said, "I wish to be your student."

"You are truly persistent," the old man smiled.

Shoupang was about to tell the Master about his vision, but hesitated when he remembered that the Master wasn't interested in talking about astral phenomenon. The boy chided himself for even considering trying to impress the Master in that manner. "I wish to purify myself," he said.

"You have no need of purification."

"I wish to learn the lessons that will set my spirit free."

"You do not need me for that. You are doing that right now."

"But I want to learn faster. I want to know truth and inner peace through solitude and austerity."

The old man looked at the early morning sun straight ahead, his shoulder-length graying hair playing in the wind. "You really think you would be happy in such a life?"

"Yes."

"You are certain? Even after having lived in richness and elegance?"

"Yes, I am certain!"

"What of the girl to whom you are betrothed? In a few years you will be of age to marry her."

Shoupang stopped walking and stood at attention, as the old man walked past him. Cali's face filled his mind. Granted, she was pretty. And, truthfully, he did feel pleasant stirrings in her presence. But she would be a mere distraction for him. Such pleasures are fleeting and can vanish without warning.

Taking a few quick steps to catch up, the boy resumed walking backward and sideways. "I... I will renounce her too. I will renounce all worldly pleasures. I wish to live a life of renunciation. It is my calling."

"You are certain it is your calling?"

"Yes, most assuredly so," he proclaimed, as another flock of birds took flight. "Please let me join your hermitage. I will earn my keep; that is a certainty. Not only that, my uncle said he will make a generous donation to your hermitage."

The old man waved his walking stick gently at the youngster. "Run along back to your uncle's shop."

Shoupang felt momentarily shaken. But the vision that was bursting forth in his mind made him impervious to rejection. "But, I wish to dedicate my life to higher consciousness, Master."

"There are other monastic orders, you know. Don't you think you might derive more benefit by choosing a retreat that is farther away from your home?"

"I suppose so," Shoupang shrugged. "But you are different, Master. Uncle Macunda says that in his travels, he has met a number of holy men, and they are all stuffy and gloomy. But you have a merry heart. You sing happily and carry a smile that shines like the sun. You bring laughter to those around you."

"I see," the old man smiled. "You have chosen me because I am a buffoon."

"Oh, no, Master! That is not the reason!"

Shoupang was becoming exasperated. The Master was so wise! Why was he being so difficult? Perhaps, he is testing me, he thought. "I wish to learn from *you,*" he said, "because you are as close to Godliness as anyone can be. Godliness is the key to happiness."

"If happiness is what you want, that is easily obtainable right now. Just smile."

"Yes, but…" He scrunched up his face, struggling to describe his aspirations without talking about his vision. "I wish to experience a certain kind of happiness. You, Master, have conquered the pains and illusory pleasures of earthly life. You have not fallen into the trap of trying to find security in the fragile things of the world that are here on this day and gone the next day." He paused to catch his breath, and then resumed talking rapidly. "I wish to know the truth that you know, so I can bring relief to a suffering world. I wish to be free and wise like you."

"Thank you for your kind words. You may go home now."

"But, Master, I wish to stay in your presence. I will give all that I have to you. Uncle Macunda says I can – if you find me worthy. In four years, I will receive my father's inheritance, which will have grown because my uncle has been investing it wisely for me." He took another quick breath and resumed talking. "I will give it all to you because I wish to support your great work."

"That is most generous of you. But you would do well to contemplate your decision a while longer. The way of the merchant has much to offer an energetic young man like you. You will travel to marvelous places and experience the richness of life."

"But surely there is more to life than working and earning money."

The old man glanced at the boy. "Quite right. You and your future wife have much mutual affection waiting to be fully realized. And, most assuredly, there are many happy children waiting to be born through Cali and you. Does that not tempt you?"

Again, Shoupang felt those pleasant stirrings in his body, as he thought of Cali. "A bit… perhaps. But that is merely a passing pleasure of the earth. It is the way of the flesh which cannot bring lasting happiness and can be taken away instantly."

"Passing pleasures cannot pass if you push them away."

"Huh?"

"You would do well to slow yourself down and think upon your decision. Contemplate why you wish to follow the way of the monk. Is there perhaps something about your life that troubles you?" The old man looked into the boy's eyes. "Has something hurt you?"

The Master's comment seemed totally irrelevant. "No," he shrugged. "I am simply moved by a higher calling. Please, Master. I truly wish to serve you." Pausing for a moment, he sighed. He couldn't stand it any longer. He simply had to tell the Master about his vision. "Last night I dreamed that you are about to do a secret work of great importance, and that you will need help."

"Really?"

"Yes. I dreamed that you were a great and noble teacher in your previous lifetime and you let yourself be killed to diffuse the forces of evil. And now you have returned quietly and discreetly to do more good work. But you may have to allow yourself to be sacrificed again, unless someone can help you. That someone is me! In my dream we were constructing a magnificent grid that extended to the four corners of the world; a grid of peace, justice and happiness."

The old man smiled. "Your imagination is as boundless as your enthusiasm."

"It is not imagination, Master. It is desti—" Shoupang slapped his cheeks with both hands. "Great mother and father of Heaven!"

"Is something wrong?" "No, not in the least! I have just remembered that in my dream I was with you and three other great masters on a mountaintop— which is where you are going right now! This is truly destiny! My dream was a most auspicious omen. Please let me join you and your noble friends on the sacred mountain. I would gladly die in your service."

"You are too young to be thinking of death."

"But death would have no meaning if you teach me your ways! I simply know that as a fact. I wish to free myself from the suffering of birth and death. I am now convinced more than ever that I am destined to learn such wisdom from you and your three exalted Master friends."

The old man continued his steady brisk pace. Shoupang scampered alongside, swiping his forehead with the back of his hand to remove the beads of perspiration.

"Now that I have thought upon this," said the old man, "there *is* one small matter you might help me with."

"Joyful day! Tell me what it is, Master. Surely, I will do it with great speed."

"No, I cannot tell you what it is yet." He gave the boy a quick sideways glance. "It is a secret," he said in a hushed voice.

"Oh," the boy nodded, earnestly.

"Go home now and join the potters in their honest work. I will reveal the task to you when the time comes."

"When will that time come to pass, Master?"

The old man chuckled. "Your persistence and candor are worthy of praise. However, since you hold the belief that death has no meaning, then you must also believe that time has no meaning, as well. Do you agree?"

"Yes, most certainly."

"So, the period of waiting is of no consequence."

"Uh…"

"You may go home now. I will call you at the appropriate time."

Shoupang stopped and watched as the old man walked on.

"Master," he said, tilting his head to one side, "are you saying this just to be rid of me?"

The old man stopped and turned. "Yes," he said. Then he resumed walking. "Now, stop pestering me."

Shoupang stood motionless as the old man disappeared behind a bend in the road.

The boy's lips trembled a bit. Glaring at the bend in the road, he clenched his teeth and made a fist with both hands. As he turned to go home, he heard the old man call out. "Be at peace, young friend. I truly will call you at the appropriate time. Until then, you can prepare yourself by smiling frequently!"

"Joyful day! Joyful day!" Shoupang sang, as he ran down the road, kicking up dust.

–6–

The image of the adolescent boy on the screen faded away. Jason Mazarosky was vaguely aware that something was out of the ordinary. Although everything was black, he could hear muffled voices and street sounds. He had a memory of having worked on the Johnson house, but wasn't sure if that was a few minutes ago or last year. Such an unusual kink in his perception of time should have been cause for alarm, but for some reason, he felt pretty okay about it.

Gradually, all outside noises faded away and were replaced by dreamy images flashing through his mind. He saw himself during his first visit to Mama Tang's Restaurant on the day of his eighteenth birthday, along with his sister, Marcy, and his new girlfriend, Katie. Jason didn't know what to do with the chopsticks, so he stuck them behind his upper lip and said, "Hey look, I'm a walrus."

He saw himself at eight years of age, receiving his first holy communion. The mass was barely over when he ran to the bathroom and threw up the communion wafer and the rest of his breakfast, after which he went to Father Henry, who had conducted the mass. "Father Henry," he cried hysterically, "I just threw up Jesus Christ! I'm going to hell!"

He saw himself shortly after birth. His mom was informing him that she and Dad would not be around very long, but Aunt Maureen and Uncle Max would take over, so he would be just fine.

Now Jason Mazarosky saw a movie screen again. This time it showed a man and woman with very dark skin, darker than the boy from the previous dream. They seemed to be relaxing by small lake.

–7–

Macunda stretched his arms as he sat on the blanket, gazing at the still waters of the oval lake he had recently excavated. He was a burly man with a massive jaw, his jet-black hair tied back in a ponytail. He wore a plain cream-colored robe, as did his wife, who slept next to him.

Picking up a flat stone, Macunda skimmed it across the sun-drenched surface of the lake. Yawning, he untied the string that held his hair in a ponytail and then shook his head side to side. He glanced down at his wife. Her right hand rested lightly on his knee. Her left hand was stretched out on the blanket; fingertips barely touching the bamboo tray containing a ceramic teapot, two cups, and a wooden bowl filled with dates and fresh figs. Not far from the blanket, a swing made of hemp rope and a wooden seat moved ever so slightly in the breeze, as it hung down from a branch of the broad carob tree that shaded them from the hot sun.

Taking a deep breath, he gazed at the forest of fruit trees and date palms all around the lake. Directly across the lake, a gravel road between the trees lead to the tall iron gate, beyond which were gently rolling hills of cultivated land and more fruit trees. An elephant pulled a plow in the distance, partially blocking the hazy mountain peaks that poked through the horizon.

"Life is good," Macunda thought. "Why would I want to jeopardize it by doing anything that would antagonize the Brahmin? They are all blood-sucking vermin that produce nothing but poverty and war, but I certainly will not improve things by stirring up trouble."

Macunda nodded thoughtfully, drinking in the serenity of his surroundings. The leaves of the carob tree overhead fluttered in the breeze, producing a barely audible melody that invited him to curl up against his wife and doze off. The only other sound came from the soft chirping of songbirds scattered among the fruit trees.

As he felt his eyelids lowering, the silence was broken by a loud adolescent voice. "Uncle Macunda, may I speak?"

Macunda eyes snapped open. Turning his head, he smiled at the intense and deeply serious round face of his nephew. "Of course, Shoupang. Here, sit by us."

The boy sat on the grass next to the blanket.

"I am puzzled," said the boy. "Before the Master left for the mountains, he said he would call me at the appropriate time so I can assist him and his Master friends with their great work. But that was nearly four months ago. Surely he will not make me wait any longer." The boy folded his arms. "Perhaps he has forgotten."

"That is an extreme improbability," said the boy's uncle as he waved away a bee that was getting close to his wife's face. "You must understand, to a being such as the Master, a few months and a few thousand years are virtually the same."

As Shoupang looked out over the water, he was reminded of his most recent vision: four stars configured into a three-sided pyramid, suspended over the surface of a lake. In his vision, the water was very calm and he could see the inverted reflection of the pyramid, directly below the real one. He was sure that it a powerful omen, though he had no idea what it symbolized.

"This morning, I had another vision," said Shoupang. "I think it is a sign from the Master, but I am not sure. He once told me that he saw Cali and me happily married. Yet, I feel driven by a higher calling."

Standing up, the boy picked a carob pod from a low-hanging branch. "I wish to be a hermit."

The woman opened her eyes. "I agree with the venerable Master," she said.

"How so, Aunt Seva?"

She sat up and stretched her arms, accentuating her substantial bosom. "Perhaps your marriage to Cali is your higher calling."

Shoupang sat on the wooden seat of the swing. He stared at the lake as he bit off a small chunk of the carob pod, chewing on it thoughtfully. "But, I think this incarnation—" He stopped when his cousin, who was not quite five years of age, ran toward them, crying.

"No fair, no fair!" she yelled.

She stopped on the blanket between Shoupang and her parents.

"Why this intrusion, Gandhari?" asked her mother, folding her arms. "Your father and I are speaking with Shoupang."

"No fair, no fair!" She said, jumping on her father's lap. "If Meta can dance in the parade, why can't I?"

"You are yet too young," said her mother.

"No, I'm not, no I'm not!"

"Yes, you are," said the child's mother, in a stern but even voice. "And throwing a tantrum will not cause you to mature any faster; it will simply earn you a spanking, if you persist. Consider yourself warned. Be patient. Next year you will be old enough to dance in the harvest parade."

"I don't want to dance anymore," said the child, in a more subdued tone. "Not ever," she cried, throwing her forehead on her father's broad chest. "And I don't ever want to go to the parade—not ever ever!"

Shoupang looked at the lake, as his Uncle and Aunt gave their attention to their daughter.

"Gandhari," said her mother, "One year is not that long."

The child remained silent, her head buried in her father's chest.

Macunda shrugged. "To a child of four," he smiled, "one year and a thousand years are virtually the same." He placed a hand gently on her temple. "Gandhari?"

"What?" she whimpered.

"Since you no longer wish to dance, I gather you will not be dancing for us when the merchants and landowners meet here in several days? I had told them what a wonderful dancer my daughter is. They will think me a liar."

The little girl suddenly composed herself and looked at her father's face. "I will dance that one time. And then, not ever ever."

"As you say my daughter. Uh… you are certain you will not be going to the parade?"

"Yes! I will stay home with Grandmother Giri and keep her company, so she will not be alone."

"Well then, your mother and I will not have the honor of having you ride with us in the procession of elephants."

"Ride on the elephant?" said the little girl, suddenly excited.

Seva gave her husband a surprised look.

"Is that a promise?" asked Gandhari.

"It is a promise," smiled her father.

Gandhari sprang to her feet. "I am happy, I am happy!" She ran toward the house. "I will go tell Meta!"

Seva shook her head slowly at her husband. "You really intend to let her ride with us?"

"Of course. There is no law against it."

She shook her head. "You indulge Gandhari too much."

"I treat her as I do our other daughter."

"Meta is quiet and well-behaved. She does not demand attention like our little hurricane, Gandhari. She must learn that she cannot always get what she desires."

"That time will come," said Macunda, "we do not need to rush it."

"But if we do not discipline her now, how will she learn?"

"Seva, my wife," said Macunda, "you know how I feel about this."

"Yes, yes," she said rolling her eyes, "no need to remind me. 'Childhood is a time of receiving. A child who is allowed to receive abundantly will embrace the responsibilities and sacrifices of adulthood.'"

"I'm glad you agree."

"I did not say I agree. I still think you are too indulgent with Gandhari."

"I am not concerned," Macunda chuckled, skimming another stone across the water. "I know that your stern hand will correct my mistakes of excess."

"You are infuriating," Seva laughed, pushing him away.

"Woman," said Macunda in a mock serious tone, "that is not the way to treat the Master of the house."

Seva picked up a date from the wooden bowl and held it next to her husband's nose. "How would you like this inserted in your nostril, Master of the house?"

Macunda grabbed the date with his teeth along with his wife's fingers, as he snarled like a dog. Seva yelled as she pulled her hand away.

When they were both done laughing, Seva removed her wind-blown hair from her face and turned to Shoupang, who was still sitting on the swing.

"Are you perhaps frightened," said Seva, "by the prospect of fathering children like your wild little cousin?"

"No," he smiled.

"She really is a good child," said Seva, "even though your Uncle tries to undermine my efforts to teach her proper manners."

Macunda looked up at the carob tree overhead and started humming.

Shoupang smiled briefly, but quickly became serious again.

"What is it, then?" asked Seva. "Is your future bride, Cali, not pleasing to your eye?"

"Cali grows fairer each time I see her," said Shoupang. "But surely, timeless wisdom is a more noble pursuit. I think this incarnation is to be my last. Therefore, I must give up the fleeting pleasures of the world and live a life of austerity and virtue."

Macunda smiled. "Perhaps that is just your vanity talking. A hermit who thinks himself too pure for this world is likely to return as a drunken vagabond. The Master once told me that."

"Our nephew is not vain," said Seva. "I think his desire for austerity is born of fear."

"Fear?" Shoupang sat up straight.

"Yes." She looked at him with her beautiful, soulful eyes. "Fear tricks us into believing that the grand things of heaven are more important than the little things of the earth."

"Fear of what, Aunt Seva?"

"Fear of loss, born of grief. In fact, this might be why you are plagued with dreams, visions, and spirits. Great pain can open the mind to other realms..." She was about to continue, but stopped when she saw her husband discreetly shaking his head side to side.

Shoupang stared at her. " I do not understand," he said.

Seva hesitated and then looked at her husband.

"Shoupang," said the boy's uncle, "The Master will summon you when he sees fit. For now, put your attention on learning the ways of commerce. I made a promise to my sister that her son would have a proper education. You are thirteen years of age, soon to be fourteen. You are nearly a man."

They were all silent.

"It is time for you to join your cousins in the study," continued Macunda. "Your math tutor approaches the gate."

The boy sighed and got up from the swing. "Yes, Uncle Macunda." Placing the palms of his hands together, he bowed respectfully. "I thank you both for giving me audience during your time of leisure."

−8−

Sam and Rusty watched the back of the ambulance roll to the end of the driveway, as it started its siren and flashing lights. It made a right turn and started weaving its way around the traffic jam on Forrest Park Road.

"Did you get a hold of Max?" asked Rusty.

"No. I left a message at the lumberyard and on his cell phone. I should call Katie at the restaurant, but I don't know her cell number. I'm going to the hospital. It's going to take a while to get there in that traffic. If Max calls here, tell him which hospital it is. And when the tile gets here—"

"No sweat, Buddy." Rusty interrupted, giving Sam a gentle pat on the shoulder. "I'll take care of things here. You go on."

Inside the ambulance, the emergency medical technician took Jason's pulse and looked at his face. He was showing signs of shock. When Jason's lips started turning blue and his skin cold and clammy, the technician covered him with a blanket and applied an oxygen mask, being careful not to disturb the restraining collar that had been placed around Jason's neck.

As was his habit in such situations, the technician placed his hand on Jason's forehead. Closing his eyes, he recited his usual prayer.

–9–

Katie picked up the sautéed broccoli and rice with her chopsticks. Chewing thoughtfully, she studied the organic chemistry equations in her notebook.

She was interrupted by a cheerful greeting with a slight Chinese accent. "Hello, Katie. What happened to Jason?"

"Hi, Mrs. Tang. Jason had to leave in a hurry."

"He needs to slow down," chuckled Mrs. Tang. "He asked you to lunch and then he runs off like that. I'm going to have a talk with that boy."

"It's okay, actually," said Katie, as she replaced the notebook in her denim bag and pulled out the organic chemistry textbook. "Now I can catch up on my studying. And, he *was* nice enough to leave lunch money," she laughed, pointing to the twenty dollar bill on the table.

"Okay, we'll let him off the hook this time," laughed Mrs. Tang, as she walked away.

Katie was about to open up the textbook, but instead she found herself staring at the cover, which showed a picture of a three-sided pyramid. It was just a model of a molecule of methane. So, why was she having dreams about it lately? Yes, methane is the basis for all other organic molecules and therefore the basis for all life on Earth, but that's no reason to be dreaming about it practically every night.

As Katie puzzled over the possible deeper meaning of methane, Mrs. Tang returned with a cordless phone. "Katie," she said, "someone's trying to reach you, but he didn't have your cell phone number, so he called the restaurant."

"Oh. Thanks," said Katie, putting down the book and taking the phone.

"Hello. Oh, hi, Sam. What's up?"

The smile on Katie's face quickly faded and was replaced by a look of horror. "Oh, my God," she gasped.

She ran her hand along the side of her head, as she continued listening. "Which hospital?" Another pause. "Yes, I know where it is," she nodded. "Bye."

Placing her organic chemistry textbook back in her bag, she stood up and walked quickly to Mrs. Tang who was standing by the cash register. "Jason had an accident," she told Mrs. Tang in a low shaky voice. "I have to go. The money's on the table," she said, as she bolted out the door.

–10–

Jason felt as if he was lying down in a moving car. He could hear the muffled sound of a siren, so he surmised that he was riding in an ambulance. A warm hand rested gently on his forehead, and he could hear what seemed to be the tail end of a prayer. As soon as the hand lifted from his forehead, things got fuzzy for a second or so, and then, he heard another voice.

"Wake up, Smiley."

Smiley? Who is Smiley? Jason opened his eyes and saw two people standing over him. By the looks of it, he was lying in a bed, in a small hospital room. Strange, he could have sworn that he had been riding in an ambulance. Oh well.

He figured the two people standing over him were nurses, but he couldn't tell if they were male or female. They were both wearing white jumpsuits—smooth and seamless. They were also glowing.

"It is time," said one of the nurses.

"Time for what?" asked Jason, propping himself up on his elbow.

"Time to build the grid, Smiley."

"Grid? What grid? And my name isn't Smiley. It's Jason Mazarosky."

The two nurses faced each other and mumbled back and forth in a foreign language that sounded sort of like staccato violin music. Jason listened more carefully and, somehow, started comprehending their frenzied musical speech.

"The extended memory is still sealed."

"The personality is tenacious."

"Quite tenacious."

"Improvisation is in order."

Jason cocked his head to one side as he listened to their babble. For some reason, he wasn't at all startled by their appearance, even though he had never seen people glowing before.

"Uh," said Jason, holding up his forefinger, "excuse me."

The two glowing nurses stopped their staccato violin conversation and simultaneously turned their heads toward Jason.

Jason glanced around the room. "This is a hospital, right?"

The glowing nurses glanced at each other, sort of confused, and then looked at Jason again.

That was when a graceful looking nurse entered the cubicle. This one looked female—for the most part. She had a soft and motherly look about her. "Summon Brother G," she said politely to the other two. Turning to Jason, she touched him lightly on the shoulder. "Yes," she said, "this is a hospital."

Besides the fact that she was glowing like the other two, she had a radiant silver star hovering a few inches above her head, but Jason decided to let that slide. "So, what's going on here?" he asked. "What's this grid thing?"

"Everything is fine, Mr. Mazarosky," said the graceful nurse, smiling at him with her big baby eyes. "Go back to sleep for now."

Jason closed his eyes. Drifting off to sleep, he saw fuzzy images of an outdoor party. Looked like a wedding. Suddenly, he was the bridegroom.

–11–

A swarm of people in elegant robes mingled inside and outside the huge circular tent next to the small oval lake. The side of the tent facing the lake was completely open. Some people were sitting, others standing; all were talking, laughing and eating.

At the center of the tent, a young girl in a festive costume danced on a round wooden stage, surrounded by a circle of spectators. Five musicians sat on one side, playing drums and assorted string and wind instruments.

Macunda stood just outside the tent, embracing several people who had just arrived. As he directed them to the food and drink, he was joined by his wife, Seva, who handed him a steaming cup.

"What is this?"

"Drink it, husband. It will prevent you from getting sick from your overindulgence."

"Thank you," said Macunda. "But, I do not think I have overindulged."

"No, but you will," she said patting his stomach. And, do ration your consumption of wine."

"Yes, precious one." He took a sip and set the cup down next to a lotus blossom in a spherical ceramic vase on a small wooden table.

"Oh, how lovely," said Seva, touching the flower.

"It is for Shoupang and Cali. A wedding gift from the Master."

A round of applause came from the interior of the tent, where the little girl had finished her dance and was taking a bow.

Macunda smiled. "Gandhari is only eleven but dances like a young lady."

"Yes. And that is beginning to concern me. Some of the boys are getting too close."

"You really can't blame them, can you?" Macunda laughed.

"It is not proper," Seva said, walking away. "She is already betrothed."

Macunda saw Shoupang through the crowd and signaled him to come over. "Yes, Uncle."

Macunda pointed to the lotus. "A gift from the Master. One of the monks brought it while you and Cali were dancing. Oh, and he also gave you this," he said, pointing to a small rolled-up parchment on the table.

Shoupang unrolled the parchment and read it out loud. "'Cherish the ephemeral beauty of this flower and you will one day know its timeless beauty.' Sounds like good advice and a wonderful blessing."

"I guess you no longer wish to be a hermit, then?"

"No," Shoupang chuckled. "Monastic life still fascinates me, but now I am looking forward to mastering the ways of the merchant. I wish to learn the art of buying things cheaply where they are abundant and selling them at a profit where they are needed. I also like the way you increase your profits by growing your own hemp, cotton, indigo, and spices, as well as manufacturing textiles and pottery in your own workshops."

"So, you no longer regard wealth as an impediment to enlightenment?"

"No," said Shoupang. It is an excellent way to help people in need."

"Oh?"

"I see how you do your good work. You do not just give to the poor as a public spectacle, like other wealthy men. You find people in need, hire them, train them, and pay them a fair wage. You quietly teach them self-sufficiency and self-respect. I'm looking forward to practicing that sort of charity."

"That is not charity. It is a sound way to run a business. In return, they will give you their loyalty and faithful service that translate into profit in many hidden ways."

"And, with that profit, you quietly acquire political power to fight the unjust laws that are creeping into our society."

"Political power? Unjust laws? Whatever do you mean?"

Shoupang laughed. "You no longer need to play ignorant with me, Uncle. You made me study history and now I know the truth. There was more fairness in the past. It used to be easier for lower class people to better themselves. They had more opportunities to gather wealth, acquire land, grow their own food, and sell their surplus. Now it is much more difficult. The change has been so slow and insidious, no one questions it."

"What about me?" said Macunda. "My father was at the lower end of the merchant class." He waved his cup of tea at his huge house and surrounding land. "Does this look like I have been unjustly deprived?"

"You are rare, Uncle. You work hard and you are shrewd. You capitalized on some good fortune that came your way, and you know how not to antagonize the higher castes. You know how to talk to the bureaucrats and religious leaders so that they gladly grant you favors. They do not consider you a threat, so they allow you to gather wealth. What really amazes me is how you manage to keep your subversive activity from their eyes."

"What subversive activity? Teaching the poor to be self-reliant and industrious is not subversive."

"That is not what I'm talking about. What will you do if the Brahmin find out that you encourage the lower castes—and even women—to learn how to read and write?"

"I do not encourage them. They ask me questions about my success and I answer them. If they happen to wander into the library and take some books, that's not my fault. I cannot control what they do when I am not looking. I am not the keeper of our laws and customs. I am just a simple merchant."

"'A simple merchant,'" Shoupang chuckled. "I suppose that is the excuse you will give if you ever get caught. But what will you tell them if they find out that you, *yourself,* read directly from the sacred books, and that you allow your wife to do the same?"

"How will they find out?"

Shoupang smiled. "Uncle, I share your vision, but not your patience. Perhaps if my parents were as cautious as you, they would still be alive."

"Then again," said Macunda, "if they had been as cautious as I, perhaps they would not have gotten married, and you would not have been born."

"True," Shoupang sighed. "I wish I had gotten to know them. I barely remember their faces.'

"Shoupang!" yelled a young lady from the tent. "Come here!"

"Your bride calls," said Macunda.

"Cali approves of my desire to become a rich merchant. But no matter how wealthy I am, the young Brahmin in the city will still regard me as dirt. They know my father was just a potter from Siam."

"Not just a potter. He also had a good mind for commerce. He did wonders for our ceramics trade."

"The Brahmin do not respect craftsmanship or intelligent commerce," said Shoupang, shaking his head. "They respect only breeding. I will never understand how such corrosive thinking got started. I will never understand why they can't see that the way to create prosperity in the land is by allowing people the freedom to better themselves. It seems hopeless."

"SHOUPANG," Cali cried.

Macunda laughed as he gently pushed Shoupang toward the tent. "As long as there are women like Cali and your Aunt Seva in our lives, there is hope."

−12−

The surface of the lake gave off a brilliant golden light, as the late afternoon sun descended toward the hazy mountaintops in the distance. Macunda walked slowly toward the lake, staggering a bit, as the servants began cleaning up. When he reached the shore, he picked up a flat rock and skimmed it across the water. He was joined by his wife, who took his arm.

"That was a grand feast," said Macunda as he let out a satisfying belch. They watched their daughter Gandhari getting up from the wooden stage in the tent, where she had been taking a nap.

"And thanks to your vigilance," continued Macunda, "our daughter is still a virgin."

Seva laughed. "Are you not the least bit concerned?"

"No. The local boys know that anyone who acts improperly around my daughter puts his life in danger. And there is no harm in letting young people flirt a little."

"I disagree. A little harmless flirting is how it starts."

They walked past the large carob tree next to the lake, where two young children, boy and girl, played on the swing. Placing the palms of their hands together, the two children bowed respectfully to the passing adults, who smiled and returned the gesture.

"Do you suppose they were flirting?" asked Macunda.

"Now you're making fun of me."

"Yes, I am. You really do need to relax a bit about sexual propriety."

"Perhaps you're right," said Seva. "Anyway, enough of that. I am very pleased with how Shoupang has matured. He will be a good husband and a good father."

"And a good merchant," said Macunda, as they strolled along the shore. "He will prosper, if he can control his strange obsession."

"You mean his obsession with monastic virtue?"

"Yes, that one. He either wants to *leave* this world or *save* it."

"Those two obsessions seem to go together."

"Do you think he will ever get over it?" asked Macunda.

"Yes, if he ever grieves the loss of his parents."

"Where do you get such strange notions, woman?"

"It is just common sense. When people are trapped in grief, they adopt vague and grandiose world-saving ambitions."

"Is this what you conclude from reading the Vedas?"

"That is another matter entirely. And that reminds me; I think you are correct in your assertion that the Brahmin misinterpret the Vedas. They suggest that transcendence involves rejecting the things of the earth. I think that true spiritual transcendence carries a deep reverence for the things of the earth."

"I do not get such an impression from reading the Vedas."

"You would if you were to read the Vedas with your heart."

Macunda shook his head. "Such strange ideas. This is what happens when women learn to read."

"Lucky for you, I am ignoring that comment," said Seva. "My point is simply that our nephew is driven by hidden grief. I am also convinced that the pain of losing both parents in such a traumatic way opened him to the spirit world. I also know that if he continues to put so much attention on monastic virtue, it will greatly affect his future incarnations, just as your secret desire to recite the Vedas in public, and your secret hatred of the Brahmin will surely have karmic consequences."

"Hatred? Me?"

Seva laughed. "You keep it so well hidden that no one can see it. You act so humble and obedient in their presence, but your ambition is to get up in front of a crowd and proclaim, "Here is the truth, my friends: the Brahmin are *not* your superiors. They are maggots! They live off your blood and sweat and give you poverty and disease in return. In the hands of the Brahmin, the pure teachings of the Vedas are turned into tools for enslaving our people." She laughed. "That is your secret wish, my husband. And of course, part of that hatred stems from the simple fact that you yourself wish to have their power!"

"I do not call them maggots," said Macunda, earnestly. "I call them blood-sucking, white-skinned vermin. There is a difference."

Seva looked at the sincere expression on her husband's face. Then, she burst out laughing. She tried to compose herself so she could respond, but as soon as she saw the innocent expression on her husband's slightly drunken face, she laughed so hard that she had to lean on his shoulder to keep from falling.

"Admittedly," Macunda continued calmly, "it would bring me pleasure to publicly expose their failings. But that does not mean I hate them."

"Call it what you will." said Seva, finally composing herself. "My point is that no matter how congenial you act in their presence, your lack of respect for the Brahmin—and your secret desire to have their power—will have karmic consequences."

"And how can I escape the karmic consequences?"

"Through compassion, of course. Not the false compassion that the Brahmin drone on about, but the true compassion described by the Master. It is the understanding that the evildoer and sufferer alike could just as easily be you. It is the understanding that both are caught in the same trap. That is the true compassion that transcends karma and liberates the spirit. In your case, it is the understanding that the same potential to abuse power that is displayed by the Brahmin also resides within you."

"Well-spoken, my wife, but I—" Macunda fell silent and stared at the tent.

"What is wrong?" asked Seva.

"Who is that boy speaking with Gandhari?" he said in a suddenly sober and serious tone.

"Oh, that is Ravi. He is Cali's cousin."

"Her cousin, you say?" He noted the boy's light complexion and light-brown wavy hair. "He does not look like he might be related to Cali. In fact, He looks like he might be Brahmin."

"He is of that lineage, yes. Apparently, he comes from a place south of here, where caste distinctions are not so strict. Marriage between castes is sometimes permitted... or at least, tolerated."

Macunda's eyes narrowed as the boy and his daughter were joined by Shoupang and Cali.

"How do we know he is not a spy from the local Brahmin?" said Macunda.

Seva laughed. "Krishna, save us! He is Cali's cousin. He is just a boy. He comes from a village far to the south. And, if the Brahmin wanted to spy on you, they would not send someone who obviously looks like a Brahmin."

Macunda continued staring suspiciously. "And why is he talking to our daughter? She is already betrothed."

Seva looked at her husband's serious countenance and once again let out a great big belly laugh.

–13–

Doctor Hauser took off her glasses and rubbed her eyes as she slowly passed Jason Mazarosky's cubical in the ICU. As she approached the exit, she slowed down, quickly raising her head like a gazelle that had just caught a whiff of a cheetah.

As she stood outside the doorway, her danger signal condensed into that familiar cold heavy feeling in her chest. Unlocking her knees, she stood very still. Sure enough, the alarm at the nurse's station went off. Instantly, she ran back into the ICU.

Jogging passed the nurse's station, she was joined by two young men in green scrubs. As the three of them quickly approached the cubical, Dr.. Hauser couldn't help but feel a sense of futility. Every time she got that cold sensation in her chest, the patient died, no matter what she did. It just didn't seem fair! What was the value of having these warnings of impending death, if there was nothing she could do about it? Just once, she wished she could use her built-in alarm to save a life, instead of having to just sit there like a dummy, holding the patient's dead hand.

—14—

Opening his eyes, Jason Mazarosky saw a tall gentleman with blondish hair, wearing a reddish jump suit. But was he really a man? He looked rather feminine. Or, maybe he was just youthful. His hair was kind of long and soft, and he had big baby eyes.

"Greetings, Smiley."

There was that name again! Jason folded his arms. "Are you the doctor?" he asked.

"No. You may call me Brother G."

The man glowed all over and was just a tad translucent. Otherwise, he looked pretty normal.

"Uh…" Jason hesitated, "… this may sound like a stupid question, but, am I dreaming?"

"In a manner of speaking."

"Good," Jason chuckled. "For a minute there, I thought I was dead."

"Well, actually," said Brother G, "that may have some truth in it too."

"Oh." Jason glanced around the cubical. "Is it okay if I get out of bed?"

"Certainly."

Jason stood up and examined his slightly translucent body. He glanced at his physical body on the bed, rigged up with a bunch of wires and tubes. "So, how come everybody calls me Smiley?"

"It is your… nickname. However, if you prefer, we can still address you as 'Jason.'"

"That's okay. Smiley's fine. It does have a familiar ring to it. Anyway, am I dead or am I dreaming?"

"I would say both."

"Huh?"

"And neither."

Before Jason could ask for clarification, the curtain at the foot of the bed flew aside and Dr.. Hauser rushed in, followed by two young men in green scrubs. The doctor glanced at the monitors overhead, showing horizontal lines, which normally registered heartbeat, respiration and brain wave activity.

Twenty minutes of applying the usual resuscitation procedures did not revive the patient. Dr.. Hauser sighed. Not knowing what else to do, she sat down and held Jason's hand between her hands, feeling rather useless.

–15–

The hospital room was gone. Brother G was gone. Jason Mazarosky was gone. Smiley rose higher and higher, surrounded by images, voices, and thoughts, all of which whirled and mingled like so many bits of fruit in a slow-motion blender. It was like being in a movie theater with a screen all around him.

He saw places that didn't look solid at all, some of which were quite sleazy and he had to be careful not to bump into someone else's thoughts. Many names flashed through his mind, most of them exotic and foreign, but the only one that consistently remained was Smiley.

Finally, he saw four stars. They were silver, blue, green, and red. Together, they surrounded him, forming a three-sided pyramid. Instantly, all semblance of order was gone. No up, no down, no here, no there. And no memories. A very strange turn of events, but he took it very calmly.

He tried to locate the boundary between himself and the world around him, but everything around him was also within him. Interesting. And what remained of his identity as an individual was dissolving. His thoughts were being replaced by a larger presence, as if he were being swallowed and assimilated by a silent amorphous giant that extended forever all around him and within him.

And then, a voice! A faint cry, as if from far away—or deep inside. The voice seemed to emanate from the past, or maybe the future; it was hard to say which one, because the two seemed to be mingling freely. In fact, he realized that the very existence of a "past" or "future" had no real meaning until the voice rippled through the otherwise undetectable sea of isness and established a point of reference... of sorts.

The voice carried a sense of urgency, in sharp contrast to the surrounding stillness, which now looked sort of violet. The voice was sort of like a rebellion against the uniformity of the great violet sea.

He tried to call out to the voice, but had no means of doing so. In fact, the very notion of "communicating" had no meaning until the voice showed up. He tried to move toward the voice, but there was no direction in which to move. The voice persisted, weak but tenacious, refusing to dissolve into the violet sea.

Suddenly, there was recognition. The voice was called Jason. Yes. Jason Mazarosky! And that's me!

Falling. Jason Mazarosky, falling. I'm Jason Mazarosky. And I'm falling! But I'm also Smiley. Anyway, whoever I am, I'm here. I have a body—more or less—and it's falling!

Noticing that he was falling rather fast, he worried about what would happen when he hit bottom. So, he was glad when he slowed down and finally landed with a rough, but painless thud into a soft chair.

Darkness all around. He quickly touched his arms, chest and face, reassuring himself with the physical-ness of his body.

Dim lights came on. Straightening up in his seat, he looked around at the big empty room filled with many rows of seats.

A theater? Yes! And, it looked very familiar. Could it be? The Vintage Theater! He was sitting in the middle of the first row, in his favorite seat!

The familiar scenery was comforting. Everything was exactly the same—except for the blank screen, which looked sort of violet. He sighed. It felt good to sigh with his own chest. He leaned his head back and relaxed. He was tired enough to take a nap, but the thought of going to sleep was scary.

In front of his feet, he saw a huge bucket of popcorn. Picking it up, he held it close to his nose. Hot with extra butter, just the way he liked it.

Looking down at the right armrest, he saw three violet buttons, arranged vertically. Each had a different engraved word: *play, stop, channel.*

He pushed the play button and the screen sprang to life, showing a major league baseball game. The Yankees versus the Phillies. Complete with play-by-play and commentary.

None of this made any sense, but what the heck. He threw a handful of popcorn in his mouth and watched the game.

After two innings, the scenery and the players seemed to be changing. By the fourth inning, it was glaringly obvious. Time was going backwards! The uniforms, the haircuts on the players, the clothes of the people in the stands—it all looked like a scene out of the 1930s.

By the sixth inning, it looked like the early 1900s. By the seventh inning stretch, it looked like 1850 or so—the very beginning of baseball. But no, that was not the very beginning! The scene faded to violet and then showed a primitive version of baseball being played as part of a Christian ceremony at Easter time. A solitary monk stood in the sidelines.

And then it changed again. Those baseball-like Easter ceremonies were now being performed by a group of Pagans. In fact, he suddenly understood that the word *Easter* was derived from *Eostre,* who was the Pagan goddess of springtime and light. And, there was that monk again! Except this time, he was a Druid high priest.

The baseball game faded and was replaced by a monk who appeared in several different places in rapid succession. Somehow, Smiley knew those places were France, Scotland, Greece, Germany, and Spain, over a period of several centuries.

Then, he saw a series of scenes with the same monk in Jerusalem, spending several hours a day staring at a picture of Jesus, as he repeated over and over, "I humble myself in the sight of the Lord," until one day a fiery hot lightning bolt shot up his back, causing certain parts of his brain to be thoroughly fried, while other parts got switched on. He spent the rest of his life in a happy, near-vegetable state, serving no useful function, except for the oddity that everyone who touched him got healed of whatever was ailing them. Smiley saw the same monk trying it again as a devout Muslim in Ethiopia, praising the name of Allah over and over again—with similar results.

Interesting movie, but Smiley preferred the baseball game. He pressed the channel button, hoping to catch another game, or at least a more normal movie that didn't include monks. He smiled when the screen showed him and his sister Marcy as children. They were sitting in their pajamas next to the Christmas tree, tearing the wrapping off their presents. But the image quickly gave way to yet another scene from the distant past. Eighth century Germany. And, there was that monk again!

Smiley shook his head. "This is getting monotonous."

The monk was converting a community of Pagans to Christianity. Smiley was about to push the channel button again, but stopped when he noticed that he was sort of thinking the monk's thoughts! The monk was enchanted by the Pagan ceremony of decorating spruce trees and exchanging gifts during the Yule. He felt that they should be allowed to keep such a lovely ceremony. He wanted to write a letter to the Pope for permission. But, he figured His Holiness would never go for it.

The images seemed to go further back in time and become progressively more grainy and blurry. The scenery became more panoramic and was eventually reduced to a satellite's view of Europe, panning slowly across the Mid East and into central India, where the camera seemed to once again come in for a close up. He saw a brief image of a group of people in ancient clothing sitting on the ground next to some wagons. But the image quickly became blurry and faded to violet.

–16–

Macunda's ten-wagon caravan, which included ten sheep and five baby Brahma bulls, was stopped by the side of a dirt road at the top of a gently sloping hill, overlooking a lush valley. The drivers and guards sat on the soft grass, enjoying a midday meal and quiet conversation, which included Macunda's lively interpretation of the Vedas that occasionally evoked rowdy laughter. The horses, sheep and baby bulls grazed close by.

Macunda looked up when he saw a rider cantering up the side of the hill. "My nephew finally returns," he said. "Let us finish our meal, strike the tents, and resume our journey before our bulls become large enough to attack us." The man laughed as Macunda stood up and walked to Shoupang.

"We were becoming concerned by your absence," said Macunda.

"I apologize for the delay," said Shoupang, as he jumped down off the horse. "I had a most productive visit with Cali's uncle. That is Ravi's Father. Do you remember Ravi?"

"The young man at your wedding," Macunda nodded. "The Brahmin side of Cali's family." "Yes. Ravi's father owns all that land between the two peaks," said Shoupang, waving his hand at the valley in the distance. "He offered to sell me the entire southeast section. Most of the land is already clear and it has good-size creek running through it. All it needs is a house. Property prices here are significantly lower than up north. Taxes are also lower, and so is the cost of labor." He paused to allow his uncle to digest that bit of information."

"And…" said Macunda, non-committally.

"And, I'm strongly considering it. I want to buy it, move down here, build on it, and establish a large business. Cali's family has a wonderful community here and they are delighted by the prospect of Cali and me moving down here."

Macunda remained silent.

"I know it means I would be moving far away from the security of your estate, but I have a very good feeling about it."

Macunda looked at the valley.

"I can easily afford it," added Shoupang, "when I combine my inheritance with your generous wedding gift. And Cali's family is begging Cali's uncle to make it as affordable as possible for me."

More silence.

"So, what do you think, Uncle?"

"Sounds like an interesting proposition. Are you certain you will have enough money to keep you funded until you start showing a profit?"

"Yes… I think. My plan is to fully utilize the local markets first, as you often recommend, before I even start thinking about distant markets. This will lower my cost as well as allowing me to sell perishables and other things that are not easily transported great distances. The growing season in these southern regions is very long, the soil is excellent, and the mineral resources are abundant. It's a little drier here than up north, but that should not be a problem if I apply your methods of harvesting rainwater."

Macunda tried to conceal his smile.

"There is great potential here, Uncle. More people are migrating to this region. There is already a demand for producers and merchants. And that demand will increase in the years to come. The laws here are more just. It is easier here for industrious men to prosper."

Macunda nodded slowly.

"And, as we gather wealth through full utilization of the emerging local markets," Shoupang continued talking rapidly, "we can gradually expand to the more distant markets. Anyway, to address your original concern, I am fairly certain that I have ample funds to begin." Shoupang paused and then resumed in a more subdued manner. "But our progress will be greatly expedited if I have an investor."

They looked at each other silently. Macunda chuckled.

"You need not answer now," Shoupang said quickly. "You can think on this for a while."

"I do not have to think on it. Your ambitious venture seems like a worthy one. You have my blessings. But before I give you my money, I want to see some signs of success. As you say, you already have ample funds to start building your foundation so you can utilize the local markets. If you show success in that area, I will consider providing the additional funding for expansion."

Shoupang spread his arms out. "Thank you, Lord Krishna," he declared, raising his head to the bright blue sky.

–17–

Smiley stared at the blank violet screen. For some reason, he imagined that it was a bright blue sky.

His mind was a swirl of random thoughts and images: people, places, religions, commerce, farms, baby bulls, wagons, markets, and lots of monks and monasteries.

He felt like there was a tug of war going on inside him. One part of his mind wanted to be Jason while another part wanted to be all sorts of strange characters doing many exotic things.

And why so many monks? He pressed the play button, hoping to call up a more normal movie. The screen showed another monk. "Damn!"

This one looked rather grim; his body withered by prolonged fasting and his mind tortured by sexual thoughts. "Please, God," he prayed, "let my innocence be reborn."

Smiley shook his head with annoyance. "What a moron," he said, as he pressed the channel button, willfully calling forth a movie that didn't have monks in it. He tried to think of baseball and his childhood.

Cramming a fistful of popcorn in his mouth, he looked at the screen and smiled, recognizing Jason Mazarosky at ten years of age, along with four other members of his little league baseball team. They were sitting on the rug, watching the opening game of the major league baseball season on TV. They were eating leftover chocolate Easter eggs, ice cream, and pepperoni pizza. Smiley recognized Sam, Rusty, Andrew, and Calvin.

"This is more like it," Smiley said, relaxing into his seat.

—18—

"What's oral sex?" asked Jason, after swallowing a mouthful of ice cream.

"I think it's when you just talk about it," said Sam, rubbing his chin.

"Oh," said Jason. Taking a big gulp of orange soda, he let out a very loud belch. "You mean like when people call those funny phone numbers and talk dirty?"

"Yeah, like that," said Sam.

"No, it isn't, you dodo," said Rusty, as he returned from the kitchen, and sat next to Sam.

"Who are you calling a dodo?'" said Sam, giving Rusty a shove.

"You, that's who," said Rusty, pushing him back.

"You're the dodo, you dodo," said Sam pushing him again.

"Fight! Fight!" two of the boys called out.

"Hey, hey, cool it," said Jason, with a mouth full of pizza. "Not in the house."

"Relax, Jason," said Sam. "Do you think we're stupid enough to start a fight in here?"

"Well, I don't know. Are you?"

Sam and Rusty glared at each other and then, apparently, decided to behave themselves.

"Anyway," said Rusty, "oral sex is when a man licks between a lady's legs and a lady licks between a man's legs."

Jason stopped chewing and grimaced.

"Yuck," said Calvin. "That is gross."

"Major gross." said Rusty. "I hear that a girl's thing is real slimy and smells like rotten fish."

They were all silent, each with a look of incredulous horror and disgust.

"And it oozes blood for no reason at all," continued Rusty.

"God, you're supposed to lick that?" said Andrew.

"Yeah, you're supposed to stick your tongue way in there!"

Still grimacing, Jason put his pizza back on the paper plate, while rubbing his stomach with his other hand.

Andrew shook his head. "There is no way in a million years that I will ever do that! You couldn't pay me enough!"

"Same here," said Calvin. "And how are you supposed to kiss the girl after she's put her mouth on your—"

Jason groaned and grabbed his stomach again. His friends watched as he bolted to the bathroom. When he started making heaving sounds, they burst out laughing.

"BARFS AWAY!" Rusty yelled.

Sam shook his head. "God, the one thing that I hate more than anything else is throwing up."

"Except when someone else is doing it," said Rusty, "then, it's funny."

"True," Sam conceded.

"Actually," said Andrew as he munched on a chocolate Easter egg, "throwing up isn't so bad. It's being nauseous that I really hate."

"Yeah, same here," said Sam, swallowing his ice cream, "You know how it is when it comes on slow and you get more and more sick to your stomach and then, just before you throw up, your mouth starts watering so much that it drips down into the toilet? Ooh, I just hate that!"

Their laughter had subsided when Jason returned with a glass of water.

"I can't help it," said Jason, "I have a sensitive stomach."

"You're lucky," said Sam. "Now you have room for more food."

They burst out laughing again.

"God," said Jason, after taking a sip. "Are you supposed to do that mouth stuff every time you make out?"

"No." said Rusty. "I think you can skip that part. Unless you want to have a baby."

—19—

The scene faded. Smiley stared at the violet screen for a while. Finally, he let out a nostalgic sigh and pushed the play button. The screen now showed Jason Mazarosky as a young adult, sitting with his feet on his desk in a cluttered office inside the lumberyard, chattering away. Sam was lying down on an old couch on the other side of the room, trying to read a paperback book over Jason's talking.

"Katie has this wisdom about her," said Jason. "She makes me see things clearly, sometimes without even opening her mouth."

Jason placed his hands behind his head looking dreamily out the window. "She's an amazing girl," he continued. "I don't know what I did to deserve her."

"What makes you think you deserve her?" said Sam, without taking his eyes off his book. "You're just a dumb jerk, who lucked out."

"Of course, I forgot. And, while we're on the subject, what about Lisa. You really have the hots for her, don't you?"

"Uh-huh," Sam nodded, looking away from his book briefly.

"So, why haven't you asked her out?"

"I intend to."

Jason shook his head. "You know, there's only one way to get over being shy."

"I'm not shy," said Sam, putting the book down and facing Jason. "I'm just waiting for the right moment."

"Sam, you are full of beans. You need to set a deadline, otherwise you'll never do it. Lisa is working the cash register right now. Just get on out there and ask her."

"No," said Sam, looking up at the slowly rotating ceiling fan. "She seems kind of moody this morning."

"Of course she's moody! She's frustrated because you haven't done your manly duty. Look, I'll help you out. How about if the four of us go on a double date? You and Lisa, Katie and me."

"No. I wouldn't feel comfortable doing a double date on the first date."

"You're right, bad idea." Jason looked out the window briefly, as a tractor-trailer backed up into the loading dock. "Why don't you invite her to a softball game? That'll be like asking her out, without actually asking her out. And she'll be real impressed when you launch one of your monstrous cannon shots over the fence."

"What if I don't have a good day at bat?"

Jason slapped his forehead. "Jesus Christ! What is wrong with you? It's not like you're going into a cage with a wild tiger. She's a nice girl."

"Lisa isn't just nice," said Sam, sitting up straight. "She's..." He closed his eyes, waving his massive arms dreamily in the air. Suddenly, he opened his eyes. "Are you sure she's not dating anybody?"

"She's definitely available. But she won't be if you keep dragging your feet. So, when are you going to ask her?"

Sam stared out the window, with a look of apprehension on his face. "I'll... do it... very soon," he said, as he stood up and walked toward the door.

"Where are you going?"

"To clear away the loading dock. The big shipment of cedar just came in."

"Chicken shit!" Jason called out, as his friend closed the door behind him. "Sam is a chicken shit!"

Smiley laughed as the scene faded away.

Staring at the blank violet screen, he had the eerie notion that he was still watching himself give advice to a friend trying to get a date with a girl, but it wasn't Sam! How strange!

–20–

Shoupang stood with his arms folded, gazing at the two men digging out the new pond. Other workers were clearing the land around the pond for cultivation, while still others were building a stable not too far from the pond. The rolling meadow all around was dotted with grazing goats, cows, and horses.

"Everything is actually progressing very well," said Shoupang, turning his head to Ravi, who stood next to him.

Ravi did not respond, looking sort of lost.

"The infrastructure is nearly complete," continued Shoupang, waving his arm around. "We are just running out of money too fast. Maybe I ought to write to my uncle and ask him again to invest in our venture. He is going to do that eventually, anyway."

Ravi remained silent with his head down.

"Ravi?"

No response.

"Ravi!"

"Huh!" Ravi quickly raised his head.

"I said, maybe I should write to my uncle and ask him again if he wants to invest in our venture."

Upon hearing Shoupang's idea, Ravi seemed even more perturbed. "Well, I don't know…"

"What do you mean, you don't know? I can assure you that Uncle Macunda already has an interest in our venture."

Ravi remained silent, looking like he was in another world.

"Ravi, what has come over you? Lately you act as if you are perpetually drunk on hashish, except that you do not look happy."

Ravi forced a smile. "I wish it was that simple."

Shoupang studied his friend. "I know why you behave so strangely," he said, pointing an accusing finger at him.

Ravi suddenly looked fearful.

"You have been spending too much time in meditation," Shoupang laughed.

Ravi relaxed.

"Meditation is a worthy pursuit," continued Shoupang, "but too much can cause you to disconnect from your earthly responsibilities. I know. I used to do that too."

Ravi stared at the pond, seemingly lost in thought.

"A little meditation is good," said Shoupang. "In fact, I have been thinking of resuming my own devotional—"

"I WANT TO MARRY GANDHARI!" Ravi yelled out. "There. I have finally said it!"

Shoupang stared at his friend. "You want to marry Gandhari?" He said in a low, well-controlled voice.

Ravi nodded. "Do you mean, specifically, my cousin, my Uncle's daughter? Is that the Gandhari to whom you refer?"

Ravi nodded.

"Please tell me you jest."

Ravi shook his head, no.

Shoupang stared at him incredulously and then looked skyward. "Krishna save us," he said in a subdued voice.

Ravi sighed and looked at the pond. "Over the past four years, I have used every excuse possible to travel to the North, so I can see her. Even when I manage to get there, it has not been easy to arrange meetings."

"And obviously, Uncle Macunda and Aunt Seva don't know of this."

Ravi shook his head. "Obviously not, otherwise I would not be alive right now," he laughed sarcastically.

Shoupang looked at his wife and Gandhari, who were walking through the new herb garden, with two of the children playing close by. The third child was being held by Gandhari.

Shoupang pointed an accusing finger at his cousin. "That little mischievous monkey. All those times that she requested to come visit us to learn about 'mothering' from Cali…"

"She was coming here," Ravi nodded, "to secretly meet with me. I've tried to break it off, but Gandhari is just— "

"GANDHARI!" Shoupang called out to his cousin. "Join us here please!"

After a pause, Gandhari started walking down the hill, followed by Cali, who signaled the two children to follow along.

"And when Gandhari was *supposedly* spending time with Cali's cousins and sisters, *supposedly* taking instruction in maternity yoga and dance…"

"She was rendezvousing with me," said Ravi, as they watched the two women approaching with the children.

"What about your parents?" asked Shoupang.

"I finally told them last year. Apparently," he chuckled, "they suspected. But they are deeply concerned, of course. This whole thing is scandalous, even in these parts. They wish that Gandhari and I would quietly end this madness."

"Why didn't you tell me?"

"Is it not obvious? By keeping this from you, your uncle cannot hold you responsible."

"So why do you tell me now?"

"We cannot keep it a secret forever. Gandhari has invented excuses to delay her prearranged marriage. My own wedding has been discreetly cancelled after much turmoil. But now, Gandhari is eighteen and I almost twenty. I need to start behaving responsibly about this, one way or the other."

Shoupang looked at Gandhari, who was now standing calmly in front of him, still holding Shoupang's youngest child and flanked by the other two children. Cali stood to the side, between Gandhari and Shoupang.

"I wanted to see you up close," said Shoupang, looking at her innocent angelic face. "I knew you were bold, but this is beyond anything that I could have imagined." Shoupang kept his reprimand at a low civil tone, since his three children were present. "My baby cousin," he nodded. "So, what do you have to say for yourself?"

"Just two things," said Gandhari. "First, I do apologize for any trouble that this may cause for you and Cali. And secondly, regardless of what anyone says, Ravi and I will not part from each other."

Ravi took a few steps to Gandhari's side and put his arm around her.

Silence. Cali smiled, almost imperceptibly.

Shoupang turned to his wife. "Cali, did you know of this?"

"Gandhari told me when she first arrived."

Shoupang placed his hands on his hips. "That was over a month ago. And finally," he said looking at Gandhari and Ravi, "you saw fit to let *me* in on your little secret."

"Yes," said Gandhari, looking him straight in the eyes with her own big dark eyes. "It seemed sensible to keep it from you as long as possible."

"So, it appears to me that you two have no shame about this," said Shoupang.

"Certainly not," said Gandhari. "We do respect our parents and are not insensitive to the difficult position this puts them in. But if parents insist on committing their children to marriage before they are old enough to decide for themselves, this sort of thing is to be expected."

Gandhari's defiance triggered old anger in Shoupang, bringing back the numerous confrontations they had as children. He heaved his chest, intending to tell Gandhari to pack her things, because she was going back home to her parents, as soon as possible. However, when he glanced at his wife's calm and steady gaze, he decided to restrain himself. After seven years of marriage, he was still amazed by Cali's ability to assert her strength and communicate wisdom without even opening her mouth.

All eyes were on Shoupang. Even the children were staring at him. He looked at Gandhari and Ravi again, their arms around each other. Much to his frustration, his anger was transforming into compassion. There was no use fighting this. Everyone was against him, including himself.

"Very well, then," Shoupang nodded. "Gandhari," he said, with a stern look, "you and Cali may return to the garden. And I will discuss this further with your…" his voice trailed off. "Future husband," said Gandhari, as she kissed Ravi on the cheek, turned and walked away with Cali and the children.

Shoupang shook his head. "That little imp continues to amaze me." He turned to Ravi. "And you are obviously smitten by her."

"Totally," Ravi said, throwing his chest out, as they started walking along the pond. "But, I *am* sorry for bringing upon you this unwanted complication," he added, in a more serious tone.

Shoupang sighed. "Under the circumstances, you—and Gandhari—have handled this madness as well as expected."

"Thank you."

"But it is madness, nonetheless."

"I agree. We have considered the possibility of running away," said Ravi. "That would simplify things for everyone."

"No need to get so dramatic. There is a more practical option."

"Oh?"

"Rather than Gandhari returning home to her parents as planned, she can just continue to live here with us, as you two make arrangements to marry. Fortunately, the customs in these parts allow for such things. I also suggest that Gandhari and you each compose a letter to her parents, explaining the situation and of course inviting them to the wedding, emphasizing how much it would mean to you and Gandhari to have them present. I will personally deliver the letters to them and assure them that Gandhari is safe, happy and well cared for. And, after they have had a chance to thoroughly express their outrage, which might take several days, I will explain to them why the most sensible and practical thing for them to do is to relax and bless your marriage. I mean no disrespect, but the fact that you are a light-skinned Brahman will not make this task easier."

"I understand."

"On the other hand," said Shoupang, rubbing his chin, "that might be to our advantage. My uncle is a rule-breaker. I will try to play on that."

"Thank you for doing this. I will forever be in your debt."

"Do not speak to me of debt. As a man of business, debt is offensive to me."

They walked silently for a while. Finally, Ravi turned his head apprehensively toward his friend. "Uh…" "Now what?"

"Are you still going to ask your uncle to invest in our venture?" asked Ravi, timidly.

Shoupang sighed, as a pained look overtook his face.

–21–

Smiley stared at the blank violet screen, feeling proud of himself for no apparent reason.

Another image of Jason Mazarosky appeared on the screen. This time he was helping Brother Jerry with some work at the monastery. They repaired some chairs, fixed a leaky faucet, and painted window frames. Eventually, they rested under an oak tree next to the lake and had lunch.

"It seems like a great thing is just falling into my lap," said Jason. "I asked Uncle Max for a small loan to finance my new construction company. But instead, he threw me a bombshell. He wants me to run the entire lumberyard. He thinks I'm ready, but, I don't know."

Brother Jerry silently nibbled on his peanut butter sandwich, while throwing chunks of it to the swans in the lake.

"Jason," said Brother Jerry, picking up an acorn, "look at this. This thing is really amazing. It doesn't look anything like an oak tree."

"So?"

"This is a seed."

"I know that."

"Which means that it has the potential to become something that is totally unlike an acorn. But to do that," said Brother Jerry, looking intently into Jason's eyes, "it has to quit being a seed. And it has to quit being little. In one sense, the seed must die."

Jason looked at the seed and then at his friend. "You know what, Bro?"

"What?"

"You are one strange dude."

"I know," said Brother Jerry, as he tossed the acorn at Jason, who caught it one handed.

"Hey," said Jason, "after the chores, you want to throw the ball around."

"Of course. Did you bring your glove?"

"Of course."

The scene faded to violet, but Brother Jerry's words lingered in Smiley's mind. As with the previous movie, Smiley had the eerie feeling that a similar drama was invisibly occurring elsewhere. This time the screen seemed to respond to his feeling by showing a blurry movie. He wasn't sure, but it looked like a man sitting at an outdoor table, deep in meditation, while construction was going on in the background.

–22–

Ravi opened his eyes. After a few seconds, he took a long breath, stretched, and rubbed his face. He studied the map on the table, showing Shoupang's property, and then looked around the land. He nodded in thoughtful silence, as several men cleared away rocks and brush.

"Ravi!" Gandhari called him from the other side of the knobby hill behind him.

"Yes?"

"Can you come here, please?"

"I am busy."

"Very well. I just thought you would like to know that Shoupang returns from visiting my father and mother."

Ravi shot out of his chair, knocking it over, along with table, as he bolted up the hill. Shoupang had been away an entire month. Ravi wasn't sure whether that was a good sign or a bad sign. When he reached the top of the hill, he looked down the other side and saw Shoupang standing in front of a loaded cart, next to the newly filled pond. He was being greeted by his wife, their three children and Gandhari. They all seemed happy, which was definitely a good sign.

Ravi ran down the hill to meet them. "How did it go?" he demanded, as he grabbed Shoupang's shoulders.

"Much better than expected! My uncle gave me more money than I asked for, as well as some much needed supplies," he said, pointing to the loaded cart. "My uncle is not merely an investor. He is now an active business partner, which means that success is guaranteed!"

"THE MARRIAGE!" Ravi yelled, shaking Shoupang violently. "WHAT ABOUT THE MARRIAGE?"

"Oh, that. All is well. You have their blessing and they will attend the wedding."

Ravi was momentarily stunned. He wasn't expecting it to go so easily. Finally, he yelled and cheered, scaring the goats and horses on the other side of the pond. He gave Shoupang a big hug, picked him up off the ground and spun him around. Then, he did the same with Gandhari, except he didn't let go of her. Then, Shoupang and Cali joined in. The four of them locked arms and formed a circle, spun around together and eventually fell into the pond, as the children laughed.

–23–

Smiley chuckled, feeling proud of Shoupang's success, as the four blurry figures laughingly walking out of the pond. And then, the screen faded to violet.

He felt a special rapport with Shoupang, as well as having a vague impression about the young man, Ravi. He seemed reminiscent of Brother Jerry. Sorting through more memories, Smiley recalled having lunch with Brother Jerry at Mamma Tang's Restaurant. He pressed the play button.

The screen now showed a clear image of Jason Mazarosky wolfing down his curry chicken and rice, while Brother Jerry's plate of black mushrooms and vegetables over rice remained virtually untouched.

"This is my first time in a restaurant in five years," said Brother Jerry, "Thanks for treating me."

"Anything for a man of the cloth," said Jason. "So does this mean that you're allowed to go to restaurants and stuff?"

"It depends. We have rules, but the abbot is willing to bend them when doing so seems more sensible than adhering to them. After I joined the monastery, he let me continue my studies at the university, so I could complete my masters."

"That reminds me. I've been meaning to ask you. How would you describe life in the monastery?"

"Why do you ask? Are you thinking of becoming a monk?"

"Me? Never in a million years! I'm just curious."

"Well," said Brother Jerry, "let me put it this way. If those walls could talk, they wouldn't say much."

"Very dull?"

"Most people would think so. There *is* a bit of drama now and then. Monks are just regular people with the usual hang-ups. Sometimes, they behave like kids in a dysfunctional family."

"What do you do about it?"

"To resolve personal issues, we're supposed to go to the abbot. But more and more, he tells them to go talk to me. I've become the unofficial shrink for the monastery. But other than the occasional mundane psychodrama, not much goes on there."

"So, what brought you there?"

"It all started with my cousin Ralph, about six years ago. It's sort of a strange story. While I was in grad school, I was playing racquetball with Ralph, and he told me about the time he and his wife were on retreat in a monastery. They are both serious Catholics. He said that after an evening of unusually evocative chanting in the chapel, he and his wife retired to their room. And, for some reason, they both became very sexually aroused that night."

"What did they do about it?"

"What do you think they did about it?"

"You mean, they actually did it in the monastery?"

Brother Jerry nodded. "Ralph said it was the best sex he ever had."

His mouth full of food, Jason tried to control his laughter.

"So," continued Brother Jerry, "I decided to check it out. I wasn't religious at all back then. I was still engaged to Nancy, and things weren't going well with us, so I figured I'd give it a shot. Unfortunately, since we were not married, they put us in separate rooms. I was bummed out, to say the least. However, after that weekend, everything changed."

"What happened?"

"Seemed like it was the chanting," said Brother Jerry, as he pushed his food around the plate with his chopsticks. "First time I chanted with a room full of monks, it did something to me. What can I say? It just seemed like the most natural thing in the world to me. Like I had been doing it for a thousand years."

"And you also sit still for five hours a day—on your own?"

"Yes. But usually, not all at once."

"Do all the other monks do that too?"

"No, that's sort of my own personal thing."

"But five hours! Don't you get bored?"

"Heck no. For the most part, I can't even tell that time is passing. If you sit still long enough, it unsticks you from the normal perception of time."

"You mean it's like being asleep?"

"No. It's more like being ridiculously awake."

"Speaking of sleep, how do you have time for it? I mean, besides those five hours, you also have to do the other monk stuff. There's all that hard work, and all those vigils, vespers, and louds."

"Lauds."

"Whatever. The point is, how much sleep do you get?"

"I try to get three or four hours every night," he said, as he picked up a piece of black mushroom with his chopsticks, looked at it and put it back down. "Otherwise, I get a little spaced out."

Jason stretched his arms and pushed his empty plate away. "You've barely touched your food," he said, pointing to Brother Jerry's full plate.

"Oh?" said Brother Jerry, glancing at his plate. "I guess I'm not that hungry. I get that way sometimes."

"Well, if you don't want it, I'll eat it."

"Sure, help yourself."

"Three hours of sleep every night!" said Jason as he took a heaping forkful of bean curd and rice. "Wow!"

"Three or four. It depends. The more I chant, the less I sleep."

–24–

As the screen went blank, Smiley got another vague impression about Brother Jerry. Without thinking, he pressed the play button, and the screen lit up into a freshly harvested wheat field, bordering a forest.

"South Wales," said Smiley pointing at the screen. "Which is in England... sort of."

Suddenly, two adolescent boys in dirty peasant clothes ran out of the woods, and into the wheat field, each carrying a live chicken under his arm.

"Open ground," one of them panted, "not a good idea!"

"I must agree," said the other.

They ran back into the woods.

Smiley watched them weaving their way among the trees and bushes and finally noticed that the boys looked alike. That's when the light flashed in his mind.

"Wait a minute," said Smiley, putting the popcorn box on the empty seat next to him. "That's me and Jerry! We're brothers! Twins! Fourteen years old. My name is Flynn, and his name is Donwald. Or, is it the other way around? No, that's right, I'm Flynn; he's Donwald."

The two boys on the screen had slowed down to a brisk walk to catch their breath.

"Blimey," said Flynn, "it's like they was waitin' for us."

"That's the last time we pinch a chicken in broad daylight."

As Smiley watched, the twins jogged through a clearing the size of a large house. It was covered with grass and bordered by a circle of stone pillars, each about three feet tall.

Smiley held up his hand at the screen. "Wait a minute," he called out to the boys. "That's not right. You two guys are not supposed to be stealing chickens. You're supposed to become monks!"

Donwald stopped. He dropped the chicken and his face became expressionless.

Flynn was all the way to the other side, when he turned and noticed his brother standing at attention in the middle of the circle, without his chicken.

"What's the matter?" asked Flynn.

"Hush!"

"Hush me arse!" said Flynn. "Why do you stand there like a statue? You want us to get caught?"

"The constable's men are running in the wrong direction," said Donwald with an eerie calm in his voice.

"The wrong direction, you say. How do you know?"

Donwald placed his fingertips on his temples. "I'm receivin' a message."

"Cripes, another one of your bleedin' messages. I'm beginnin' to think you're possessed. Me own brother turnin' into a witch!"

"Hold your tongue." Donwald closed his eyes. "A spirit is here with us."

"Aye, I might 'ave known." Flynn wiped the sweat from his forehead. "Another one of those busybody ghosts who has nothin' better to do than pester honest Earth folk."

Donwald squinted, as if he was struggling to hear.

"Why don't they all just go on home and leave us be?" continued Flynn.

"Be quiet, I tell you," said Donwald in a hushed voice. "This spirit isn't like the others. Powerful 'e is. Most powerful. Resides in a magical land far away."

"Bully for 'im. What's 'e want?"

"First off, you need to let go of the chicken."

"Let go of me chicken? Why? I stole it fair and square."

"It's important that you let go of it."

"I'll do no such thing! Now, come along, and tell that demented spook to piss off. We need to be movin' on before the men catch up with us."

"Relax, we're safe—for now. But we must pay 'eed and do exactly like the spirit says or we'll be hangin' from a rope by tomorrow morning."

Flynn dropped the chicken.

Donwald fell deeper into his trance. "We must journey to Scotland. Once there, we are to present ourselves at the Ar… Arb… Arbro… Arbroath Abbey."

"An abbey? Isn't that where they keep monks?"

Donwald seemed to go deeper still. "We are to become monks."

"Monks, you say! I don't means any disrespect to the spirit, but what sort of deranged priest would accept the likes of us as monks? We can't read or write! And we 'aven't been inside a church since our mum passed on."

"No matter," said Donwald, his eyes still closed. "We will be accepted."

"Cripes, this is too strange." Flynn placed his hands on his hips and looked round at the circle of stones. "What do monks do anyway?"

"I don't know. But we must do this. Our lives depend on it."

"Well… if we must, we must. But, does this mean we have to give up stealin' chickens?"

"I suppose so," said Donwald opening his eyes. "I never heard of monks stealin' for their livelihood. I think they just beg."

"That doesn't make any sense. Seems to me that stealin' is more honorable than beggin'."

"Aye," said Donwald rubbing his chin. "But it's not for us to question the ways of God."

They stood in silence for a while. The circle of stones seemed to have a soothing presence.

Donwald closed his eyes again. "Wait. There's another message. This one is for you."

"Me?" said Flynn, taking a step back.

"The spirit says you must remember this day and think upon it often. It will help you in the future...way off in the future."

"Really now," said Flynn. "And who might this spirit be who's takin' such an interest in us?"

Donwald paused. He opened his eyes, suddenly looking puzzled. "You."

–25–

As that scene faded, Smiley contemplated Brother Jerry's devotional practices. The violet screen looked like it was trying to get his attention. It was trying to form another image. Though he could not see much detail, it seemed very ancient. And it seemed to convey a feeling of foreboding.

He tried to concentrate and make the image clearer. Instead, it became blurrier. Instinctively, he closed his eyes and found himself entering into a state of unusually deep relaxation and monastic silence. It happened very easily, as if it was second nature to him. As his mind became still, he felt as if he was drifting back in time.

Opening his eyes, he pressed the play button on the armrest. The screen now showed two young men. At first, Smiley thought they were Flynn and Donwald again, but they turned out to be Shoupang and Ravi from the other blurrier movie. This time, the image was very clear and he finally got a good look at their faces. Yes, they both looked hauntingly familiar.

–26–

"You need not worry," said Shoupang, as he removed the string from around the rolled up map, "by the time you and Gandhari are married, your house will be completed. For now, we need to concentrate on the task at hand."

Ravi sighed. "You are right, as usual."

"Yes, always heed the words of your elders," he said, placing the map on the table. "Well… not *always*."

They laughed.

Shoupang placed his index finger on the map and drew a circle around one small area. "As I was saying, the bottom land, here, will not provide enough space to grow all the spices, cotton, hemp, and indigo we will need. So, we will shift the main growing area to here," he poked another spot on the map, "the high-ground, next to the hills. We will use the bottomland to expand the vegetable garden and plant fruit trees that require more moisture. Also, by using the bottomland, we will be able to utilize a secondary pond, which we will dig on slightly higher ground, right here," he pointed to another spot on the map. "It will be fed by the same stream that feeds the main pond. From that secondary pond, we will dig a small canal that will allow us to more easily irrigate the bottomland, so we can make full use of it."

"Most efficient," nodded Ravi. "But what about the high-ground?" he said, pointing to the other side of the property. "Will it have enough moisture to support our production?"

"That is a certainty, my friend. During my uncle's visit, he said this land might just well be a gold mine, given its potential. And, as you have so astutely observed, the key to our success is water. We will dig a series of trenches," said Shoupang, waving his arm at the hills. "They will be used to collect the monsoon rain from the entire hillside and guide it into the drier portions of our land. We will collect the water in a cistern and a third pond we will dig in that area. Both will be positioned so as to allow us to utilize canals that we will use to easily irrigate the land, minimizing the need to carry water. That will free up our hired laborers for other tasks. If we construct the third pond and cistern properly, they should provide additional water for quite some time during the dry season to irrigate the land and water the animals. Only the highest corner of the land will remain arid; and only during the dry season."

Ravi laughed. "That is brilliant!"

"The only issues with the use of irrigation canals is that we lose water through seepage into the ground. But I think it's a good compromise; we waste a little water to save on labor."

Ravi rubbed his chin. "Actually," he nodded pensively, "we need not compromise. We can fashion a number of curved ceramic tiles in our workshop and place them in the canals. This will not only reduce water loss, but also minimize soil erosion in the years to come."

Shoupang thought for a second and then burst out laughing. "Brilliant," he said slapping Ravi on the back. "Anyway, during very long dry periods, we can use the main pond in the bottomland as a secondary source of water, since it will obviously retain water longer than the other two ponds. For added assurance, the two deep wells, which we will dig at either end of the property, here and here," he pointed to the map again, "will provide emergency water in the event of a prolonged drought."

Ravi nodded, as he gazed at the land.

"Think of it," continued Shoupang, excitedly. "We can become a major food provider for this entire region. We will be virtually impervious to drought. People will come to know that we can grow food when no one else can. What's more, when they come here for their fruits, vegetables, staple foods and spices, they will also buy our manufactured products. This way, we can sell some of our wares without having to travel at all, which means that our profit margin is higher. This estate will be like a small self-contained market place," Shoupang waved his arms, "where the local residents can obtain their needed goods without making a day's journey to the city. Our operation can be the focal point for the growth of a new village. It will be a most prosperous village with an abundance of food and a thriving commerce. No one need go hungry."

"A worthy vision," Ravi nodded.

"I agree. I wish I could take credit for it. But most of this was my uncle's idea. He believes that poverty and hunger are totally unnecessary with intelligent planning. He also reminded me of the two main factors that maximize profits. The first one is, of course, to get supplies as cheaply as possible. That means we grow and make most of the merchandise we sell. The second point is that before we even think about distant markets, we take full advantage of local markets, because the further you have to travel, the more it eats into your profits. In that sense, the ideal situation is where people just come to us. As our profits increase, we will acquire some of the surrounding land while it can still be obtained inexpensively, so we can later expand our operation and produce enough to sell to the distant markets.

"Ingenious," Ravi smiled.

"I am delighted that you approve. Here you go, Master Architect," said Shoupang, handing Ravi the map, "round up the men, and make it happen."

"Yes, my Lord," said Ravi, as he bowed ceremoniously and walked off.

Shoupang flopped into the chair and placed his feet on the table, feeling very satisfied with himself. And then, in the silence, out of nowhere, he got an urge to meditate, which he had not done in many months.

He removed his feet from the table and placed them flat on the ground, kicking off his sandals. Taking a deep breath, he closed his eyes. The whirlwind of thoughts settled down and he gradually became relaxed. His mind gradually entered into a deep silence. He was surprised how easily it all came back to him. Eventually, he lost track of time. Random images flashed through his mind in rapid succession. Remembering the Master's instructions, he did not try to analyze them or push them away, but simply let them pass in their own time. However, the last image shattered his peace.

His eyes snapped open. He quickly got up from his chair and called out to a worker standing outside the stable. "Ashuk!"

"Yes, Sir."

"Saddle the fastest and strongest horse, immediately. Include a sword, knife, and bow and arrows."

Shoupang ran up the hill to the main house. Bolting through the front door, he called his wife.

"Cali! Cali!"

No answer.

"Cali, where are you?"

The back door opened and his wife walked in. "I am here, husband. Why the shouting?"

"Pack enough food and water for a three-day journey on horseback. Immediately!"

"Why? What's wrong?"

"Now, woman!" he said, running out the door again. "I will explain before I depart."

–27–

The screen went blank. Smiley drummed his fingers on the armrest.

"I'm Jason. And I'm other people, too, like maybe this Shoupang character. But most of all, I'm Jason. No, most of all, I'm Smiley. But who the hell is Smiley? Am I dreaming, am I dead? Am I Jason dreaming about Smiley, or am I Smiley dreaming about Jason?"

His mind was overloaded. The theater disappeared. So did his body. Everything went black, which was nice; he needed the rest.

When he became conscious, everything was jumbled. Many places and non-places, many identities, many monks. The only point of reference was Smiley, who was sort of like Jason—but more so.

When he silently asked for clarification, four stars appeared. They surrounded him, forming a three-side pyramid. Instead of getting clarity, however, he found himself merging into a sea of amorphous violet stuff that had no up and no down, no past and no future, no here and no there. All memories and personalities were dissolving into nothing. All names, all faces, all places, gone. However, the dissolving stopped abruptly when a single voice cried out... faint but tenacious... far away, or maybe deep inside.

"Jason! Jason Mazarosky!" The voice would not dissolve. It seemed to be getting closer—or stronger. Suddenly Jason was back, body and all. Falling, falling.

He stopped with a thud on a soft chair. The lights came on. He was seated in the Vintage Theater, middle of the first row.

Looking around, he realized he had done this before. "Okay," he said, folding his arms, "will somebody please explain what's going on here?"

Silence. And then, muffled footsteps approached from the back of the theater. That tall gentleman appeared again, this time wearing khaki slacks, blue sport shirt, and cream-colored loafers with red trimming. He also looked a bit more masculine and business-like.

"Greetings, Smiley."

"Greetings to you. Brother G, right?"

"Yes. Perhaps I may be of assistance?"

"Sure. Have a seat."

"Thank you." said Brother G, as he sat next to Smiley.

"So, what's going on here?"

"In the past twenty-four years, did you ever wonder about who you are—besides Jason Mazarosky?"

"No. Was I supposed to?"

"Well...never mind."

"So, am I dreaming, or am I dead? And, don't say 'both and neither.' You have two options—dead or dreaming. Or neither. And I guess 'both' is a possibility too. But don't say 'both' *and* 'neither'."

"Very well. But, you must understand that it's all a matter of perspective. From Smiley's perspective, we would have to say 'neither.' However, Jason is still very much in charge, so I guess we should address your question from *his* perspective."

"Okay, go ahead."

"From Jason's perspective, we would have to say 'both,' because there is an equal probability that he is dreaming or has passed on."

"So, you're saying that maybe I'm dreaming and maybe I'm dead?'

"Yes—from Jason's perspective."

Smiley waved his hand around the room. "So, what's all this about?"

"The simplest explanation is that this is a dream going on inside Jason Mazarosky's head."

"And you're a figment of my imagination?"

"Uh, yes," said Brother G, "that's pretty close to the truth. More specifically, I'm a figment of *Smiley's* imagination, and the imagination of all those that Smiley has any relationship with."

"Does that mean you don't really exist?"

"I sort of do, but not in the way that you might think. It's somewhat complicated to explain and not immediately relevant to the issue at hand."

"Alright, skip it."

"Very well."

"So, who is Smiley?"

"Well, you might say that Smiley is a container."

"A container?"

"Let's back up a little. Let's say that Jason Mazarosky is a container. Let's say that he contains twenty-four years of experience. Smiley is a bigger container that holds about twenty-four *hundred* years of experience, which includes Jason Mazarosky. If Smiley is a tall glass of beer, Jason is the foam on top."

"Cute."

Actually, the glass-of-beer analogy may not be quite right. I would say that Jason Mazarosky is more like the crown on the head of the king."

"Yeah, I like that better than the foam on the beer," said Smiley. "Anyway, how come I still feel like Jason?"

"You still *feel* like Jason because you, as Smiley, are still trying to find your way through the circuits of Jason's brain."

"Oh." Smiley looked around. "Why am I here in the Vintage Theater?"

"So you can watch movies, obviously."

"Why?"

"Because, you like watching movies— that is to say, Jason likes watching movies."

Smiley picked up the bucket of popcorn from the floor. "Want some? It's good."

"No, thank you."

Smiley looked at the violet screen. So how come I'm seeing all this stuff from different time periods?"

"Well, if you think of time as being like a river, we are at the river's edge. You can stick your toes in and feel the water and then pull them out again."

"Oh," Smiley nodded . "So, what do we do now, just watch more movies?"

"If you wish."

"Okay." Smiley pushed the play button. "Roll 'em!"

The screen now showed Macunda, sitting by his lake. He did not look well.

—28—

Macunda gazed across the small oval lake, which was now littered with debris. His long, graying black hair was matted and unkempt, falling all over his shoulders. The carob tree behind him and the fruit trees around the lake were bare of leaves and blackened. Some were burned to the ground.

All the buildings, including the main house were destroyed. Most of the wood was burned and the stone walls torn down. The crops beyond the north gate had been either burned or trampled or both.

When Macunda heard a horse approaching from behind at a fast trot, he did not turn. He figured someone came in through the south gate or through one of the gaps in the wall. When the horse stopped just to his right, he turned his head and saw Shoupang dismounting quickly.

"Uncle Macunda," Shoupang said, incredulously.

Macunda stared at him and then signaled for him to sit, as the horse walked directly to the pond and started drinking.

As Shoupang sat on the ground, he said, "Aunt Seva?"

Macunda looked at his nephew and then resumed staring at the lake in front of him. His eyes welled up.

"No," Shoupang said, in a weak, shaky voice. He managed to swallow the lump in his throat. "What about your children and their families."

"All safe, miraculously. Meta is with her in-laws, and all three of my sons and their families are attending the Mela in Calcutta. I was called to a hearing north of here. That is why I was not here when this happened." With a slight break in his voice, he added, "And I am very grateful that Gandhari is with you."

That was the last thing that was said for a while. During the silence, Shoupang finally buried his face in his hands and sobbed. And then they were silent again.

For the first time, Shoupang noticed a knife on the ground, next to his uncle. He made a point to stay at his uncle's side whenever possible.

"Bandits?" Shoupang finally said.

Macunda slowly shook his head no. "They were too thorough." He looked around. "They took their time. And at least part of this was done during daylight hours. Apparently, they were not concerned about the patrolling peace officers."

More silence.

"If they *were* bandits," Macunda continued, "they were the same sort of bandits that attacked your mother and father." He paused and then sighed. "Which means that... I am to blame. My beloved is gone," his lower lip trembled, "because of my arrogance."

Shoupang resisted the temptation to tell his uncle that he was not to blame.

Instinctively, he knew this was not the right time. His uncle needed to give voice to his pain and then just sit with it in silence.

Standing up, Shoupang walked around the immediate area to fully assess the damage. It triggered old forgotten fear and grief from his early childhood. But he pushed the feelings down and sat by his uncle again. For the first time, he noticed a painting in a wooden frame, leaning against the blackened carob tree. It depicted a beautiful long-necked bird with colorful plumage, surrounded by flames. He was curious as to why his uncle had salvaged it, but decided not to ask.

"Gandhari painted it," said Macunda. "She always was a talented child."

More silence.

"When did this happen?" asked Shoupang.

"Three days ago, said Macunda staring at the ground.

After another long pause, Macunda raised his head and looked at his nephew. "How did you get here so quickly. Surely, news of this could not have reached you this fast." He paused again. "One of your visions?"

Shoupang nodded.

"That is least a six day journey," Macunda continued. You did it in just three days?"

Shoupang nodded.

More silence.

"Did you sleep?" asked Macunda.

"A little."

Macunda looked at the horse, now grazing.

"That is not the same horse I started with," said Shoupang.

As they looked at each other, Shoupang thought he detected the barest hint of a smile on his uncle's face.

–29–

The scene faded and the screen became violet. Smiley remained respectfully silent for a while, as the grief vibration that surrounded him resolved itself.

And then, he pressed the play button and the screen sprang to life, showing Macunda again, now sitting on a porch swing overlooking a peaceful meadow, as he gently rocked himself.

Rubbing his chin, he gazed at the small bamboo grove next to the main pond. The water in the pond glistened in the morning sun. In the foreground, servants were still cleaning up after yesterday's celebration. Turning his head to the other side of the property, he looked at the new pond and cistern, which had recently been filled by the monsoon rains. At the edge of the meadow, workers were chopping down trees and clearing brush.

"Good morning, Uncle," said Shoupang, as he fell down on the swing, sending it into wild undulation.

"Good morning, Shoupang," said Macunda, steadying himself.

"That was a grand feast."

"I agree," Macunda nodded, patting his belly. The food was exquisite."

"We grew most of it here, including all the spices," said Shoupang. "My goal is for us to eventually be totally self sufficient." Another tree fell at the edge of the meadow. "That land is being cleared to make room for trees that bear edible nuts and seeds, such as almonds, chestnuts, and walnuts. Eventually, we will be a major supplier of staple foods for the local residents. All available space will be planted with productive trees and bushes." Shoupang pointed to the workers. "And the wood from those felled trees will be used to construct the new buildings and furniture."

Macunda nodded, as Ravi and Gandhari walked hand in hand at the edge of the meadow where the land was being cleared. They stopped briefly, as Ravi gave instructions to the workers.

"My daughter was an exceptionally beautiful bride," said Macunda. "And, I must admit that after spending time with Ravi these past few weeks, I am inclined to agree that he will be a worthy husband for Gandhari."

"Most worthy. I did not realize until recently that he is a deeply spiritual young man. But he is also quite industrious and has a good mind for commerce."

Macunda raised his eyebrows. "Unusual for a Brahmin."

"I think you will find that the Brahmin here are different. And the relationship between the castes is also different. I think you would find it is most to your liking. You have already met Ravi's father, so you know what a fair and generous man he is. There is opportunity here for all men to better themselves. The rapid growth and early success of our enterprise is testimony to—"

"If you are trying to tempt me to migrate to this area and be an active partner in your venture, you may save yourself the effort. As I have already said, commerce no longer interests me."

"You don't have to be involved in commerce, Uncle. Just move down here so you can be close to your family. You still own a fifth part of this estate. And your sons have already decided to migrate even further south of here. You can live here or you can live with them."

"I find that I am enjoying my solitude."

"But it is not safe for you in the North. I fear it will be just a matter of time before they send the assassins after *you*."

"So be it, then," said Macunda, with a blank look on his face. "I should have been the one they eliminated last year, not my wife."

Shoupang sighed, tactfully refraining from responding to his uncle's comment. He decided to wait a while and then play his last card.

"Well, Uncle," said Shoupang, "can you at least extend your visit a few days so you can show us how to organize the new workshop and warehouse... and perhaps a few other items?"

Macunda paused. Then he nodded, with a sad smile on his face.

Shoupang remained silent. He had pushed his uncle as much as he dared. He sat back, as the swing gently rocked back and forth, its barely audible squeak reminiscent of a whimpering child.

Finally, Macunda tilted his head to the side and pointed to the bamboo grove next to the main pond. "Is that all the bamboo you have?"

"Yes."

"I suggest you gradually increase production four-fold over the next ten years."

"Why? It provides plenty of material for baskets and other items."

"In the years to come, more people will be moving south to escape the oppression of the North. Some of them will be people of means. They will acquire land. They will build. As wood becomes scarcer, bamboo will see wider usage. The greater demand for bamboo will raise the price, generating greater profits for the bamboo growers, craftsmen and merchants. Since you engage in all three phases of the bamboo market, your profit margin will be quite high."

Macunda pointed to one of the other ponds, newly filled by the monsoons. "I suggest you grow the additional bamboo next to the new pond. The root system and the added shade provided by the foliage will allow the pond to retain water longer during the dry season."

Shoupang nodded, but deliberately remained silent, as his uncle gazed at the surrounding land.

"And, it seems to me," continued Macunda, "that if you rearrange the trenches on the slopes and support them just right with earthworks on their low side, the high ground will retain almost as much moisture as the bottom land." He paused and then pointed to the highest corner of the land. "Even the most arid region can be green and productive all year round."

They watched as the workers felled another tree.

"It is good to fill your property with productive trees and bushes," Macunda continued. "However, always leave room for plants that simply add beauty to the land."

Shoupang smiled.

As Shoupang and Macunda faded from the screen, Smiley turned to Brother G. "So, I'm Shoupang, right?"

"Yes."

"And I'm also this bigger dude called Smiley. But I still feel like Jason."

"Shoupang is the reason why you, Smiley, have devoted so much time to being a monk." Shoupang is, in one sense, the beginning of the consciousness called Smiley. The experience called Shoupang is complete... more or less. However, Jason is not complete, and that is why you are still strongly identified with him. Jason's memories and desires are overpowering Smiley. You are literally trapped in Jason's brain."

So, do I continue watching movies until I, that is, Jason, has had enough?"

"That seems like a good plan."

Smiley rubbed his chin. "Is it possible for me to actually be in the scene instead of just watching it like a movie?"

"Yes."

"Cool. Can I drop in on any of those scenes that we're looking at."

"Yes, theoretically. But if you just relax and go with the flow, you will probably be pulled to the event that is most emotionally significant for Jason. That would probably be the most productive move."

Smiley nodded. "Okay. What do I do?"

"Just press the play button and close your eyes."

Smiley did so. When he opened his eyes, he found himself standing on the sidewalk, next to the juniper hedges, just outside Forrest Park. A screaming ambulance with flashing lights passed by, weaving its way through the stalled traffic. The man in the suit, sitting on the secluded park bench just beyond the juniper hedges, looked up briefly to look at the ambulance, and then resumed reading the newspaper. Across the street, in the garage of Forrest Park Auto Service, Raffi was hoisting up Jason Mazarosky's red pickup truck on the hydraulic lift.

The scene was familiar, but somehow it looked foreign. Smiley felt disoriented.

"You can retreat to the theater any time you wish."

Smiley turned quickly and saw Brother G, who was once again translucent. His smooth seamless body glowed all over. He seemed more like himself now. His eyes were a little bigger and rounder and his hair was longer. He looked rather feminine.

"If you would like to leave," continued Brother G, "just imagine that you are in the theater with your eyes open."

Smiley nodded. "Yeah, I might do that real soon." He noticed that his own body was now translucent. He glanced around. Everything was so strange. Empty space wasn't empty anymore. It seemed to be made of some kind of jelly-like stuff.

He could feel its texture. Everything he saw seemed to be made of the same stuff. The dogs, people, and cars weren't really solid objects moving through empty space. They were all just bulges and waves in that same field of jelly-like stuff. Even the thoughts and emotions that flew around were made of the same stuff.

His luminous body resonated with the waves of emotion that were flowing by. He felt smothered and sluggish. It was like walking through maple syrup.

For the first time, he noticed that he did not sense things in ways he was used to. He wasn't really seeing things with his eyes, which seemed to be strictly ornamental. Neither did he hear voices, or smell the air, or feel the ground under his feet. There was just an amorphous awareness that he could only compare to radar. It was rather bland. The richness and diversity of his five senses were reduced to just a bunch of vibrations in a field of homogeneous stuff. He didn't like it. Granted, his memory allowed him to translate this new way of perceiving into something that resembled sight, sound, taste, and smell, but it just wasn't the same.

Suddenly Smiley became amorphously aware of Brother Jerry walking by quickly along the sidewalk. He was probably at the scene of the accident and was now going to the parking lot, presumably to get his car and follow the ambulance to the hospital.

Smiley wondered what Katie was doing. He closed his eyes. When he opened them, he found himself sitting in the back seat of Katie's car. Brother G was sitting next to him.

Katie was sitting in the driver's seat. Smiley felt the waves of fear emanating from her. He wanted to reach out and touch her, but realized he was no longer capable of doing that. Being amorphously aware of her was not the same as seeing her face, smelling her body, and feeling the texture and warmth of her skin.

He remembered the emotions he used to feel when he was physically with Katie. He wasn't sure whether he was missing Katie or missing those emotions. Maybe there wasn't any difference!

He closed his eyes. When he opened them, he and Brother G were at the entrance of Forrest Park Auto Service. Raffi was working on Jason's red pickup truck on the hydraulic lift. Another mechanic waved to the man in the business suit who was still reading the newspaper as he sat on the secluded bench in the park. The man stood up and started walking across the street by going through the narrow gap in the juniper hedges.

Smiley felt the waves of low-grade anger emanating from the man, apparently due the fact that his car wasn't ready yet. That was when Smiley realized that he could get a pretty good replica of the sensory and emotional experience of the people around him just by being in their vicinity. He felt Raffi's mild low-back pain, the hunger pangs of one of the other mechanics in the garage, and the visual delight of another mechanic who was watching an attractive woman walk by. It was almost like being physical again!

Almost, but not quite. He decided that being a peeping Tom wasn't nearly as much fun as full participation, so he backed off.

Katie came to mind. Yes, he could easily plug into the right person and experience a facsimile of the emotions he used to feel with Katie. But, he could not duplicate Katie.

He decided to retreat to the theater.

Opening his eyes, Smiley stared at the blank screen. He was more confused than ever. Contorting his face, he drummed his fingers on the armrest.

"Perhaps you should watch this," said Brother G, now wearing the shirt and pants and looking masculine again.

The screen now showed Katie walking slowly on the grass of Forrest Park. She had a pensive expression on her face.

Smiley sat up straight. "What's the time frame?" he said quickly.

"About two hours before Jason gets conked on the head."

–31–

Katie Sprite's tennis shoes dragged along the grass. Her sparkling green eyes were downcast and her brow furrowed. She adjusted the strap of the blue denim handbag that hung over her left shoulder. Her lips, normally full and sensuous, were squeezed together, as if she was trying to answer a tough question on a calculus test.

A gust of wind blew her long, strawberry-blond hair across her face. Raising her head, she combed her hair back with the fingers of both hands, momentarily exposing the full beauty of her moon-face.

As she walked past a large oak tree, she was startled by a voice. "Hello, Katie."

Turning her head quickly, she saw a bearded young monk sitting against the trunk of the tree with his shoes off.

"Brother Jerry! What a surprise!"

"Beautiful day for a walk in the park, hey?"

"Actually, I was looking for a place to sit and study, and then I'm going to meet Jason for lunch at Mama Tang's Restaurant. What are *you* doing here?" she smiled.

The young monk flipped his hands in the air. "Just hanging out."

"I mean, what are you doing in *town*."

"I have a meeting at Marist College downtown. They want me to teach a psychology course and maybe do some counseling."

Katie looked down at the books in her denim bag. "You know, this is such a coincidence—meeting you here, I mean. There's something I've been wanted to discuss with you. I guess it sort of falls within the ballpark of counseling." She paused. "Remember about six months ago? The Thanksgiving dinner?"

"Yes."

"After everyone left, you, Sam, Jason, and I were sitting on the porch, and you were telling us the story of how you became a monk."

Brother Jerry smiled. "Uh-huh."

"At the time, it seemed like just a really cool story. And funny as heck," She chuckled. "I laughed so hard I thought I was going to p——. Anyway," she said, looking away quickly. "I'm having an issue that's sort of related to some of the things you talked about… I think. Except that my story isn't funny."

"Well," said Brother Jerry, glancing at the big digital clock on the wall of the bank building across the street, "my appointment downtown isn't until later this afternoon. Would you like to discuss it right now?"

"Yes. I would really appreciate that."

"Please step into my office," he said, waving his hand at the ground, "and pull up a chair."

Katie sat on the ground across from Brother Jerry, sort of at an angle so that they were both facing the big fountain and children's playground in the distance. Just beyond the fountain, the surface of Murphy Lake glistened under the cloudless sky.

"First I want to say that, as of three weeks ago, Jason and I are officially engaged."

"Oh! Congratulations."

"Thanks," Katie smiled briefly. "That's part of what I wanted to talk to you about. Marriage, children, school, my future. It's all very confusing right now. I realize that lots of people face this kind of thing, but there are other things going on here that I can't quite put my finger on. It's almost… spooky." She sighed.

"Spooky, hey?"

"It's like I'm in a theater watching a play. And backstage there's all this activity that we don't see, so everyone just forgets about it and watches the drama on stage. For example, my relationship with Jason feels so right, but at the same time, there's an equally strong feeling that we will separate. It's downright eerie."

"I relate," Brother Jerry nodded. "Let's try this: Just for now, let those conflicted spooky feelings just be as they are, without trying to fix them. And just consider how you would conduct your life, if you weren't getting married to Jason."

"That's easy. I see myself going to medical school and eventually opening up a family practice, with an emphasis on good nutrition and healthy lifestyle."

"Can you do all that while being married to Jason?"

"Yes... I mean... I think so." She laughed and covered her face with her hands.

"It's okay," Brother Jerry chuckled. "Let those doubts speak."

"If I become an MD, it means that education will always be a big part of my life. Jason is not interested in that. He also doesn't seem to be the least bit concerned about it. And, it's easy for me to get pulled into his freewheeling non-academic world. I'm doing my homework and he calls and says, 'hey, want to go see a movie?'"

"Are you saying that he trivializes your education?"

"No," she laughed, "it's just that *I* have a hard time saying no. Other than that, he's very supportive. I tell him about the sacrifices we would have to make, and he says, 'Honey, whatever you need to get through school, I'll be there.' I tell him that once I graduate from med school, I would have little time to cook, and he says, 'We'll order a pizza.'"

Brother Jerry smiled.

"He's just so busy enjoying life in the moment," continued Katie, "that he isn't the least bit concerned about the future."

"Hmmm," said Brother Jerry, "sounds serious."

Katie looked at him, at first not knowing what to say. And then she burst out laughing. "Okay, I know my concerns may sound kind of ridiculous, but..."

"Not at all," said Brother Jerry. "Your main concern isn't who will cook dinner. Your concern is how a medical doctor/vegetarian can share a life with a construction worker who devours everything except books."

"Precisely. I might become dissatisfied with him. Jason is not stupid. But, he has no interest in developing his mind. And I feel like, eventually, that will cause a problem. This nagging feeling won't go away and I don't know what to do about it."

They were silent for a while, looking at the children playing around the lake in the distance.

"Do you pray?" asked Brother Jerry.

"Yeah," she said with a touch of defensiveness. "Why do you ask?"

"In my experience, after a person has said everything that needs to be said about a problem, the next step is to pray about it. If you are so inclined, we can apply a little prayer power right now. I hear that two heads are better than one."

Katie folded her arms.

"Unless you just don't feel like it," Brother Jerry added.

"I *do* feel like it," she replied, unfolding her arms. But, first I need to clarify something." She put the palms of her hands together, gathering her thoughts. "And, of course, this is a totally separate issue from my situation with Jason."

"Of course."

Katie reached into her denim bag and took out the organic chemistry textbook. She started to show Brother Jerry the picture of the three-sided pyramid on the cover, but changed her mind.

"Never mind," she said, putting the book back in the bag. "That's not really relevant. The main thing is that when I seek divine guidance, like when I pray, I generally call upon Mother Mary." Her eyes darted to the organic chemistry book. "In fact, quite frankly, if it weren't for her, I wouldn't go to church at all. Truthfully, she is the one thread that keeps me connected to Catholicism."

She fell silent, staring at the children in the playground area.

"Is that all?" asked Brother Jerry.

"No… there's more." She paused again. "When I pray to Mother Mary, I feel this…"

"Yes?"

"Energy."

Brother Jerry laughed. "Oh that."

She leaned forward. "Are you saying that you know what I'm talking about?"

Brother Jerry nodded. "I went through that myself a few years ago."

"That's wonderful. I just knew you would understand," She leaned forward some more. "So, tell me about it."

"Well, I didn't feel inclined to do anything with it. I just sort of let it be there. Eventually, I got used to it and stopped noticing it."

"Not me. In fact, it's gotten very strong. It has…"

"Substance?"

"Yes! You *do* understand! It has a rich texture. It's earthy and soft and warm." Katie looked at the lake for a while and then slapped her thighs and looked at Brother Jerry. "Let's pray!" she said.

"Okay." He looked at the digital clock on the wall of the bank. What time did you say you were going to meet Jason for lunch?"

"12:15." She looked at her wristwatch. "My God, it's 12:15 right now!" She leaned over and gave Jerry a sitting hug. "Thank you. You have helped me so much."

Standing quickly, she slung her bag over her left shoulder. "I'll pray later," she said, prancing away.

The screen went blank, as Smiley continued staring at it.

"Maybe you should also watch the next scene, as well," said Brother G.

The screen came to life again and now showed Jason Mazarosky and Katie sitting in a restaurant. Smiley watched as Jason's index finger slid down the laminated page of the menu.

"Hmmm," Jason nodded. Having made his selection, he dropped the menu on the table and stared out the window at the parking lot, but quickly got bored with that. So he examined the picture of the red dragon against the glossy white cover of the menu, admiring its intense red eyes, teeth, and scales. But he soon lost interest in that too, so he picked up his chopsticks and placed them vertically behind his upper lip, letting them hang down like fangs.

"Hey, look, Katie, I'm a walrus."

Katie lowered her menu and looked across the table. "Oh, Jason!" she groaned, raising her menu again and retreating behind its red dragon. "Why must you always do that?"

"Seems like a reasonable thing to do," he garbled, as the chopsticks wiggled around. "And besides, you like it."

Katie lowered her menu just enough to see Jason's shaggy brown hair, freckled face, and whimsical eyes; his upper lip pressing against the dangling chopsticks. She ducked behind the red dragon again and tried not to laugh too loudly.

Jason removed the chopsticks and started tapping them on the table like drum sticks.

"What is it with you today?" asked Katie. "You're as hyper as a chipmunk."

"Hyper? Me?" He looked at the parking lot again. "You know, now that you mention it, I have been racing a little."

"What's the matter?"

"Nothing. The crew is getting behind on the Johnson house, but, otherwise, everything's cool." He picked up his chopsticks and started drumming again. "Hey, do you want to go to the ball game tonight?"

"Sounds like fun. But no," she sighed. "I really shouldn't. I'm getting behind in school. I was going to study this morning at the park, but then I got into that conversation with Brother Jerry—"

"HOLY COW!" said Jason, slapping his forehead.

"What's the matter?"

"I forgot about Rusty!"

"Rusty? The plumber guy?"

"Yeah." He glanced at his watch. "Jesus, it's 12:40!" He felt his pockets. "Damn, I left my cell phone back at the Johnson house. " He stood up and reached into his back pocket. "I'm sorry, Katie. I gotta go. I'm supposed to meet him in five minutes at the Johnson house for an estimate."

He placed a twenty-dollar bill on the table. "I'm really sorry about this."

"No problem," Katie chuckled. "I came prepared." Reaching into her denim bag, she pulled out a spiral-bound notebook. "I have an organic chemistry test at three o'clock today. I really should be studying right now."

"I'm a bad influence on you." He leaned over and gave her a quick kiss on the lips. "I'll see you later," he said, walking quickly away.

–33–

As the scene faded to violet, Smiley slouched in his seat and remained silent, feeling like he was being quietly torn in half. He tapped the side of the popcorn box with his fingertips. "It's pretty clear," he said, "that Katie has this whole life ahead of her, and that I—Jason—might sort of mess things up for her."

He stood up and paced along the front row of theater seats for a while, as Brother G sat patiently with his hands on his lap.

"Okay," Smiley said, finally sitting down again. "I'm really this dude named Smiley, but I still think that I'm Jason."

"Correct."

"And as much as I want to continue to be Jason, it's clear that if I do that, it will mess things up for Katie. So, obviously, the right thing for me to do is to remember that I'm Smiley and move on. I should just let the Earth folks get on with their lives."

"Seems reasonable."

"So, how do I do that?"

"Normally, you would remember by simply being complete with Jason."

"Okay," Smiley nodded, "How do we do that?"

"Under the circumstances, the most direct way to bring completeness to Jason's experience is for you to remember that you are Smiley."

"But you just said I can't remember that I'm Smiley as long as Jason is not complete."

"Correct."

Smiley stared into space.

"Actually, it's not as paradoxical as it sounds. Since we are at the edge of time, it is doable."

"Well, let's have a crack at it."

"Very well. Close your eyes and concentrate."

"On what?"

"Nothing. Just concentrate."

"I can't concentrate without having something to concentrate on."

"Sure you can. Concentrate on nothing."

Smiley tried to concentrate on nothing. To his surprise, he found it easy. His mind quickly settled down into a deep monastic silence. When he opened his eyes, the screen had lit up. It now showed an image of four people on a mountaintop. He tried to determine what they were doing, but it all seemed incomprehensible. They were strikingly different from one another in appearance, but in their eyes they were almost exactly the same—sort of baby-like. Two were more or less female, two were more or less male.

Suddenly, one of the four, an old heavy-set man, filled the entire screen. He glowed with majestic blue light. And, he had a goofy grin on his face.

"Do you remember the garden?" asked the smiling old man.

The screen now showed a little garden next to a cottage, high up on the side of yet another mountain. Standing in the garden was Shoupang, talking with the Master.

–34–

"Yes, Master, I am happy with my life. Our caravan is full, and my wife, Cali, is a joy. She carries our fifth child."

"May your joys continue to multiply," said the old man.

"Our profits have been substantial and we were able to distribute a fair sum to families in need."

The old man nodded silently as he leisurely tilled the soil.

Shoupang slapped his forehead and grimaced. "Forgive me, Master. I said that only to ingratiate myself in your eyes."

"Quite all right. And, since you are wanting to gain my favor, I would guess that you want something of me?"

"Yes, Master. Ever since the tragedy with Aunt Seva, I was reminded that worldly pleasures are fleeting. It awakened my old restlessness. Once again, I wish to learn how to transcend the earthly life. Now that I am meditating again, mundane reality sometimes seems silly to me."

"You cannot transcend it if you regard it as silly."

"Why not?"

"To truly ascend to the highest octave of Heaven means that you respect and value the smallest things of the Earth. Therefore, you will depart from this world when you are simply thankful for having had the experience."

Shoupang nodded. "Aunt Seva used to say such things. I must confess, it seems paradoxical to me."

"Well then, you may look at it this way: You regard earthly life as silly because you do not understand the fullness of it. If you do not understand the fullness of it, you cannot transcend it."

"Surely then, I wish to understand the fullness of it. How can I do so?"

"You would do well to take a lesson from your friend, Ravi. He is devoted to monastic virtue, but in ways that are harmonious with his earthly life."

Shoupang nodded. "Yes," he chuckled. "With me, it is more like a tug-of-war."

"Be at ease, my friend. The understanding you seek is simply the fruit of the happy life you are living. Return to your family and your honest work."

Shoupang sighed. "Very well, Master. I thank you for giving me audience." Bringing his palms together, he bowed respectfully and walked away, as he carefully stepped over the rows of freshly tilled soil. When he got to the edge of the garden, he paused and turned back to the old man.

"Master, may I ask one more question?"

"Certainly."

"I do not want to seem impatient, but…"

"Your impatience is beautiful. Speak freely."

"When will I be ready to help you with your great work?"

"What great work is that?"

"I continue to have dreams that our society is slowly degenerating. Our rules of social order are gradually being perverted into tools of slavery. The oppression in the North seems to be gradually creeping to the South. You never speak of it, but I know that you are helping to diffuse such evil so it doesn't completely destroy us. When will I be ready to help?"

"You will be ready…in no time."

Smiley was about to press the stop button, but hesitated. He continued watching the scene, as Shoupang walked away from the garden and approached his horse.

–35–

Shoupang guided his horse down the mountain, still deeply puzzled by his strange discontent. Suddenly, he got the eerie feeling that he was being watched. He stopped his horse and looked around. The Master's cottage and the monastery were out of sight in the slopes above. Far below at the foot of the mountain, he saw the caravan.

The low-grade tension in his stomach he had been feeling recently became more noticeable. Feeling dizzy, he dismounted, and sat cross-legged on the grassy slope. In the silence, the feeling of being watched grew stronger.

His stomach became tenser and he felt dizzier. Grabbing his temples, he closed his eyes. Holding his body very still, he felt a series of clicking sensations in his head, followed by an intense pressure between his eyebrows.

An image formed in his mind. He saw a young man in a darkened room filled with chairs. Shoupang was startled, but quickly regained his composure.

As he became more relaxed, the image became clearer and richer in detail. Transfixed by the strange image, Shoupang got the notion that he was being watched by *himself* from a vantage point just beyond the normal flow of time. Suddenly, his future became like a brightly lit corridor.

The vision lasted for just a few seconds. When it faded, the tension in his stomach dissolved. Keeping his eyes closed, he became deeply relaxed. And then, to his surprise, the face of his mother appeared in his mind, followed by his father. They both smiled at him, and silently told him how proud they were of him.

Long forgotten images of his early childhood flashed through his mind. He saw his mother bathing him, and his father showing him how to create a cup on a potter's wheel.

As the images continued, tears emerged from behind his closed eyelids; tears of sadness that gradually became tears of joy. A smile formed on his face.

When a gentle breeze ruffled his hair, he opened his eyes. He had no idea how long he had been sitting. He looked back up the mountain and silently thanked the Master.

Standing up, he got back on his horse and resumed his journey down the mountain. As he approached the caravan, his mind drifted to the business contacts he and Uncle Macunda would make in Babylonia, Egypt, and the other emerging markets of the West.

—36—

Smiley continued staring at Shoupang on the screen. Suddenly, he felt as if an electrical circuit had just been completed. The immense span of time between Shoupang and Jason became like a brightly lit corridor. And he remembered himself fully as Smiley.

The screen now showed a stony mountaintop. It was dome-like, ancient and weathered, covered with patches of lichen and numerous cracks filled with grass. Without bothering to press any buttons, he projected himself into the scene.

His body glowed. It was smooth and seamless. He felt a little groggy, as if he had awakened too quickly from a deep sleep. He was aware of many names and faces, all nested within the container called *Smiley*. However, as soon as he got used to the idea that Smiley was his deeper identity, he became vaguely aware that Smiley was just one of many names nested within an even bigger container. In that very instant, four luminous stars appeared in front of him, forming a three-sided pyramid.

Silent musical notes emanated from the pyramid, asking Smiley if he was ready to build the grid and move on.

Smiley silently gave permission. The pyramid responded by enveloping Smiley. He looked up at the silver star directly over his head. The other three stars formed a triangle on the ground. The four stars started giving off beautiful soothing tones that embraced Smiley. The silver star had a tone that was gentle and kind. The green sphere radiated peace. The red sphere radiated a sense of safety. The blue sphere was playful and funny.

The tones swirled and throbbed all around and through Smile's body, causing it to vibrate with confidence. The silent musical tones from the pyramid reminded him that the task he was about to perform was not their creation, but Shoupang's.

Smiley nodded in silent remembrance and his electromagnetic body exploded into a gigantic smile. And it was a most proper smile; its precise frequency was established by the pattern of affection initiated by Shoupang and perfected over twenty-four hundred years. The radiance spread evenly in all directions from the mountaintop and became part of a vast energetic grid of remembrance, designed to help the human inhabitants of Earth smile properly.

Task completed.

Another signal from the pyramid. Now that Smiley had fulfilled his purpose, he was ready to gain full access to the multidimensional freeways into the higher octaves.

Again, Smiley gave permission.

The pyramid abruptly disappeared.

Standing alone on the lichen-covered mountaintop, a portal, oval in shape with a black interior, opened in mid-air directly in front of him.

It was pulling him in. As he approached it, his seamless body started dissolving, along with all his neatly ordered memories and personalities. Swallowed! I'm being swallowed! Should I fight it? No, this is why Smiley came into existence—to dissolve into this moment—the moment that contains all moments! The ecstasy that contains all ecstasies. Swallowed by...me; it's just me—the me that existed before Smiley existed. It was a summation and multiplication of every joyful experience he ever experienced in linear time. It had a sweet familiar quality to it, like going home, and yet it had newness, a freshness, and joyful expectancy that evoked a sense of "birth."

Smiley was on the verge of joyfully dissolving into his own deeper primordial state, but suddenly, it all stopped. A faint impulse, a tiny voice spread through his dissolving field and caused it to stop dissolving.

The impulse was like a persistent desire; something about sex, Chinese food, and... softball tournaments? What's this?

The impulse refused to go away. It was causing Smiley's electromagnetic body to condense even more. Suddenly, he became very frightened. The bliss of the emerging Self became the terror of the disappearing self, as if he was about to fall into a great abyss and vanish forever.

"HOLD EVERYTHING!" he roared.

The portal closed. And he found himself falling through space. He landed with a painless thud on a soft chair.

–37–

Smiley was once again seated in the Vintage Theater, in a body that resembled Jason Mazarosky's. Jason's thoughts, memories, mannerisms, and desires were at the forefront. The four stars, still configured as a pyramid, were now on the screen, against a violet background.

"What's the matter?" said Brother G, who was sitting in the next seat.

Smiley turned his head quickly, startled. He glanced at the four stars on the screen and then looked back at Brother G. "You're one of them, right?"

Brother G nodded, grinning sheepishly.

"But you're not Shoupang's Master."

"No, I'm the red star," said Brother G pointing at the screen. "Shoupang's Master is blue star."

"I thought I was ready," said Smiley, "but I'm not. Jason Mazarosky simply won't go away."

"Well, that's understandable," said Brother G, "This drama is, in a very real sense, occurring entirely in his head. It seems only fair that he should have a say in this."

"I won't argue with that. The way I feel right now, there is no way that I'm going though that portal. I don't mind losing something like a chariot race or all my worldly treasures or a physical body or two. But, I don't think I can let go of every bit of my identity without making a fuss about it."

"Your fussing is most beautiful to us," said the four stars, in a collective human voice that had the quality of a musical quartet.

"I'm glad you think so," said Smiley, looking briefly at the screen, and then turning back to Brother G. "This doesn't feel safe to me."

"It's perfectly safe, I can assure you," said Brother G.

"Oh, sure, for *you* it's perfectly safe! You've never been down in the trenches!"

"Trenches?" Brother G looked puzzled. "What trenches are you referring—?"

"I have so many stray thoughts and images!"

"Time-bound memory fragments," said the Master's musical voice from the blue star on the screen. "I have a few myself. Delightful, aren't they?"

"Uh... no, not really."

"No need to be concerned," said Brother G. "Once you let go of everything, you will realize that no part of you is ever lost."

Smiley placed his hands on his hips. "I feel so not ready," he said shaking his head. "I still feel so... human."

"Your humanity is beautiful to us," chanted the stars.

"This training period was supposed to prepare me to have free access to the galactic freeways. But when I started to go through, I went into chaos. It was like...hell."

"Naturally. You were attempting to gain access to the galactic freeways without fully liberating the emotional body."

"Why didn't you warn me?"

"Warn you?" the four stars chanted. "You would have us steal your experience from you?"

Smiley watched as silent musical tones and multidimensional equations bounced playfully among the four stars. He could not comprehend the exchange, but it was reminiscent of young children dancing around a unique and wondrous gift.

Finally Brother G spoke. "We are not skilled in that area, but we are willing to learn, if that would serve you."

Smiley felt very confused. "Look, I'm just not ready for this. Maybe I need more time in a body of flesh."

"Perhaps," said Brother G. "Your training period as Smiley *was* rather brief."

"Here I go again," said Smiley, "back to the cradle. Perhaps I should be a monk again so I can finally learn some real patience."

"You are certainly free to do so," said Brother G. "However...uh...wait a moment, please."

Smiley watched as the four stars on the screen exchanged silent musical tones. When they were complete, Brother G spoke. "Before you begin the birth sequence," he said, "do you wish to be... uh... warned?"

"Yes."

"Very well." Brother G pointed to the screen. "Watch."

The screen now showed two bearded young monks sitting at opposite ends a rectangular wooden table. They appeared to be twins. Each had a quill in hand, as they carefully copied old tattered scrolls onto fresh parchment. Smiley leaned forward, looking intently at the scene.

One of the monks stopped working and looked blankly into space, turning his head to the side, as if trying to hear something. Then he sighed and looked out the window. Tapping his quill slowly on the table, he gazed at the rolling hills and blue sky, partially obstructed by the stone wall and bell tower in the foreground. Leaning back in his chair, he looked at his companion who seemed oblivious to everything except his work.

—38—

"Donwald?"

No response.

"Donwald!"

"Huh?" Brother Donwald quickly raised his head.

Brother Flynn folded his arms and looked down at the table in front of him. "This passage says that honesty is the companion of prayer; both being necessary for the salvation of the soul."

"Something troubles you?"

"Aye."

Brother Donwald put his quill down and sat back. "Speak."

Brother Flynn looked at the pile of work stacked against the far wall of the room. "If I were to be honest, I would have to say that I feel like I am in prison here. How about you?"

"I feel as free as any man can possibly be."

Brother Flynn nodded. "I feared that you would say that."

"Well, Brother, it is no secret that you dislike sitting indoors copying texts. Your real passion is to be outdoors, building things."

Brother Flynn nodded. "Yes, but…"

Brother Donwald nodded. "But it's not as simple as trading the quill for a spade?"

"For me, it feels somewhat like the early days again. Do you remember the early days?"

"Aye," Brother Donwald chuckled. "It was a miracle we weren't thrown out."

"But even then, it felt right to be here. For most of these seven years, it has felt right to be here. I feel like I've been a monk for centuries. But now, for some reason, I grow restless."

Brother Donwald remained silent as Brother Flynn stared at the old text in front of him.

"I don't know," continued Brother Flynn. "Maybe if I patiently endure this madness, it will pass."

They looked at each other, for a while.

"Do you honestly believe that?" asked Brother Donwald

"No. In fact, it grows stronger by the day. What is wrong with me?"

Brother Donwald smiled. "Nothing, I suspect."

"Do you say that just to comfort me?"

"No. I mean it."

Brother Flynn leaned forward, resting his elbows on the table. "If you have a clue as to what stirs inside me, please speak."

Brother Donwald thumbed through the old text in front of him. "Perhaps the notion that you have been a monk for centuries is not altogether fanciful. This ancient book claims that every soul is born into a body of flesh many times."

"Really?"

Brother Donwald smiled at his brother. "Why the look of surprise? We already suspected as much."

Reaching down to the floor, Donwald picked up a wooden sign he had painted earlier. He held it up and read it out loud: *"Arbroath Abbey: location of the signing of the Declaration of Scottish Independence, in the year of our Lord, April 6, 1320."*

"So?"

"That was four hundred and five years ago." Brother Donwald's voice became hushed. "Yet, sometimes I feel like I was there. If I'm not mistaken, the sun was shining and the air was crisp on that day." He looked at Brother Flynn. "Maybe you *have* been a monk for centuries. Maybe it's simply time for you to do something else."

Flynn gazed at the huge rock-face on the hillside, smiling, as British soldiers tried to wash off the bold black letters that had been painted on the rock during the night: "British go home. Long live Caledonia."

He looked back at his Brother. "I feel torn. And, the fact that you do not feel the same madness, makes it all the more disconcerting."

"For me this place is home," said Brother Donwald, "and will probably remain so for the rest of my days. However, it appears that your destiny is elsewhere."

"So, why did I even come here?"

"To discipline your mind and learn your craft, I suspect," said Brother Donwald. "And to prepare you for your next adventure."

"You really think so?"

"Your eyes glitter when your duties take to the home of the architect— and his daughter. Elizabeth awaits you, Brother."

Brother Flynn slapped his forehead. "Is it that obvious?"

"Glaringly so. I would guess that she probably stays up nights, as you do, wishing for what she thinks she cannot have."

"If you saw all this, why did you not speak earlier? Why did you allow me to struggle in silence?"

"One does not intrude on a young sparrow learning to fly. Your wings are flapping, but your talons cling to the nest. When your wings are strong enough, your talons will let go."

Brother Flynn nodded as he stared out the window. "I fear that if I let go, I will fall into a great abyss."

"Fall or fly, it would appear that your time as a monk is coming to an end. When the architect said you would make a worthy apprentice, he wasn't just paying you a compliment. He was extending an invitation. I believe he was serious when he spoke of you studying at Cambridge."

"You really think so?"

"Aye. It is time for you to be a builder."

–39–

The scene disappeared and was replaced by the four stars against a violet background.

"Very well," said Smiley, "scrap the monk idea. And thank you for the warning."

"Perhaps you would also benefit from watching this," said Brother G, pointing to the screen, which now showed a middle-aged Shoupang, standing in a garden with the Master.

"My third grandchild is now one year of age," Shoupang said, as he walked around the freshly turned soil "And, Cali is still beautiful to me."

The old man nodded as he leisurely tilled the soil. "Your joy emanates from you like music from a happy flute."

"My three cousins and I have a become a major economic force in our region, thanks to my uncle's guidance. And, with the fair and just leadership provided by my wife's Brahmin relatives, we now live in a land of peace and prosperity." Shoupang picked up a basket of flower bulbs at the edge of the garden and carried it toward the Master.

"I'm also happy," Shoupang continued, "that Uncle Macunda got to learn that even Brahmin can be kind and decent. In his latter years, he even became friends with Gandhari's father-in-law," he chuckled, placing the basket of bulbs on the ground. "Now, there is just one thing that puzzles me."

The old man looked into the basket. "Oh, they are beautiful. Thank you for this wonderful gift."

"You are most welcome, Master. If it is not too obtrusive of me, I would ask you a personal question."

"Certainly," said the old man, as he took one of the bulbs from the basket.

"In my youth, I had the notion that you came to this world to save us from evil, and to teach us noble truths. If that is not so, then tell me, why did you come here?"

The old man smiled. "So I can do this," he said, waving his hand at the freshly tilled soil.

–40–

"Okay," said Smiley, clapping his hands together in front of his chest. "Now I really get it. It's about symmetry." He extended his arms to the sides, palms up. "Shoupang is sort of the mirror image of Jason. Shoupang's desire to fly off to Heaven became earthly bliss. And Jason's desire for earthly bliss…"

"Will propel Smiley to the heavenly octaves."

"We have to reactivate Jason," said Smiley.

"As you say."

"So, how do we do this?"

"Well, a course change of this magnitude requires that you get an extra boost from a few locals in the flesh."

"So, it's simple and straightforward, no complications?"

"That depends on your helpers. As you know, humans can be quite unpredictable."

"I understand that. But, assuming everything goes according to plan, will Jason's life be pretty much the same?"

"Almost. Jason will have to make some adjustments. For example, his relationship with Katie will have to change so as not to interfere with her flow. As you have already surmised, her life-plan doesn't include being married to a lovable ignoramus."

"I understand that. How do we fix it?"

"Obviously, she and Jason would either have to separate or Jason has to become more scholarly."

Smiley closed his eyes for several seconds and then opened them again, smiling. "Jason would prefer the latter."

"And so would Katie. A little rewiring of the brain should take care of that. The only possible complication is that Jason might have to endure some annoying ESP."

"Great. So, how do we put this plan into action?"

"You already have, simply by giving it your approval. Now, you can sit here, eat popcorn to keep Jason pacified and watch the show, as your friends go through their temporal drama and get into position to give you that extra boost."

"Oh, you mean I get to watch the whole thing on the screen?"

"That would be very helpful, yes. You see, by watching, you also participate. Specifically, you help to weave everything together. From this vantage point, you have one foot in time and one in timelessness, which gives you great leverage."

"Great," said Smiley, pressing the play button.

"The first scene should be pretty simple and straightforward," said Brother G.

The screen now showed Brother Jerry walking quickly on the sidewalk just outside Forrest Park. Smiley could hear the fading sound of an ambulance in the distance.

"Oh, I remember this," said Smiley. "Brother Jerry is going to the parking lot so he can go to the hospital."

Suddenly, Brother Jerry stopped. He stood at attention. His head tilted to the side, as if he was trying to hear something. Rather than continuing along the sidewalk, Brother Jerry turned right and went into Forrest Park by walking through the narrow gap in the juniper hedges. Taking several more steps, he sat under the same oak tree and closed his eyes.

"Wait a minute," said Smiley. "That's not what he did last time." He also noted that the secluded bench close to Brother Jerry was no longer occupied by the man in the business suit, but rather by an unshaven, shabbily-dressed man who apparently had just awakened from a nap.

Across the street, Jason Mazarosky's pickup truck was still on the hydraulic lift, but Raffi wasn't working on it, this time. Instead, he was standing by the entrance of the garage, talking to an attractive lady with a flowing pink dress and bright green floral shirt.

"Looks like you have succeeded in altering the flow, slightly," said Brother G.

"How did I do that?"

"By watching."

Suddenly, Katie Sprite came running along the sidewalk and approached Brother Jerry.

–41–

"Brother Jerry," said Katie, standing breathlessly in front of him.

The young monk opened his eyes, startled.

"I just got a call from Sam," she said, her voice breaking and her eyes welling up. "Jason just had an accident at work. It sounds really serious."

Brother Jerry nodded. "I know," he said in a subdued voice. "Why did you come back here?"

"I don't know. But now that I'm here, I guess I want to sit down and pray with you, like you suggested. And then I'll go to the hospital. Can we do that?"

The young monk nodded. "Of course."

"So, how do we do this?" asked Katie.

"I suggest we keep it simple. We'll start by praying silently. You can do your Mary/energy thing, and I'll do my thing. And we'll just take it from there"

"Sounds good to me."

Brother Jerry closed his eyes and Katie followed.

Katie did her usual silent prayer and invocation. She became progressively more relaxed and strangely detached. Then, for some reason, she got an urge to use the spoken word. At first, she felt obliged to ask Brother Jerry for permission, but then decided that it was unnecessary. She cleared her throat. "Blessed Divine Mother," she said reverently, "I call on your loving presence to surround and enfold Jason. I bring to you all my thoughts, desires, and concerns for Jason's health and safety, knowing that you will translate them in accordance with his highest good. For this I give thanks. So mote it be."

After a few more minutes of silence, Katie opened her eyes. Brother Jerry followed.

She wiped a bit of moisture from her face, looking calmer now. "I feel like I want to go to the hospital now."

"Of course."

"Are you coming too?"

"I'll be along in a little while," he said. "You go on."

She stood up. "Thank you," she said, as she turned and walked away quickly. She squeezed through the gap in the juniper hedges and started walking along the sidewalk.

Brother Jerry closed his eyes again.

–42–

The screen went blank, but Smiley continued staring at it. Finally, he rubbed his face and turned to Brother G. "I hope the other movies aren't as tough to watch as that one."

"Probably not," said Brother G.

They sat in silence for a while.

When Smiley felt ready, he took a deep breath and smiled. "Okay," he said, as he pressed the play button. "Roll 'em."

The screen came to life, now showing a young lady with long auburn hair and glasses, sitting at a desk.

"What's the time frame?" asked Smiley, as he picked up the box of popcorn.

"About eleven years before Jason gets conked on the head."

PART TWO
The Story of Sarah

−1−

Sarah Chazinov looked up from the test paper she was grading and sat back in her chair. Feeling a slight tingling in her spine, she wondered what else was going wrong with her body.

Removing her glasses, she rubbed her eyes, as her mind drifted back through the day. She remembered her answer to a question asked by a student. "Tachyons are particles that supposedly travel faster than light and can, therefore, travel through time. Most physicists regard the existence of tachyons with skepticism."

She smiled briefly, recalling her run-in with that bratty kid, William. "That's a good question, William, but it goes far beyond the Newtonian physics that we're working with right now."

"Oh, come on, Miss Chazinov, that's a cop out."

"No, it is not, young man. If we were to discuss that now, it would confuse you royally, not to mention the rest of the class. Just be patient; we'll get there."

"Ah, yes, patience is a virtue."

"And please refrain from being a smart ass."

"Smart ass? What do you mean?"

"And don't play dumb. It is not cute."

Sarah yawned. The pain medication was making her drowsy. Her mind drifted to her car. Leaky radiator… need to find a good mechanic… maybe buy a new car—no, too many other bills to pay. Taking a deep breath, she put her glasses back on and resumed grading the tests.

Her eyes were half closed when she entered the last exam score into the roll book. She looked across the page to make sure the grade was recorded next to the right name. Yes, Jan Mackey. She glanced at Jan's other text scores: 95, 96, 100, 100. Her class attendance was perfect, and she was never late. Sarah smiled as she remembered Jan's enthusiasm and the intensity with which she listened and asked questions in class. "And she's not just a goody two-shoes," Sarah had said to the department chairman. "She's a free thinker. She'll probably go to some prestigious university, graduate with honors, and then begin a wonderful career as a research scientist. Twenty years from now, they'll be quoting her work in the literature."

Sarah remembered her own high school days, when similar predictions were made about her. She sighed and closed her roll book.

After clearing off her desktop, she crumpled a sheet of scrap paper into a ball and tossed it toward the wastebasket next to the desk. The ball hit the rim of the basket and rolled under the bed.

Her eyelids gradually descended. As her chin drifted down to her chest, her mind flew into a reverie of images and voices. She settled into a familiar dream. She was sitting in a theater, watching a movie. The scene showed a drunken Dominican priest raping a young lady. This version of the movie was set during the Spanish Inquisition, and the priest had accused the woman of being a witch. Another version took place during the crusades in Jerusalem. But the basic plot was always the same. And the ending was always the same: Sarah would watch the scene for a while and then awaken, sometimes with a scream, as the woman was about to die.

This time, the only sound she made was a startled gasp, as her eyes snapped open. As usual, the dream seemed very real. The images lingered in her mind.

The dream seemed to occur with more frequency since she became sober. She remembered Betty's words. "Careful, Sarah, dear. Once the alcohol is removed, all the issues that drove you to drink in the first place will probably re-emerge."

She looked up at the signs posted over her desk: *THIS TOO SHALL PASS. EASY DOES IT. SMILE.*

She stared at the words. Then she slumped forward, running her fingers through her long auburn hair. Examining her fingers, she noticed a few more fallen strands. Leaning to the side, she looked at the mirror next to the desk. Her hair still looked rather full, but it did seem to be losing some of its luster. She shook her head. Such vanity! Here I am worried about my hair when I have all these other problems.

Her Persian cat, Sir Thomas Mallory, walked up to her and snuggled against her leg. Sarah did not respond.

On the desk, she saw the book on brain exercises she had borrowed from Betty. She closed her eyes and attempted to do the laser beam exercise. Straightening her spine, she breathed deeply and tried to place her attention at the center of her brain, but the dull pain in her upper back was too distracting. Just as well. That exercise had worked well at first, but now its only effect was to induce bizarre dreams filled with snakes and demons.

She almost stood up to get an extra dose of pain medication but stopped when she remembered Betty's words. "...And be careful with those pills; they make your thinking foggy. I should know, I used to take that stuff just to get a cheap high."

In the last few months, less and less exertion was needed to aggravate the pain. She picked up the paper on which she had written her two alternatives.

A: Die within two years.

B: Surgery to remove the tumors in the uterus and left breast, and chemotherapy and radiation to remove the tumors that were beginning to form in the spine. The side effects were hair loss, nausea, vomiting, and general poor health.

Dead by age twenty-nine. She was no longer frightened of that.

The answering machine on the desk showed seven messages. Three of them were probably from Betty. Her left hand was not too far from the answering machine, but listening to the messages seemed like a cumbersome chore. She looked at the digital clock on the night table next to the bed—11:30. Too late to return phone calls, anyway. Poor excuse. As Sarah's sponsor, Betty gave her instructions to call any time of the day or night if ever there was a crisis. Was this a crisis? Of course not! No need to wake her up. Wake her up? Betty rarely went to bed before midnight. Glancing at the floor, she smiled when her eyes caught sight of the rubber snake that Betty had gotten her as a joke.

As she reached for the phone, her arm and shoulder seemed to creak and grind, as if she had sand in her joints. She turned the phone belly-side up and pushed the first six digits of Betty's phone number. Then, the voices came.

She was never sure whether she was hearing actual voices or just her own morbid thoughts. Lately, they seemed to show up more frequently, especially when she was very tired.

As Sarah held the receiver in hand, the voices faded in and out. "…Don't call Betty. Put the phone down and get it over with. You can die painlessly now, or you can die much more painfully later."

Sarah looked over her shoulder to the other side of the room. The bathroom door was open. In the darkened interior, she saw the medicine cabinet with its sliding glass door half opened, revealing silhouetted bottles and jars.

The room became a little blurry. She turned her head away as Sir Thomas Mallory brushed against her ankle and sat across her feet. She nudged him lightly with her toes. "Hello, Tom," she mumbled."

"This is it," said the voices. "Stop procrastinating."

She looked at the medicine cabinet again, as her cat stroked her leg with his tail.

"What are you waiting for?" the voices continued. "No one will rescue you."

Sarah nodded mindlessly as her eyelids drifted down. She placed her hands on the edge of her desk and was about to stand, when another voice—a new voice—suggested that she write a letter first.

Removing her hands from the edge of the desk, she reached for a large yellow writing pad with her right hand, and picked up a pen with her left. Suddenly, she

found herself reliving the last time she was drunk. She vividly remembered staggering into her apartment, followed by Betty, who kept a hand on Sarah's back.

—2—

"The dragon in the long cave was actually a mutated dinosaur," said Sarah,
dramatically, as she walked through the doorway. "Within the fearsome monster
lived a spirit who was quite lost and had forgotten the proper way to sustain itself.
So, it became a dinosaur with sharp teeth and a small brain, along with other
spirits who had also forgotten the proper way to sustain themselves..."

Betty guided Sarah to the living room couch and gently made her sit.

"But that was okay," continued Sarah, "because even though they seemed
quite confused, they were all pretty much doing what they wanted to do, and
they weren't really bothering anyone who didn't want to be bothered..."

Betty walked away.

"Where are you going," said Sarah. I haven't quite finished yet."

"I'm going to the kitchen to make you some special tea."

"Special tea, hey? That means it will taste like crap."

"More than likely."

"Will it at least make me undrunk?"

"Probably not," Betty called out from the kitchen, "but, your liver will appreciate the support. Go ahead, finish your story."

"Oh yeah, I forgot. So, anyway, some other spirits condemned the dinosaurs
for being dinosaurs. Eventually, they too became dinosaurs. And that was also
perfectly all right because, eventually, all of them quit being dinosaurs and were
just thankful for having had the experience. Except for the dinosaur that became
a dragon. He was hard core. He still hung out in the long cave, attacking attractive young women so he could steal their psychosexual energy. But Sir Isaac
Newton put a stop to it, and they all lived happily ever after."

Sarah took a deep breath and leaned back on the couch. She closed her eyes
and continued talking randomly about dragons and drunken Dominican priests,
until Betty returned from the kitchen and sat on the couch next to Sarah.

"Drink," said Betty, handing Sarah a cup of steaming brown liquid.

Sarah quieted down long enough to take a sip. "Not bad. It's not yucky this
time," she said, taking another sip.

"I added some liquorice root to this batch, which takes the edge off."

"Liquorice, I love liquorice," said Sarah, taking a big gulp.

Suddenly, Sarah became quiet. She stared at the blank screen of the TV set
across the room. Then she looked at Betty. "I don't know what happened," she

said, her voice a bit more sober. I didn't think I was capable of slipping. Certainly not this bad. At the meetings, I've heard stories of people losing control like that, but I didn't seriously think that it could happen to me."

"Join the club," Betty smiled.

"If I wasn't drunk right now, I'd be really freaked." She rubbed her eyes with one hand. "I'm sorry. I feel like I've failed you."

"You can feel whatever you feel, but I want to be very clear that you haven't failed me. I'm your sponsor, not your wife."

Sarah smiled. "You know, if I was a lesbian, I would really go for you."

"I'm touched."

Sarah took another gulp of tea. "Anyway, thanks for coming to my rescue. I know you were studying for your big nursing exam. Sorry."

"No problem. I'm going to ace it, anyway."

Sarah drank the last of the tea. "My mother was a nurse. And my father was a drunk. Bad combo." She stared at the TV screen for a while. "So, what do *you* do when you feel like you're losing it?" she asked, as she placed the cup on the coffee table.

"I pray to Mother Mary."

"Yeah," Sarah nodded, "she's a nice lady, even if she is a fictitious person. Sorry, that was disrespectful. I hate being drunk, it makes me say disrespectful things."

"No offence taken. I know she's for real, even if I was the only person on the face of the Earth who believes it."

"So, how do you know? And I don't mean that as a criticism. It's a purely academic question. I sincerely want to know how you know."

"I know because I know."

"But how do you know that you know?"

"I know that I know, because I know. That may not remove your skepticism, but I don't have any other explanation."

"Right now, I'm not being skeptical, I'm being jealous. I wish that *I* knew that I knew."

"You will."

"When? When will I know that I know?"

"You will know that you know...when you know."

Sarah laughed. "Okay, I get it. We have reached the limit of logic." Then she frowned again. "I still feel really crappy about this. Six months of sobriety down the tubes."

"It's okay to feel crappy, but just so you know, it's not a requirement. In my opinion, you'll come through this more gracefully and with less likelihood of slipping again, if you restrict your self-flagellation. We can analyze and pick though this experience later when you're fully sober and alert. For now, just relax and enjoy the buzz."

Sarah burst out laughing and continued for quite some time. Then, she quieted down and began sobbing, as her forehead descended on her friend's shoulder. Betty just smiled and patted her gently on her upper back.

—3—

Sarah continued seeing the image of herself crying on Betty's shoulder, as if she was mindlessly watching a movie of someone else. Then, she looked down at the paper and began writing.

To Whom it may concern,

She looked up at the lamp above her desk. The frosted spherical glass cover seemed to grow more luminous. Suddenly, she became dizzy, and felt a slight pressure between her eyebrows. Shaking her head, she looked down. The shadow of her left hand holding the shadow of the pen quivered slightly on the paper. Quite automatically, she resumed writing:

A beam of light! A simple beam of light. It is such a miracle, such a profound mystery, such an incredibly fantastic and awesome phenomenon of nature! I get goose bumps whenever I think about it. A few months ago when I first learned about light, I said, 'My God! Is this really true? This isn't just far-out science fiction?' Our excellent physics teacher, Mr. Koozman, has done an excellent job of explaining the properties of light, but I can't understand how he could stand there with a straight face and talk about such an amazing thing and not be totally blown away.

I am totally convinced that if we can comprehend the nature of light, we will know the secret of life itself. So, fellow students, I am writing this article for our excellent science magazine because I wish to share with you that if you are looking for wondrous miracles, just consider ordinary light; it is quite miraculous. In fact, there are, NOT ONE, but TWO reasons why light is so miraculous. Let me tell you about it.

Sarah paused and became dimly aware that she was doing something out of the ordinary. She resumed writing, watching the words flow out like she was playing an old video.

The first reason that light is miraculous has to do with the fact that it is made of waves. There is nothing mysterious about waves, per sé. A wave is a very simple thing. If you take any object at all, a lump of Jell-O for instance, and kick it on the side, waves move through it, which is a fancy way of saying that it wiggles and shakes.

However, pretty soon, scientists learned that there was something mighty strange about light. As far as they could tell, light was made up of waves. In other words, it is made up of something that is wiggling and shaking. The problem was THEY COULDN'T FIND THAT SOMETHING! This must have driven them crazy! It's like having water waves without water. How could that be?

Well, that was just ridiculous, there has to be SOMETHING to make up light waves, something had to be there, wiggling and shaking. So, to maintain their sanity, they decided that the entire universe is filled with a mysterious undetectable SOME-THING, which they called 'ether'. And they figured that when this invisible ether stuff is kicked on the side, it wiggles and shakes like Jell-O. And, when this vibrating ether supposedly bumps against the eyeball, we see it as light. It was a reasonable assumption; don't you think so?

So, for a while, everyone was happy. But then, along comes Dr.. Einstein. And he said there is NO ETHER, which leads to the embarrassing conclusion that light, the basic stuff of all Creation, is a vibration (a wiggling and shaking) of NOTHING!!!! It's totally illogical.

And so, fellow students, in the beginning, there was NOTHING. And God placed His hand in the NOTHING, like a child playfully dipping his finger in a lake, producing waves in the sea of nothing. And, the waves in the sea of nothing is what we call light. I said to myself, 'Isn't that interesting, God created light by disturbing NOTHING!'

Anyway, that's one reason why light is so miraculous—it appears to be a vibration (a wiggling and shaking) of NOTHING!

Now, here is the second reason that light is miraculous. Actually, the second reason is so bizarre that I'm afraid to even talk about it. When our physics teacher first told us about it, I said, 'Mr. Koozman, do you realize what you're saying? This is totally illogical! This isn't science. This is magic!'

You see, right around the time that scientists were scratching their heads over the fact that there was no ether to account for the existence of light waves, another discovery was made about light, a discovery that probably made the physicists of that time go completely bonkers. Are you ready for this? It was discovered that light, in addition to behaving like it's made of waves (and very strange waves at that), also behaves like it's made of PARTICLES. In other words, it acts like zillions of teensy-weensy golf balls zipping through space. Now, this is a blatant contradiction in logic that causes my brain to become cross-eyed if I think about it too much. Think about it. A ripple in a lake (a wave) expands out in all directions, while a golf ball can only move in one boring little direction at a time. And, here we are, saying that light is simultaneously like a ripple in a lake and like a bunch of little pellets. These little pellets are called photons, by the way.

Now, don't get me wrong! I believe that everyone is entitled to their opinion. If you want to say that light is like ripples in a lake, that's fine. If you want to say that light is like a bunch of golf balls traveling very fast, that's fine too. However, to say that light is simultaneously like BOTH of these things, is too much for my brain to handle. It's like saying that a bathtub is full of water and bone dry at the same time. It's like saying that two people who are trying to destroy each other also love each other deeply. How can that be? It's a blatant contradiction. It's a total paradox!

This is how ordinary light actually behaves! It behaves like a total paradox! Maybe that's why life seems so contradictory sometimes. Maybe life is contradictory because the primordial stuff of Creation—light—is contradictory! It's like God creating the Garden of Eden, and then putting a snake in it.

On the other hand, maybe life isn't contradictory. Maybe there is a hidden order behind it all. But, if there is, I sure as heck don't know about it! Mr. Koozman says that the paradox about light can be explained logically by using something called the Heisenberg Uncertainty Principle, which I won't bore you with here because it's complicated, and, quite frankly, I really don't think it explains anything. I just think there is something deeply mysterious about light that defies all attempts at logical explanation.

My conclusion about light and life in general, is this: It is all a miracle. It is simply a miracle that we are alive! And, I feel so privileged to be in this grand theater and participating in the grand drama and the great symphony of life.

Sarah stopped writing. She remained motionless for several minutes, staring at the last sentence. The digital clock changed from 12:59 to 1:00 A.M. "The sleeping pills, the sleeping pills, the sleeping pills," said the voices in a lyrical and hypnotic tone. She nodded, paying no attention to Sir Thomas who had just jumped on the desk. Her brain felt foggy, and her eyelids drooped.

She stood up and was turning to go the bathroom, but stopped in mid-stride, feeling like a strong and gentle hand had settled on her shoulder. The many voices became silent, and a single soft voice touched her mind: "Lie down and rest awhile; you'll feel better."

As soon as the side of her head settled on the pillow, she started drifting off to sleep, still dimly aware of the invisible hand that touched her shoulder and the voice that had prompted her to rest.

−4−

When the luminous red numbers on her digital clock changed from 6:44 to 6:45 a.m., a musical chime filled the room. Sarah half-opened her eyes and looked at the clock.

"Ohhhh," she groaned.

Taking a deep breath, she reached toward the night table and pounded the top of the clock. Then she closed her eyes again. She thought she could hear her eyes saying, "Please let me stay closed." Her limbs were pleading, "Please don't make me move," and her brain was saying, "Please let me sleep just five more minutes." As she took a breath and prepared to pry her body out of bed, she heard another voice. "Very well, rest for another five minutes."

She dozed off again and immediately began dreaming. She was six years old. Little Sarah opened a door and walked into a room filled with happy people and decorated with balloons and brightly colored ribbons crisscrossing along the ceiling. It was someone's birthday. She stood by the door as two men and two women gave beautiful gifts to the children.

As little Sarah watched, one of the women walked over to her.

"Ah," she said, "and you must be Sarah. Would you like to join our party?"

"I can't."

"Why not?" she said, as she got down on one knee.

"I have a boo-boo, and it hurts."

"Oh, I see. Well, if you would like, I'll ask my friend to help you. He's very good with boo-boos. Okay?"

"Okay," she pouted.

The scene faded and was replaced by another. This time, she was sitting in her counselor's office in graduate school. Her thesis was going nowhere, and she was starting to drink heavily. In the dream, however, the discussion ended differently than it had in real life. Rather than arguing with him and storming out of the office, she remained seated and calm. "I have thought about it carefully," she said, "and I have decided to give it another try. Your assistance would be appreciated."

The dream faded. The last image was that of the counselor's kindly face.

Sarah was back in bed. But, her limbs seemed to sway side to side and her entire body gently bobbed up and down, like an air-filled balloon on a pool of water. A gust of wind seemed to be blowing through her head, and there was a whirling sound in her head, like a rapidly spinning turbine. Another dream, obviously. But…wait a minute! She felt like she was wide-awake! So, why was her body losing interest in gravity? And, why did her head feel like a wind tunnel? Such things don't happen when you're wide-awake!

Somehow, it was all very familiar. Of course! Her fun dreams! She recalled her early childhood. Right in the middle of quiet sleep, she would suddenly find herself fully awake. Little Sarah would jump out of bed, walk around the room, inspect her sleeping body on the bed, and even fly out the window under the protection of her fairy friends.

Sarah's fun dreams stopped at about the age of six. Were they actually returning? Controlling her excitement, she decided to determine if this was, in fact, a re-emergence of her fun dreams. She tried raising her arm first. Focusing her attention, she lifted her left arm. She did it slowly, so as not to disturb her sleeping body. Sure enough, there it was— a translucent image of her arm. She waved it across her field of vision, wiggling her fingers and making a fist.

The next move was more challenging. Slowly, she sat up in bed and looked around the room. Satisfied that she was in her room and not in some distorted dreamland, she stood up. Taking several steps to the center of the room, she turned and looked back at the bed.

The sight of her sleeping body was scary for some reason, but the memory of her fun dreams reassured her that everything was okay.

She started feeling giddy, but restrained herself. There were two ways of looking at this, she told herself. She was either standing in the middle of the room wide-awake— without her body, or, more likely, she was just having an unusually vivid dream.

She looked around the room. If this was just a dream, there was bound to be some distortion of details. Looking around, she took note of the closet door and the half-opened bathroom door through which she saw the sink and medicine cabinet. On the adjoining wall, she noticed the pink curtains on either side of the window, the potted umbrella plant in the corner, the electric socket, and the framed picture of Sir Isaac Newton. Through the glass of the closed window, she saw the rooftops and the stars against the black sky. In the distance, she saw the lake at the center of Forrest Park, glistening under the full moon. Below the picture of Sir Isaac Newton, she noticed the bubbling fish tank with its aquatic plants. She saw the two goldfish, named Archimedes and Sushi, and the one snail, named Flash. By the side of the bed, she saw her fuzzy bunny-rabbit slippers. In the far corner of the room, she noticed several stuffed animals and other little toys, including Betty's rubber snake.

On her desk, she noticed the physics textbook and several days' worth of unopened mail. On the wall above the desk, she saw her signs: *THIS TOO SHALL PASS. EASY DOES IT. SMILE.*

Clothing was strewn randomly on top of the dresser and sticking out of half-opened drawers. Behind the answering machine, she noticed Betty's brain exercise book sitting on top of the laptop computer, which was in need of repair.

The physical details of the room seemed accurate, and she noted again that her thoughts were real awake thoughts, with full access of her mental faculties and memories. Maybe this was more than a dream.

She was still skeptical, however. Was she really observing the room in the here and now, or simply recalling and visualizing it as she last saw it before going to sleep? She decided that a good way to test these two possibilities was to observe little things that she would not have noticed when she was awake, and then she would see if these details were present when she woke up.

Looking around again, she saw two pencils in "v" formation on the desktop, the right bunny-rabbit slipper slightly toed in toward the left, and the bottom drawer of her desk partially opened. In the far corner of the room, at the foot of the bed, several books were piled randomly on top of each other and were partially covered by the mountain of stuffed toys. Looking more closely, she recognized The Koran, the Baghavad Gita, and three versions of the Bible. She looked at Betty's brain book again on the desk and noticed the page marker sticking out at an angle, about three quarters of the way through the book. On the floor, next to the bed, was another small pile of partially-read books. She counted five.

She memorized these details for future reference. However, she questioned the validity of her little test. All those little details could already be stored in her subconscious mind. She recalled a magazine article in which people under hypnosis were able to remember trivial details, like phone numbers that they had seen on the walls of public bathrooms many years before.

Nonetheless, she continued observing, hoping to notice something new, something she couldn't possibly have seen when she was awake. Finally, she looked under the bed. As she expected, she saw the crumpled paper that had bounced off the rim of the wastebasket.

Then she gasped in delight. Directly behind the crumpled paper was the very object she needed to make her test scientifically valid. A rubber duck!

Betty's two-year-old daughter, Christy, had lost her rubber duck about a month ago, while visiting. Sarah observed the duck's details—the big blue eyes, the big smile, and the four wooden wheels on the bottom.

She recalled Betty's visit in great detail. Betty had just gotten back from visiting her family in Venezuela.

"...I also saw Mother Eva," Betty had said. "Did I ever tell you about Mother Eva?"

"Yes," replied Sarah, "You said she practically saved your life."

"That she did. During this last visit, she gave me a book on brain exercises."

"Brain exercises? Why?"

"I don't know. But Mother Eva is not your average nun..."

As Sarah recalled, during that conversation, Christy ran around, dragging the rubber duck by a string, wandering through the apartment. When she returned, she did not have the rubber duck. It had been missing ever since.

Sarah looked at the rubber duck under the bed. What a stroke of luck! She reminded herself to look under the bed as soon as she awoke. "Yes," she said. "If that rubber duck is still there when I'm awake, it would strongly suggest that this was no ordinary dream."

As soon as she said that, a cheerful masculine voice filled the room. "Excellent, Sarah. Now we can begin."

–5–

"Who's that?" said Sarah, quickly raising her head.

"A friend."

The voice was pleasant enough, but under the circumstances, she was not comforted by it.

"What do you want?" she said, standing quickly.

"I'm here to help."

"Help?" Sarah looked around searching for the source of the voice, ready to apply what little she knew of karate. "Help with what?"

"Do you remember the dream you just had?" said the voice.

"Yes. How do you know about that? Who are you, mister?" She was just about ready to run out of the room, but then she remembered this was just a dream too. But, what if it wasn't a dream? She couldn't just run out and leave her body unguarded on the bed. Such bizarre thoughts! She shook her head vigorously and tried to wake herself up. Didn't work. She glanced at her sleeping body, which was now wincing and grimacing.

"Sarah, what do you make of those two dreams you had?"

"What business is it of yours?"

"I am an interested party. Tell me about it, please."

Sarah hesitated. There didn't seem any harm in telling him. "I was a little kid. And there were four adults. One of them was talking to me."

Her eyes darted across the room, still trying to find the source of the voice.

"And what about the second dream?" asked the voice.

"In the second dream, I was back in grad school. I was talking to my counselor." Sarah relaxed a bit. "Now this is interesting. You sound just like the counselor in the dream. Is that who you're supposed to be?"

"Yes... in a manner of speaking. Are you still interested in reversing your decision to drop out from your current life?"

"That was just a dream. Just like this is a dream. Doesn't feel like a dream, but obviously it is. Are you supposed to be my guardian angel or something—not that I believe in angels," she added quickly.

"I'm just here to help. Now, do you wish to reconsider your decision to drop out?"

"Wait a minute. My personal life is none of your damn business, until I say otherwise. I don't mean to be rude, but I think you ought to know that I get nervous when I'm alone with strange men. And an invisible man, no less. Where are you standing, anyway?"

"Actually, I'm not standing anywhere."

"So, where is your voice coming from?"

"Nowhere in particular. We might say that I'm just everywhere, sort of like a wave. It has to do with particle-wave mechanics. Would you like to give it a try?"

"No. And, I don't like talking to a voice that's coming from nowhere in particular."

"Would you like for me to become visible?"

"Yes. I mean, NO! Just stay like that for now."

"Of course. I assumed that you would want it this way. That's why I'm here without form."

"Yes, you're a perfect gentleman. Now, who the hell are you?"

"Who do you think I am?"

"Oh, brother. How the hell am I supposed to know? You're a disembodied voice in my room. So, again I ask, who are you?"

"I am who you think I am, in a manner of speaking."

"I don't think that you're anybody. Look, mister, I would like to emphasize that this whole encounter is very disturbing to me, even if it is just a dream."

"Why is this so disturbing? You've been hearing voices all your life. You used to be able to discern them quite well. Now you can't even distinguish them from your own thoughts."

"But even when I used to hear the voices clearly, I was never able to have a running conversation with them, like we're having now. They were just a few words here and there, just before waking up in the morning or going to sleep at night."

"Well, right now you just happen to be in top form. So, do you want to reconsider your decision to drop out? After all, you did call me."

"I did not call you!"

"Yes, you did. I could not be here if you didn't call me. Just like the other voices couldn't be here without you calling them."

"Look, this is irrelevant."

"I agree. The point is, are you interested in continuing your present life?"

Sarah paused. "Of course, I am. I was just feeling crazy last night, not to mention that I was doped out on pain meds."

"And do you wish to proceed with this encounter?"

Sarah shrugged. "Maybe."

"Excellent! You're a brave woman."

"Don't give me any compliments yet; I may change my mind."

She glanced at her sleeping body. "And, exactly what is it that you're going to do, wave your magic wand and make everything better? I don't believe in magic."

"Neither do I. It's a rather crude way of doing things."

Sarah suppressed a mild desire to smirk. "So, what is your plan of action?" she asked.

"It's simple really. How did Brother Einstein discover relativity?"

Sarah shrugged. "He extrapolated upon Newtonian mechanics using the quadratic equation and the Maxwell field equations, but that's not what you mean, is it?"

"Uh… no. Brother Einstein pulled the idea out of what you call his subconscious mind""

"So, you're going to dig into my subconscious mind, is that it?"

"Yes. But, we don't have to do much digging really, because according to your own assessment, we're already there."

"Fine, fine. So, exactly what is it that you plan to do?"

"Quite frankly, I don't have a specific lesson plan. But since you're raising such a fuss about it, let's just give you a chance to ask all the questions you want, and basically talk about whatever you want to talk about, so you can feel comfortable with this encounter. And then, we'll take it from there."

"Okay. The first thing I'd like to have clarified is this: who the hell are you supposed to be?"

"Well, it's sort of complicated. We can just keep its simple by saying that I'm a projection of your subconscious—"

"Yes, yes, I know. But you're supposed to be someone. I can feel it."

"In manner of speaking, yes. But, you see, it's not actually a fixed identity. And it really isn't all that important—"

"Look, you said I could ask whatever questions I want."

"Yes, I did say that."

"So, I'm waiting."

"All right. Close your eyes and be still a moment."

"Oh, brother! Why don't you just tell me?"

"Because I can't actually tell you. What I mean is, theoretically, I can. But, from a practical standpoint, you have to tell *me*. Come on now, close your eyes, and relax."

Sarah hesitated. She looked around the room to convince herself that he wasn't hiding somewhere. She thought she detected a friendly smile in his voice. She decided to trust him— for now.

She closed her eyes and waited.

Nothing happened.

"This isn't working," she said, with her eyes still closed.

"Of course it's not working; you're not doing it properly."

"What do you mean?" she said, opening her eyes. "I did what you said."

"You're supposed to relax."

"That's what I was doing, for Pete's sake!" she said, throwing her arms in the air.

"All right then," said the voice, "close your eyes, and be tense."

Sarah was ready to tell him to get lost, but when she considered his instructions, her anger quickly turned into a concerted effort to keep herself from laughing. She sighed, closed her eyes, and tried very hard not to smile.

Immediately, she saw an equilateral triangle, which then became three-dimensional and took on the shape of a tetrahedron. Each of the four corners of the tetrahedron consisted of a pulsating star. The top one was silver. The other three were red, blue, and green.

Suddenly, the green star grew very large and took the form of a bearded young man, wearing a gray robe. He had a pleasant smile, and his presence was rather soothing. Sarah instinctively smiled back, but then she figured out who he was supposed to be. Her smile vanished and her eyes snapped open. "That's ridiculous!"

"Why?"

"Because," she said, throwing her arms in the air, "I... I'm Jewish!"

"So am I. In a manner of speaking."

"This is absurd! Aside from the fact that this whole setup is totally bizarre, and aside from the fact that I don't put any faith in any of that Bible crap, it would at least make more sense if you were one of those Old Testament prophets, like Moses. Not that I believe that he's any more real than you are. At best, you're all just... personified images of archetypal phenomenon."

"Wait 'til Moses finds out that you called him a personified image of an archetypal phenomenon."

"That's what all of you are, for Pete's sake. You're all just elaborate projections of our collective human consciousness." She composed herself. "Of course, I keep forgetting, I'm having a dream, a very vivid dream, but a dream nonetheless. I am talking to a mere projection of my subconscious mind."

"Fine, I don't have a problem with that."

"I still don't see how I can be standing here having this running conversation as if you were a real person."

"Well, the vividness of this experience can be attributed to the obvious fact that you are very proficient as a conjurer. The flip side of that is you are equally proficient at conjuring up tormenting demons."

"Maybe you're one of them."

"Be that as it may, I am the teacher you have presently called forth."

"I did not call you!"

"Well, believe what you will. I am here and at your service. And you can command me to leave whenever you wish, and I will be obliged to honor your request. That would be true whether you believe me to be an angel, a demon, or your Aunt Rivka."

"I still say that Moses makes more sense."

"As you wish. I will call him. Hey, Moshe!"

"YES?" A booming voice filled the room.

"Sarah would like to meet you."

"Very well," said the booming voice. "Greetings, Sarah. Now, tell me, exactly what is a 'personified image of an archetypal phenomenon?'"

"THIS IS PREPOSTEROUS!" Sarah yelled. "How do I know you're really Moshe—I mean, Moses?"

"How do you know that he's really Jesus?" asked the booming voice.

"I don't!"

"Well, there you are."

"Huh?"

"Now listen, Sarah," said the booming voice, "all things considered, this is a job for Brother Josh. Of course, if you want to speak with me on any specific matter, just conjure me up again and I'll be at your service. See you later."

Sarah stood still, with her mouth opened. She considered going back to bed and ending the whole show. But the very absurdity of the situation made it just too tempting. She had a suspicion that her guest knew this and was skillfully exploiting her curiosity. She placed her hands behind her back.

"Well?" she said.

"Well, you heard the man... I mean, the personified image of an archetypal—"

"Oh, shut up!"

–6–

Sarah's guest remained silent.

"So, now what?" asked Sarah.

"As I said, I'm just here to help."

"Terrific, can you fix the radiator in my car?"

"Are you kidding? I can't even drive."

Sarah smiled briefly. "And I always thought that *real* men are natural mechanics."

"That might be so, but I know even less about cars than you do, because all my information about cars comes from you."

Sarah shook her head. "None of this crap is real."

"So, what are you worried about? If this is just a dream, why not relax and roll with it?"

"I don't care if it is just a dream. It's the principle of the thing."

"What principle?"

"Well...Number one, you are a symbol of Christianity. So, like it or not, you symbolize centuries of Christian persecution of the Jews. Number two, the mere fact that you are a religious figure rubs me the wrong way. And to top things off, you're a *male* religious figure. You are a product of the patriarchy. So, why you of all people?"

"Because I am a male, Christian, religious figure— in your mind."

Sarah opened her mouth and closed it again. "Is that supposed to make sense?"

"Certainly. You see, we have to be economical and efficient with energy, which means we must accomplish as much as we can in as little time as possible—"

"In other words, you're going to be a pain in the ass. You're going to try to irritate me as much as possible."

"Well, that's entirely up to you. Anyway, the bottom line is, you called me here."

"I DID NOT CALL YOU!" she yelled. "Please, understand," she said, composing herself, "this isn't anything personal, but I just don't like you."

"Fine, I have no problem with that."

"And, thus far, I don't think much of this... process. If I *do* have to meet a fictitious biblical person, why don't you send me your mother, she seems like a nice lady."

"We can do that. But she will surely tell you the same thing that Moshe told you."

Sarah shook her head. "I'm not buying any of this."

"You don't have to. You don't have to do any of this. You can just go on back to bed."

"And, in case you haven't figured it out by now, I certainly don't intend to put you on a pedestal."

"Good. It's lonely up there."

"I would trade you in for a good auto mechanic any day."

"Sorry, I can't help you there. So, what would you like to talk about, besides automotive repairs?"

"I don't know. I've talked about everything there is to talk about in therapy." She glanced at Betty's rubber snake on the floor. "Maybe we can discuss my fear of snakes. That's probably the only hang up I haven't talked about."

"Very well."

"No, I'm just being facetious. That's trivial."

"Alright."

"I really don't feel a need to talk about anything in particular. You pick something."

"How about religion?'

"Absolutely not!"

"Very well."

They were silent for a while.

"Why do you want to bring up religion?" asked Sarah with a look of annoyance.

"You asked me to pick something. I picked something."

More silence.

"But why religion, of all things?"

"Well, you must admit that over the years, you *have* given considerable attention to the Bible."

"I don't give a damn about the Bible."

"And, you have read through a bunch of other holy books."

"So?"

"Several times."

"I read fast."

"And, while you were in college, you took a graduate level course called Religions of the World."

"Since you're poking your nose into my memories, I will point out that the entire course was white-washed bullshit. I did my own study on the religions of the world and what I discovered simply nauseated me. Anyway, I don't mess with religion anymore."

"Be that as it may, it would appear that you do have some interest in... let's call it extra-corporeal intelligence. As I recall, before I introduced myself, you were busily engaged in trying to prove to yourself that you are not merely having a dream; that you are, in fact, awake and aware, independent of your physical body. I believe that your primary piece of evidence was a rubber duck."

"Look, Mr...."

"Jesus is fine."

"But that's not really who you are. You're just saying that to annoy me."

"Certainly not. I am who I am; and I am exactly who you believe I am."

"That is such double talk."

"Why don't you just call me Brother Josh, like Moshe did?"

"I'd feel silly calling you 'brother'."

"Well then, just call me Josh."

Sarah folded her arms. "Okay... Josh." She paused. "I forgot what I was saying."

"You were explaining that you are indifferent to religion and holy books."

"Oh yes. I was about to say that I have read such books in the past, just as

I sometimes read mythology. But when push comes to shove, I don't believe in myths and fairy tales, and I don't put any faith in all this religious mumbo-jumbo, whether it's clothed in the language of the ancients or modern lingo."

"Sarah, you may interpret this situation any way you wish. You may look upon this encounter as a dream inside your head. You may see it as the result of the awakening of dormant parts of the brain, triggered by a combination of emotional trauma and those exotic brain exercises that you've been doing. These explanations have a measure of validity. But you cannot deny that religion has been a powerful presence in your life, one way or another."

Sarah noted that his voice had become stern, but somehow managed to retain its annoyingly unshakable benevolence. His mannerism reminded her of a physics professor she had once admired in college. Was he being that way on purpose?

She looked at her body lying in a fetal position under the blanket. Her long flowing hair extended forward over her shoulder, while her eyes moved rapidly under the lids, as if watching a tennis match inside in her head.

"As for the mumbo-jumbo, I suggest that you don't sweep it away too quickly, because you may find some value in it. For example, you've been exposed to the idea that much of what you experience as reality isn't as real as you think it is; gravity, for instance."

Before Sarah could argue, the voice continued.

"Anyway, I know all this is a little difficult for you to believe, but that's because you've trained yourself to be so skeptical; after all, that is your job. 'Show me proof, show me your references, show me your late-pass, show me the equations, show me, show me, and show me.'"

Sarah opened her mouth to speak, but she wasn't fast enough.

"But it's all right that you're so skeptical. It's rather charming. It does mean a little extra work for me, but that's no problem at all—"

"DO YOU MIND IF I GET A WORD IN EDGEWISE?" Sarah yelled. She was about to give him a piece of her mind, but stopped when she heard a sound coming from the bed. Her sleeping body had inhaled abruptly, emitting a single loud snore.

"Shhh," said Josh. "You'll wake yourself up."

Sarah used every bit of will power to maintain a stern and serious countenance, and almost succeeded. She grinned only slightly. "All right, maybe some of that stuff does have a basis in reality. However, I certainly am not going to jump off some cliff just because you're telling me that gravity is an illusion, because I can assure you that Sir Isaac Newton's Third Law of Motion, illusion or not, will still take effect, which would compel me to accelerate toward the earth at 9.8 meters per second squared."

"Good point."

"You might be able to prove to me that Newtonian physics is an illusion, but you still can't run your car without it."

"Well, I wouldn't know anything about that. I'll just take your word for it."

"And, I am still not convinced that this situation is anything other than an extremely vivid— and very bizarre— dream."

"No problem. That is a perfectly valid way of looking at it."

"Okay. So, let's stop all this nonsense and get to the point."

"Of course. There are actually several points that we have been skirting around. With your permission, I shall enumerate them."

"Proceed."

"They are as follows. Number one: You feel as if you are rotting away as a babysitter in high school, rather than completing your doctoral studies.

"Number two: You don't relate well to your professional colleagues. You either feel contempt or excessively competitive toward them.

"Number three: You feel unfulfilled because you've never had a healthy relationship with a man."

Sarah looked skyward. "Oh, spare me."

"Shall I stop?"

"Just say what's on your mind. But let me warn you, I won't necessarily agree with what you say."

"Number four: You don't get along well with women in general. Again, you either feel contempt or overly competitive toward them, except for Betty, of course.

"Number five: You have a strong longing to reach out and touch people in sweet and loving ways.

"Number six: There is the fiery spirit of the rebel within you that is just itching to do battle with just about everyone. This of course stems from number five.

"Number seven: You don't trust men because they appear to be quite unreliable. You think they are just after your body. This is particularly painful for you in light of number five."

Sarah shifted her feet.

"Number eight: You have an obsession with God and religion that you don't quite know what to do with."

"Obsession!"

"Number nine: Over the years, you have developed many creative ways of coping with your various challenges. One of them was not so creative."

"You mean alcohol?"

"I mean denial."

Sarah looked skyward and shook her head slowly. "Before this session is over, you are going to make me puke. I've already looked into the denial issue."

"Yes, yes, and you're doing a fine job. But that's not what I'm talking about."

"Well, what else is there?"

"Your heritage."

"What's that got to do with anything?"

"Denial of anything that's yours robs you of self-respect. It has contributed to a deep sense of self-hatred, and—"

"Oh, put a lid on it," said Sarah, waving her arm in the direction she thought the voice was coming from. "I get really pissed off when people play psychiatrist!"

"And, naturally, you compensated for that self-hatred by demanding perfection of yourself in all worldly endeavors, which has added to your frustration."

"You really are trying to irritate me, aren't you?"

"Number ten: Underneath the cool, rock-hard, business-like person, there is a lake of smoldering lava. The internal pressure is tremendous and is obviously reaching the critical point. Things look fine from a distance, but when people get close enough to you, they sense the tension and the strain, they feel the tremors, they hear the deep rumbles, and feel the heat rising from within."

"Oh, God, he's a poet, too."

"But I will say this. Your courage and determination have been nothing less than heroic."

Suddenly, Sarah felt the welling up of emotions. She stopped the wave in her throat where she felt the familiar lump. She tightened her throat and sent the wave back down again. Glancing at her body in bed, she noticed a reflexive grimace on her sleeping face.

"You haven't mentioned my physical problem at all," she said with deliberate casualness. "The tumors."

"That's number eleven," he said softly. "That was your body's way of saying, 'I quit.' It's saying, 'I quit,' because for many years, you've been telling it, 'I hate you.'"

Sarah stood silently at attention. She noticed another grimace and shudder of her sleeping body. "Oh, hell, I'm just being an arrogant bitch, I know it, and you know it, so quit being so damned nice." She unfolded her arms. "Okay, what do we do now?"

"Well, your friends would probably tell you to begin at the beginning— the bottom step on the stairwell, as it were."

"What do you mean?"

"You know what I mean."

"No, I don't."

"Yes, you do. And please don't play dumb; it is not cute."

Sarah paused. "All right. But, as I understand it, that bottom step essentially translates into surrender."

"Precisely."

"But that's ridiculous," she said, folding her arms again. "Just before I went to sleep, I was thinking about surrendering everything."

"We are speaking of surrender of excess baggage, of your demand for perfection. It is surrender of your pretense of being in control. That sort of surrender can only come forth on the heels of firm determination. That sort of surrender gives birth to new life, whereas the sort of surrender that you were contemplating results in throwing out the baby with the bath water, which obviously wasn't what you really wanted to do; otherwise we would not be having this conversation—"

"All right, all right, I get the point. God, you are such a chatterbox. Let's just get down to business." Sarah ceremoniously stood at attention. "I'm taking the first step. I admit that my life has become a bloody mess and that I feel pretty damned powerless to do anything about it. So, now I'm ready to surrender all beliefs and attitudes that have made me a sick puppy. So, what's next?"

"Faith."

"Faith?"

"Faith."

"Faith in what, for Pete's sake? What do you want me to do, become a good Christian again?"

"No, certainly not. A good Jew would be more like it."

"Now wait a minute!"

"You see, Sarah, your heritage will be as an invisible chain around you, until you discover the truth contained in it."

"Well, those are real nice sounding words, but I don't see any reason to accept them as the *a priori* truth. The only way I can accept the tenets of any religion, including my— including Judaism, is to put blinders on. No, thank you. I accept only what is rational and tangible, heritage or no heritage."

"Judaism is quite rational."

"On the surface maybe."

"Do you really believe that?"

"Let me put it this way: it's partially rational. They talk a lot about each person being free and self-responsible and refusing to yield to any authority except God. Sounds real nice. But, to me, that is just paradoxical. It is not rational to say that we answer to no one except an unseen and unproven God. It's baffling as hell. Religion, any religion, is just one paradox after another, one contradiction after another, one inconsistency after another."

"Why do you think that's so?"

"Hell, I don't know!" Sarah noticed that she was becoming more agitated. "Time and time again, I've encountered religious beliefs wherein rational thinking and benign philosophies are mixed in with bizarre superstitions, asinine theologies, holier-than-thou arrogance and horrible cruelty. And the fact that some aspects of their beliefs are sensible and humane apparently prevents them from seeing their dirty underside. I mean, damn it, just look around. Every religion has its own stupid spiel to convince the followers that they are somehow better than the religion next door. Some are very blatant about it, others are amazingly subtle, weaving it into prayers and sneaking it in between their grand declarations of love, so the members are too emotionally enraptured to question the crap that's being implanted in their minds."

"But surely you see this has nothing to do with the religion in question per sé, which according to your own assessment, is often humane and sensible. The problems you just described are a function of unresolved self-esteem issues that become generalized in the collective—"

"Let's just drop it, okay? This whole discussion is upsetting me."

"As you wish."

She glanced at her body curled up in bed. "When I wake up, I'll probably have a headache from all this."

"Would you like to terminate this session?"

"Don't tempt me."

"I'm certainly not tempting you. I'm simply reminding you that you don't have to continue this conversation if you find it objectionable."

Sarah felt her anger dissipating, which then made her even angrier. "Oh, I get it. You're using reverse psychology on me. Telling me I can go, so that I'll want to stay. Well, it won't work. I'll decide when I've had enough, regardless of what you say."

"Of course. So, what else would you like to discuss?"

"Hell, I don't know. Since you're already inside my head, you pick the topic. Just make sure it isn't about God or religion."

"Very well. May we speak about your father?"

Sarah stood silently at attention, feeling like she had just been ambushed. She searched her mind for a legitimate reason to veto the request. "Sure," she finally said with a shrug, "go ahead."

"Why do you think he drank?"

Sarah relaxed. This was familiar territory. "He had no self-respect," she said, with another shrug. "He hated himself. The only reason he converted to Judaism was so he could marry my mother. He even went so far as to change his name to 'Chazinov' just to please his in-laws. He figured he couldn't be a proper Jew with a name like 'Sullivan.' He didn't have to do that. He did not have to turn his back on his family and completely disown his heritage. That's why he drank and that's why he became so argumentative." Sarah paused and then folded her arms. "Now, wait a minute!"

"Yes?"

"My father's issues have nothing to do with me."

"Really?"

"What I mean is… I haven't abandoned Judaism to chase after another fairy tale. I'm just being rational about things."

"Well, if you think that being rational and scientific excludes religion, I'd like to point out that a number of the great geniuses that you admire, like Sir Isaac Newton, were deeply religious."

"I know that. They were also all males. I don't hold that against them, either."

Sarah waited for Josh to comment on her brief exploration of Christianity, but he remained silent. "The only reason I started to attend Catholic Church as a college freshmen was because I was young and confused and far from home. I hadn't given up on God yet, but the Jewish version of God was just too impersonal for me. I was starved for love, so I was looking for a version of God that was more personal. Boy, was I disappointed."

"Well," said Josh, "since I'm here, the Catholic Church must have made some kind of impression on you."

"Look, that's not the point. The point is; I'm through with that all that biblical stuff. Do you really expect me to follow a religion that believes in a God that is supposed to be benevolent and wise, and then burns babies and separates humanity into so many warring nations? Is that what you're asking me to believe in?"

"Certainly not. I'm simply suggesting that there is more to life than what you presently perceive and believe. I'm suggesting that you consider the possibility that a presence permeates the universe… like a great unified field. I am suggesting that you consider the possibility that this presence is very real, very tangible in its activity, and is as close and as readily available as your next breath."

Sarah shook her head slowly. "You are turning out to be a real corn-ball prophet, you know that? You're trying to trick me into doing the second step again. I do not like that second step stuff."

"I merely asked you about your father. You're the one who started talking about God and religion again. I don't have to trick you into addressing the role of religion in your life. You're already obsessed with it. No matter what we talk about, it will come back to that."

Sarah momentarily felt cornered, but quickly found a logical way out. "I am not obsessed with religion. The subject is just annoying to me, so naturally it's easy for me to get sucked into it." Sarah threw her arms in the air. "Look, this just isn't working. Why don't you bring in the Buddha? Maybe I'll relate to him better."

"Yes, if you wish. However, I can tell you right now, he's too laid back for you."

"What's that supposed to mean?"

"Of all the time and energy you have expended on various religions, you have given little attention to Buddhism. Not enough action and drama for you. You secretly see him as a wimp."

"So what are you saying, that I'm too argumentative? You know, you're not exactly Mr. Mellow yourself."

"That is understandable if I am a projection of your own mind."

"Whatever. The point is, if you're trying to maneuver me to accept that Judeo/Christian crap, forget it. I've read every version of the Bible and I'm just not interested."

"Not *every* version."

"What do you mean?"

"You haven't read the five books of the Torah, in the original Hebrew."

Sarah paused. She glanced at her sleeping body, as it flinched under the covers.

"What difference does that make?" she asked.

"For you personally, it would make a great deal of difference."

Sarah looked out the window. "My Hebrew is rusty. And the old Hebrew is tricky. The words have no vowels, for Pete's sake. You can interpret it lots of different ways. It would take me ages to figure out what the hell they're really trying to say."

"Not necessarily. There's a form of holographic speed-reading that would speed things up considerably."

"Holographic speed-reading? Are you putting me on?"

"Certainly not. It has to do with tracking the collective vibration of symbols. I can teach it to you, if you wish."

"Well," she said, folding her arms, "that's irrelevant. The point is that I don't feel comfortable with all this talk of God and religion. It's… irritating."

"Fine. So, for now, let's see if we can just translate this into something that less biblical and a bit more palatable." He paused. "Ah yes! Earlier, you mentioned Sir Isaac Newton's Third Law of Motion."

"Yes?"

"Can you recite it?"

Sarah relaxed. "'To every action there is always opposed an equal reaction, or, the mutual action of two bodies upon each other is always equal and directed in contrary parts.'"

"Very nice. Sir Isaac couldn't have said it better himself."

"Naturally, it's a direct quote."

"More simply stated, 'To every action, there is an equal and opposite reaction.' Now, an obvious implication of this law is that no force in the universe can exist without its opposite."

"Of course."

"However, during your quiet moments, you have often contemplated the existence of a force that has no opposite. In fact, it was the focal point of your post-graduate studies."

"I was simply investigating magnetic monopoles, which is a legitimate area of study."

"So, I'm asking you to contemplate the possibility that your idea might even have ramifications that go far beyond magnetic monopoles; a force that has no opposite— a presence that is entirely self-contained; a force that unifies everything else."

"So, where do you fit into this picture?"

"I'm just a projection of your own mind, as you said."

"You're being evasive."

"I merely answered your question according to the model you accept. If you wish for me to respond in a different context, please specify."

"Yes, that will do. But first, I would ask you why you changed the subject. My role in the so-called creation myth is irrelevant to your current—"

"Look, you said I can ask anything I want."

"Yes, I did say that."

"So, are you going to answer, or not?"

"Of course."

"And keep it simple. I don't like high brow philosophy."

"Very well. Let's talk about forces again, simple Newtonian forces. Let us consider a rubber band."

"Okay."

"Or better yet, a spring, like the slinky toy that you were so fond of playing with. Let's say that you stretch out the ends of a spring, and then let them go. What happens?"

"It snaps back to its original position," she said.

"Right. So, there you have it."

"There I have it? There I have what?"

"I have answered your question regarding my involvement in the current creation myth."

"You haven't told me anything," said Sarah.

"You said, 'Keep it simple'."

"That wasn't simple, that was nonsense."

"Well, it's not my fault you equate simplicity with nonsense."

"Okay, never mind. Go ahead and get a little technical."

"As you wish. So, we have this spring, which we stretch out and then it snaps back."

"Yes, I know that part."

"I know you know it. I just want to make sure that you are aware of the basics before we elaborate."

"I'm not dumb, you know. I mastered Newtonian mechanics in my first year in college."

"So, who said you were dumb?"

"You're talking to me like I'm a dumb little girl." Sarah noticed that even though they were arguing, she felt more at ease. "Alright," she said, "so, we have a spring, we stretch it out and it snaps back again. So what?"

"Now let's look at this spring as Sir Isaac Newton might look at it. Sir Isaac would say that the spring stretches out because we have introduced a force that causes the ends of the spring to repel or pull away from the hypothetical center of the spring."

"Okay."

"Let's call this force, 'the repulsive force'. Now, in accordance with Sir Isaac's Third Law of Motion, another force, an attractive force, gets activated within the spring. And this attractive force counters the repulsive force, thus causing the spring to bounce back to its original position. In other words, this attractive force tends to pull the proverbial spring back to the 'hypothetical center'."

"Wait a second," said Sarah. "Is this 'hypothetical center' that you speak of a metaphor for God?"

"Yes, it can be. But, if we look at it strictly from the standpoint of Newtonian mechanics, we would simply say that it is a condition in which there are no forces opposing each other."

"And that's supposed to be God, right?"

"Yes, but I'm refraining from making that correlation because you indicated the concept of God is offensive to you."

"I did not say the concept of God is offensive to me! Don't put words in my mouth."

They were both silent.

"Well," said Sarah, "go on."

"Very well. To make an extremely long story short, the creation myth, as you call it, may be compared to a repulsive force pulling away from the hypothetical center, followed by an attractive force that pulls back to the hypothetical center."

"So, life is like a yo-yo."

"Only if we look at it from the standpoint of Newtonian physics."

"I understand that," said Sarah. "Go on."

"Now, the periodic excursions of the repulsive force pulling away from the hypothetical center are essential for creation to occur, but they can show up in human behavior as anger, jealousy, deception, and so forth. But regardless of how it shows up, its presence activates the attractive force."

"Okay, so the attractive force is the good guy and the repulsive force is the bad guy."

"I didn't say that."

"You implied it."

"I did not. That is simply an assumption on your part."

"It's a reasonable assumption."

"Let's not make this more complicated than need be. What we have here are two simple forces. Their behavior follows the same fundamental laws as the forces that interact to produce the motion of a spring, or a seesaw, or a violin string, or a yo-yo. Would you say that the downward force of the yo-yo is bad and the ascending force is good?"

"Never mind. Go on."

"Now, since the repulsive force causes all things to move away from the hypothetical center, the result is separation of everything from everything else. Surely, you can see that this is essential for creation, as you know it. Consider the expanding universe; it's about things separating and moving away from the hypothetical center. In order for anything to be created, it must, in one sense, have a separate identity. The repulsive force is the beginning of creation, and the attractive force brings it to fulfillment. This, of course, is a grossly over-simplified explanation. In reality, the attractive force and repulsive force are occurring simultaneously. In other words, separation and joining must occur as a single harmonic unit involving specific frequencies and octaves. The whole thing has to do with rhythms and patterns. These patterns are generally not discernible within the framework of space/time, except maybe as music—"

"All right, enough!"

"What's the matter?"

"You're supposed to be helping me with serious life and death issues. Instead, you're talking about art appreciation."

"I was merely answering your question."

"No, you weren't. You were going off on some silly pseudoscientific tangent."

"My answer was not tangential at all. It was most decidedly centripetal—"

"Look, can you keep this cosmic flatulence down to a minimum and just talk on a practical human level?"

"Well, if we have to describe these two forces in human terms, it still has to do with creation. For humans, creation has to do with desire. The repulsive force is the emergence of desire. The attractive force is the fulfillment of desire."

Sarah nodded, "Okay. I think I see that."

"We might also say that the activation of the repulsive force involves forgetting, while the activation of the attractive force involves remembering. Both are important to creation. One or the other isn't intrinsically good or bad. It's all a matter of timing and rhythm. Which, on a human level, simply means that there is a time to forget and a time to remember."

"Forget and remember what?"

"It."

"It?"

"Yes, It. The hypothetical center. Unity."

"Otherwise known as God."

"Yes, but you find that annoying."

"Don't patronize me, all right? That really pisses me off."

"I was merely respecting your wishes."

"Well, whatever you're doing, it's making me angry, which you're probably doing on purpose. You're deliberately pissing me off because you know that it will keep me engaged."

"I can assure you I'm not trying to make you angry. I don't have to. You're doing it quite beautifully all by yourself."

"Get off it, will you?" she yelled.

"I am just telling you the truth."

"OH... JUST STOP IT!"

"Stop it? What do you want me to do? Lie?"

Sarah paused. "This whole conversation," she said in a controlled tone, "has become irrelevant and absurd."

"I agree. Shall we get back to the second step?"

"Not yet," she said. "First, I want to get straight on this so-called repulsive force— on a human level."

"All right. Let's just say that the repulsive force is saying, 'I want to explore; I want to be noticed; I want to be recognized as an individual.'"

"So what's wrong with that?"

"Who said there's anything wrong with it?"

"Never mind. Go on."

"Getting back to your original question, my role in the creation myth is simply to act as a vehicle for the attractive force to interact harmonically with the repulsive force, so that springs and violins and civilizations and yo-yos can oscillate properly. Understand?"

"I understand your metaphor. But that doesn't explain the actual nature of this so-called repulsive force, and why it came into existence in the first place."

"That's a very good question, Sarah, but it goes far beyond the simple Newtonian model that we're using right now. Just be patient, we'll get there."

Sarah opened and closed her mouth.

"Now," continued Josh, "are you ready to address the second step?"

"No. I will rephrase my question. Why does the repulsive force sometimes go out of control and turn into a monster?"

"What monster?"

"You know, the devil, the beast."

"Since you are the one who makes that correlation, you tell me."

"I don't make that correlation. People do." She paused. "What I mean is… wait a minute. I'm getting confused here. Before we started this conversation, I never thought of the repulsive force and attractive force. But from what you said, the repulsive force can obviously be interpreted as Lucifer's rebellion against God."

"Again, Sarah, you are the one who makes that correlation."

Sarah sighed. "I don't know what to say to that." She glanced at the rubber snake on the floor.

"Perhaps, this might help," said Josh. "In your mythology, the repulsive force 'gone bad' is often depicted as a snake."

"Yes?"

"The snake symbolizes deception, seduction, sneakiness, and so forth. Perhaps, you might ask yourself what is the true nature of the snake beyond all the exotic qualities that you have projected on it?"

"It's just an animal. A reptile."

"And how would you describe its behavior."

"Instinct."

"Precisely."

"So?'

"So, free of all your projections, the snake is just an animal living according to its instincts."

They were silent for a while.

"I don't get it," said Sarah. "How does this relate to the repulsive force going bad?"

"Well, think about it."

Sarah sighed and glanced at her body in bed. "Okay," she said, throwing her arms in the air, "Time out! This is not the direction in which I want to go. Forget about the devils and rubber snakes and things."

"All right."

"What I want to know is, why has the so-called repulsive force run amuck in *my* life?"

"You called it into action, of course. That's the only way that it can act. You told it to act and you told it how to act."

"I don't recall doing any such thing."

"Obviously."

"So, how did I call it into action?"

"With your prevailing thoughts and beliefs. Which, in turn, emanate from the underlying major and minor harmonic—"

"Never mind that, let's just get to the point. Assuming that what you say is valid, what can I do about it now?"

"The second step."

Sarah sighed and then folded her arms. "Not yet."

"Very well."

"I have another question, if you don't mind. Why is it that every religion on earth seems to think that they have the only hot-line to heaven and that everyone else is just a variation of 'bad'?"

"Once again, you are asking a question that cannot be intelligently addressed within the framework of the Newtonian model. We could possibly explain this in terms of high energy physics and quantum mechanics, but we would have to use an exotic form of multidimensional calculus that you haven't—"

"Screw the Newtonian model and all that other stuff! I just want to know why so many religions absolutely think they are IT and everyone else is just bad or deceived or both. I think my question is very straightforward and simple."

"But the answer is not."

"I don't accept that. Since you are a projection of my subconscious mind, I command you to give me a simple straightforward answer!"

"Very well. The simple straightforward answer is that there is no simple and straightforward answer."

"Why are you being so evasive?"

"My response was not evasive. You simply can't draw a straight line in a curved universe, and you can't put things into neat little separate compartments when faced with harmonic parameters specifying that everything is contained within everything else."

"What are you talking about?"

"Those behaviors that you mentioned can be understood only when we see they are not isolated to certain segments of the greater symphony, or creation myth, as you call it. As in any wave phenomenon, they have a statistical existence everywhere you can point to."

Sarah threw her eyes skyward. "Oh, so there are no bad guys. And those idiots who spew out their venomous accusations and dictatorial laws in the name of 'Godliness' are just a projection of my own mind!"

"Precisely. You see, you *do* understand how this works."

"I do understand the concept. But that doesn't mean I accept it as true. You're saying that everything on the outside reflects my insides. I say, there's more to it than that."

"Well, if it will make you feel better, I can assure you that those things that bother you do have a basis in external reality."

"Of course they do! And what really infuriates me," she said, raising her voice, "is that these assholes get to be narrow-minded, hypocritical, and cruel, while they walk around swaggeringly, feeling very sanctimonious about themselves, as they lead us around by the nose."

"There is such a thing as free will, you know."

"WHAT!" Sarah raised her fist in the air. "THAT IS SUCH A GOD-DAMN JOKE! How can you talk about free will when they have a vice grip on our emotions that reduces us to an infantile state of dependency? They make us believe that we're damned if we go our own way or feel anything that they don't want us to feel. WE'RE SLAVES; THAT'S WHAT WE ARE!"

"I assure you, it's all perfectly symmetrical and harmonically—"

"It is not symmetrical," said Sarah, trying to control herself. "I know how the game works. The followers are given a taste of security and togetherness, but while they are emotionally open, they're imprinted into the organization. And the vice grip is re-enforced with cute little stories that play on our deepest fears. We grow up programmed to believe that if we don't submit to their authority, we'll miss the boat and drown with the rest of the infidels, or burn in hell. Scaring people into submission by threatening them with drowning and burning is the oldest and cheapest gimmick for population control."

"However, I must again remind you that if you look deeply enough into the harmonic patterns, it is all perfectly symmetrical."

"IT IS NOT SYMMETRICAL! IT'S INDECENT!" Sarah braced herself and lowered her voice. "Granted, they do nice things like support family life. But they support it so they can siphon energy from it. Why do you think religious people historically have had big families?"

"Copulation I suppose—"

Sarah raised her voice again. "I'LL TELL YOU WHY! PEOPLE WERE PUSHED TO HAVE LOTS OF KIDS TO INCREASE THE SIZE OF THE FLOCK. AND THEY WANT TO BE SURE THAT THE WOMAN IS SO BUSY RAISING KIDS, ALL HER ENERGY IS SPENT BREEDING MORE BELIEVERS AND MORE SOLDIERS, SO SHE HAS NO TIME TO DEVELOP HER OWN MIND! TO THOSE MEGALOMANIACS, WOMEN ARE JUST... JUST..."

"Cattle?"

"YES!" Sarah roared. "WE'RE JUST CATTLE TO THEM!"

She deliberately toned herself down when she realized that she was beginning to seriously lose control. "I mean, let's tell the truth here. The most brutal and repressive dictatorships in history were religious and patriarchal. Do you remember the Dark Ages?"

"About as well as you do—"

"They had control of education, health care, commerce, you name it. They would do it again today if given the chance. Can mere politics justify such horrors as the Inquisition?" She stopped momentarily, remembering her recurring dream in which she was sitting in a theater, watching a movie from the Spanish Inquisition, in which a Dominican priest was raping a young lady. Feeling slightly disoriented, she quickly gathered herself and continued. "Can politics train fanatical soldiers to go on a genocidal rampage or a suicide mission? Hell no! Only religion can do that."

"But that has nothing to do with the pure essence of Judaism, which is your—"

"HORSE SHIT!" Sarah exploded. "NO RELIGION IS PURE. EVERY ONE OF THEM HAS COMMITTED ATROCITIES IN THE NAME OF GOD!" Sarah paused. She tried to compose. "And when it looks like they're becoming benign, watch out!"

Sarah focused on her feet to calm herself, as she had learned from her Tai Chi instructor. But it just did not work as well without her physical body. "Look," she said in a painfully soft voice, "I'm not being paranoid."

"Who said you're being paranoid?"

"I'm just facing facts. The psychosexual programming that goes on week after week in religious institutions does more harm than any child molester."

"Surely you don't mean that?"

Sarah tried to count to ten but only as far as two. "YES, I DO MEAN IT!

THEY ROB US OF OUR INNOCENCE. AND THEY CONTROL OUR THINKING TO THE POINT THAT WE'RE TOO FAR GONE IN LALA LAND TO KNOW THAT WE'RE BEING RAPED!"

Sarah's sleeping body convulsed in bed and sat up, eyes open. "SO DON'T TALK TO ME ABOUT FREE WILL! HARDLY ANYONE HAS FREE WILL! IT'S SYSTEMATICALLY BROKEN AND CRUSHED WHILE IT'S STILL IN THE CRADLE…" As she continued yelling, her words became a blur and her outburst became surreal to her. As she felt the bursts of anger that could have blown up every house of worship and incinerated every holy man on the face of the Earth, a tiny corner of her mind calmly asked a question: "Where is all this rage coming from?"

In the midst of her fury, she had the impression that she was reunited with her physical body. The floor felt more solid under her feet. Her stomach muscles strained and her throat felt raspy from all the yelling. When she glanced at the bed, it appeared to be empty, though she could not be sure, because the rage that was roaring out of her was so intense, it was like a blinding light that obscured her vision.

Finally, with great effort, she lowered her voice, still shaking with anger. "And that schmuck of a Rabbi at the temple!"

"What about him?"

"Do you know what that dick-head said to me?"

"Not specifically."

"He made a big show about how open-minded we are, how we encourage our members to ask questions of God and scrutinize the law. Sounds really nice, huh? But every time I spoke to him, he made it very clear that he knows everything and I know nothing. His sickening show of liberalism conceals an attitude that clearly says that he speaks for God, therefore, any member of the congregation who disagrees with him must be wrong, especially a young *girl* like me. 'Dear Sarah,' he says, 'why do you have the need to rebel against God.' I politely held my tongue and listened to his condescending spiel. That was the last time I went to Synagogue. Ever since then, I've been mad at myself for not telling him what I was really thinking."

"What were you really thinking?"

It was a simple enough question, but Sarah noticed that it triggered that blinding light again. Before she could control herself, she started yelling again. "I WANTED TO SAY, 'NO SIR, I'M NOT REBELLING AGAINST GOD I'M REBELLING AGAINST TYRANTS LIKE YOU WHO LIKE TO PLAY GOD! I USED TO THINK THAT SORT OF DICTATORIAL, KNOW-IT-ALL BULLSHIT WAS JUST A QUIRK OF THE CHRISTIANS, BUT IT'S IN *OUR* RELIGION, TOO!"

Sarah composed herself when she realized she had said *our* religion.

She sighed, feeling a strange sort of tranquility, a sublime exhaustion.

"Sarah, if you feel that strongly about this, you will undoubtedly have the opportunity to participate in the symphony in a way that you will find meaningful. But first you must learn to manage your internal energy so it can do something else besides explode."

"I suppose you're right."

"You would probably be a bit less accusative if you were more precise with your analysis."

"What do you mean?"

"In your passionate testimony, you did not prove there is anything inherently faulty with religion. In order to bring yourself all the way through this cathartic experience, you must punctuate it with scientific precision by acknowledging that your own personal experience with religion is just that— your own personal experience."

"I never said otherwise."

"You must also recognize there are many persons whose experience of religion is entirely different from yours, yet no less valid."

Sarah thought of Betty. "Granted."

She glanced at the bed and saw her body, lying sideways on top of the covers and breathing heavily. Her long hair was spread out in all directions on the pillow, as if she had literally fallen into bed.

"I usually don't use this much profanity," she said, ready to defend her freedom of speech. "I hope it doesn't offend you."

"Not at all. Your use of graphic expletives serves a useful function."

"Really?" Sarah felt herself inwardly stumble. She had expected another argument, but found herself with nothing to push against. "How so?"

"It's a means of generating energy that allows you to break inertia."

"Oh," she said, suddenly feeling disarmed.

"There are other ways of generating energy, of course. Ways that are more elegant and energy efficient."

"Such as?"

"The second step."

Sarah felt herself becoming tense again, suddenly feeling like she had been ambushed. Her body winced a bit, in bed. "Look, you are asking me to do something that I find uncomfortable and distasteful."

"I understand that."

"And quite frankly, I still don't know what to make of this whole situation. The most reasonable explanation is that everything I'm seeing and hearing right now is simply the result of the electrochemical activity of my brain cells," she said pointing to her body in bed.

"Again, that is a valid way of looking at it. In fact, if you want more details, we can say that most of the significant brain activity associated with your current experience is occurring in the areas of the brain that you call the thalamus and hypothalamus, with some significant contribution from the rest of the limbic system, as well as the area known as the old reptilian brain. The cerebral cortex thinks that it's running the show. But, frankly, it has an inflated opinion of itself."

Sarah smiled briefly. She relaxed a bit. "For some reason I have to remind myself that this is just a drama unfolding in my sleeping mind. Including you."

"Most certainly."

"That doesn't bother you?"

"Not at all. I don't mind being a projection of your subconscious mind. I find it rather amusing."

"You don't mind, huh? What if we proved beyond a shadow of a doubt that you really don't exist except in my mind and in the collective minds of humanity? What if you found out that if everyone stopped believing in you, you would go poof and disappear forever?"

"No problem."

"No problem?" Sarah folded her arms. "Okay, let's back up a little. You previously described yourself as an expression of that so-called attractive force, whose sole purpose is to counteract the effects of the repulsive force."

"In a manner of speaking, yes. Although, the term 'counteract' really isn't—"

"HA! If what you say is correct, then, as soon as you succeed in doing your job, you cease to exist!"

"Yes, in a manner of speaking."

"Don't give me that, 'in a manner speaking' stuff. According to what you said, WHEN THE REPULSIVE FORCE IS GONE, SO ARE YOU!"

"Stop yelling at me; I said I agree with you!"

Sarah composed herself. "So, you don't have an ego?"

"Certainly I have an ego. I have yours."

Sarah tried to suppress her smile.

"More precisely, I have a slightly altered version of your ego. I rather like it."

Sarah paused. "Fine. But, if you're a projection of my own mind, shouldn't you be saying things that reflect my own beliefs?"

"Certainly."

"So why are you saying so many things that I totally disagree with?"

"Quite simple. You really don't disagree with them. The ideas I have expressed simply reflect beliefs you have repressed, because you're unable to integrate them.

You called me here so you could, in effect, argue with yourself."

Sarah felt like she had been outmaneuvered again. "Okay, I'm just going to drop all assumptions about who you are and who you aren't."

"Alright."

"And I'm going to ask you a simple question. Are you a mere projection of my subconscious mind, or is there more to this picture?"

"The only way I can adequately answer that question is to respond with another question."

"That's cheating."

"Is it cheating when *you* respond to a question from your students with a question of your own?"

Sarah paused. "Proceed."

"My question is this. Does an atom consist of a cluster of tiny pellets called protons and neutrons, and many orbiting electrons?"

"That depends on how you look at it."

"Well, there you are."

Sarah opened and closed her mouth. "Your analogy is inappropriate," she snapped out. "Protons, neutrons, and electrons have both a particle nature and a wave nature. The model of the atom to which you refer is valid and legitimate if we are considering the particle nature, but not the wave nature. It is an oversimplified model, but it does have a basis in reality and it serves a useful function."

"Precisely. And, if you want to see me as a mere projection of your subconscious mind, it is entirely appropriate. Like the simple model of the atom, it fits the observable facts and it serves a useful function."

"But you're cleverly implying there's more to it than that, so as to put doubts in my mind."

"I'm certainly not trying to put doubts in your mind, and I am being quite explicit regarding your interpretation of my presence here, which, like your model of the atom, is functional, has a measure of validity, but does not tell the whole story."

"So, what is the rest of the story?"

"Something, which, at the present time, cannot be communicated in words."

"HA!"

"Ha, nothing! Would you ask someone to learn calculus before they've learned algebra?"

"There you go again, trying to weasel your way out by throwing in a clever analogy that you think I will find acceptable."

"And there *you* go again, assuming that I am concealing something. The purpose of my analogy was clear and simple. I was communicating to you the need to follow a certain linear progression of understanding."

"Why?"

"Because right now, your mind is operating in a linear fashion, whereas the answer you seek is more… holographic. If you will pardon yet another analogy, you cannot fully comprehend the wave nature of atoms if you have no knowledge of wave mechanics. If you stop trying to force the issue, your linear thinking will reach its natural destination and allow you to step into four-dimensional and eventually higher understanding with ease and grace. Surely you, as a teacher, can appreciate the need to follow a linear order of progression in learning."

"I don't accept that analogy. My question is simple. Do you have a basis in objective reality or are you just a figment of my imagination?"

"The simplest answer is that I exit in a realm where such a distinction has no meaning. From a mathematical standpoint, we would have to say there is an equal probability of both."

"Would it, at least, be safe to say that you are a… spirit?"

"It's safe, but that's about it."

"What do you mean?"

"I exist in a realm where the distinction between flesh and spirit has no meaning."

"Okay, whatever you are, could we say that you reside in a physical location other than the Earth— another planet or galaxy?"

"By a wild stretch of the imagination, perhaps."

Sarah remained silent for a while. "You're just not going to give me anything are you?"

"I'm giving you everything that you are capable of receiving. I'm being as explicit and accurate as possible under the circumstances. If I tried to be more explicit, my words would become less accurate. If tried to be more accurate my words would become less explicit."

Sarah paused. "So, if we were being completely rational…"

"If we were being completely rational, we would have to say that I exist only in your imagination. Other than that, I am nothing."

"A very peculiar nothing." Sarah nodded.

"Granted."

"All right. So, what's next?"

"The second step."

"I wish you'd stop pushing me to do that damned second step."

"I am not pushing you, I am merely encouraging you to do it because it's the next logical thing to do."

"According to whom?"

"According to me, obviously. But, it's still your choice."

"Well then," Sarah folded her arms; "I choose not to do it at this time."

"Fine. If you have any other solution, besides sitting in your room with your thumb up your ass until you drop dead, I'm very open to hearing it."

After recovering from the shock of Josh's response, Sarah sighed and relaxed. "Look, it's not that I don't want to do it. The truth is, I'm afraid to do it. It feels like I'm setting myself up for..." Sarah felt herself trembling. "What I mean is, trusting God seems as ridiculous as trusting my..."

"It's all right. You don't have to force anything to happen. As long as you know where you stand, the next move will come naturally."

Sarah silently looked at her body in bed.

–7–

"So, what else is on your mind?" asked Josh.

Sarah flinched. "What makes you think that I have something else on my mind?"

"A hunch."

"Well...there are lots of things on my mind."

"Pick one."

"Uh, I used to be curious about the parable of the lost sheep. First off, it implies that we are mindless domestic animals. It also implies that we are property. Other than that, I think it's a rather poor analogy. I mean, obviously, it's designed to make us feel loved and cared for, but when you look at it from a practical standpoint, that shepherd was rather foolish. He was risking the entire flock to go after one animal."

"It seems foolish because you're looking at it from the perspective of linear arithmetic."

"Are you going to fall back on that non-linear excuse again?"

"Well, it's not my fault that you keep asking for linear answers to issues which are basically non-linear. Yes, the behavior of that hypothetical shepherd makes no sense, but only if you assume that the value of each sheep is a fraction of the entire flock. From that perspective, as the size of the flock grows, the relative value of each animal diminishes."

"You're saying that it is not so?"

"I'm saying there's another way of looking at it."

"If you're going to tell me that the parable is really about God's infinite love for us, you can stop right there. That parable is just playing on our existential anxiety."

"What existential anxiety?"

"You know. That feeling of being an insignificant grain of sand in a vast desert; the feeling that you're a very expendable dumb animal lost in a huge herd. That sheep story is cleverly designed to subdue that anxiety."

"Since you already have the parable all figured out, why did you even bother asking me about it?"

"I didn't say I have it all figured out. I'm just telling you about the part that I see. But, I was also thinking that...maybe there's more to it."

"There most certainly is."

"So, what is it?"

"Without making reference to God's infinite love?"

"Correct," said Sarah with deliberate firmness.

"Very well. But again, the answer is non-linear and therefore—"

"There you go again!"

"And there *you* go again, trying to force linear parameters upon non-linear issues. Look, let's say there is a certain quality within that lost sheep. If that quality had a tug-of-war with the same quality in all the other sheep put together, the result would be a tie."

"Huh?"

"Let's say it another way. If that quality is like weight, and we placed it on one side of a seesaw and put the same quality of all the other sheep on the other side, the two sides would balance. This is what I mean by non-linear—"

"Yes, yes, I understand what you're saying. It sounds real deep, and mysterious, and miraculous. But it's all gibberish until you prove it."

"Prove it? Prove what?"

"Hah! I knew it!"

"Hah, nothing! If you wish, we can explain this in greater mathematical detail, but we would have to consider certain aspects of integral calculus that are currently regarded as mathematical artifacts because they only have meaning in four dimensions or higher, and then we must apply those equations to particle-wave mechanics."

"Particle-wave mechanics again! Do you have a thing about particles and waves?"

"No. You do. And, as I have already said, you can get a first-hand experience of that particle-wave relationship, if you wish. It would surely give you an understanding of this lost sheep thing in a way that you would find satisfying."

Sarah suddenly felt herself becoming disoriented. "I don't think I'm quite ready for that. Anyway, that's not really the main thing that was on my mind." She inwardly flinched, wishing she hadn't said that.

"What *was* the main thing on your mind?"

"Uh… Actually, I don't know if there was really one *main* thing. There were several things."

"Oh?"

"For instance, I have general questions about you as a man."

"You consider me to be a man?"

"Oh, that's right, you're not a man. If you *were* a man, you would know how to fix my car."

"How much longer are you going to jab me with that one?"

Sarah caught herself giggling. "Then again, maybe you *are* a man."

"So, what questions do you want to ask about me?"

"Well, for example, in the Bible, there is no mention of what you were up to between the ages of thirteen and twenty-nine. What is that about?"

"Don't ask me. I didn't write it."

"No, seriously. There is no mention whatsoever. Were you hibernating or something?"

"What do you care? I'm just a figment of your imagination."

"Oh, stop it! For now, let's assume you really did exist as an actually historical person the Earth."

"All right."

"A while back, I heard some speculation that you did quite a bit of traveling between the ages of thirteen and twenty-nine."

"I was moonlighting as a Buddhist sage, okay?"

Sarah laughed. "That's very funny. I wish I had thought of that."

"You did. Now please say what's really on your mind."

As Sarah started to formulate her question, she remembered her recurring dream: the one in which she was sitting in a theater, watching a drunken Dominican priest raping a young lady. She mentally brushed it aside.

Sarah sighed. "Well…I…It's not important."

"Not important? So, why are you carefully avoiding it?"

"What I mean is that I've already explored this in therapy. I was just wondering about… theology… and its relationship to…"

"Sex?"

"Yeah," Sarah nodded quickly.

"With regard to theology, we might say that sexual desire is the flesh and blood translation of a deeper desire to return to the hypothetical center."

"I see," she said. "Is that why certain cults—"

"Sarah, we're going off on a tangent again. Is that what you wish to do?"

"No. Sarah started to feel a bit weepy. She reflexively pushed it down with anger. "I don't know," she said throwing her hands in the air. "We're not going anywhere here. We're talking about a lot of different things, and they're all disconnected and pointless. I'm going back to bed." She turned around and faced her sleeping body.

"Very well. Pleasant dreams."

—8—

Sarah did not remember actually going back to bed. As far as she knew, she had been standing on the floor, and then, instantly, she was back in her body in bed. She was in a half awake, half asleep state, feeling rather disoriented, as she heard a voice say, "Pleasant dreams."

She immediately drifted into a dream, in which she found herself in a theater. The Vintage Theater, no less. Her favorite get away. She looked at the violet screen, which sprang to life. Oh no, not that same movie! The screen showed a drunken Dominican priest raping a young lady in basement of a church.

Sarah shut her eyes and willfully forced herself back to bed, where she once again found herself in a half awake, half asleep state. She remembered the dream. She also vaguely remembered the bizarre conversation with an invisible man in her room. That memory was fading quickly. A quiet sort of panic filled her chest, as if a door was closing that she did not want to close.

Instinctively, she quieted her mind, causing it to perform a bit of a somersault. First, she felt herself drifting more deeply into sleep, and then suddenly, she was wide-awake. Without hesitating, she stood up. Her luminous body walked quickly to the middle of the room, as if racing to go through a door before it closed.

Not quite sure what to do next, she looked back at her bed. The sight of her physical body did not evoke any fear this time. What did scare her was the thought that maybe she had severed a line of communication that she would not be able to reopen. What was that man's name again?

"Uh…" she said, timidly waving her hand in the air. "Josh?"

"I'm here."

Sarah felt relieved. She looked at her sleeping body again. Her face seemed to carry a deep sadness. She really didn't know what to say or what to do.

"What might bring some cohesion to this experience," said Josh in a gentle voice," is for you to become more aware of what you really want."

More silence.

"What do you want, Sarah?"

"I… I just want to understand."

Suddenly, she felt embarrassed, as if her desire to understand was synonymous with wanting to have sex. She felt dizzy and the room became wavy.

"And what do you wish to understand?"

Her sleeping body heaved a bit in bed. Suddenly, Sarah felt very naked.

"Your physical body," said Josh. "Perhaps this is what you are wanting to understand? That body is a body of knowledge, living vibrating knowledge. And, as a living body of knowledge, it wants only one thing. It wants to be understood. And, it wants to be told that it is good."

Her body in bed seemed to relax.

"Over the years," continued Josh, "regardless of whether you were having a good day or bad day, there was always that nagging feeling that there was something important that you couldn't quite understand, a piece of information that was hidden, a memory locked in your body."

Sarah stared at her body.

"Well," she said, "you certainly have some interesting ideas, some of which I would tend to agree with. So, now that you have given your opinions, can you translate all of this verbiage into a specific how-to solution?"

"Yes."

"Good. Let's have it," she said, reminding herself not to expect too much.

"You have to wake up in the morning, get out of bed, do your bathroom things, get dressed, clean your room, eat a good breakfast, go to work, do your job well, get some exercise, balance your checkbook, play with your friends, get enough sleep, see funny movies, and eat carrots and walnuts; they're good for you."

Sarah smiled, shaking her head slowly. "I should have known." He was giving her exactly the same sort of advice that she gave her students.

"Surely," said Josh, "you didn't expect me to wave a magic wand?"

Sarah felt her insides shifting again. Something in her chest wanted to move. She felt the wave rising again. And this time, it felt like she might have a tough time persuading it to go back down.

"I know, but…" Her lips quivered. "It still hurts."

The wave in her chest rose quickly into her throat and refused to sink back down. And then a face appeared before her. It was the face of a bearded young man.

To her surprise, she wasn't the least bit startled. His eyes conveyed deep serenity and compassion; the kind that only comes from having experienced everything that a human being can possibly experience.

"I understand," he said softly.

The lump in Sarah's throat exploded. Suddenly, she was back in bed. She was curled up into a ball, her closed fists against her throat and her forearms covering her chest. She sobbed deeply, feeling a grief that seemed to have no end.

A searing electrical current shot up her back, setting free an avalanche of images. She saw herself sitting in the faculty cafeteria eating an apple, and then sitting in her high chair, eating Gerber's applesauce. She saw herself sitting in the university library, reading a research paper on magnetic monopoles. Then she saw herself at home sitting on the couch intensely reading *The Cat In The Hat*.

She saw herself leaving graduate school. She saw herself at age six, crying in bed because Mamma had become an angel and would not return.

She saw her father. On the one hand, he was a dear sweet man and on the other hand, she had often wished that he would just die. Sometimes his eyes would twinkle and he seemed so lovable; other times, she couldn't stand to be around him. He was either weak and spineless, or he had no control of his temper. Either way, he was just unreliable.

Too many conflicting feelings. Little Sarah had to escape. Fantasies were fun. Eventually, she discovered science books, which were logical and consistent. It all worked out so well because by being smart and studying a lot, she was able to get lots of money and go to high school far away from home.

She remembered her anxious grade school days when she methodically avoided inviting her friends to her house because she didn't want them to see how shabby it was. She was afraid they might see Daddy staggering around or smell the alcohol on his breath because there was just no way to predict when he was going to drink. She remembered how she avoided talking about her home life, and when she couldn't avoid it, she lied about it.

She remembered how infuriated she felt in her freshman physics course, when her lab partner, a boy she liked, insisted on setting up the bar magnets himself because, as he laughingly said, "Girls don't understand physics." So, she politely informed him of how disappointed she was that he was such an ass and told him what he could do with his bar magnets. She made it a point to be exceptionally brilliant in every physics course she took throughout her college years. Every lab assignment had to be perfect. She zipped through her undergraduate studies in three years and then was accepted at Cambridge University, where she began an accelerated MA/Ph.D. program. And, that's where it all fell apart.

She remembered the terror and the rage of being sexually assaulted. She remembered her disillusionment on discovering that her sage-like meditation instructor was really a horny old goat.

She remembered how slowly the alcohol crept up on her. She remembered how she was sure that nothing was wrong, right up to the day she woke up in the detox unit of the hospital, with a nasty bump on her head and a blood alcohol level of 0.75. She remembered the doctor's words. "It's simply a miracle that you're alive!"

And, there was always that feeling; the feeling there was something in her brain she couldn't quite retrieve. No matter how much she prayed and meditated, no matter how much she analyzed her dreams, she just couldn't figure out what it was.

–9–

"Can we put this on pause?" asked Smiley.

"Certainly," said Brother G, as the image of Sarah in bed became motionless.

"This isn't going to disturb her, is it?"

"No. You are putting Sarah on pause in *your* frame of reference, not hers. There are some connections of course, since we are at the edge of time and not full blown timelessness, but as long as we don't tinker too much on this end, she won't know the difference."

"Cool," Smiley nodded. He looked down into his bucket of popcorn. It was still full, though he had been eating it for quite some time. "Anyway, I still can't quite figure out where I know her from. She doesn't live that far from Forrest Park, so maybe I've seen her at the lumberyard. Or, since this movie happens eleven year before Jason gets conked on the head, she could be a teacher in Jason's old school."

"Perhaps this will help," said Brother G, turning his head toward the screen, which now showed a woman lying in the narrow bed with a moist cloth on her forehead.

On one side of the bed were two boys, both around nine years old— twins, apparently. Removing her arms from under the blanket, she reached out with both hands. The two brothers, dressed in gray peasant's clothes, took a step forward, each taking a hand.

She smiled, her eyes welling up. "I shan't be with you much longer, she said, straining to keep a clear and cheerful voice. I'll be joining your father. The plague will pass soon, but not soon enough for your mum. I am very grateful that you two are among those who are immune."

The brothers tried to hold back their tears. Their lips trembled. When one of them lost control, the other quickly followed.

The woman squeezed their hands. "Be comforted," she said, after they quieted down. "You may find this difficult to believe it now, but I know something good will come of this for both of you. I just know it."

She turned her head out the window. "Look. See that tower in the distance?"

The two brothers turned their heads.

"That is Cambridge University. A great professor teaches there. I used to be his housekeeper, before you two were born. He was very stern, but also very kind. Even with his great learning and reputation, he always treated me with kindness and respect."

She inhaled deeply, wheezing a bit. "Last winter," she continued, "I ran into him in the market place, and, I guess he could tell I was in need of money. He pulled out his money purse and handed me ten pounds! That is a lot of money. I tried to refuse, but he said, 'Madam, if your children go hungry because you have no money, that's one thing; but if they go hungry because of your vanity, that simply is not acceptable.'"

She laughed weakly and then coughed, placing the palm of her hand on her chest.

"He's not just a great man of science," she said, catching her breath. "He is also a true gentleman, and a devout man of God."

"I have often prayed that you two would be given the same opportunity to go to school and grow up to be men who are worthy of respect. Such doors are generally closed to the likes us, but I know that with God, the impossible becomes possible. The professor said that education should be for all, not just the privileged few.

"I know this is asking much of you, but I want you to have faith that, somehow, when these difficult times have passed, it will all work out for the best." She looked to one and then the other. "Flynn, Donwald."

She squeezed their hands gently. "Know that I love you, and that I will be watching over you in the years to come."

The scene faded and was replaced by Sarah lying on the bed— on pause.

"So, Sarah was my mother," Smiley nodded. "Okay," he said, grabbing a hand-full of popcorn. "Roll 'em."

The movie did not resume, but remained on pause.

"Roll 'em," I said.

Still, no response from the screen.

"What's wrong?" asked Smiley.

"Apparently," said Brother G, "Sarah has become aware of our presence. This is an unexpected twist."

"Is this going to mess things up?"

"On the contrary, it presents her with the possibility of altering her temporal flow in a way that both she and Jason will find pleasing."

"Sounds good to me." He looked at the motionless figure of Sarah on the bed. "So what's going to happen now?"

"That is an unknown, in our current frame of reference. Right now, things are happening that we are not privy to. She is actually tapping into a higher octave and is therefore invisible to us. We shall see what comes of this, after Sarah's brain is done rebooting itself."

"That is way cool," said Smiley, throwing some popcorn in his mouth.

−10−

When Sarah opened her eyes, she was standing in a large room that looked like the lobby of a movie theater. In fact, it looked like the Vintage Theater. She wasn't at all startled by the abrupt change in scenery. In fact, she was unusually calm and detached.

The floor was covered with an industrial-grade maroon carpet, and the ceiling had florescent lights that were fashioned to look like chandeliers. To her left, was the concession stand. To her right, were four doors, leading to the four auditoriums.

On the walls, were posters for coming attractions. One poster showed a giant colorful picture of a brain. Another showed a man sitting by a lake, fishing, while four stars configured into a tetrahedron hovered over their own reflection in the water. Yet another poster showed a man and woman sitting on a park bench, with their eyes closed, praying, apparently.

Sarah took it all in dispassionately. And then, without thinking, she walked to one of the doors, pushed it open and stood in the doorway. She was in the back of an auditorium with a large screen at the front. The room was empty except for two men who sat in the front, talking quietly, as one of them munched on popcorn. They were looking at a screen that showed a still-picture of Sarah, sleeping on her bed.

Without thought or emotion, Sarah looked at herself on the screen for a moment and then retreated from the doorway. Walking to the next door, she pushed it open and looked inside. Another empty auditorium. The screen showed four stars configured into a tetrahedron, hovering over its own inverted reflection in the still waters of a lake. The water disappeared, but the two tetrahedra remained. They each rotated ninety degrees in opposite directions and moved toward each other, becoming intertwined and forming an intricate version of the Star of David.

Sarah recorded the image for future reference and proceeded to the next auditorium. This time, she pushed open the door and walked directly to the closest seat. As soon as she sat, the screen immediately lit up and showed a drunken Dominican priest forcing himself on a young lady in a room lined with granite blocks.

Sarah recognized the scene, but this time, she watched it with calm detachment. Another difference was that she was aware of other details, as if she had already seen the rest of the movie. The girl was a rabbi's daughter, and the scene took place in the basement of a church, just outside Jerusalem, during the crusades. The entire region was in chaos. In spite of Saladin's chivalry and civility, King Richard had refused to make peace. Bloody fighting had resumed, the Christian forces were frazzled, and Saladin was about to recapture Palestine. Looting and raping had become the rule of the day; therefore, the Dominican priest was sure his crime would go unnoticed.

Suddenly, the priest and the terrified girl looked up. The basement door was slowly opening. A bearded little monk stood at the doorway. Sarah noted that the drama was unfolding differently from the previous times she had seen it. She did not recall a monk being present in the previous versions.

The monk paused for a moment and then started walking calmly to the side of the room where the priest was restraining the girl on the granite floor. The priest released the girl and hastily staggered to his feet. Towering over the monk, the priest tried to intimidate him with a stern look. The monk just looked at him calmly and steadily.

"Brother Jason," said the priest, trying to muster some semblance of dignity.

The monk then took a few more steps to the girl and got down on one knee. Using his limited knowledge of Hebrew, he tried to reassure her, as he helped her stand. Taking off his cloak, he placed it around her shoulders to cover the areas that had been exposed by her torn clothes. As the girl whimpered, he placed his arm around her shoulder and escorted her out the door.

Sarah stood up and walked to the next auditorium. Pushing open the door, she looked at yet another empty room full of seats. But something was very different here. The screen showed an identical auditorium, including the back of her own head in the foreground of the screen, as if she was standing just behind and above herself, looking at an infinite number of smaller versions of the same image on the screen. Each successive screen was symmetrically nested in the center of the next larger screen, so as to form a long corridor that seemed to extend into infinity. However, there was only one image of herself, standing in the foreground, because each successive smaller image of herself was perfectly centered in the larger.

As she walked down the center aisle toward the front of the room, a tiny corner of her mind was wondering why she wasn't having a massive emotional reaction and bursting with curiosity about all this. Instead, she continued walking quietly and observed the approaching screen, as it rapidly filled with the growing image of her own back. When she reached the screen, she did not slow down, but simply walked effortlessly into it, after which everything disappeared.

–11–

Sarah was lying down on her side, breathing quietly with her eyes closed. She felt as if she was waking up from a dream, which she barely remembered, except that it had to do with a drunken Dominican priest. So, what else is new?

She opened her eyes, expecting to find herself in bed. Instead, she was looking at the rough surface of a small rectangular granite block, right under her nose. Startled, she stood up quickly. She was in a wide corridor that seemed to extend into infinity.

"Good grief," she exclaimed, throwing her arms in the air. "Now what?" Her voice echoed all around. "I hate it when I wake up from one dream into another dream."

She looked at the ceiling and walls. It was about thirty-feet high wide, fifty feet wide and perfectly rectangular, sort of like a movie screen, she fancied. Movie screen! Hmmm. She tried to remember her previous dream, but it was too fuzzy and jumbled.

The walls, floor, and ceiling were composed entirely of granite blocks. She thought of the previous dream again. In front of her, the passage was dimly lit by a series of kerosene torches that extended as far as she could see. The air was damp and smelled of mildew.

She turned around. The passage behind her was jet black, as if it did not even exist. "Well," she said, facing the illuminated side, "I guess I'm supposed to go thataway."

Her footsteps echoed softly as she walked slowly through the corridor. The only other sound was the "bloop, bloop, bloop" of water droplets falling into a puddle, close to the wall.

The torches became extinguished as she walked past them, so that the corridor immediately behind her was completely dark. "Cute," she nodded.

The air seemed to be vibrating. With each step she took, the vibration seemed to increase slightly. She also noticed wooden doors on both walls, spaced about twenty feet apart. The doors seemed to extend forever, just like the corridor. Was she supposed to open one of those doors?

Each door had a white sign with red lettering. She took a few steps toward one of the doors, so she could read the sign. "Been there, done that." She assumed that she did not need to enter any of those doors, which was good enough for her.

She stopped when she saw a big red sign on the wall: *No access control beyond this point. Proceed with caution.*

"What does that mean?"

Spider webs descended from the ceiling and merged with the adjoining wall. The thought crossed her mind that some of those webs might have real spiders. Suddenly a large black spider descended on a single thread not too far in front of her. She hesitated, made a detour around it, and walked on.

"What? No bats?" she mumbled.

Two small bats fluttered past her left ear. She gasped and watched them disappear into the darkness behind her.

As she walked on, the vibration was getting stronger.

"I could be mistaken," she mumbled, "but I think I'm expected to do something akin to facing the proverbial dragon."

A large reptilian beast appeared before her. It stood upright and let out a roar.

"Gevaldt," she gasped, so startled that she barely noticed that she had reflexively exclaimed in Yiddish, which she was not inclined to do.

The beast approached.

"GO AWAY!" she yelled.

The beast disappeared.

She stood motionless, regaining her composure. "Well, now," she said, still smelling the musty odor of the dragon's breath. She tapped her chin with her index finger, telling herself to be very careful with her thoughts.

An idea formed in her mind. Her heart started racing. It seemed like a preposterous notion. But, she simply had to give it a try. She straightened her spine and cleared her throat, feeling a bit embarrassed. She was thankful that she had total privacy. "I now hereby call forth Sir Isaac Newton," she said with authority, "to appear before me...uh...right now."

She recalled how she used to idolize the man, dreaming about him at night and praising his achievements during the day. On many a star-filled night, in the presence of frustrated adolescent male suitors, she would stare out into space: "What was Sir Isaac Newton really like," she would say, "this giant among giants, who forever changed the way we look at the universe? It's so amazing to think that all the other great scientists who shaped our view of the universe were standing on the shoulders of this one man. Great thinkers like Maxwell, Bohr, Heisenberg, just to name a few. It's incredible," she said, as she jabbed her elbow into the ribs of her confused boyfriend, "Sir Isaac Newton invented calculus. He actually *invented* calculus, the mathematical language by which Mother Nature reveals to us every one of her intricate movements, from galaxies spinning their way through the cosmos, to an apple falling from a tree."

That was years ago. Nonetheless, when she heard the footsteps behind her and turned to see the tall man in eighteenth century garb emerging from the darkness, her eyes became wide and her jaw dropped, like a boy in the 1920s, who had just come face to face with Babe Ruth.

The man stood just a few feet from Sarah, hands in his pockets. Though still partially shrouded in darkness, he looked just like the picture in her room: the oblong face, the dimpled chin, and the aristocratic nose with just the slightest hint of a hyperbolic curve. Every detail was accurate, right down to the lines on his face and his rich and curly hair that fell about his shoulders.

As the images from her youth flashed through her mind, she recalled how she had directed an enormous amount of mental energy fantasizing about meeting the great professor. She wanted to ask him questions about his views of the universe and maybe even a few personal questions, like what sort of women he liked, and why he was so much into religion.

He was just as handsome as she had imagined him to be. He was a tower of steel, perfectly poised and in control. Only such a man could have established order in a chaotic universe.

Even though she was a bit nervous, she felt very safe in his presence. She just knew that he was, above all else, honorable and trustworthy, a man of principle. Yet, as she looked into his intense eyes, she thought she detected a deep vulnerability. She wondered, was his keen intellect a shield to protect that vulnerability? Or was the vulnerability a product of a keen intellect that saw more than he could comfortably handle? She didn't dare ask him. His entire being seemed to consist of deep passion, contained magnificently within an equally deep well of dignity. Everything about him was just...deep.

She finally opened her mouth to speak. "Is that really your hair?" she asked in a hushed voice. As soon as she said that, she cringed. How inappropriate! How anticlimactic!

"Certainly not," the professor responded. "It's a wig."

"Oh," Sarah nodded. "It's very nice."

"Thank you."

She started to regain her composure. "Uh, Professor, are you...real?"

"I was, until you made an hallucination out of me."

"Oh. Sorry."

The vibration she had detected earlier seemed especially strong around the professor. "Uh, Professor, what's all that..." her voice trailed off as she waved her hand around the professor's head.

"It isn't anything that can be explained in English," he said, waving his hand casually in the air. "For your purpose, you may think of it as a field of tachyons, or some such fictitious thing."

"Oh."

They stood in silence looking at each other.

"So, tachyons aren't really real?" Sarah asked.

"They're as real as the other fantasies that mar the advancement of science."

More silence.

"That reminds me," said Sarah. "What do you think of how physics has evolved since your days?"

"I can answer that with just one word: Timid."

"Timid?"

"The fundamental principles of mechanics that I developed were intended to give you young scientists the foundation to uncover the real secrets of how the universe works. Instead, you cling to my elementary equations as a child clings to his security blanket."

Sarah lowered her head a bit, suddenly feeling guilty. "So, relativity and quantum mechanics—"

"Both are hopelessly flawed. The mere fact that the two are mutually exclusive is testimony to their respective failure of imagination."

They looked at eat other silently.

"Have you any other pressing inquiries?"

Sarah shook her head, no.

"Good. Now then, even though time is ultimately irrelevant, I suggest you stop wasting it."

"I beg your pardon?"

The professor rolled his eyes. "How much longer do you intend to continue with these inane proceedings?"

"Uh, I... I don't know. This is all very strange to me. You show up, and just a moment ago, there was a dragon—"

The dragon appeared again— bigger and more ferocious than before. Standing on its hind legs, its head reached almost to the ceiling. It roared louder than before, baring its teeth, and breathing fire as it moved toward Sarah.

"OH, NO!"

The dragon continued on and seemed to swell even bigger after Sarah's fearful cry.

"Stop that, stop that!" said the professor, stepping in front of Sarah and shaking his finger at the beast. "Stop that brutish behavior at once."

The dragon stopped walking and became silent.

"Taking advantage of her ignorance," continued the professor, placing his hands on his hips. "Have you no sense of decency?"

The huge beast stood with its head down, eyes downcast and mouth closed, its forelimbs hanging down in front of its belly, as tiny wisps of smoke drifted out of its nostrils.

The professor folded his arms. "How do you expect to evolve yourself when you conduct yourself in such an abominable manner? Go on now, move along, move along! And take off that ridiculous costume. You shan't steal her psychosexual energy, and that's final."

After another moment of hesitation, the dragon disappeared.

The professor shook his head. "Bloody twit! Doesn't have the slightest understanding of thermodynamics and countercurrent exchange systems."

The professor turned back to Sarah. "Well, cease all this playing around and move along. You're keeping many people waiting."

"Yes, sir."

"All right then. Good day." He bowed politely and started walking off into the shadows.

"But...professor?"

"Yes?"

"What's this all about?"

"Good heavens, child!" he said. "It's patently obvious!"

He walked on, his footsteps echoing in the darkness. "God gave you a brain, use it!"

"But—"

"Unless you want to spend the rest of your life conjuring up demons to justify your failings and prophets to tell you what you already know." His voice trailed off in the distance. "Vanity, that's what it is. You have yet to free yourself of vanity."

She waited until the sound of his footsteps faded away. Placing her hands behind her back, she walked on. "He's right," she said. "It's all very obvious. I'm having a rather vivid dream in which the hypothetical barrier between the world of objective reality and the world of ideas has been lifted." She nodded pensively.

The vibration in the air continued to intensify. She could just about hear it as a deep and resonant hum.

When she realized the dragon might appear again, she started whistling and tried to occupy her mind with anything except dragons. Nonetheless, the translucent image of the beast started appearing in front of her. She furiously tried to remove it from her mind—which seemed to make the beast materialize more quickly. However, when the beast tried to take a step forward, it stopped in its tracks with a look of astonishment on its face, as if a giant hand had suddenly grabbed its tail.

"Persistent little bugger, aren't you," said the voice of Professor Newton.

The dragon abruptly disappeared. Seconds later, another sign appeared on the wall: *Access control partially restored—verbal command only.*

Sarah sighed and walked on. Now that she was no longer in danger of her own stray thoughts, she found it easy to not think about dragons.

"Well, whatever this is about, when I reach my destination, I'll probably see a big heavy wooden door."

A big heavy-looking wooden door appeared next to one of the other, smaller doors. She stopped walking.

It was about eight feet high, five feet wide and was set within a heavy metal frame. Large iron hinges with hexagonal rivets held the door in place. The door handle was part of a huge bolt that penetrated the door frame and was secured by the biggest padlock she had ever seen. A thick layer of cobwebs surrounded the door.

"Me and my big mouth."

Taking a few more steps, she saw a square piece of parchment with writing on it. She hoped it would say, "Been there, done that." Instead, it said, "HEREIN SLEEPS YOUR REAL DRAGON," in big red gothic lettering.

A feeling of terror was building inside her. However, she quickly realized that if she made the door appear just by speaking the words, she could make it disappear in the same manner.

"I command the door to disappear!" she proclaimed with confidence.

The door vanished, revealing, to her horror, the darkened interior.

"NO, NO! THAT'S NOT WHAT I MEANT!"

Closing her eyes tightly, she squeezed her head between her hands. "Uh, I command the doorway…to be sealed with granite blocks, like the rest of the wall."

Granite blocks immediately filled in the doorway.

The terror subsided. But, in its place was curiosity. She reminded herself it was all a dream.

"I command the door to reappear— safely locked."

The door reappeared.

"And one more thing." said Professor Newton's echoey voice emanating from the shadows. Sarah gasped and snapped to attention.

"You have yet to ask a simple question," said the Professor. "Why have you, for so many years, been consistently drawn to and repulsed by religions that have a strong patriarchal influence?"

Out of respect for the great professor, Sarah contemplated his words. But in that moment, the question seemed irrelevant. She decided to put it aside and consider it later.

"Actually," continued Professor Newton's voice, as Sarah snapped to attention again, "my question is relevant to the hallucination you are about to conjure up. As the sign on the door suggests, that demented behemoth back there was but a symbol of your real demon."

–12–

Sarah took a deep breath and closed her eyes. "Okay," she said timidly. "Open sesame!"

Nothing happened.

She opened her eyes and put her hands on her hips. "In other words," she said with deliberate irritation in her voice, "open the damn door!"

The padlock snapped open and the huge bolt slid out of the way as flakes of rust fell to the floor.

Sarah straightened her back and took a step backward as the door creaked open, stretching and breaking the cobwebs adhering to it.

She didn't remember making the decision to walk in. Nor was she aware of her feet stepping one in front of the other as she crossed the doorway. There was an instant when she did not feel the floor under her feet and had no sense of up, down, left, right, front, or back. If the feeling had persisted, she would have panicked, but it came and went in a fraction of a second. When she felt the floor under her feet again, the heavy door closed behind her with an echoing boom.

She stood in the darkness, her heart pounding.

"Okay, let there be light, already!"

A dim light gradually came on. At first, she expected to see a creepy dusty cave housing a fearsome fire-breathing monster, or a bunch of poisonous snakes, at least. Instead, she saw a child's bedroom with a soft pink carpet and pink curtains. She recognized the little dresser, the canopied bed, and the large picture of a Teddy Bear on the wall. Next to the bed, she saw the little table, with its lamp and the Mickey Mouse play phone which she knew would play, "Twinkle, twinkle, little star," when she lifted the receiver.

On the bed was a little girl, about age six. She was lying on her side with her hands together and tucked just under her chin, her forearms against her chest and her knees close to her tummy. Sarah recognized the bright red T-shirt and little green shorts. The little girl didn't seem to be aware of Sarah approaching her. Her little nose was red, her eyes were bloodshot, and her long hair looked uncombed. Her lips seemed to be saying, "Mamma, please come back."

Sarah stooped over the bed. As she touched the little shoulder, she became the child.

Through the child's eyes, she saw the silhouette of a huge male figure approaching her. At first, she expected him to comfort her.

But this time, he just stared at her, as if he didn't recognize her. His eyes did not twinkle. His eyes didn't even look like his eyes. They looked almost reptilian.

"Daddy?" she whimpered.

He didn't answer.

Seconds elapsed. And then he crouched down and touched her. From that point on, the scene became a blur. She felt his rough, clammy hand, pushing her clothes aside. She felt the weight of his body against hers and smelled the alcohol on his breath. His touch was not painfully rough, but the little girl sensed that something was wrong. In the past, it felt good to be touched by him. But this time it was scary, though she did not know why. Even without the pressure of his body against hers, she was too stunned to move, too scared and confused to say anything. She felt suffocated. A sick, contracting feeling enveloped her stomach.

Her father was no longer her father. He looked more like a snake. Little Sarah screamed.

Sarah became an adult again and looked upon the scene, suddenly remembering the event. All the energy which had been hidden as vague, silent shame, exploded into murderous rage; the rage of being helpless, of not being able to enjoy her own sexuality, and of being horribly betrayed by one she trusted.

Instantly, she became the little girl again, just in time to hear her own adult voice fill the room: "GET AWAY FROM THAT CHILD, YOU PIG!"

The voice was like thunder. It got little Sarah's attention. It was almost like her mother's voice. Just before she heard the voice, she had made a decision to escape into one of her fun dreams, never to return. She wanted to become an angel, like her mother. Little Sarah felt safe in the presence of the voice. She decided to stay, even though she was still scared.

A door appeared on the wall facing the side of the bed. It opened easily and silently. The other side was absolutely black. As little Sarah looked at it, the darkness burst into brilliant white light with wisps of gold. It shone on the face of little Sarah, who looked upon it and immediately became big Sarah again.

Her father was gone. The room was gone. Only the snake remained. It looked up at her and seemed to be saying, "Well?"

Sarah returned a look that said, "Well, what?"

"Do you remember your recurring dream about the drunken Dominican priest raping a young lady?"

"What about it?"

"Were you the girl or the priest?"

Suddenly, Sarah felt extremely disoriented. She had absolutely no idea how to respond. "Huh?" she finally said.

The snake rolled its eyes. "Never mind," it said, "you still have some loose wires in your brain."

−13−

Sarah was back in bed in that half awake and half asleep state. Without thinking, as if by instinct, she began doing some of the brain exercises in the book she had borrowed from Betty. She placed her attention at the center of her brain and imagined she was breathing into that point. However, before she could proceed to the next part of the exercise, she drifted off to sleep.

She now found herself standing inside a vast dome-like chamber. The walls consisted of an amazing labyrinth of ultra-fine wires and circuits. She gazed around at the intricate circuitry, which she imagined to be sort of like the inside of a computer that housed a colossal amount of memory. Looking around the dome, the whole setup seemed scattered and inefficient. There were tangled wires all over the place. Ragged holograms floated everywhere, and there were vast pockets of inaccessible memories.

What a mess! She was embarrassed until she realized that the set-up was fairly typical. "God," she said, "No wonder people can't get along."

Contemplating what might be done about it, she remembered that a hologram is made with lasers, reminding her of Mother Eva's brain exercise, which she had started to do, before drifting off to sleep.

She decided to do the rest of the exercise. She felt a little silly about it, but figured that as long as she was dreaming, she may as well have some fun with it. In fact, doing the exercise from this unique vantage point might produce some novel results.

Looking up, she imagined a laser beam extending from the top of the chamber to the bottom. Then she imagined a second laser beam that connected the left and right sides of the chamber and intersecting the first beam. This resulted in the formation of many clear three-dimensional holographic images emerging from the point of intersection of the two laser beams.

She then conjured up a third laser beam connecting the front and back of the chamber, intersecting the other two, so that all three beams came together at the center of the chamber.

"Easy as XYZ," she said.

Immediately, the images changed from three-dimensional to four-dimensional, extending into the past and future with exceptional clarity. One of them was a four dimensional image of the snake. It stared at her with its reptilian eyes.

"Now do you understand?" said the snake.

"Sure," said Sarah, pointing to the tangled circuits all around her. All this mess is the result of pure animal instinct that was not allowed to evolve."

"How do you allow it to evolve?"

"Simple," said Sarah, "Just don't mess with it."

The snake laughed. "Now that it's been messed with, what are you going to do about it?"

Sarah shrugged. "Beats me."

"Same here. Let's ask the boss," said the snake, as it disappeared.

Sarah paced around, looking at the décor. She was wondering how to fix it without messing it up more, when she heard a knock on the wall of the chamber.

"Come in," she said casually.

A hand reached inside the chamber through a portal, which she fancied to be the ear canal, and offered her a small white compact disc. It sort of reminded her of the large communion wafer that the priest ceremoniously consumes during the Catholic mass. The hand holding the disc seemed feminine and rather elderly.

"Mother Eva?" asked Sarah. "If that's you, I just want to say that these brain exercises of yours," she said, pointing to the three laser beams, "are turning out to be a bit much."

The hand moved closer, and Sarah saw that the compact disc had writing on it: *The Torah— In extremely ancient Hebrew.*

"Sure, go ahead," said Sarah. "I didn't realize I had my own built-in CD-ROM."

The hand tossed the disc like a Frisbee. It stopped in mid-air at the point of intersection of the three laser beams. A luminous and very intricate four-dimensional hologram formed around the disc. Suddenly, the hologram divided itself into the twenty-two characters of the Hebrew alphabet, which then reconfigured themselves into a single multidimensional figure that defied all description, although it did have a sort of spiral flavor to it. In a matter of seconds, she understood all five books. She immediately understood the meaning of Chosen People—from a four-dimensional holographic standpoint.

"Oh, I see!" she said. "Chosen to remember! Chosen to be the first to remember that no one is first. Simple enough."

She scanned the old books again and did some crosschecking with other documents. "Of course," she said. "And, when we reach that Promised Land, we will remember that the first and the last—the alpha and omega—are one and the same. And that is God's kingdom. The land overflowing with milk and honey, where all things are provided."

She understood why the Jewish version of God had to be relatively impersonal, and why the Christian version had to be very personal. And she understood why both needed to be symmetrically present in the collective consciousness of humanity in order for each to fulfill his purpose.

Sarah nodded. "So how did things get so twisted?" she said looking at the tangled wires all around. "Oh, yes. Animal instinct that was not allowed to evolve."

The snake reappeared in the midst of the hologram, directly over the compact disc. It smiled, incinerated itself, and then emerged as a respectable-looking long-necked bird. "Good job," it said. "Now I can go home."

As the bird spread its wings, Sarah called out. "Wait!"

"Yes?" said the bird, its wings extended.

"You sound just like Josh. You're Josh!"

"In the flesh... as it were."

Sarah laughed, throwing her arms in the air. "Vey ist meir."

"Your Yiddish is excellent, by the way," said the bird.

"Thank you. Now, for umpteenth time, I must ask, who are you really?"

"You mean underneath it all?"

"Yes."

"Beyond the beyond the beyond?"

"Yes."

"I am all things," said the bird, as it flew away and disappeared through the wall of the chamber. Then, it briefly stuck its head back in and looked at Sarah. "And so are you."

–14–

Sarah walked around the chamber. The holograms hovering around seemed a little clearer but the hard wiring was still rather tangled. Finally, she grabbed the sides of her head in frustration and threw her arms out to the sides. "I still don't get it," she called out to no one in particular.

"Seems like you do," said the long necked bird, now hovering just inside the chamber wall.

Sarah was startled. She opened her mouth and closed it again. "Not really. I have to be very honest here. Yes, understanding the Torah in the old language was very helpful. But..."

"You don't feel it in your bones yet."

"Correct."

"Relax, Sarah. Lighten up a little."

The long-necked bird now changed into a smiling white rubber duck. With its big cheerful blue eyes, it looked up at the tangled wires on the ceiling. "The more you relax, the more easily your brain can rewire itself." The smiling duck gave her a wink and flew out of the chamber.

−15−

Sarah found herself resting in bed, feeling the rising and falling of her chest. She wondered if the bizarre dreams were finally over. Apparently not. The creature's parting words seemed to reverberate through her body. As she relaxed, she felt a stirring deep inside her belly. It was a wave of some kind. It was like music, except that it was silent. It was like a thought, except it could not be put into words. It was like an emotion, simple and genuine, but otherwise indescribable. It was like a sensation, except she couldn't tell what the sensation was. It was just a wave—or maybe a series of waves, emanating from deep inside her uterus.

Whatever it was, it was deep and visceral. It seemed to have a mind of its own, distinct from her personality, yet inseparable from it. If it was a sound, she could only describe it as a musical tone. If it was a thought, she could only describe it as a prayer. If it was an emotion, she could only describe it as a feeling that seemed to say, "Everything is okay." If it was a sensation, it was like a quiet and unhurried orgasm caressing her body. Yet, she felt like she was experiencing only a tiny portion of this wave or series of waves, as if there was a tremendous symphony going on and she was hearing just the flute.

She decided to just relax, figuring she could do a better job of experiencing it. Sure enough, as she stopped trying to analyze the wave, it increased in strength—by a factor of ten, she estimated. A moment later, it increased again by a factor of ten.

The wave continued increasing exponentially, occupying more and more of her awareness, until she fancied that she became the wave, expanding in all directions, existing simultaneously everywhere, past, present, and future.

At first, she was astonished by the abrupt change in her identity, but then it just seemed normal. Obviously, she was an infinite-ever-expanding wave of everything. And, simultaneously, she was a single tiny particle among countless other particles. No big deal. Not only was she okay with the notion, but she was aware of the communion between the grandness of her wave nature and the smallness of her particle nature; sort of like the infinite and the finite making love.

The whole thing was elementary and easy to comprehend as long as she was an infinite ever-expanding wave of everything. Yes, she was a single flesh-and-blood particle who was capable of taking some things seriously (which was entirely appropriate) and, at the same time, an infinite ever-expanding wave of everything, to whom every created thing was a precious and utterly perfect artistic event. However, she knew that such awareness, if maintained long enough, could have some potentially adverse side effects. For example, her body might vaporize.

Sure enough, she noticed that her physical body— which was already not very noticeable— was becoming even less noticeable. It was emitting a low rumbling sound, somewhat reminiscent of a herd of horses stampeding in the distance. She had the impression that all the atoms in her body were about to let go of each other and leisurely drift away. "Interesting possibility," she mused. However, she decided that she didn't want her body to vaporize just yet, so she respectfully told her atoms to stay together. While she was at it, since the atoms were looser than usual, she took the opportunity to rearrange them a bit.

The infinite ever-expanding wave toned itself down. She became plain old flesh and blood Sarah again, though she was still aware of a soft vibration emanating from her tummy. She imagined that it was causing her brain to gradually rewire itself.

–16–

"Hey, it looks like the movie is playing again," said Smiley, pointing to the screen.

They watched Sarah curled up on her bed. She was breathing rhythmically but very deeply, almost like she was hyperventilating. Her face was flushed bright pink and seemed to glow.

"Whoa," said Smiley, "Where has she been?"

"A place where only she can go, I suspect."

They watched Sarah for quite some time, as she continued breathing deeply. Finally, she stopped abruptly. Smiley waited for her to resume breathing normally, but she remained perfectly still.

"Is the movie on pause again?" asked Smiley.

"I don't think so," said Brother G.

"Well, she looks like she's not breathing."

"Apparently."

"Is she okay?"

"We will see."

She remained in an apparently breathless state for several minutes. Smiley glanced occasionally at Brother G's unconcerned facial expression to assure himself that everything was okay. Still, he was relieved when Sarah's chest started moving. And then, without warning, Sarah was drifting through a dark tunnel, whose walls played soothing music.

"What's happening now?" asked Smiley.

"I don't know, but this is turning out to be an intriguing adventure."

When Sarah emerged on the other side, she was standing next to a small lake surrounded by burned trees. Another dream. She took in the scene, more or less emotionally detached, though the landscape had a hauntingly familiar look to it.

Walking toward the lake, she noticed a man sitting by its shore. He had very dark skin, long graying black hair and wore ancient clothing. Standing next to him was a younger Oriental-looking man with slightly lighter-tone skin and long black hair tied back in a pony-tail.

The young man was speaking softly in a foreign language that Sarah guessed was Hindi. She heard him say, "Macunda," a few times, which she gathered was the other man's name.

The younger man kneeled on one knee and put his hand on the older man's shoulder. Then, he stood up and walked quickly toward a horse that was grazing by the lake. Mounting the horse, he cantered away, saying a few parting words and making a gesture with his hands. Somehow, Sarah knew he was reassuring the other man that he would return shortly.

Sarah walked closer toward the other man, who was now staring blankly at the lake. For some reason, she suddenly felt aggravated toward him. The feeling was like a wave of ancient anger, whose origin was too far back to be connected to any memory. But when she looked into his tired blood-shot eyes, her anger turned into compassion.

The man closed his eyes and his facial expression became more grim, as if he was in deep and continuous pain. When he opened his eyes, he looked down and picked a long pointed knife from the ground. Slowly, he rotated it so that the tip faced his heart.

Instinctively, Sarah, kneeled next to the man and placed her hand on the man's chest. The knife's point reached the back of Sarah's hand, and then stopped.

The man lowered the knife and dropped it on the ground. Then, he leaned forward and sobbed, as Sarah continued holding her hand on his heart.

Sarah's rational mind could not explain what was happening, but she was awake enough to know she was dreaming, and so, she found it easy to just follow her instincts, without needing to make sense of the events.

When the man stopped crying, Sarah took her hand away and stood up. She looked around again. The property looked like marauders had attacked it. All the buildings and trees were burned and the surrounding stone wall was destroyed in several places.

For the first time, she noticed a large framed painting leaning against a nearby burned-out tree. She walked right up to it and saw that it was a picture of a brightly colored, long-necked bird, surrounded by flames. It too looked hauntingly familiar. She stared at it long and hard, until suddenly, she found herself in the tunnel that played soothing music. And then, she was back in bed.

–17–

Cool air rushed into Sarah's nostrils. When she first became aware of her limbs, they seemed to be swaying gently from side to side. Eventually, they settled down. The last odd sensation was a mild throbbing pressure between her eyebrows, which quickly subsided.

Half opening her eyes, she saw Sir Thomas Mallory, sitting on the bed, purring with his eyes closed. She closed her eyes again.

Suddenly, she gasped and her eyes popped open. Turning her head quickly, she looked at the clock on the night table. 6:50 a.m.

"Huh?" Glancing out the window, she saw the first light of early dawn. She recalled the alarm having originally awakened her at 6:45, but figured that was just one of the many dreams she had. She probably forgot to set the alarm.

Turning over on her back, she let her head relax on the pillow. She looked at the physical details of the room to see if they matched her observations during the dream: the half-open bathroom door, the sink and medicine cabinet, the bubbling fish tank, the partially opened drawers with clothes hanging out.

She picked up Sir Thomas Mallory and placed him on her stomach, gently scratching behind his ears as she continued looking around the room.

Suddenly, she held up Sir Thomas by the shoulders. "I saw Christy's rubber duck under the bed," she said to the startled cat.

Putting Sir Thomas down, she reached under the bed with one hand while bracing herself on the floor with the other hand. After a few seconds of probing, she pulled out a white rubber duck on wheels.

Staring at the cheerful blue eyes and the big smile on the duck's face, she gave it a squeeze and it quacked. Putting the rubber duck on the bed next to Sir Thomas, she took a deep breath and rested her head back on the pillow.

Closing her eyes, she drifted into a semi-sleep state. She felt the gentle waves again. She imagined they were waves on a vast ocean. She saw her body as a tiny boat bobbing up and down on the waves. She marveled at the majesty and awesome power of the ocean, which somehow saw fit to create from her womb that tiny and fragile boat, while never once thinking itself to be greater than the boat.

Her body jerked slightly as the phone chimed. When it chimed a second time, she reached for it and turned over on her back.

"Hello," she mumbled.

"Good morning, Sarah!"

"Hi, Betty."

"Were you sleeping?"

"Yes."

"Oh, I'm sorry. I figured you'd be up by now."

"Yeah, I know," said Sarah, stretching her arms. "I'm being bad."

"I was thinking about you last night. Actually, 'thinking' isn't the right word. I was worried. Are you okay?"

"Yeah, I'm fine. And how are you?"

"Terrible. My precious little darling woke me up four times during the night. But, I didn't call to bitch about my baby. What's going on with you?"

"Nothing much," Sarah yawned.

"Why is your voice so hoarse?"

"I'm not sure. I think I was yelling in my sleep."

"Really! I didn't realize such a thing was possible. Who were you yelling at?"

"Jesus, mostly."

"Jesus?"

"Actually, I don't know who he was, or if he was anyone, for that matter. I think he told me to call him Brother Josh, which is what Moshe called him, but I just called him Josh."

"Moshe?"

"Moses. He dropped in too.

There was a silence on the other end of the phone.

"Okay, let's back up a little. You have just told me that you've met Jesus and Moses?"

"And, Sir Isaac Newton. Oh, and I think your old friend, Mother Eva, dropped in too—"

"CHRISTY, GET AWAY FROM THERE!" Betty yelled. "Do you believe that kid? She was chewing on my maidenhair fern. God, she is all over the place! Yesterday she managed to poke a hole in the screen door. Those things can be expensive. Fortunately, they were on sale at Mazarosky's Lumber Yard. Anyway, it sounds like you had quite a night."

"Oh... yeah. It was like this very long drawn-out dream that just went on and on." She glanced at the clock. "Very strange. I don't remember most of it. Sir Isaac Newton popped in wearing the cutest wig and just told me to stop wasting time. And Mother Eva, or somebody, gave me a CD. Josh said a lot of goofy things. I asked him if he could fix my radiator, but he knows nothing about cars and I think he was sort of defensive about it."

"So, what does all that mean?"

"I'm not sure. Anyway, we'll talk more when we go to the meeting tonight.

Right now, I really should move my ass. My car has a leaky radiator. I need to find another mechanic."

"Oh, go to Mahmoud! He's one of the mechanics at Forrest Park Auto Service. Their rates are reasonable and they do a good job."

"Oh yeah, I've seen it." Sarah yawned. "I can just drop it off and take the bus to school."

"Make sure you ask for Mahmoud. He doesn't own the place; he just works there."

"I'll do that. Anyway, I'll see you later. And, thanks for waking me up."

"Anytime, dear."

"Bye." Sarah reached over to the night table and hung up the phone.

She stared at the picture of Sir Isaac Newton.

"Well, professor," she said, "what do you think of all this?"

She imagined Professor Newton was saying, "It's all bloody nonsense. Remove your bottom off the bed, and get to work."

Stretching her arms, she yawned and stood up. She looked out the window at the rooftops in the early morning light. In the distance, the lake at the center of Forrest Park reflected the fiery red of the eastern horizon.

Looking down at the desk, she picked up the letter she had written the night before. She thought about possibly using it— with slight revision— in her physics class. She glanced at the clock on the night table. 7:05. Putting on her glasses, she walked out of her room, reading the letter.

PART THREE
The Story of Preacher Roy

–1–

As Sarah walked into her kitchen, Roy Dobbs, a newly ordained minister in the state of Kentucky, rolled over in his bed and farted loudly. Opening his eyes, He looked at the certificate on the night table, pondering how it would look in a frame made of unfinished oak or walnut. Maybe he would go to Conrad Simmons' shop and ask him to build a frame. Yes, that would give him a chance to ease some of the ill feelings between them. Now that he was a minister, he figured he really should try to clean up little things like that.

Rubbing his scruffy face, he glanced at the digital clock on his cluttered night table. 7:05 AM. Turning his head, he looked out the window at his empty cornfield. There was no frost. The ground was almost ready for planting.

Beyond the cornfield, the clouds on the eastern horizon were beginning to blush pink. He heard the muffled crow of the rooster in the hen house.

Running his fingers through his dirty blond hair, he thought about going into the kitchen and making coffee. However, the bed was warm and cozy. His sleep had not been very restful that night—lots of strange dreams. He yawned.

His meeting at the church was still five hours away. He figured he would get up in an hour or so and leisurely walk through the cornfield to see if it was dry enough to turn the soil. Then he would clean the barn and milk Agnes.

There was lots of time. He figured he would stop by Charlotte's house on the way to his meeting and surprise her with a dozen eggs and a quart of ultra-fresh goat milk, which she loved. However, he then remembered that Charlotte was going to spend the day putting the final touches on her wedding dress. She probably wouldn't want him to walk in while she was doing that. Some sort of pre-wedding superstition.

Closing his eyes, he tried to think about what it would be like to be married. There didn't seem to be much to think about. He and Charlotte would just move in together and he would love, honor, and protect her. Simple enough. He didn't understand why everyone made such a fuss about it. Anyway, he'd find out in a few days. He yawned and scratched his buttock.

The real question was whether or not he would ever make enough money as a preacher to quit his part time job at the auto parts store. Probably not. Even if he did become pastor some day, the church just wasn't that big. A more feasible option was to make his farm more profitable. He certainly knew how to do that. He just needed to set his mind to it.

As he drifted into a semi-sleep state, his arms seemed to sway side to side. But that was impossible—one arm was wedged under the pillow and the other was curled against his chest. His legs were doing it too! And, there was a funny little pressure between his eyebrows, again. And there was a whirling sound in his head.

Drifting into a semi-sleep state, fantasies and images flashed through his mind. He saw the elderly Reverend Smith dying. He saw himself conducting the memorial service. The board members had an emergency meeting and voted unanimously to appoint Roy Dobbs as the new pastor— the youngest in the history of the county. They would call him 'the boy wonder from Hickory Ridge.' He saw the congregation doubling in size; a bigger church building needed to be built. He saw himself becoming too busy as pastor to work in the auto parts store, or even to run his farm. He saw himself doing Sunday services and weddings, and judging homemade pickles and pies at county fairs. And, he heard people say, "Preacher Roy is the best minister we've ever had." He saw himself traveling around, preaching in other churches.

Suddenly, he grimaced and shook himself fully awake. "Lord," he said silently, "please purge me of these evil, arrogant thoughts."

Closing his eyes, he fell asleep again and forgot the whole thing.

–2–

Five months later

Preacher Roy stood with his hands in his pockets, looking at the grave of Reverend Smith.

"What's troubling you, Roy?"

Preacher Roy stared at the headstone as the breeze pushed a few dry leaves across the grave. He leaned against an oak tree.

"Nothin'."

Mrs. Bailey glanced at the preacher's face. She looked around the churchyard. The air was thick with the smell of pine straw baking in the sun.

"Are you sure?"

The preacher removed his shoulder from the tree. Putting his hands in his pockets, he walked a few steps away from the headstone.

"I just came out here for a breath of air." He rested his massive forearms on the split-rail fence that separated the churchyard from the meadow. He took a deep breath and caught the fragrance of the wildflowers that blanketed the area. The air was warm, but the wind had a tiny bite to it. He detected the smell of autumn in the air.

"You're not getting cold feet, are you?" asked Mrs. Bailey.

The preacher kept looking straight ahead at the meadow, resisting the temptation to turn his head and glare at Mrs. Bailey in defiance. Removing his elbows from the fence, he straightened his spine. His stocky frame dwarfed the petite figure of Mrs. Bailey. Throwing his chest out just a bit, he readied himself to respectfully say no, but changed his mind when he looked into her eyes. He remembered his own words in church when he once described Mrs. Bailey as having a benevolent gaze that can pierce concrete.

"Yeah, I guess my feet are gettin' a mite chilly." He ran his fingers through his short, neatly combed hair.

"What's the problem?"

"I'm not sure. I've been pastor one week, and so far everything seems to be goin' fine." He rubbed his massive jaw, being careful not to touch the spot where he cut himself shaving. "I was afraid some of the folks would frown on me fillin' Reverend Smith's shoes. But so far, they've been kindly. I do appreciate that you convinced the other board members to give me the job. But..."

"I didn't have to do much convincing. It was a unanimous vote. Reverend Smith already had you picked out as his replacement."

"Yeah, I figured that. But I didn't think it would happen so quick."

"It's what you always wanted to do, isn't it?"

"Well, yes and no." The preacher looked at a tractor in a distant field, puttering away as it harvested corn. "Years back, when Reverend Smith hired me to help him out with chores around the church, I'd daydream about bein' a preacher myself. But I was just a kid." He lowered his head and picked at the tree bark with his fingers. "Charlotte seems okay with it."

"Speaking of Charlotte, how are things at home?"

"Great. I'm as happy as a pig in a mud hole. Charlotte gets a little out of sorts now and then. Misses her friends in Lexington. But I guess that's normal early on."

They turned their heads as a black pickup truck pulled up next to the church.

"Hey big brother!" said the young man, sticking his head out of the window.

"What is it, Amos?"

"I dropped off those bags of buckwheat in the tool shed."

"Thanks, I appreciate it."

"Are you going to need help spreading it?"

"Maybe. I have been a mite short on time lately."

"By the way, Mamma wants to know if you and Charlotte are still comin' over for supper tonight."

"Yeah. Why? Is there a problem?"

"No, we was just worried that maybe you've become too important for us."

The preacher laughed. "Get out of here, you little weasel."

He shook his head, still chuckling as Amos drove off.

"You know," said Mrs. Bailey, "a while back, Reverend Smith said that no one can give a sermon better than you."

The preacher gave her a little sideways glance and tried not to smile.

"There are just a few areas where you could stand a little polishing."

"Oh?"

"For one thing, you might try wearing this job like a loose fitting garment." The preacher was relieved. He was afraid that Mrs. Bailey would say something about his anger. "Loose fitting garment?" he said. What do you mean?"

"Lighten up a bit."

"About what?"

"In particular, go easy on the fire and brimstone. You have the ability to hold their attention. You don't need to scare them or shame them."

"I do that?"

"Just a bit. On occasion. All preachers seem to do that now and then. When they get stressed, they take themselves too seriously. That's when they resort to browbeating and scaring folks."

The preacher nodded. "I'll keep an eye on that."

"You might also think about being a bit more genteel with your use of the English language."

"Yeah, I'm workin' on it." He folded his arms and looked down, slowly rolling the gravel under his feet. "And, there's also the matter of my…temper. I have been known to pop off now and then. Is that just me takin' myself too seriously?"

"Yes. But, it's not all bad. Your temper is passion looking for elbowroom. Every preacher needs passion."

He put his hands in his pockets and kicked a stone. "Truth is, I just don't feel like a real preacher, let alone a pastor. That piece of paper don't mean squat. I don't have a proper clergy education. I haven't been to college. I don't even look like a pastor. Pastors are supposed to be tall skinny fellers with silvery hair. I just turned twenty-eight last month! A pastor, at twenty-eight?"

"So? You'll be the youngest pastor in the history of the county. Nothing wrong with that. Folks are already taking a fancy to it. 'The boy wonder from Hickory Ridge,' that's what they're saying."

The preacher made no attempt to hold back his smile.

"Besides," continued Mrs. Bailey, "you've been speaking at church services since you were fifteen. You're already an old hand at it. And, it's what you love to do."

"I also love fishin'," but I'm not about to run off and get a job on a fishin' boat."

Mrs. Bailey smiled. "Well then, consider this. If you don't do it, you'll be repeating your father's pattern."

The preacher's stomach tightened. "How do you figure that?"

"His problem wasn't his drinking or his temper," said Mrs. Bailey.

The preacher's stomach tightened some more.

"His problem," continued Mrs. Bailey, "was that he hated himself because he couldn't be the man that he wanted to be. The way this town was growing back then, his business should have boomed. Instead, he let it wither away and he went back to coal mining and moonshining, while his niche was filled by Conrad Simmons' daddy. And that's why he ended up in a mental hospital," she said calmly. "It wasn't his liver that killed him. It was his unwillingness to step forward."

The preacher tried to keep his jaw from tightening up. He stared at the cows grazing on the hillside beyond the meadow.

"It's your choice, of course," said Mrs. Bailey.

The preacher paced along the fence and then leaned against the oak tree. "It *is* scary, but I guess I've already made up my mind to do this. I just needed to get this off my chest."

"Nothing wrong with that," smiled Mrs. Bailey.

"Remember, you told me I should pay attention to my dreams because they're symbolic?'

"Yes."

"Well, I had a doozy last night. I dreamed that Jesus was talkin' to me."

He waited for Mrs. Bailey to respond, but she remained silent, so he continued. "Jesus said 'Roy, make up your mind. Are you in or out?'"

He paused again, but still no comment from Mrs. Bailey.

"I guess Jesus really is callin' me to do his work," he said, looking into the distance.

Not even a nod from Mrs. Bailey. Finally she said, "By the way, I finally sold the old farmhouse, did you hear?"

"Yeah," he said, irritated that Mrs. Bailey had changed the subject. "Rumor has it that you practically gave it away. Seems most peculiar."

"What do you mean?"

"Seems peculiar that you sold it so cheap after you let it sit idle for years, turnin' down them big offers from the mining companies."

"Well," she said, "the buyers seem like such a nice young couple."

"Who are they?"

She adjusted her glasses. "Their names are Mahmoud and Elimma Mossavi. He's an auto mechanic. Wants to set up shop in the barn. I met them while I was traveling. I sort of stayed in touch with Elimma."

The preacher nodded and tried not to act surprised. "Foreigners?"

"Yes. They should be moved in by next week if you want to pay them a visit."

The preacher put his hands in his pockets. "Are they Christians?"

"I don't think so."

The preacher nodded as he pushed a pinecone around with his foot.

"Well," said Mrs. Bailey, "what do you say we get back inside? We have lots of work to do."

–3–

Three years later

A whirlwind of apple blossoms fluttered against the blue sky. They descended all around Preacher Roy, as he sat on the wooden dock, arms folded, and a troubled look on his face. He stared at the ripples moving across the water. His fishing pole stood on its end, projecting out of a knothole on the dock.

Yawning, he glanced at his watch. 4:30 already. He wished he didn't have to go back to town. And he wished he hadn't sold his log cabin in the hollows.

Remembering the church service earlier that day, he wondered if he had made a bad impression. The county fair last week wasn't much fun either. He did a proper job of judging the pies, and he was polite enough, but he wasn't very sociable otherwise.

After packing up the fishing gear, he took out Charlotte's letter. He wasn't sure why he felt inclined to bring it to the lake today. He had certainly read it enough times the last two months. Taking a deep breath, he read it again.

Dear Roy,

I'm sorry to break the news to you this way. I've tried to tell you this many times, but you were so preoccupied.

Roy, you were a lot more fun to be around when you weren't running the church. Ever since you became the pastor, you've just been trying too hard to bury your past. You've been so concerned about those few backbiting busybodies, like Conrad Simmons, you didn't realize that the majority of the congregation consists of decent folks who understand that you are human like they are.

But even if you had been a perfect husband, I don't think I would have been happy here. It was making me crazy to have to put on a pleasant face appropriate for the pastor's wife. I think that was the real reason that I used to bitch about you not cleaning up after yourself and replacing the cap on the tube of toothpaste, and picky things like that. The real reason I was unhappy is simple: I was denying myself to help you maintain this cozy little religious community. There's nothing wrong with it, I just don't feel at home here. Now I know it was a mistake for me to give up my own plans to study theater at Bowling Green University.

What's more, I was never really sure you loved me. Sometimes it seemed like you did, and sometimes I felt like I was just part of your grand plan to save the world or conquer it or something. Every time you tried to fix things between us, I wasn't sure if you were thinking about our relationship or if you were just concerned about making our marriage look good. Did you really love me, or was our marriage just part of your empire. I just didn't know. I don't think you were clear on that either.

Your sermons are so inspiring. They're almost mesmerizing. But sometimes I think you're so busy talking, that you don't really listen to what you're saying, or to what anyone else is saying. You better watch that, or it will get you in trouble. No matter how smart you are, if you don't listen to what others have to say, you can get pretty twisted.

You were so slick at talking me out of whatever I was feeling. Every time I tried to leave to think things over, you talked me out of it without really hearing what I was saying. I became very confused, and I'm still confused. What I do know is that I felt like a prisoner here.

Maybe if you weren't a minister, it would be different. Maybe if we were just two normal married people living somewhere else, we wouldn't have all these problems. The more I write this letter, the more I feel like you really do care about me. But everything is just so tangled now. I have to leave.

Anyway, now that I'm gone, you can court Candra Winfield. She does have her eye on you. You tried to convince me she was just being neighborly. But you just didn't see—just like you didn't see that you enjoyed her subtle flirtation.

Under the circumstances, I'm grateful I had the miscarriage. If I had a child right now, I don't know what I'd do. Even so, this was a very difficult decision for me.

I'll have my lawyer draw up the papers and send them to you. Please don't make a fuss. Let's just get this over with. I won't ask for anything that isn't rightfully mine. But if you want to keep everything, go ahead. I just want my life back.

Charlotte

Quite a one-two punch. His mother dies, and, three months later, his wife leaves.

No matter how many times he read the letter, he still felt that same sense of shock and disbelief. He had no idea it had been this serious. He felt like he had been blind-sided and ambushed.

Glancing at his watch, he stood up and walked away from the dock. Maybe he would stop by Mrs. Bailey's house. She seemed to be the only one who wasn't shocked by Charlotte's departure.

As he contemplated chatting with Mrs. Bailey, his body relaxed. He stopped walking. His sense of shock and disbelief gradually faded. His perception of having been blind-sided gave way to another perception. "Maybe my blind side is bigger than I realized," he mumbled.

Putting the fishing gear down, he took the letter out of his pocket again. He unfolded the letter and stared at it. To his surprise, he found himself talking to her out loud. "Charlotte, I'm sorry. I was a dumb jackass, too wrapped up in my own world and my own ambitions to notice your pain."

He folded the letter slowly and gently, stepped off the trail, and meandered along the trees. When he reached a relatively clear area, he went down on his knees. Picking up a flat rock, he cleared away the fallen leaves and dug a hole in the ground. Placing the letter in, he stared at it for a while, as his eyes welled up. Sighing deeply, he replaced the dirt and leaves in the hole, wiped his nose on his sleeve, and walked away.

With Charlotte still lingering in his mind, the preacher mentally went over the backlog of church business. Most of the folks had been understanding and kind, but the church had to be tended to. Since he became pastor, the congregation had doubled in size, but lately he had noticed a decline in attendance. Once again, he pondered the possibility of resigning. The board of directors placed no pressure on him either way. Mrs. Bailey assured him that they could find a replacement if he felt the need to resign or take a leave of absence.

–4–

He had been on the road less than ten seconds when the oil light came on the dashboard. "Shouldn't be low," he muttered.

Pulling over to the side of the road, he got out, still half absorbed with the logistics of resigning. Looking under the car, he saw oil drops trickling down to the ground. He reached in and ran his finger along the rim of the oil pan. "Bad gasket," he mumbled, as he rubbed the dab of oil between his thumb and forefinger.

Wiping his fingers on the dry grass, he stood up. The twenty miles of road between the lake and town were still free of convenience stores and gas stations. Somehow, that area had been spared from the strip-mining operations and road-side construction that had crept into the surrounding counties.

His mind drifted. Lately, he was starting to feel claustrophobic living in Hickory Ridge, which was still well secluded in the foothills of Eastern Kentucky. The residents didn't travel much. He had lived there all of his life. Only once had he traveled as far as the Tennessee border. Might be fun to travel and broaden his horizon.

The nearest house along the road was about four miles way. Then he remembered Mrs. Bailey's old farmhouse, which was now owned by a mechanic. How convenient! If he cut through the woods, the house was less than a mile away.

Putting on his jacket, he walked into the woods and picked up a side trail that climbed up the side of the gently sloped mountain. He felt irritated that he had to be social when he had already made up his mind to be alone the rest of the day. Then he considered the possibility that God was guiding him to the old Bailey place to preach the gospel to this stranger. He quickened his pace.

After reaching the top of the ridge, he paused to catch his breath and followed a switchback trail down the other side. Walking downhill, his pace quickened and his spirits lifted. Maybe he just needed to exercise more to blow some cobwebs out of his brain.

Farther down the mountain, the steep slope leveled off some, and the trail widened as he approached the Bailey's old coal bank, which was cut into the hillside next to the trail. He smiled, remembering in his childhood the times his mother warned him and Amos not to play in there because of the rotted timbers and the danger of cave-ins. Slowing his pace, he looked inside the entrance. The once spacious interior was now filled by numerous cave-ins and windblown debris.

Farther down the hillside, the Bailey place appeared from below. The red roof of the barn showed up first through the thicket along the trail, followed by the barnyard, the tool shed, the cedar house, and the split rail fence. When all thirty acres came into full view, a heavy, sweet sadness welled up in his chest.

As he approached the barnyard, he gazed at the ring of hardwood trees in the clearing around the barn. The house was clearly visible on top of the little knobby hill close by. A huge oak tree formed an umbrella that shielded the barn.

The familiar shape of the land was comforting. However, the neatly mowed grass that matted the barnyard was a strange sight. The last time he had seen the barnyard, it was overgrown with weeds and thorn bushes.

He saw two people kneeling near the open door of the barn. One of them was a pudgy young man with a thick black beard and wearing dark gray overalls. He looked like he was in his mid-to-late twenties. He was tinkering with an automobile transmission and speaking slowly in broken English. The other, to the preacher's surprise, was Timmy, Joe Potter's son.

The preacher walked up to the barn door. "Howdy," he said.

They both turned and looked at the preacher. "Oh, hello," said the bearded young man. "I beg your pardon, I did not see you." He stood up and wiped his hands with a rag.

"Gee," said Timmy. "What a surprise seeing you here!"

"I'm a bit surprised myself, Timmy. And by the way, it was good to see you in church again today."

"Thank you, Reverend. You gave a right good sermon."

"Oh," said Mahmoud. "You are Minister of church! I am honored to meet you." Having succeeded in wiping the grease from his palms, he held out his hand. "Timmy says you are very good."

The preacher shook Mahmoud's hand, but not too firmly. "Well," he chuckled, "I do my best."

"So, Mr. Dobbs, how may I help you?"

"My car's down the road yonder. The oil light came on. Do you have a quart of oil I might buy from you?"

"Yes, I have oil. What kind you like?"

"It don't matter. The gasket on the oil basin went bad. I just need somethin' to keep the engine greased up 'til I get to town."

"Bad gasket? I replace it for you, if you like."

"That's all right. I'll have my mechanic replace it when I get back to town."

"Of course. Let's go into shop and get you oil."

The preacher walked into the old barn and saw the fresh coat of paint covering the walls. The cobwebs and rusted farm tools were gone. Also gone was the aroma of old hay and mildew. The walls were lined with tables and shelves filled with auto parts and mechanic's tools. The dirt floor was replaced with concrete. It all looked so foreign. The only object he recognized was Mr. Bailey's old wooden plow standing in a cleared area against the far wall.

He took in the scene as Mahmoud removed a quart of motor oil from the shelf and walked cheerfully back to the preacher.

"Here you are, Mr. Dobbs. It is two dollars and forty-five cents."

The preacher pulled out two-dollar bills from his wallet. Then he reached into the pocket of his jacket and came up with two quarters. "Keep the change," he said with a tight smile.

"Thank you, Mr. Dobbs. Would you like for me to drive you to your car?"

"No thanks," said the preacher walking away. "It's a nice day for a stroll."

Walking briskly past the oak tree, the preacher waved to Timmy who was tinkering with the transmission. "See you later, Timmy."

"Bye, Reverend."

"It was nice meeting you," said Mahmoud, as he walked out of the barn. "Maybe we will meet again soon, yes?"

"Yeah…real soon."

As the preacher finished putting the oil in the car, he realized that he had neglected to mention the gospel to Mahmoud. Just as well, he didn't feel like preaching anyway.

He wondered how Mahmoud could possibly expect to run a successful business at the old Bailey place. He was basically surrounded by small farms and hillbillies.

As the car started moving forward, the oil light came on again.

"Now what?" he mumbled.

He looked under the car and saw a substantial trickle of oil from the bottom of the engine.

"Durn!"

Twenty minutes later, he was back in the clearing, where Mahmoud was once again on his knees tinkering with the transmission, while Timmy looked on.

"Hello again, Mr. Dobbs!"

–5–

Mahmoud was flat on his back, replacing the gasket on the oil pan, as he talked about the antics of his two-year-old son. The preacher squatted close by and watched, waiting for an opportunity to mention the gospel.

"This is very nice old Corolla," said Mahmoud, as he got out from under the car. "Is good car. I can tell see you take good care of it."

"Yeah," the preacher smiled proudly. "Before I became a full-time minister, I used to sell used cars and I worked in an auto parts store."

"Really! My first job was in my uncle's auto parts store. That's how I started learning about cars. By the way, before I forget, freeze plugs getting rusty."

"Yeah, I've been bad about servicing my car lately," the preacher chuckled.

"One of the plugs looks like it might rust through in a few months. You might want your mechanic to check it out."

"I certainly will do that. Thanks for the heads up. And by the way, have you seen the light yet?"

"I beg your pardon?"

"Have you been introduced to Jesus Christ yet?"

"Oh yes. I have read about him in the Koran."

"Huh?"

"Not only that, a few years ago, I was going through a most difficult time, and then I dreamed that Jesus talk to me and said I need to pay closer attention to the teachings of Mohammed. After that, I feel better. It is amazing you asked me about Jesus. Timmy is right, you are very wise."

−6−

Two months later

The preacher whistled softly, staring at the smooth surface of Possum Lake. Looking at his watch, he quickly reeled in the line. Joe Potter had said the plans for the new cabin would be ready at three o'clock.

He threw the remainder of his lunch into his backpack and jogged off the dock.

Walking briskly and whistling, he thought about his new project. According to Joe, getting electricity to the cabin site would be expensive. The more he thought about it, the more he liked the idea of having no electricity. He also liked the idea of digging his own well and rigging up a hand-pump. Real simple, low maintenance.

As he approached the road and saw his car, he slowed down a bit and stopped whistling as his mind drifted to his first encounter with Mahmoud, two months ago. He thought about what he had said and what he wished he had said. For some reason, he felt a need to redeem himself. But why? He hadn't said anything offensive or foolish. He quickened his pace and whistled as he tried to direct his attention to church business.

As his car sped past the gravel driveway that led to the old Bailey place, he glanced at the red and white sign by the side of the road. *MAHMOUD'S AUTO REPAIR.*

His mind returned to the logistics of gathering logs for his new cabin. He was looking forward to building it pioneer style, using trees and stones on the property, with some help from his brother and Joe Potter.

His musings stopped when a light on the dashboard signaled that the engine was overheating.

Stopping by the side of the road, he looked under the car and saw water dripping from under the bottom of the engine. One of the freeze plugs of the cooling system seemed to have rusted through.

"Durn."

He figured he could safely drive the car for a few miles, but he certainly wasn't going to drive all the way to Hickory Ridge with his car in that condition. Standing up, he put his hands on his hips and looked back at Mahmoud's red and white sign down the road.

–7–

Meanwhile, back at Forrest Park...

"She loves the first grade," Betty laughed. "She feels so grown up!"

"I know how Christy feels," said Sarah. "I loved the first grade too; that is, until my mom passed away, and things went to—"

"Look out!" Betty interrupted. They both ducked as a wayward Frisbee flew by.

"So let's sit down already and eat," said Sarah.

"Sure. Where do you want to sit?"

"Right over there," said Sarah, pointing to the curved row of tall rhododendrons at the edge of the field.

"On the ground? I don't think so. The grass looks dry, but the ground is still damp from the rain."

"No," Sarah chuckled, steering her by the elbow. "There's a bench behind those bushes."

"Speaking of your troubled past," said Betty, as they walked toward the bushes, "I still marvel at how things have evolved for you over the past three years. I know I've said this before, but this is as close to a genuine miracle as I have ever seen."

Sarah nodded. "The doctor called it spontaneous remission."

"And you really think it was Mother Eva's brain exercises that did it?"

"I think that's part of it. Let me know next time you visit Venezuela," said Sarah, "I'd like to tag along and see her personally, if it's okay."

"Sure, that would be a blast. How about next June, after final exams?"

"No, I will most probably be taking a graduate course in quantum mechanics."

Walking around the rhododendrons, they sat on a secluded bench that faced the four-foot tall row of hedges at the edge of the park.

"This is my favorite place to sit," said Sarah.

"Yes, very cozy," said Betty as they fished their salads out of their plastic bags. "The bench is nicely nestled in rhododendrons behind, juniper hedges in the front, and a big ginkgo tree for shade and added privacy."

"A ginkgo tree. So, that's what it is."

"Also known as the maiden-hair fern, even through it's not a fern," said Betty, as she opened a small plastic bag of walnuts. "It's prehistoric. Today, it survives only in cultivation. A tea made of the leaves is very good for circulation, especially in the brain. During final exams, I always drink tea made from ginkgo leaves. I also eat walnuts," she said, holding up the bag, "because they have about sixty different chemicals that benefit the brain."

Sarah chuckled. "Are there any plants on the face of the Earth that you don't know about?"

"What can I say," she said, as she sprinkled walnuts on her salad. "Botany is my bag." Betty sighed and looked around. "Yes, this is nice little place to sit. I'm going to come here more often."

"I discovered this spot about three years ago, when I first took my car to Mahmoud on your suggestion," said Sarah, pointing to Forrest Park Auto Service across the street.

"Speaking of Mahmoud," said Betty, "did you ever get the full story on why he left so suddenly?"

"No. His wife, Elimma, and I sort of became friends. She called me just before they left, to say goodbye, but she hesitated to give any details. I think he had some issues with his brother-in-law."

"Oh yeah, his brother-in-law. I never did like that guy," said Betty, shaking her head. "I stopped taking my car there after Mahmoud left."

"Actually, Mahmoud's brother-in law sold the place last year to his cousin, a very nice man, named Raffi Hamid."

"Good," said Betty. "Maybe Mahmoud will return now. Do you know where he is?"

"Last I heard from Elimma, they were living in Kentucky, somewhere out in the boonies, surrounded by hillbillies."

—8—

The preacher chewed on a twig, arms crossed, shoulder leaning against the big oak tree. The sun filtered down through the branches, shining on his face. "So, Jesus is really mentioned in that book of yours? What's it called again?"

"The Koran," said Mahmoud, his feet sticking out from under the jacked up car.

"Where did it come from?"

Mahmoud paused as he pried off one of the rusted freeze plugs. "Same as Bible," he said. "It is inspired word of God revealed to man so that we may live in righteousness. Mr. Dobbs, all freeze plugs badly rusted. You want I should replace all of them?"

"Yeah, go ahead."

"Most unusual to see car with metal plugs," said Mahmoud, as he got up and walked quickly into the barn. "All newer cars have plastic plugs. I just happen to have them because a while ago, I found an old abandoned Corolla, so I towed it to my shop and stripped it for parts. The engine was no good, but still have good clutch assembly and transmission."

The preacher paced around until Mahmoud came back out.

"But who actually wrote the book?" asked the preacher as he leaned his shoulder on the oak tree again.

"I beg your pardon?" said Mahmoud, as he disappeared under the car again.

"The Koran. Who wrote it?"

"It was written by the prophet, Sayyidina Mohammed, as revealed to him by the Archangel Gabriel."

"The Archangel Gabriel! He's in your religion, too?"

"Yes. My wife has her own special name for the Archangel Gabriel," he laughed. "She call him 'Brother G.'"

"And Jesus is actually mentioned in the book?"

"Yes. By the way, before I forget, there is small amount of transmission fluid seeping from the casing. Have your mechanic check it out."

The preacher paced around slowly. "So what's it say about him?"

"I beg your pardon?"

"What has the Koran got to say about Jesus?"

"It say many things."

"Such as?"

"Well…he is the Messiah."

"And you believe that?"

"Of course."

"So… do you pray to him?"

Mahmoud did not answer. His feet remained motionless. Then, he slid out from under the car. Leaning on his elbow, he looked at the preacher. "For me, that would be a sin," he said politely. "We are instructed to pray only to God."

–9–

Two months later

The full moon over the big oak tree illuminated the barn. Crickets chirped in the cool night air.

"Yes, olive leaves!" said Mahmoud.

The preacher leaned against the door frame of the barn, arms folded and feet crossed, his shadow extending out into the barnyard. "Are you puttin' me on?"

"No! My grandmother used to give us tea made from olive leaves." Mahmoud picked up a thermos bottle from the table. "It taste terrible, but we hardly ever get sick."

Mahmoud removed the top from the thermos and poured out a steaming greenish gray liquid into a cup. He walked to the preacher and offered him the cup.

The preacher took the cup and stared at it.

"Drink. You feel better."

The preacher took sip and then grimaced.

Mahmoud laughed. "Yes, very bad." He walked back to the table. "But I always drink it this time of year. My grandmother also say to never eat cheese by itself, because it make your thinking not good. She say to eat cheese with nuts, especially walnuts, because walnuts good for brain. She was right. When I was a boy and I go to school, I always do better when I eat lots of walnuts and not too much cheese. That was easy because where I lived, they grow the best walnuts in the world."

"Your grandma still around?"

"Yes. She is ninety-five years old. She still healthy. Mind very sharp. She still cleans house, works in the garden." Mahmoud poured himself a cup of tea from the thermos. "And then there was my Great-Uncle Mustafa. He was my grandmother's older brother. He also heal people." Mahmoud took a sip. "Uncle Mustafa was the one who taught my grandmother about olive leaves. He never went to school. He teach himself to read and write. He work hard. He build factory for making bricks. But in his spare time, he heal people. Sometimes, he use herbs, sometimes massage, sometimes he push on your back, sometimes he push your stomach around."

Mahmoud searched the toolbox on the table. "And he never charge money. He was very devout man. He say all his remedies are gifts from God and must be given free."

The preacher twirled his cup slowly in his hand.

"Anyway," continued Mahmoud, "one day, a man come to village. He could not walk. His brothers bring him on a cart pulled by a donkey. They come from far away. They ask an old man in village, 'Where is Dr.. Mustafa?' The old man take them to the brick factory. Uncle Mustafa was standing next to oven," Mahmoud laughed, "his face and arms and hands all black from the soot and his clothes all sweaty and dirty. The old man point to my uncle and say, 'This is Dr.. Mustafa.'"

The preacher smiled. Taking another sip of tea, he grimaced.

"My uncle say the man dislocate both hips," Mahmoud continued. "I don't remember the story of how he do that. But my uncle know how to fix it. He say to bring the man back tomorrow. And also to bring a cow!"

"A cow?" chuckled the preacher.

"Yes. He also say—"

The cordless phone on the table rang.

"Excuse me," said Mahmoud. "Hello... Yes, Mr. Waddell. I call you yesterday because I think I overcharge you when I put battery in your car. What kind of battery is it?" Mahmoud held the phone against his ear with his shoulder as he continued fishing though the toolbox. "That's what I thought," he nodded. "I overcharge you ten dollar and fifteen cents. I will mail it to you." Mahmoud smiled, still fishing through the toolbox. "You are welcome, Mr. Waddell. Good bye."

The preacher looked at Mahmoud. "Waddell never would have known the difference," he said. "That was mighty good of you."

"Oh no," Mahmoud chuckled. "I am not good. Only God is good. I'm just being practical. It would be silly for me to keep that money, because on Judgment Day I will have to answer."

Mahmoud opened another toolbox and started looked through it. "What were we talking about?"

"Your Uncle Mustafa and the cow."

"Oh yes. So, my uncle say to bring a cow tomorrow and to not give cow any water for twenty-four hours! He say to give cow all the things cows like to eat—corn, oats, alfalfa—but no water! The strangers were puzzled, but they do what Uncle Mustafa say because they did not know what else to do."

Having found the right bit for the ratchet, Mahmoud walked back to the car. "The next day, the strangers come back with the cow. And do you want to guess what my uncle did?" he laughed.

"I don't have a clue," said the preacher.

"My uncle say to put the man on cow's back and tie his feet around cow's stomach. After they do that, my uncle give cow all the water it want to drink. And cow drink and drink and drink. Stomach got real big and then you hear POP! And when the man come down from cow, he walk, no problem."

The preacher burst out laughing. "And this is a true story?"

"Yes," Mahmoud said. "My father was there as a boy, working in factory. He see it."

The preacher continued laughing as he walked to the interior of the barn and put the cup down next to the thermos bottle on the table.

"Please, take more," said Mahmoud, "We have more in house."

The preacher refilled his cup and sat on a chair next to the table. "Say, if you don't mind me askin', whatever possessed you to move down here?"

Mahmoud smiled, shaking his head slowly. "Very strange story," he said, shining a flashlight on the newly installed transmission.

"When I first come to America, I work in garage owned by my brother-in-law. In those days, I was—how you say it—stuck up. I talked about God, but it was all empty words, arrogant words. It was my way of being big shot."

The preacher nodded.

"I had just got married. I used to argue with my wife because she say many strange things about religion. For example, she say that the Archangel Gabriel is really a woman! I told her she was being sacrilegious, but she just laugh at me. She say the only thing that is sacrilegious is when we are not kind to each other. Anyway, that was just the beginning. One day, a woman come to shop with bad radiator. That's when things really go crazy. She was science teacher in the high school close by. She teach physics. Very smart lady."

The preacher tilted his chair back against the wall, resting his cup on his belly.

"This woman keep coming back to get her car fixed; first the radiator, then vacuum pump and so on. Sometimes she go sit on park bench across the street and read, but usually she stay in garage and she talk and talk and talk about religion. I could not argue with her. She knew the Koran better than I did. She say the main problem with the great holy books of the world is that people don't read them. They just blindly follow the leaders who want to use the sacred teachings for their own ambitions."

The preacher took another sip of tea as Mahmoud dug through another toolbox.

"Every time she talk about God, I became more confused," Mahmoud chuckled. "And to make things worse, she became friends with my wife. You should have seen them when they first met. You think they were sisters!"

The preacher took another sip and looked down at the greenish liquid in the cup. The taste seemed to be improving—a bit. And, his throat seemed to be less scratchy.

"I did not know what to think," continued Mahmoud. "Suddenly, my faith, which used to be like a rock, became like scrambled eggs. Then, something very strange happen. I had a dream about my great grandfather. He was a most unusual man. He lived to be one hundred and twenty years old."

"A hundred and twenty! Was he the father of your ninety-five-year old grandma?"

"Yes. He pass way when I was nine years old. He always go to bed right after dark and wake up at 3 AM. He pray until four AM and then he go to work. He had big, big garden, many acres, many vegetables, many fruit trees. He work 'til sunrise, then eat breakfast, work 'til one o'clock, then eat lunch. Lunch was big meal of the day. After lunch, he take walk, talk with friends and family and then take nap in little open hut in middle of garden. Very quiet, very peaceful. Then, he do some light work for rest of afternoon, like grind up wheat into flour for bread. They always grind wheat and make bread fresh every day. He grow all his food for his family. Everything fresh." Mahmoud pointed to the Bailey's old plow leaning on the far wall of the barn. "He had plow like this one. People come to great grandfather's garden to buy food, but if they had no money, he just give it to them because he have so much. He grow all kind of fruits and vegetables, dates, almonds, walnuts, everything. His apricots very big, and taste like no other apricots I ever taste. Grape bushes so full of grapes, you no see bushes, you just see grapes. People come from all over to learn from him. He say when pick apricots or grapes, must pick them gently and give thanks. Don't just grab, because next year they not grow so good."

"And he actually lived a hundred and twenty years?"

"Yes. After he die, some men from the government come to check his papers so they could put him in record books. And, the whole time he was alive, he never go to doctor. No shots, no pills. Teeth good even when he was very old. He never eat sugar or candy or cakes. He eat simple. Fruits, vegetables, not too much meat. He never stuff himself with a lot of different foods. Was healthy and strong right up until he die. He always happy, never say bad things about people, talk to everybody, joke around."

Mahmoud became silent as he made some fine adjustments under the hood. "I forget," he chuckled. "Why was I talking about my great grandfather?"

"You said you had a dream about him when you were having problems with that science teacher?"

"Oh, yes. In dream, he say to me, 'Mahmoud, what happen to you? You used to be such a good boy.'"

Mahmoud looked at the preacher. "When he say that, I just cry and cry. And, when I stop crying, my great grandfather was gone, and I see Jesus standing in front of me. He spoke to me for a long time. It was a long, long dream."

The preacher sat up in his chair. "What did he say?"

"I'm not sure. I don't remember most of it. All I remember is he ask me to explain to him how cars work. So I did."

The preacher chuckled.

"Very strange," continued Mahmoud. "But, I felt much better when I wake up. I was calm and happy. I read the entire Koran for the first time in my life. I read it very slowly, and felt like I understood it like never before. I told my brother-in-law about it and he throw me out of garage, which is okay because he didn't like me anyway, and he was just looking for an excuse to fire me. That's when Elimma say to call Mrs. Bailey. We had met her earlier when she was visiting the city and I fix her car. She offer to sell farm real cheap. It was crazy idea, coming to strange place out in the middle of anywhere! I still don't know why I did it."

The preacher gulped the last of the olive leaf tea. His throat definitely felt better. "So, business is okay here?"

"Is slow. We don't know anyone here. There is nice little Muslim community in Lexington. We go there once or twice a month for worship. If business not get better, we move to Lexington and I find work. But, I hope we can stay here. We like the mountains. Is peaceful, mortgage is low, and cost of living is low."

"The cost of livin' would be next to nothin' if you grow your own food. You got lots of room for a garden and fruit trees. You can grow potatoes and squash and do enough canning to have food for the whole winter. You can also get yourself a couple of goats and some chickens and have fresh eggs and milk. You can even make your own yogurt, cheese, and butter. It's real easy. Heck, if you want, you can produce enough surplus to sell. That's what I did, until the church got so big, it took up all of my time."

"That is a most excellent idea," Mahmoud nodded. "But Elimma and I don't know anything about raising animals, growing vegetables, or canning."

Mahmoud tightened the last bolt that secured the transmission and lowered the hood. "Okay. Let's take it on the road and see how it is. We might still need to adjust the clutch."

—10—

Three years later

They walked through the forest in silence, their elongated shadows dragging behind them. The preacher's boots kicked up pebbles and dust along the trail. His hands were buried in the pockets of his fishing jacket, which he could no longer button due to the twenty pounds he had put on.

Mountain laurel in full bloom lined one side of the trail. On the other side, hazy sunbeams filtered through the thicket of oaks and hickories, creating a tapestry of light and shadow on the forest floor.

"So, why you visit so early?" asked Mahmoud.

The preacher lifted his chin and looked straight ahead. "I'm through as a preacher. I'm goin' away for a good spell."

Mahmoud's thick black eyebrows shot up. "Why?"

"I'm not sure. But I think it's kind of like the reason you left your brother-in-law's garage."

"You mean they throw you out?"

"No, not exactly."

"My God, what did you say to those people?"

"Well, I didn't think I said anything offensive. My worst fear as a preacher has always been that the entire congregation gets angry and shouts me off the stage. It certainly wasn't anything like that."

"So, please tell me," said Mahmoud, "What happened?"

"I don't rightly know. But last week I had the durndest dream. Most peculiar."

"What did you dream about?" asked Mahmoud.

"I don't know. I sort of forgot it."

Mahmoud scratched his beard and looked straight ahead, putting his hands in the pockets of his metallic gray overalls. "So, what did you say to them that was so bad?"

The preacher recalled his words: *My friends, the presence of God is like a vast ocean. And each of us is like a tiny boat bobbing up and down on the waves of that ocean. And even with all of its power and majesty, it holds each boat tenderly. If the presence of God is anything, it is accessible to all. God shows up in our lives as the love we share with our family and community. But once in a while, a few individuals experience the presence of God in a more direct way that most of us couldn't handle. It's like looking at the sun. The sun brings life to the Earth, but we can't look directly at the sun because it would blind us. That is, until we have become pure enough. And when we are pure enough to directly experience the fire of the Holy Spirit, we can also walk on water...*

"Well," said the preacher rubbing his chin. "I started by telling 'em how God's presence is like a vast ocean and we're all like tiny boats supported by the ocean."

"That is beautiful. What is so bad about that?"

"Nothin,' if I had just left it at that. But then... well, I guess I sort of went off the deep end. A few of the folks got real upset, and the more I tried to explain myself, the worse it got."

Mahmoud nodded. "Just like me talking to my brother-in-law."

They stopped walking at a grassy patch next to Possum Lake. Several cardinals were foraging in front of the wooden dock. The water moved in ripples that shimmered with golden light as the morning sun skimmed over the surface. The only sound was that of the water splashing gently against the four-by-fours that supported the dock.

"What about the new church building?"

"They'll just have to complete it without me. It's almost done anyway."

"And, what about that school teacher, Candra Winfield?" asked Mahmoud.

"What about her?"

"You said she likes you."

"I've never formally approached her," said the preacher. "She teaches Sunday school and such, so we've become... acquainted. We've had dinner a few times, but it was all very proper. I've only kissed her once—on the cheek." He folded his arms. "Anyway, this past week, with everything else that's happened, I've also realized that Candra and me ain't quite right for each other. She's a bit too high-brow for me."

"What is high-brow?"

"Stuck up, arrogant. I had the impression that my bein' a country preacher wasn't good enough for her. Seems like I was always havin' to prove myself to her."

They stood in silence for a while.

"I am sorry that my wife and son are not here to say good-bye."

"They ain't?"

"No. They left yesterday. Her brother is sick."

The preacher shrugged. "Well, that's okay. I figure I'll be back in six months or so. I'll go back to bein' plain old Roy Dobbs."

They stared at the lake for a few minutes and then resumed walking in silence.

"You are very quiet, Mr. Dobbs. Most unusual for you."

"Yeah."

"Usually, when you visit, you have such wonderful stories to tell. I always like the stories about your camping trips by the lake with your boyhood friends."

As they passed by a large beech tree, the preacher remembered one of his adventures. "Did I ever tell you about the marks on that tree?"

"No."

"I was twelve years old. I spotted Conrad Simmons carvin' his name on it. Mrs. Bailey had told me a few times that she wished people wouldn't mutilate the smooth and beautiful bark of beech trees. I told Conrad Simmons to stop. Not only didn't he stop, but he made a comment about my mother. I flattened him with one punch. Later that day, I felt guilty, so, on Reverend Smith's advice, I composed an appropriate prayer to set things straight. I said, 'Dear Jesus, please forgive me for what I done to that no-good varmint, and forgive him too, because he didn't rightly know he was doin' somethin' wrong. But now he does.'"

Mahmoud laughed.

"What does Mrs. Bailey have to say about this?" asked Mahmoud, as they walked past several chickens in the barnyard.

"She's been pretty quiet about it. She just keeps tellin' me to lighten up a little."

The preacher looked at the huge vegetable garden next to the house. The two goats were grazing next to the fence surrounding the garden. "Looks like you're gonna have a bumper crop of green beans this year."

"Yes, thanks to you. My son is now big enough to help pick them. He is looking forward to it. But canning them is going to take long time. Maybe we just freeze. I picked up a very big deep freezer in junkyard. I fix it. Works good."

They stopped walking under the oak tree. "I still do not understand why you have to leave," said Mahmoud.

"That makes two of us. But it seems like it started with that durn dream."

As they walked on into the barn, the preacher was filled with more vivid images of his boyhood. He recalled himself and his buddies, barreling into the barn, chasing each other through the stalls and climbing up and down the hayloft, pretending they were jet pilots or knights.

"Oh, yeah," said the preacher, "now I remember."

"What?"

"That dream. It was about knights."

"Night? What do you mean?"

"You know, knights. The fellers that used to ride horses, savin' damsels and such."

"Oh... knights!"

"I saw three knights ridin' by. One of 'em was sort of goofy lookin'. When they rode by, I ran after 'em."

"Why?"

"I don't know. I followed 'em to a mountaintop, and they bowed before a beautiful queen. And then something most peculiar happened: one of the three knights turned into a woman. And then, a young kid comes along and starts pesterin' 'em to save the world."

"Then what?"

"Nothin'. I woke up."

Mahmoud looked out the window, scratching his beard. "And for this, you are leaving home?"

"What do you mean?'

"You are leaving because you dreamed about goofy knights?"

"I know it sounds stupid, but after I woke up, I felt like I understood somethin.' It's hard to explain now. You see dreams are symbolic."

"What does symbolic mean?"

"It means that whatever you're dreamin' about isn't really what you're dreamin' about."

"Oh."

"For instance, a horse in a dream isn't really a horse. It's somethin' related to a horse."

Mahmoud, stroking his beard pensively. "You mean, like a donkey?"

"No, no, I don't mean that it's related *that* way." The preacher rubbed his face. "You see, everything in a dream has a message. It's tellin' you somethin' important about yourself."

"Oh!" Mahmoud smiled. "Of course! I knew that. So, what is the meaning of goofy knights?"

"I don't rightly know. And they weren't all goofy. Only one of 'em was goofy." The preacher sighed. "We're not gettin' anywhere."

"Is this what happened when you tried to explain it in church?"

"Worse. What really threw them over the edge was when I started talkin' about walkin' on water. You see, when I woke up that mornin', I had the notion that I could walk on water."

"I have not felt that way since I was a teenager," said Mahmoud.

"Very funny."

"No, really," Mahmoud chuckled. "I actually tried it."

"What happened?"

"I got wet."

The preacher nodded. "I guess I got wet, too. But it's not like I told them that I could really do it. I just felt that we could learn how if we wanted to. And…"

"And what?"

"I just remembered some of the other things I said to the congregation." He rubbed the back of his neck. "Yeah, some of it was sort of crazy. And then, I started fantasizin' about establishin' a new and bigger church in Lexington. I figured I would do sermons on TV and such. I thought about how impressed Candra Winfield would be."

"That's all right, Mr. Dobbs. My great grandfather once said, 'When a young man is first given sacred knowledge, he will probably try to use it to impress women.'"

"Quit tryin' to cheer me up. What I did was shameful."

"So, you are leaving because you are ashamed?"

"I don't know why I'm leavin'. All I know is, every time I walk through town, I feel like the third tit on a bull."

Mahmoud puzzled over that one.

The preacher walked to the old plow standing in a cleared area against the wall. "Are you ever goin' to get rid of this thing?"

"Oh no," Mahmoud laughed, "that would be a sacrilege."

The preacher ran his hand over the wooden body of the plow, nicked and pitted with age, but still sturdy.

After taking a deep breath, he looked at his watch. "Well, I guess I better go."

"Do you want me to check your cabin while you are gone?" asked Mahmoud.

"Yeah, I'd appreciate that. But, be careful. Some of them folks who live back in the hollers ain't quite civilized. They'll look for any excuse to start a fight, especially when they're filled with their own corn whiskey."

"Yes, I have heard. Have they given you trouble?"

"Nah," said the preacher, "I know how to talk to 'em." He walked slowly toward Mahmoud. "Well," he said, holding out his hand, "good-bye."

"Good-bye, Mr. Dobbs. God be with you."

The preacher slapped him on the shoulder and walked out of the barn.

"So, this is it? You go right now?" asked Mahmoud.

"No. I have to go to the bank and sign a few more papers." He paused and his face showed a bit of anger. "Then I have to do one more thing." He turned the ignition key and revved the engine forcefully.

–11–

Three hours later, Preacher Roy sat down with a grunt on the edge of the wooden dock that extended into Possum Lake. He removed a small black cassette recorder from his backpack and placed it on the dock. After he assembled the fishing pole, he baited the hook and cast the line into the water. Then he placed the end of the fishing pole upright in a knothole on the dock.

He wiped the sweat from his forehead with the back of his hand and glanced at his wristwatch. 12:45. He wasn't hungry yet, but he was thirsty. He removed a beer can from the cooler and looked at it. His first in six years. He simultaneously felt a sense of guilt and a sense of freedom.

He took a long draw, savoring that first swallow. After wiping his mouth on his sleeve, he picked up the cassette recorder and pressed the record button.

"Dear, Amos—" He stopped abruptly when the fishing line became tight. The pole bent like an archer's bow and then slipped out of the knothole. He dropped the beer can and the recorder, reflexively reaching for the fishing pole with both hands, but the motion of his left elbow knocked over the cooler, causing the remaining beer cans and ice cubes and several sausage and biscuit sandwiches to fall onto the lake. Feelings like he was moving in slow motion, he found himself lunging at the recorder, grabbing it just as it was falling over the edge, but in so doing, his center of gravity shifted well beyond the edge of the dock. He managed to drop the cassette recorder on the dock as he fell belly first into the water.

He was submerged briefly, sprawled out face down on the muddy bottom.

Springing to the surface like a breaching whale, he stumbled and fell again belly first into the water. He stood up again, this time more carefully.

Waist deep, he slapped the water with his hand. "DAG NABBIT!" he yelled at the top of his voice.

He placed his hands on his hips, his voice echoing through the valley.

Meanwhile, Mahmoud stuck his head out of the barn window with great astonishment, certain that he had just heard a camel calling in the distance.

The preacher grabbed the fishing pole before it drifted too far. The fish had gotten away. He waded to shore and stepped onto the dock, dragging his fishing pole, his shoes squishing and bubbling with muddy water. His long hair hung down slick and smooth, covering his ears and forehead and most of his neck. He thought about walking back to his car and changing clothes, but remembered he had given away all his clothes to the church charity and planned to buy new ones when he left town. He thought about going back to Mahmoud and borrowing clothes. No, that would be embarrassing.

Taking off his jacket, he slammed it on the dock. He stood silently, hands on hips, water dripping from his head and arms. The lake gradually settled down. A duck quacked in the distance.

Sitting with thud, he grabbed the recorder, which was still running. He held it close to his mouth, scowling at it. Without bothering to rewind it, he yelled into it. "ALL RIGHT, AMOS, I KNOW I'VE DONE A PISS POOR JOB OF EXPLAININ' MYSELF," he said, spraying water from his lips, as he said piss poor. "BUT YOU HAVEN'T MADE THINGS ANY EASIER! THE PROBLEM WITH YOU IS YOU DON'T KNOW WHEN TO SHUT UP AND LISTEN!"

Realizing that he was getting out of control, he switched off the recorder. He wiped the water from his hair and face and shook his arms out. Taking several deep breaths, he looked out across the water.

Removing his boots, he emptied the water and mud into the lake. Then he took off his socks, wrung them out, and placed them flat on the dock.

After a few minutes, he stood up and took off his shirt. Wringing it out, he placed it flat on the dock.

Taking a deep breath, he picked up the recorder again, rewound it, and switched it on.

"Alright, Amos. Now that you're not standing over me, interrupting me every five seconds, I'll tell it from start to finish… and, maybe that way I'll be able to make some sense of this myself."

He paused the recorder, watching tiny ripples expanding across the lake. "What in blazes is the beginnin' anyway?"

"I guess if I have to pick a beginnin', it was one Sunday afternoon three, maybe three and a half, years ago. I never did tell you about this, because, well, it didn't seem important at the time."

He spoke briskly into the recorder. "I was in my car and the oil light came on. So, I went to Mahmoud Mossavi's place. When I got there, he was fiddlin' with a transmission and talkin' to Timmy, Joe Potter's boy. That's when I remembered that I'd seen Timmy in church the last three Sundays, which was a might peculiar because his Mamma done everything she could to get him there and finally gave up. After service, I ran into his Daddy, and I said to him, 'Joe, is that really Timmy?'

"'I reckon he is', Joe says, just as puzzled as he could be."

He looked at the recorder and shook his head. "I was tellin' myself that Timmy was comin' to church because I was such a hot-shot preacher. Wasn't 'til later I realized Timmy started comin' to church after he started workin' for Mahmoud."

"They turned out to be nice folks," he said into the recorder. "They don't drink alcohol, and they don't touch pork. They get up at six o'clock every mornin' to pray. Every day at six o'clock in the evening, no matter how busy he is, he stops what he's doin', washes the grease off his hands, gets on his knees, and prays."

Pausing the recorder, he placed it on the dock in front of the cooler. His upper body was becoming warm and dry, reminding him that his lower body was cold and wet. He stood up and he took off his pants, wrung them out, and placed them flat on the dock, next to his shirt. After a moment of hesitation, he looked around. "Oh heck," he mumbled, as he took off his jockey shorts, "nobody ever comes here, anyway."

Glancing down at the wooden planks, he thought about splinters. He started to reposition the cooler so he could sit on it, but in doing so, he knocked the recorder into the water. He watched it disappear into the murky water.

He sighed and sat on the cooler. He watched a frog sitting on a partially-submerged log, the floor of its mouth bobbing up and down. Not far from the frog, a fish was nibbling on a floating biscuit. A duck quacked in the distance.

Crossing one leg over the other, he cleaned out the specks of debris from between his toes. He looked straight down at his naked reflection in the water.

For a while, he just stared across the lake, watching the ripples, losing track of time. Closing his eyes, he became deeply relaxed. Through closed eyelids, he saw four stars in the shape of a three-sided pyramid hovering over its own reflection in the water. His eyes snapped open. What was that? Oh well, one more mystery.

He looked down at his clothes. They would take a few hours to be reasonably dry. Not knowing what else to do, he baited his hook again, cast the line into the water and placed the end of the pole in the knothole. He figured he would just write a letter to his brother tomorrow. Or maybe the next day. No rush. He was going to be away a good six months, so he would have a lot of time on his hands.

–12–

Six months later

"Jesus said, 'I am the way, the truth and the life,'" droned the hypnotic voice of Reverend Mathew McCann, as he conducted the opening invocation of the monthly Inner Sanctuary meeting.

The preacher sat with his eyes closed, along with the rest of the crowd. He tried to relax, but that nagging suspicion crept up again.

"Trust in Jesus," continued Reverend Mathew. "Let your doubts dissolve."

The preacher sighed. He recalled having used the exact same words when he was pastor at Hickory Ridge. Taking a deep breath, he tried to silence the war that was going on inside him.

"Relax," said Reverend Mathew, "you don't have to do battle with the voice of Satan. The light of Christ will set you free…"

The preacher took another deep breath. Once again, Reverend Mathew's words seemed to exactly address his silent thoughts. The man obviously had a gift. "What's wrong with me," he said silently.

Suddenly, Mrs. Bailey flashed through his mind, followed by a wave of peace. He felt like a fog had finally lifted from his brain. His five months with Reverend Mathew's church paraded through his mind. He recalled the grand promises, doomsday prophecies, and the all-day Gospel Gatherings consisting of hour after hour of quiet browbeating, camouflaged as sweet religious platitudes. And, there was just enough truth in his words to make him very convincing.

The preacher opened his eyes. *My God,* he thought, w*here have I been?*

He looked around at the forty-five or so people sitting with their eyes closed. Then he looked at the tall and thin figure of Reverend Mathew pacing slowly on the stage in the front of the room, with his hands behind his back. His intense penetrating eyes seemed to be looking off into the distance. He wore a neatly pressed dark three-piece suit that matched his short, neatly combed jet-black hair.

He spoke of love and Christian ideals, yet every sermon and class included subtle attacks on other churches. Even when he had something good to say about other churches, he threw in something invalidating; sometimes it was just a hesitation in his voice, or a tonal inflection.

"Welcome everyone," said Reverend Mathew, as the rest of the people opened their eyes. "Welcome to our *50th* Inner Sanctuary meeting."

The group applauded. "Wow," came a voice in the crowd. "50! Already?"

"Who is here for the first time?" Reverend Mathew called out. "Please stand."

Two women stood. The preacher hesitated and then stood. He considered just walking out, since he had already decided to quit the church, but decided to stay for awhile and leave quietly later. No need to make a scene.

"We bid you a special welcome to our Inner Sanctuary," said Reverend Mathew. He started clapping, and the rest of the group joined in. "The fact that you three are here means you are, perhaps, ready to go further than those who only come to Sunday services, Gospel Gatherings and such. You are here because you have heard the calling to be more committed in your service to Christ and to humanity."

After the three sat down again, one of the new women raised her hand.

"Yes, Joyce?"

"Is it true that we have to give up eating meat to be admitted into the Inner Sanctuary?"

"No, of course not," chuckled Reverend Mathew. "That's entirely up to you. The only requirement is a willingness to reach out—to be the voice of Jesus. This meeting will give you a chance to check out the Inner Sanctuary, to see, if in fact, it is for you. God willing, all three of you will return in one month to our next meeting to be formally initiated. If not, you are welcome to continue as general members. General membership is about receiving. The Inner Sanctuary is about giving. It is for those who feel nourished enough to reach out and feed God's flock. Don't worry, though," he smirked, "we won't ask you to go knocking door-to-door."

The crowd chuckled. "You won't?" remarked a young man. "What a bummer!"

The laughter picked up. "Can't we at least sell pictures and greeting cards on street corners?"

More laughter.

The preacher nodded. Apparently, the subtle attacks on other churches were not so subtle in the Inner Sanctuary.

When the laughter died down, Reverend Mathew continued. "I also want to emphasize to the new potential initiates that whatever we talk about in these Inner Sanctuary meetings is not to be discussed with anyone who has not been initiated into the Inner Sanctuary. Whatever is shared in these meetings should be held as sacred, no matter how trivial it seems."

"Naturally," the preacher whispered sarcastically.

Reverend Mathew motioned to the young lady standing by the door at the back of the room. "Jane," he said, "the Announcements, please."

The young lady picked up a clipboard from the chair and walked up to the stage. She had a slender pretty face, long blonde hair, glasses with large plastic frames, and wore a blue business suit.

"Actually," she said stepping up to the stage, "I made all the major Announcements at the last Sunday service. The one thing I want to repeat for those who didn't attend on Sunday is that we are severely, and I do mean severely, shorthanded for our community outreach program. So, please, please, if you have any free time at all, see me after the meeting. Also, please note that the Prosperity Class is going to be moved from Tuesday to Wednesday, starting next month."

She started walking away, but Reverend Mathew stopped her. "Jane."

"Yes?"

"What about the news regarding John and Sylvia?"

"Oh, that," she said, with a smile that seemed to conceal a generic discontent, like a child being forced to do an unpleasant chore. "Well, I found out why they disappeared. It seems that John's parents talked him into going back to their church."

"We send them our love," said Reverend Mathew raising his hands and closing his eyes.

"John and Sylvia separated two weeks ago and are planning to get divorced."

Many nods and *Uh-huh's* from the crowd.

Reverend Mathew turned to Jane. "And you said you spoke with our friend, George Mack, who left us three months ago."

Jane nodded, again with that camouflaging smile on her face. "His business is floundering again. On Reverend Mathew's suggestion, I pointed out to George that his business was thriving while he was a member of the Inner Sanctuary. The prosperity classes had really turned things around for him. He said he's coming back to us, even if he has to start as a general member."

The room burst into applause and cheers, among shouts of "Amen," and "Well done, Sister," as Jane maintained her forced smile and returned to her post by the back door, where she finally sighed and dropped her clipboard on a chair.

Reverend Mathew paced around slowly. "There is no magic here. We simply apply the plain truth of the gospel in an uncompromising way. In *our* church— especially for the members of the Inner Sanctuary— we are not content to remember God on Sunday and forget about Him the rest of the week. We say 'Thy will be done' everyday, in our home life and at work. I cannot tell you how many people have tried to graduate from general membership to the Inner Sanctuary, but ended up running away from our church altogether. And that's all right. There are other churches that can serve their needs."

He stopped walking and looked at a young lady in the front row.

"Nicki, why the tears?"

"It's silly," she said shaking her head.

"Nothing that pains you is silly," said Reverend Mathew, as he stroked her cheek with the back of his hand. "Tell us what troubles you."

"I miss my mom."

"Why don't you go visit her?"

"I… I don't know. I've been wanting to for the longest time. But, since I was initiated into the Inner Sanctuary, I've been very busy. I was planning to visit her over Thanksgiving, but that's when you're having the next Clarity Class. Things just keep coming up, like maybe I'm not supposed to see her."

"You are certainly not required to attend the Clarity Class."

"I know. But, you said it's an important class for those who eventually wish to be ordained."

"'Important' is a relative term. The question is 'what is important to *you* right now?' And, you should also know the issue here is not whether to visit your mother or attend the Clarity Class. If that was the issue, the answer is simple, just do one or the other. And, God knows, I fully support you in honoring and respecting your mother."

The preacher's jaw became progressively tighter.

"Thank you," said Nicki, "that makes me feel better. My mom and I have been distant from each other in the past several years. The last time I saw her, she said some bad things about the church, and I felt myself wavering." She sighed. "I don't know why I'm making such a big deal about this."

"Because you have not forgiven her," said Reverend Mathew, "Not the sugar-coated and popularized version of forgiveness that we often see beyond these walls, but the true forgiveness that allows us to let go of the past. My own mother died when I was ten, leaving me in the hands of a drunken and brutal father. Through God's mercy, I have forgiven them both. Now, I know that I am no one's child, except God's."

Nicki wiped her eyes.

"Dear one," said Reverend Mathew, "ultimately it doesn't matter whether you join us in the Clarity Class or visit your mother. What's important is that you forgive your mother. And also remember that regardless of what decision you make, we still love you, and you are still part of this family."

The preacher started drumming his fingernails on the wooden armrest of the chair. Several people in his vicinity turned their heads.

Nicki sighed. "Is there a reason why you scheduled the class on Thanksgiving Day?"

"It was not my decision. Several of the board members received strong guidance to hold the class on that morning. Which reminds me, for anyone who is interested, we will be having a festive Thanksgiving gathering after the class. Bring your family and friends and your favorite dish."

"I do want to come to the class," said Nicki. "But, I still want to see my mom. She hasn't been feeling well, and it got me thinking; she won't be around forever. I want to spend time with her while—" She started crying again.

"Go ahead and cry," said Reverend Mathew. "Whatever decision you make will be the right one. You will learn in your own time and in your own way to simply let the dead bury the dead."

Preacher Roy slammed his fist on the armrest and stood up. "BY GOD," he yelled, "THAT'S ENOUGH!"

All eyes were on him as he marched quickly to the front of the room. "Sir, what you are doin' here is twisted, perverted, and indecent." He turned to the teary-eyed young lady who now looked shocked. "Nicki, there's nothin' wrong with you bein' with your mom on Thanksgivin.' It's just good healthy instinct, and that's all there is to it."

"I did not say there was anything wrong with it," said Reverend Mathew, calmly, as if he had been waiting for the outburst.

"Like hell, you didn't." The preacher went nose to nose with him.

Reverend Mathew stepped back and smiled. "My words were quite clear. She is free to choose."

"I don't give a damn about your words."

Several people gasped.

Surprised by his own fury, the preacher calmed himself. "Your intention is obvious."

"My intention is to spread the truth of the Gospels."

The preacher backed down some more when he realized that Reverend Mathew believed his own words.

"Roy," said Nicki angrily, "your interference is inappropriate."

"It's all right, Nicki," said Reverend Mathew. "The Inner Sanctuary is, among other things, an open forum. We encourage free discussion and open expression of feelings." He turned to the crowd. "Your opinions, concerns, and complaints are welcomed here. " We have enough angels in this room to sweep away any demons that are released." He turned back to the preacher. "Thank you for your honesty, Roy. And now, I will be lovingly honest with you. Your attempt to rescue Nicki is understandable. You want her to feel grateful to you," he said, as his voice became hypnotic again. "After all, you do find her attractive."

The preacher glanced at Nicki. Yes, she was attractive—very attractive. However, that certainly wasn't what motivated his outburst? Was it?

"We speak the plain truth here," continued Reverend Mathew. "And sometimes, speaking the truth is uncomfortable or even painful because we do not dilute it or sugar-coat it. That is why many individuals choose to leave the Inner Sanctuary. We are not given to coarse language or obscenities," he said with compassion in his voice, "but we do speak the plain truth. Roy, instead of trying to save Nicki, perhaps you should save yourself."

The preacher's face got hot. Sweat formed in his hands and armpits. Should he argue? No, that would only make him look even guiltier.

Suddenly, his body spontaneously took a deep breath. A wave of peace moved through him like cool water. He wasn't sure whether it was divine intervention or his decision to just give up trying to save face.

The preacher looked at Nicki. "I am sorry if I interfered with your…process." He paused for a moment and then turned back to the Reverend, unexpectedly becoming angry again. "As for you, you pious slime ball—"

There were a few gasps from the audience, but the tone quickly changed to quiet mirth as Reverend Mathew responded with, "Pious slime ball?" in a tone of mock surprise.

Reverend Mathew started pacing with his hands behind his back. "Roy, remove the mote from thine eye. When you look at me, you do not see me as I am. You see only your own dark past. It is time for you to own up to your own abuse of power as pastor of that… church of yours, such as the times you used your position of authority to quietly indulge your lust."

The preacher's newfound poise crumbled. He felt like he had been kicked in the crotch. He was being attacked with the very same information he had been encouraged to reveal during one of the Forgiveness Classes." But why was he feeling so flustered? He hadn't done anything immoral as pastor. Had he? Glancing at Nicki, he furiously went over his seven years as pastor.

Reverend Mathew continued. "You may have controlled your overt behavior, but you sinned in your heart repeatedly. You spoke in Jesus' name, but you did not heed your own words." He paused, as his face took on a look of compassion, again. "Roy, I am not trying to humiliate you. However, the sacredness of our Inner Sanctuary demands that the plain truth be brought to light. You were given gifts—the gift of seeing, of eloquence and persuasion— and you used them for self-glorification. It was God's mercy that removed you from your position of authority and brought you here to us so you could start cleansing yourself. However, don't just take my word for it. Just be honest with yourself." He lowered his voice and spoke with that hypnotic tone again. "Since you have joined our church, have you or have you not been reminded of your own shadowy past?"

The preacher quickly realized the question was intended to trap him. If he said "no," it would be an obvious lie. If he said "yes, but…" everyone would hear the "yes" and ignore the "but." Taking a deep breath, he carefully weighed his words before he spoke, making sure he did not start his response with "No," or "Yes, but…"

As the preacher opened his mouth to speak, Reverend Mathew waved his hand side-to-side and leisurely walked away. "You don't have to struggle to respond," he said, "your silence speaks volumes."

The preacher was feeling horribly guilty for no apparent reason. His body trembled with a fear that seemed unnatural. Setting his jaw, he took a deep breath, and the fear ignited into indignation. He was about to unleash it like a cannon shot, but the feeling quietly dissolved when he looked more deeply into Reverend Mathew's eyes. That intense look around his eyes seemed to conceal deep sadness and grief.

Reverend Mathew walked closer to the preacher. "Roy, you are being given a blessed opportunity to repent. Please take it. I implore you to heed the message, rather than attacking the messenger." Reverend Mathew paused. Many nods and uh-huh's emanated from the group.

The preacher glanced around. For a moment, he felt the loneliness of an outcast. Then, another wave of peace moved through him. He smiled and looked back at Reverend Mathew.

"Tell you what, Rev." He folded his arms and took a step toward Reverend Mathew. "I'll admit to my sins if you admit to bein' a self-righteous egotistical bastard." Leaning toward Reverend Mathew, he lowered his voice so that no one else could hear. "If you stay on your present course, you will lose everything, just as I did."

For the first time, the preacher saw a hint of fear in Reverend Mathew's eyes.

Nicki quickly stepped between the preacher and Reverend Mathew. "Roy," she said with new-found power and authority, "get out of here. You have violated this temple. And, for your information, I have decided not to visit my biological mother. This is my real family right here, and I will not allow you to attack my family with your vulgar language and angry ways."

The group applauded and cheered. A few members called out. "Yes, leave us. Leave this house."

The preacher looked around. His worst nightmare had just come to pass. Overall, it wasn't so bad. Another wave of peace flowed through him.

"You see, Roy," said Reverend Mathew, calmly, "I don't run this church. They do. "The preacher's eyebrows lifted. He remembered the many times in Hickory Ridge, when he had said, "I don't run this church. You folks do!"

He sighed. Placing his hands in his pockets, he stepped off the stage. Glancing back, he thought he detected a slight softening in Reverend Mathew's determined stare.

As he walked down the center aisle, most of the forty-five or so people in the room were gazing at him with parental compassion. A few had their eyes closed, hands up, palms facing him, sending him love.

As he approached the door, Jane stepped aside. He glanced into her eyes, expecting to see that same syrupy stare. Instead, she had a look that seemed to say, "I wish we could sit down and talk."

–13–

Four months later

The preacher sat naked on the floor of the darkened hut, along with a group of nine other men. His arms were wrapped around his knees, as the hot steam swirled around him. He couldn't decide whether he was more bothered by the steam or the ridiculous conversations. Dripping sweat, he grimaced when the old man sitting on the other side of the hut took another scoopful of water from a bucket.

The water pouring from the scoop hissed and bubbled as it washed over the hot rocks that filled the pit at the center of floor. Another wave of hot steam enveloped the preacher's body. He sighed, irritated that he let Debby talk him into doing this silly thing.

The steam burned his nostrils with every in breath. He wished he could stop breathing for a while. Closing his eyes, he lowered his head, hoping to make the heat more tolerable. It seemed to work. This wasn't so bad now! He figured he would just sit like that for the remainder of the session; maybe take a snooze for himself.

The old man poured more water on the rocks, sending another wave of steam through the hut. The preacher let his head drop down to his chest. Suddenly, his head started spinning and the voices in the hut became echoey.

As he attempted to wiggle his torso to get more comfortable, he realized that he no longer felt his buttocks on the ground. Nor did he feel the hot steam against his skin. The voices of the other men? Gone.

Opening his eyes, he saw that his body was still in a seated position with his arms around his knees. However, with his head still down, he could not help but notice that his testicles were no longer safely parked on his folded-up beach towel on the ground, but were suspended over a pastel violet abyss. Looking around, he saw the same violet in all directions.

He figured he was dreaming. He felt wide-awake, but, obviously, he couldn't be awake. Things like this don't happen when you're awake. So, obviously, he was dreaming.

Or…maybe… all those years on Earth, he was actually dreaming all along, and only thought that he was awake; and now he really *was* awake and wondering if he was dreaming. Either way, he was okay with it.

He recalled a phrase that Debby used a few times: *Infinite Void.* He nodded. Yes, this was the infinite void… or some such thing. Frankly, he couldn't understand why Debby made such a fuss about it. There was no horizon to speak of, and everything was the same in all directions, whether you looked very close or very far. Rather bland.

Debby said that if you enter the infinite void (and don't go crazy or vaporize in the process) you can do anything and go anywhere. It is the realm of infinite possibilities. The trick is to dip into the void while still maintaining some sort of time-sense. Looking around again, the preacher knew (though he didn't know how he knew) that he could do exactly what Debby said.

The more he floated in the pastel violet stuff, the more he liked it. Bland, yes, but it was a nice sort of bland. In fact, maybe "bland" wasn't quite right. No, definitely not bland. It was more like an easy and continuous orgasm that made everything okay. He glanced down at his body. It was translucent and violet, pretty much like his surroundings. Funny, he hadn't noticed that before.

Infinite possibilities! Creating anything you want! Interesting concept. He considered his life on…where was it again? Oh yes, Earth. He contemplated the changes he might like to make. He thought about what he would like to do and what he would like to have. He searched for his deepest desire. Try as he might, however, he couldn't come up with anything. Everything was just fine, as far as he could tell.

He looked down at his body again. It seemed even more translucent now. Maybe he would just go back to… Earth. What had he been doing? Oh, yes, the sweat lodge. He figured he could just go back to the lodge and hang out for a while. That seemed fine. Or, he could just continue to float in the infinite void, which obviously meant that Preacher Roy would be no more. That was fine too.

He was calmly watching his personality and memories dissolve forever into the void, when a tunnel appeared directly ahead, about ten feet… or maybe ten miles. The opening was black and roundish, sort of like the entrance of a small coal mine, except the interior had a kind of vortex flavor to it.

Next to the tunnel was the petite figure of Mrs. Bailey.

He was about to wave hello, but she spoke first. "This is no time to get drunk," she said, pointing to the entrance. "Go on in and get to work."

"Work?" he said, as an invisible force pulled him into the tunnel. "Oh, yes! I remember work. What a peculiar concept."

He drifted leisurely though the blackish vortex. Soft and pleasant music, the sort that is played in elevators, emanated from the walls of the tunnel. It seemed like the music was gently propelling him along.

When he emerged on the other side, he found himself standing by the doorway of a bedroom. The change in scenery was very abrupt. He felt a little wobbly and his vision was wavy, as if he were under water.

At the far end of the room, he saw the darkened figure of a young woman with long auburn hair, sitting at a desk. In spite of the blurriness, he could tell the woman was deeply troubled. A storm of emotions swirling around her—heavy clouds of dingy gray, muddy green, dirty dark blue, and deep blood red, mingling with one another with no clear boundaries between them; some parts clashing as in a turbulent whirlpool, while others seemed stagnant and covered with a greasy brown scum.

Part of the problem was obvious. She was surrounded by a gang of demented spooks that were firing a barrage of ridiculous commands and accusations in her direction. As the preacher approached her desk, they quieted down. He silently suggested that she write a letter to compose herself.

She seemed to hear him. Picking up a pen, she commenced writing. Sure enough, the emotional turbulence around her subsided a bit.

Instinctively, the preacher said a prayer on her behalf. The swirling colors around her became clearer and brighter. The turbulent areas settled down even more, while the stagnant areas started moving.

As she continued writing, her thoughts took shape as clearly defined geometric forms dancing about her head—spheres, polygons, and lots of three-sided pyramids. The preacher prayed continuously until she completed the letter and sat back in her chair. She looked more settled, but exhausted and still deeply troubled.

As he completed his prayer and moved a little closer to her, the demented spooks that the preacher had been holding at bay with his presence suddenly started threatening him. He gave them a stern look and they all left.

The preacher placed a hand gently on her shoulder. "Lie down and rest a while," he said silently, "you'll feel better."

The preacher watched the woman as she drifted off to sleep. She was quite beautiful. He was wondering what else he could do to help her, when he suddenly found himself back in the tunnel that played elevator music.

When he emerged on the other side, he was once again floating in a pastel violet void, apparently the same one as before, although all infinite voids were pretty much alike, as far as he knew.

Without warning, the pastel violet faded to black. Then, he felt his naked rear end and feet on the beach towel, and the heat and steam all around him.

Eyes closed, he was vaguely aware of having had a bizarre dream, but could not recall any specific images. When he opened his eyes, the old man was looking right at him. "Is he upset with me because I took a nap," he wondered.

Taking a deep breath, the preacher looked around. He noted that the other men seemed to be taking the heat pretty well. Or, maybe they were just too embarrassed to admit that they couldn't take the heat. Debby was undoubtedly enjoying it in the women's sweat lodge. She probably did this sort of thing on a regular basis.

"...The really advanced ones communicate through music," said the crazy-eyed young man on the other side of the hut. "It came to me in a vision during the last sweat lodge."

The preacher rolled his eyes. That weirdo was talking about aliens again. No wonder he was excommunicated from the Mormon Church.

"Actually," continued the young man, "music isn't even the right word for it. It's just the closest thing in our reality that describes *their* reality. In fact, like music, their technology has a component that is mathematically precise and another component that defies description."

The preacher rubbed the back of his neck. How did such a diverse group of men come together like this, he wondered. Maybe they all had wives or girl-friends, like Debby, who dragged them to strange places. Although, he figured the man sitting to his right didn't have a wife or a girlfriend. The preacher felt a little queasy about sitting naked next to him.

Taking an inventory, the preacher noted that the group included an atheist from Australia, an excommunicated Mormon who claimed to talk to aliens, a voodoo enthusiast from Haiti, and several others. All of them seemed to have a lot to say, most of which made no sense. The exception was the old man, who sat quietly with his arms around his knees.

"They do have some similarities to us," continued the young man, "otherwise, they would not be here. Some are playful; others take themselves very seriously... just like us. The most advanced ones are totally benign. Their technology is so far beyond ours, we can't even call it technology."

The preacher glanced around. The men in the hut seemed to be getting bored.

"In our terms," continued the young man, "their behavior is whimsical and childish. But they basically prefer to stay in the background and enjoy the show without being detected. The only way we learn about them is when some ridicu-lously sensitive individual runs into them and pulls them into our drama."

The preacher yawned. Others followed. He wondered why the old man didn't just put a stop to it.

"And another thing," continued the young man. "From our standpoint, the communication among themselves is sexual."

The men in the hut suddenly became very attentive.

"It looks like they communicate with each other by giving each other highly organized orgasms," continued the young man.

The young man paused. The men seemed very interested now, but confused, expect for the old man, who smiled, ever so slightly.

"But it's not sexual, really," said the young man. "That's just how we would experience it if we tried to communicate on their level. Most people would freak out. To visit their world and hang out with them, we have to be totally free of all our sexual hang-ups."

No one commented. However, since everyone was obviously attentive, the young man continued. "When they do get very involved in our world, they are so powerful, they are likely to change the course of history because they have the capacity to manipulate time, space, and matter. I think that some of the stories about prophets, saints, and gods are based on encounters with these particular aliens. And, calling them "aliens" may not even be accurate," he chuckled. "This is where the line between natural and supernatural gets really fuzzy. And distinctions like 'here and there' go out the window."

"So, what do these highly advanced, horny aliens want from us?" asked the atheist from Australia.

Quiet laughter from the other men.

"Nothing, really. They're basically just playing—at least, that's what it would look like to us. The only reason that they're here is because we call them without realizing it. In particular, they respond to deep sincerity. It has a vibration that pulls them in like a magnet. There's just something about the vibration of deep sincerity, as expressed by humans, that resonates with their own evolutionary history—except that they really don't have a history in our sense of the word, because they exist outside of regular time. But somehow, in some inexplicable way, we are related to them.

"The coolest thing about them is that they can change physical reality like a musician changes the pitch on a violin. It's really wild. In fact, we might even say that their very nature is musical."

"I think that music is basically what all of us really are on a soul level," said the man of questionable sexual orientation who sat next to the preacher. "We are the music and God is the musician," he continued, with a funny inflection in his voice that made the preacher even more uncomfortable. The preacher discreetly inched away from him.

"Well," said the atheist, "if any of this is true, my vote is that all these aliens, good and bad, get off our planet and leave us the 'ell alone, so we can get on with our lives without their bloody interference."

The preacher smiled. Finally, someone finally had said something sensible. He was even more pleased when someone changed the subject from extraterrestrials to world politics.

The preacher's mind drifted. After eight months on the west coast, he was mostly unimpressed and was about ready to return to Hickory Ridge. The past month, however, had been more enjoyable, primarily because he had met Debby. He wasn't looking forward to saying good-bye to her. Maybe he would extend his trip one more month. No, the cost of living out here was higher than he expected. He did not want to look for another temporary job, and he was tired of living at the YMCA.

Turning his attention back to the sweat lodge, he noticed that the political discussion had become rather heated. He glanced at the old man, who remained quiet. He seemed like a level-headed fellow. Level-headed? If he was level-headed, why was he taking part in this foolishness? What was his name, again? He hadn't really introduced himself, even though he was clearly in charge. Debby had mentioned his name a few times. Oh yes, she called him Jake. Jacob Clear-Water. Strange name. Probably wasn't even his real name. He probably made it up to project some sort of image. Remembering Reverend Mathew, the preacher's eyes narrowed as he studied Jacob Clear-Water.

The men in the hut continued debating world politics. They frequently glanced at the old man, apparently waiting for him to comment, but he remained silent.

Finally, the old man slowly threw several scoopfuls of water on the hot rocks, and the men quieted down for good. After the steam and heat subsided, the old man looked down at the smoldering rocks. "If you take away a person's dignity," he said in a soft voice, "if you take away his home, his freedom to come and go, and his right to govern himself, what do you get?"

The preacher's stomach knotted up as he remembered his ex-wife.

"A very dangerous animal," said the old man, still looking at the rocks.

The men remained quiet. The old man looked around. "Does anyone have any *personal* stories to tell?" he said softly.

The men looked at each other. No one responded. The old man resumed gazing at the hot rocks, apparently content to sit in silence.

The preacher looked around. "Well, then," he said, "does anybody know any good jokes?"

The men looked at him like he had just belched at a formal dinner. Jacob Clear-Water slowly picked up his head and looked at the preacher, maintaining a steady poker face. Then, he burst out laughing.

The other men joined in. They spent the remainder of their time in the hut telling jokes.

As they crawled out into the night air and rinsed off under the outdoor showers, the preacher felt surprisingly invigorated, yet calm and relaxed. Maybe the sweat lodge wasn't such a dumb idea after all.

He dried himself with his large beach towel and stretched his arms, vaguely remembering the tunnel dream. From behind the tall bushes, he could hear the women laughing and screaming as they took their cold showers. He recognized Debby's voice.

As the preacher looked up at the star-dotted sky, he realized that he had been on the West Coast almost ten months, and he still had not seen the redwood trees. He decided to stay another month after all.

–14–

Seven months later

"First and foremost, you must remember to smile!" The tall, well-dressed gentleman paused and took a sip of water. As he tipped the glass up, the stage lights glistened off his neatly combed, silvery black hair. "The smile is inviting," he said placing the glass down on the small table next to the podium, "and encourages the customers to converse with you, and they will be more likely to make a purchase. But make sure your smile is genuine; otherwise, it will backfire."

The preacher, who sat in the last row, suppressed a yawn as he discreetly looked at his wristwatch. He hoped that no one would ask questions so that Mr. Langley would finish his talk and allow everyone to go home early.

"Look into the customers' eyes," continued Mr. Langley. "The eyes give you information you need to encourage a sale. This is particularly important with high-priced items such as jewelry and large appliances, because the customers want to be reassured that they are making the right decision. Another key principle is to avoid talking about yourself excessively..."

Mr. Langley smiled and brought his hands together. "Any questions?" The people looked around at each other. No hands were raised.

"Well," said Mr. Langley, glancing at his wristwatch, "looks like we might finish early this evening. Let's take a quick recess, and then we'll wrap things up and go home."

The forty people who filled the conference room rose up almost in unison out of their chairs and started drifting about the room. A few went straight to Mr. Langley and struck up a conversation with him.

The preacher walked slowly to the window to get some fresh air. He gazed down at the city lights, the traffic below, and the Golden Gate Bridge in the distance.

He enjoyed selling shoes, and he was more than happy with his salary. But these monthly meetings were useless. Furthermore, the sales strategies were hauntingly similar to what he used to do as pastor of the church.

He did try to show some interest in Mr. Langley's teachings. However, the preacher's impatience was beginning to show through. And, the feeling seemed to be mutual.

The preacher had wondered why he had not been fired, until Debby told him that shoe sales had increased noticeably in the six months he had been working there. He looked back at the small crowd of sales people around Mr. Langley. Mostly females. Women seemed to get along with him.

The preacher shook his head slowly when he remembered a rumor that Mr. Langley had an affair with his former secretary, who was barely twenty-one. In all fairness to Mr. Langley, his former secretary was sexy enough to induce an erection on a eunuch, but that was no excuse.

Of course, Mr. Langley's private life was nobody's business. The preacher was just irritated that Mr. Langley went out of his way to look polished and proper, when he was obviously just a lecherous old goat. He did pay the sales staff well, which explained why they put up with the military-like atmosphere and these ridiculous sales meetings.

As the preacher walked slowly toward the rest room, he looked briefly at Debby who was conversing with Mr. Langley.

"He's a good man," she had once said. "He just needs to lighten up a little."

The preacher's attention shifted to Debby. With each passing day, he felt as if a web of confinement was being woven around him.

He glanced at her again as he pushed open the door to the restroom. Maybe it was time to move on.

As he stood in front of the urinal, he thought about how he might gently let go of Debby. The fact that they both worked in the same store made it tricky. And, the fact that he lived in the house of Debby's best friend made it even trickier.

His train of thought was broken when Mr. Langley walked briskly into the restroom. For the first time, the preacher noticed that the restroom had only two urinals. And the sit-down toilet was occupied.

Mr. Langley's hesitation was barely perceptible. He walked to the urinal next to the preacher.

"Mr. Langley," the preacher nodded cordially.

"Roy," Mr. Langley nodded back.

The two men stared straight ahead at the wall in front of their noses. The only sound was the hushed splattering of urine against porcelain.

The preacher contracted his belly to empty his bladder more quickly. He zipped up and walked out of the restroom, being careful not to appear that he was in a hurry.

The sales staff was still settling down in their seats when Mr. Langley stepped up to the podium and began speaking. "In summary, be mindful of the basics. Remember, this is an upscale store. Our customers expect the best. Be well-dressed and well-groomed from opening to closing. Keep your shirts tucked in, jackets on, ties straight. Be courteous and use proper English; avoid the use of colloquialisms, such as 'ain't.'"

Mr. Langley looked to the back of the room where the preacher was the last to settle down in his chair.

"And, of course, always be hygienic," continued Mr. Langley as he leaned his elbow on the podium. "Where *I* come from, we were taught to wash our hands after using the restroom. What do you say, Roy?"

The preacher felt his stomach contract. His face flushed with embarrassment. He figured Mr. Langley would get nasty eventually, but he wasn't expecting it so soon—and in front of the entire sales staff, no less!

Suddenly, the preacher remembered the joke Jacob Clear-Water told in the sweat lodge, four months ago. It was an old joke. He was surprised that Mr. Langley walked right into it. The preacher relaxed into his chair and delivered the punch line: "With all due respect, sir," he said with a smile, "where *I* come from, we are taught not to piss on our hands."

<h2 style="text-align:center">–15–</h2>

The preacher thumbed through Webster's pocket dictionary, looking for the definition of *troglodyte*. It wasn't easy because he wasn't quite sure how to spell it. Unable to find the word, he tossed the dictionary on the pile of scattered papers that covered the table. Sitting back in his chair, he stretched and yawned, extending one arm out the opened window.

He picked up the glass of orange juice from the table and took a sip, slurping it just a bit, as he gazed out the window at the expansive lawn surrounding the house. Beyond the row of tall bushes and sycamore trees at the edge of the yard, he heard the last of the morning traffic.

Placing the glass back on the table next to the empty cereal bowl, he pushed the dictionary aside and dug through the pile of papers, until he found the letter he had received from Mahmoud. He held it by the window and read it again:

Dear Mr. Dobbs,

How you doing? When you come home? Everybody ask about you. We doing good. My son grow fast. Tomorrow, I take him fishing for first time at Possum Lake. He is excited. Elimma pregnant two months. She say hello.

Business was slow but now a little better because funny thing happen. Your friend, Mr. Hamlin, needed work on truck but had no money, so he gave me chicken parts from his chickens that walk around free and did not eat bad chemicals. Then, he ask me if I want to sell them and split profit. I still have big deep freezer that I found in junkyard. I put it in garage and put chickens in it. All my customers buy them, even those who have their own chickens, because they are fresh and cheap and already cleaned. They very popular. Other people besides customers come to buy chickens, and then they come back to fix cars.

Last month, something else funny happen. Mr. Dole bring old tractor. It was sitting broke long time. I took it apart and put it together. I got a book on tractors and study it. I learned much about tractors, but I could not get it to start. Finally, Timmy say, "Gas sitting in tank long time. Maybe gas go bad?" So, he took out old gas and put in new gas, and tractor start, no problem. I call Mr. Dole. I say, "Timmy fix tractor." He say, "Good, what was wrong with it?" I say, "It had bad gas." We all had good laugh.

Fruit trees getting big and garden is most excellent. We have more apples, peaches, and plums than we can eat. We sell some of them, and we dry some of them. Some customers like to go to orchard and pick fruit while car is being fixed. But goat is not making as much milk as before. We don't know why...

The preacher smiled as he read the rest of the letter. He placed it back on the table and dug through the pile of papers until he found a pen and large yellow writing pad. With his forearm, he cleared off part of the table, pushing some papers and pamphlets to the floor. He gazed out the window for a moment and then began writing.

Dear Mahmoud,

Give your goat alfalfa. That should increase milk production. Alfalfa tends to be expensive, so shop around for a good price in the Farmer's Market Bulletin. You may want to think about growing your own next year.

Sorry for not staying in touch. My life has taken a few peculiar turns. Up until last night, I had a job selling shoes at a fancy department store. But, the owner suggested that I might be happier working on a pig farm. I agreed with him in principle and respectfully added that although a pig farm would be quite a step up, my experience in his store gave me excellent preparation for such a move.

The preacher stopped writing when he heard a knock.

"Door's open."

A young lady in blue jeans, green sweatshirt, and long blond hair in a pony-tail stuck her head in the doorway. "Good morning, Reverend Dobbs, venerable man of the cloth!"

"Hi, Julie. How you doin' this mornin'?"

"Terrific. I have fantastic news," she said, tugging on her sweatshirt. "But first, tell me what happened last night?"

"Last night? I guess that means you spoke with Debby this mornin'?"

"Yes," she said with a huff, throwing her eyes skyward. "I just got off the phone with her. She talked a lot but didn't say much. All I know is that you have no job and no girlfriend. How do you feel?"

"I feel fine. I wish Debby didn't take it so hard."

"She'll get over it. What happened with Mr. Langley? I hear you two got into a bit of a joust."

"Yeah, that we did. After I told him I quit, I could have just walked out, but I guess both of us wanted to make a showing while we had an audience handy."

"Did it get ugly?"

"Nah," said the preacher as he stretched. "He called me a Barbary ape and I called him a pig with an upturned pinkie."

Julie laughed out loud, as she leaned on the door frame.

"He told me that he wouldn't give me a reference," continued the preacher, "and I told him to go piss up a rope."

Julie laughed harder.

"He called me an uncivilized troglodyte—whatever that means—and I called him Emily Post with a mustache. He said I was stubborn and uncooperative and a poor team player, and I said he was a control freak who takes himself way too seriously."

"Is that all?" said Julie as her laughter trailed off. "Hardly worth mentioning."

"Actually, this mornin', I realized Debby was right. Mr. Langley ain't such a bad feller. Me and him are just too different."

"Speaking of Debby, she asked me to get the book she lent you last month."

"Sure," said the preacher. He looked around the room. "I think that's it on the dresser."

Julie walked carefully around the clothes, shoes, and boxes scattered about the floor and stopped by the cluttered dresser next to the unmade bed. She slid the book out from under a loose pile of socks and underwear.

"*The Egyptian Book of the Dead*," she said. "Deep stuff. Have you read it yet?"

"No. But if they're dead, I suspect their qualifications are limited."

"I'll return it to her when I go shopping at the store tomorrow," said Julie. "Right now, she doesn't want to come here."

"I hate to think that she's goin' to stay away from here on my account."

"It's okay. I've seen her do this before. Even though she's older than me, she can be quite immature. She gets attached real easily and then gets pushy and demanding and drives men away. Then she broods for several days, sitting in her apartment, channel-surfing and eating popcorn. In a few weeks, she'll find someone else, and she'll just regard you as a friend." The preacher stretched his arms and looked out the window. "Did you and Kevin have that little talk yet?"

"Yes," she said, jumping in the air, arms stretched out over her head. "And, it was terrific! Last night, we had a no-nonsense, heart-to-heart talk. And, do you know what he did at one o'clock this morning?"

"I wouldn't want to guess."

"He proposed to me! We are now officially engaged."

The preacher gave a bitter-sweet smile, thinking of Debby. "Congratulations."

"I figured, why not! I'm done with college. I love Kevin and he loves me. You were right; the only thing holding us back was that we were both scared. And, what you said about the ring was really helpful."

"What ring?"

"You said we don't have to be afraid of the ring around the finger as long as it doesn't become a ring in the nose."

The preacher rubbed his chin. "Oh, yeah, I did say that."

"Besides," she laughed, "Kevin said that since we have a preacher living in the house, we should stop living in sin. Which reminds me. If you're still here in June, we definitely want you to perform the ceremony."

"I'd be honored. But, I will most likely be goin' home soon."

"Well, okay. We'll miss you. Are you still going to visit Grandpa Jake today?"

"Yeah."

"Kevin and I are going too. Would you like to ride with us?"

"Sure. I was goin' to a write a letter, first."

"No problem. Kevin and I figured we'd go right after lunch."

"That sounds good to me."

"Great. See you later."

After Julie closed the door, the preacher looked down at the pad and resumed writing his letter to Mahmoud:

I almost came home about seven months ago. But while I was in a parking lot, I met a gal named Debby. She had locked herself out of her car and it was late at night, so I couldn't very well leave her there. We sort of became friends. She helped me get that job at the store by convincing the owner I was a natural born salesman. She's a pretty little thing, but a might peculiar. She told me that to get close to God, you have to quit eating meat and just eat fruits and vegetables because that makes you peaceful. But, I'll tell you, she is about as peaceful as a badger.

Not long after we met, she decided I needed to attend an American Indian ceremony. While we were there, she introduced me to an old feller named Jake. His full name is Jacob Clear-Water. He's 50% Apache and 50% You-Name-It. Him and his wife have a farm an hour south of San Francisco. I'm going there later today to help him bale up his alfalfa crop. He also used to be a Jungian analyst. I'm not sure exactly what that means, but it's some kind of psychotherapy.

Anyhow, I figure I'll be back in Hickory Ridge in about one month.

Best Regards, Roy Dobbs

–16–

Nine months later

The preacher stepped out of the elevator and into the short corridor of the penthouse. He was about to knock when he saw a sign next to the doorbell: *Door is open, please enter.* That was strange. He figured a woman living in a big city would be more careful about such things.

He opened the door and stepped into a spacious foyer furnished with a tall bookshelf, desk, water cooler, and couch. Soothing harp music played from an expensive-looking stereo next to a huge window overlooking the skyline of the city.

Lying down by the window was the biggest German shepherd he had ever seen. The dog stood up and walked toward the preacher, who decided to just wait by the door and not move.

With her huge snout, the dog sniffed up and down the preacher's pants leg and then licked his hand.

The preacher sighed and sat on the couch. The dog sat up next to him. Placing her head on the armrest, she looked up at his face. When the preacher failed to respond, a low, deep rumble emanated from the animal's closed mouth. Taking the hint, the preacher rubbed behind the dog's ears. When he tried to stop, the rumbling started again. The preacher chuckled and resumed his task.

While he was waiting, the phone rang and the answering machine clicked on, followed by a woman's voice. "Hello, Aunt Mona, this is Vera. I got your message. Thank you for inviting me to your party; I'll be there…" The preacher's ears perked a bit. The voice was sensuous, playful, and hauntingly familiar, though it had a trace of a foreign accent that he couldn't quite place. "…I probably won't have a date," the voice said, "but I fully expect that when I get there, you will introduce me to a dashing young knight. After your little pep talk, I've decided that the next man I date has to be an officer and a gentleman. I love you. Bye."

The preacher's mind drifted back to Charlotte and Hickory Ridge. He looked out the window at the blue sky and rooftops, feeling like he was a million miles from home. The door next to the couch opened, and a smiling black woman with shoulder length hair tied back in a ponytail greeted him. "Good morning," she said, with an accent that was sort of British.

"Good mornin', Ma'am."

"Sorry, I forgot to turn the volume down on the answering machine," she said, walking toward the phone. She was barefooted and wore blue jeans and a loose fitting flowery white shirt. "And you are…?"

"Roy Dobbs, Ma'am. I have an appointment with Madam Bell."

She looked at him with a puzzled look on her face. And then she burst out laughing. "Madam Bell," she howled, holding her tummy and throwing her head back, exposing her beautiful, decay-free, perfectly straight teeth. "Touché, Jake!"

Now it was the preacher's turn to be puzzled. He looked at her, as the dog sat next to him, nudging his fingers with her wet nose.

"My name *is* Mona Bell, but you can skip the 'Madam.'" Still laughing, but more in control, she looked at the dog. "Fluffy, go lie down."

The dog walked slowly to the window and lay down.

"Quite a guard dog you got there."

"She certainly is. Her bark can scare the pants off any burglar. However, she wouldn't hurt a flea. She just wants to stay close to people and get stroked… especially if she likes the person's energy." She extended her hand toward the open doorway. "This way, please."

The preacher stood up and followed her through a corridor.

"I saw your name on the appointment book two days ago," she said, "but it wasn't 'til this morning that Helena mentioned you are a friend of Jake's. No doubt he's the one who told you to address me as 'Madam Bell.'"

"Yes, ma'am," he said.

They stepped into a large oval room with lots of plants, two chairs facing a small round table, and plenty of floor space. The walls were covered with shelves filled with books. Some of them looked very old. At the far end of the room, French doors led to a large terrace with numerous plants, some of which were enclosed within a greenhouse.

Mona sat in one of the chairs and beckoned the preacher to sit in the other. "'Madam Bell', indeed," she chuckled. "That old rascal. He was teasing me from a distance."

"I don't understand."

"About thirty years ago, I was seeing Jake for counseling. That was when he had first started teaching at NYU. He used to be called Dr. Millman in those days. Did he tell you why he changed his name back to Clear-Water?"

"Well, Jake said 'Millman' was his mother's maiden name, which he used professionally."

Mona smiled mischievously. "Oh, there was more to it than that. You see, because of the counseling work I had with Jake, I decided to drop 'Madam Bell'. I was twenty-six years old, he was thirty-two. He was so inspired by my decision that he decided to drop 'Dr.. Millman'. He said, 'Mona, you put me to shame. It's time for me to stop hiding behind my mother's apron.'"

"That certainly sounds like somethin' Jake might say."

The preacher noticed a poster of a beach with palm trees. Printed on the bottom was the word *Haiti* in flowing letters.

"Is that where you're from?" he said pointing to the poster.

"Yes. Though, growing up, I spent most of my time in London."

"Oh." The preacher managed to keep a straight face as he envisioned witch-doctors and bloody sacrifices. "Jake didn't say anything about you bein'... Haitian."

"Relax," she chuckled. "I'm not going to perform voodoo on you."

The preacher felt his face blushing.

"So, you and Jake are old friends?" asked Mona.

"Not *old* friends. We've been acquainted for almost two years. And I've been livin' at his farm for the past six months."

"I visited Jake's farm four years ago," said Mona. "He was converting the hayloft into an apartment. Is that where you lived?"

"Yes, ma'am," the preacher smiled. "I helped him put in a patio while I was there."

"A patio! Does it face the mountains?"

"Yes."

"Oh, the view from up there must be gorgeous!"

"That it is."

"So, you actually worked at the farm?"

"I helped out here and there. But my regular job was at a car dealership, closer to San Francisco."

"Are Jake and Beth still together?"

"Yeah. Married and happy."

"Wonderful. That makes..." Mona silently counted off numbers on her fingers. "...ten years," she said with a sigh. "I guess the old sweetheart really has settled down."

The preacher wondered if Jake and Mona had been intimate together. Jake certainly gave no clue.

"Are you planning to live in New York?" asked Mona.

"Well, I'm not sure. That's one of the reasons I wanted to see you. And," he chuckled, "Jake said you might direct me to some places of interest."

"Oh, I'd be happy to! In fact, I'm free the rest of the day! I was hoping to go to an art fair in the Village this afternoon and meet my niece. You are welcome to join me."

The preacher's eyebrows raised. Join her? They had just met!

"But first let's get on with this session. You are a minister by profession?"

"Uh, I guess technically I still am. Two weeks ago, we had a wedding on Jake's farm for his granddaughter, Julie. I performed the service. I left there a few days after the wedding."

"So, what made you decide to come here?" Mona seemed to be looking through him.

"I'm just travelin' around, lookin' for a place to settle in for a while." The preacher's mind drifted back to Julie's wedding. He remembered Debby, who was there with yet another boyfriend. "I've been sort of confused. Jake says you're real good at seeing into things. So, what do you see?"

"I see that you are confused."

"I was hoping you could offer more than that."

"Well, for whatever it's worth, there are four stars hovering over your head forming a tetrahedron."

"A what?"

"It's a..." Mona pointed to a pink three-sided pyramid candle sitting at the edge of table. "It's like that candle. My niece, Vera, made that for me. Isn't it lovely?"

The preacher glanced briefly at the candle. "Yeah, it's right nice. And you're sayin' I got four stars shaped like that, hangin' over my head?"

"Uh-huh."

"What's it mean?"

Mona's face was expressionless for a moment. Then she resumed smiling. "Do you believe in karma?"

"Well, I've heard of it."

"I don't have much specific info on the four stars, but they're somehow helping you work through some karmic patterns."

The preacher became annoyed. He certainly wasn't paying one hundred dollars an hour to hear about this woman's hallucinations.

"So tell me, Roy, what is it exactly that you would like to get from this session?"

"I'm not sure. Like I said, I'm just confused. My life has become most peculiar."

Again, Mona seemed to be looking through him. "Usually, when there is confusion there is also emotional unrest. Do you feel emotionally unsettled about anything?"

"Yeah, I guess so. But mostly I'm just confused."

Mona was silent for a moment. "Well then, let's just talk about your confusion. What are you confused about specifically?"

"I'm not sure. Everything, I guess—life."

"That is a rather broad subject. If you're confused about life in general, one option is to stop thinking about life altogether, and just live. Just get moving, even if you don't know where you're headed. If you're confused about what to do, you probably have two or more specific courses of action that have become entangled and blurred together. To determine your course of action, simply look at each option individually."

The preacher counted them off on his fingers. "I can stay in New York. I can go back to the West Coast. Or, I can go back home to Kentucky. But heck," he said, glancing at the candle again, "seems like there's a heap of other things goin' on that I can't make heads or tails out of."

"That's all right. Just handle the basics and the other details will come on line. So, the first question is, do you seriously see yourself living in New York?"

"No." He was surprised at how quickly he responded.

"That was easy. One down, two to go."

"But I would like to stay in town a few days and see the sights," he added.

"Of course. And, I'll be happy to show you some places of interest," she smiled.

Mona had a warm and inviting smile. For the first time, the preacher also noticed that she had a pretty face and pleasant figure. She was a bit on the plump side, but it was quite becoming. Jake said she was in her mid-fifties. She didn't look it.

"Next question," said Mona. "Would you seriously consider going back to the West Coast?"

"Yeah. Jake said I can live on his farm again. And, I'm pretty sure I can get my job back at Wesley Cobb Toyota. The owner is a Kentucky boy."

"And, third question, would you seriously consider going back home to Kentucky at this time?"

The preacher stared blankly into space. "I think so."

"Good enough. You have two major options. So, what you can do, after you're done visiting here, is just get in your car and drive west. When you reach Kentucky, if the steering wheel wants to turn, just go on home. If it doesn't, just keep driving until you want to stop, or until you reach the Coast, and then, just take it from there. If you want to ponder what you're going to do before you do it, go ahead and ponder. But, in your present state, you'll probably change your mind dozens of times before you get there. So, rather than wasting energy worrying about what you are going to do, just do things and go places—and don't think or plan a whole lot."

The preacher nodded. "Seems like a simple and practical solution."

"Unfortunately most people who go to psychics aren't looking for simple and practical solutions. They want to be told they have pretty auras. They want to be told that the person they are attracted to is their soul mate. They want to be entertained and mesmerized. I used to do that quite well when I was 'Madam Bell'," she laughed, "until Jake came along and ruined my act. The real gullible clients are the ones who want to be told they've come to Earth because they're on an important divine mission to save humanity. Truth is, the world doesn't need to be saved, except from those who think they are here to save it."

The preacher shifted a bit in his seat.

"And do you know the cause of such notions?" asked Mona, as she leaned forward in her chair.

The preacher quickly shook his head, no.

"Grief!" said Mona. "These folks who want to save humanity, create a utopia, establish a new order or whatever you want to call it; these are the same folks who are so immobilized by their own frozen grief that they can't accept the simple joy of honest relationships and honest work. Your mission, Roy, if you want to call it that, is to free yourself from the morbid idea that you are part of God's elite, which is just the flip side of believing you are a worthless piece of shit."

The preacher tried not to look shocked. He did not expect to hear profanity from such a graceful looking lady who spoke the King's English.

"It doesn't really matter which side you act out," continued Mona. "Whether you fancy yourself to be divinely illumined or a worthless sinner, it makes no difference. If you have one, you have the other. Either way, it's just self-indulgence, designed to hide frozen grief—a sense of loss and desolation so vast and so deep, it seems big enough to encompass all of humanity. When you're ruled by so much frozen grief, it makes you want to save the world. It's a very common condition. That's why we have so many saviors ravaging the world."

The preacher furiously tried to come up with an intelligent comment.

"However, you can relax," continued Mona. "You are instinctively taking the right steps to melt that frozen grief, so that you won't be so confused about who you are and what you're doing, and you won't be so easily seduced by those who would try to mesmerize you with visions of grandeur."

The preacher decided not to ask the other questions he had formulated in his mind.

Mona stared in silence at the preacher. "Do you have any other issues you wish to discuss?"

He quickly shook his head, no.

Mona's eyes looked away and then looked at him again. "Did either of your parents drink when you were a child?"

The preacher hesitated. "Uh… My daddy drank some."

After another moment of silence, Mona asked, "Was he a serious, habitual drunk?"

The preacher forced himself not to raise his eyebrows. He was surprised that she asked such a blunt question, but the look in her eyes was so earnest and non-accusatory, he couldn't help but relax.

"Yes, ma'am," he sighed, "it was pretty bad."

"Your grief is understandable. It's the grief of a lost childhood. You had to spend a good bit of your early years taking care of your mother and younger brother, rather than getting on with being a child."

The preacher's eyebrows shot up before he could stop them. How did she know he had a younger brother?

"Anyway," said Mona, "there really isn't anything for me to do here. Lady Grace seems to be doing all the work for now. Just let things take their natural course. You have experienced great changes recently, external and internal. And more changes are on the way. It doesn't have to be unpleasant, though. The more you flow with what is, rather than clinging to what was, the more you will enjoy the journey."

The preacher sighed and nodded. "Okay."

"It's summer, you're in New York City. Enjoy."

Mona seemed to be looking through the preacher again. "Well, I guess we're done for today." She turned and looked at the clock on the wall. "I won't charge you for this session since it took so little time. But you *can* take me to lunch. And then, if you wish, you can come to the art fair with me."

The preacher was stunned. His mind started racing. Is she making a pass at me? Is this normal in New York City?

On the bookshelf, he noticed a picture of an older black man with his arm around Mona, with the United Nations building in the background. Is that her husband? Her father? Maybe she had loose morals. Maybe she was part of a voodoo sex-cult and was trying to lure him in. Jake had told him practically nothing about Mona, except that she was "unique." As his mind furiously tried to decipher the implications of Mona's offer to go to lunch, he found himself smiling, as he said, "Sure, I'd be honored."

–17–

Two months later

The organ music played and the choir sang melodiously in the balcony, as the preacher sat in the crowded church. His eyes were on the altar at the front of the room, where Vera stood with other worshipers who formed two single lines in front of the two priests. When it was Vera's turn, she cupped her hands together reverently in front of her chest, as the priest placed the communion wafer on her open palms. Vera placed the wafer in her mouth and performed the sign of the cross.

As she walked back to her seat, palms together between her breasts, she appeared to be in another world. She kneeled next to the preacher and went into prayerful silence. Her smooth melano skin seemed to glow with violet light.

The preacher looked around the room again, amazed that something so familiar could seem so foreign. In a funny sort of way, it was even more of a culture shock than last night's adventure. He respectfully contained a smirk as he remembered their night out at Esqualita, a gay Latin dance club and cabaret. He remembered how utterly shocked he was, and how completely cool he acted, when he discovered that the beautiful female vocalist on stage was actually a male. He continued to act cool as two half drunken men danced together on the crowded dance floor, openly expressing affection to one another. Such a bizarre sight! Even more bizarre, everyone (except for him) seemed oblivious to it.

He imagined trying to describe Esqualita to Joe Potter back at Hickory Ridge. He would first explain that it was not unusual for normal people to visit such establishments in large cities. He would further explain that the only reason *he* went to Esqualita was that one of the owners was Vera's uncle, from Peru, who provided yet another surprise for the preacher. Vera's uncle, Arturo, turned out to be a husky fellow with a calm and manly mannerism.

His attention back at the mass, the preacher turned to Vera, who was still kneeling with her eyes closed and her palms together. A look of deep tranquility and quiet ecstasy was on her face.

He could not imagine being able to describe Vera to Joe Potter. Watching Vera in her prayerful silence, he felt a bit unsettled when he realized that the barely-audible sighs and miniscule movements of her face were reminiscent of the sounds and facial movements she exhibited during sexual intercourse. In fact, the look was so similar, that he found himself getting somewhat aroused. He distracted himself by imaging that he was laughingly describing Esqualita to Joe Potter again. As he thought about Hickory Ridge, he received another one of those waves of restlessness that he had been getting lately. It was almost like a voice in his head that was saying, "It's time to go." He glanced at Vera. "But, I don't want to go," he silently replied to himself. As Vera continued to commune in silence, the preacher occupied himself by listening to his inner debate.

–18–

Early Next Morning

Drifting, drifting, no sounds, no images, no light, no darkness, just drifting, with no memory of ever not drifting, no thought of what was behind or ahead, no direction, no separate identity from the space all around, just a ripple drifting through an endless sea.

Suddenly, contraction. Limitless expansiveness condensed and focused into a single point, by the lens of time and space.

Linear movement. Accelerating. Falling. Falling from a tremendous height. Falling through a huge funnel, from a vast place to a small place far below. The pull was irresistible. He could not fight it. He did not want to fight it. He felt the impulse to descend, the yearning to condense further into solidness.

Falling faster, getting denser, heavier. The funnel became a narrow tube. He was feeling more and more like an individual, while still immersed in the last lingering memory of…

Out through the mouth of the funnel. Eyesight, vision. Something far below in the distance. Pulsating light, a beacon. Sound. He could hear now. The pulsating light was musical.

The pulsations became more and more rapid, changing into a single steady hum. A song, soft and sweet. It was alive.

No longer falling. Gliding now, drawn by the pull of the song. As the sound grew louder and closer, he slowed himself down.

He finally stopped when he felt surrounded and caressed by the angelic song. He felt his body against the mattress. The song became muffled and whispery.

A gust of wind moved through his head. He felt a gentle throbbing pressure between his eyebrows. His arms and legs seemed to sway side to side.

The cool air rushed into his nose. As he felt his heart beating slowly in his chest, he remembered who he was. Roy Dobbs. He was vaguely aware of having had weird a dream in which he was walking though a field of violet grass that was waving in the wind, as he listened to an angel sing.

Feeling the rising and falling of his belly, he remembered where he was. New York City. The angelic song was the sound of air moving in and out of Vera's nostrils, which were right next to his ear. When he finally half-opened his eyes, the outer world was not quite distinguishable from his own thoughts. He was feeling a blend of his thoughts and Vera's thoughts, with a light scattering of other people's thoughts, at first not knowing whose thoughts belonged to whom.

Eventually the boundaries solidified. What day was it? Monday. It had to be Monday because yesterday was Sunday. He knew yesterday was Sunday because he had attended his first Catholic mass. That certainly was an unusual experience. Evocative, to say the least. He wondered if that had anything to do with the dream he just had.

He gazed at the tall ceiling of Vera's loft apartment. In a matter of seconds, his eight weeks with Vera flashed through his mind. He smiled as he recalled meeting her at Mona's party. He remembered his first impression of Vera: wide-eyed, exuberant, and interested in just about everything from hiking to physics. She seemed particularly interested in something called "quantum fields." His weird dream flashed through his mind again.

During the party, she played the harp like she was making love to it. He wasn't surprised when he found out she also taught music history at City College, where she was working on her doctorate. Her musical interests spanned from early Christian hymns to Haitian voodoo drums. She was also a yoga enthusiast, which explained why she was so adept at getting her body into so many exotic positions that challenged the preacher's flexibility to the limit and demummifed his notion of innocence.

Listening to the sound of Vera's soft breathing, he felt a tingling in his groin, which drifted up his spine and became a warm glow in his chest. She had insisted that all music is the language of the soul and that all acts of creation are musical. He had heard such ideas before, but never had he been so thoroughly convinced.

She easily talked him into extending his visit another week, and another, and another. He even considered living in New York, and was starting to think of how he might earn a living. However, eventually, the feeling of restlessness began stirring inside him.

As he listened to the muffled sound of traffic in the street below, the feeling grew. Drifting back into a semi-sleep state, random images flashed through his mind. Finally, he saw an image of Mrs. Bailey smiling at him. She was wearing a long black robe with white trimming, looking somewhat like a Catholic nun. She was standing next to a freeway that ran in the direction of the setting sun.

When he awoke, the feeling of restlessness was stronger still. Opening his eyes, he stared at the clouds through the window. He figured it was time to go home. He raised himself from the bed, moving slowly so as not to disturb Vera. Walking to the window, he gazed over the Hudson River to the apartment buildings and rolling hills extending westward beyond the coast of New Jersey.

He was deep in thought when he heard the hardwood floor creaking ever so slightly under Vera's bare feet. Standing behind him, she leaned her firm naked body against his and rested her chin on his shoulder. Reaching around, she placed her hands on his broad hairy chest.

Silence.

He placed his hands over hers, caressing them.

"I have to go," he said softly.

"I know," she pouted.

–19–

As the car sped past the Virginia border and into Eastern Kentucky, the preacher yawned. The exit for Hickory Ridge was about ten minutes away. In about an hour and twenty minutes, he would be home.

His mind was flooded with the sights and sounds of Greenwich Village, SoHo, Little Italy, China Town, a sea of yellow cabs, countless museums, bridges, and unusual taverns and clubs. He remembered the smell of the subway stations, exotic restaurants with exotic names, street vendors with their hot dogs, giant pretzels, and knishes. And, the steady roar of traffic.

He still couldn't believe he let Ann talk him into going to a Shakespeare play. What was the name? Oh yes, *A Midsummer Night's Dream*. Even more surprising, he wasn't bored like he expected. In fact, he had never laughed so hard in his life.

He figured life in New York City wasn't really that wild. It just seemed that way because it was summer and because he was a guest in Mona's huge penthouse in the sky. The house would be quiet as a church for days, and then it would explode into a circus of activity: a steady stream of visiting friends, family, caterers, dignitaries, and people who had just stepped off the plane from Haiti, England, Hong Kong and so on. Tables and chairs were littered with trays of every kind of food imaginable, as people chatted, laughed, cried, and strolled through the spacious kitchen, living room, and terrace. And then, just as quickly, the house would be quiet and neat once again.

And then, there was Mona. Yes, she had remarkable abilities and, yes, her husband was an official at the U.N. But those were mere details. Her four grown children and troop of grandchildren were a testimony to Mona's boundless energy and love. He recalled how the kids would crowd around him, insisting on hearing his richly detailed stories of life in the foothills of Eastern Kentucky.

He smiled and looked dreamily into the horizon as Ann came to mind. The smile became a quiet laugh, as he remembered sitting naked next to her on her bed at midnight, as they ate corn chips and discussed Einstein's theory of relativity, time displacement, and quantum fields.

His eyes welled up a bit as he remembered their last kiss. Looking back, he marveled at the level of intimacy that he had established with Ann and Mona in just eight weeks.

As the whirlwind of images continued parading through his mind, he turned his head slightly, watching a rider on horseback just beyond a white wooden fence. Looked like a young lady training a thoroughbred.

Thoroughbred! Shaking himself awake, he realized he was well into the central part of Kentucky. Glancing at the clock on the dashboard, he sighed deeply. He had passed the exit for Hickory Ridge about an hour ago.

As he approached the next exit ramp, he had every intention of making a U-turn and driving east, but his hands refused to turn the steering wheel. Sighing deeply, he reached for the tall plastic cup of ice tea, took a big swig, and drove on.

—20—

One year later

The preacher and Tamara walked briskly side by side along the crowded street on the outskirts of Caracas, Venezuela. He started to put his arm around her shoulder, but pulled his hand away, sensing she did not want to be touched. She had been rather quiet since they stepped off the plane, though she seemed to be more talkative with the other two members of the party. He was glad to have this time alone with her.

He wondered if she was becoming dissatisfied with him. She had stopped prodding him to resurrect his career as a minister. Now he wished that she would nag him again. Not that he would do it! The two presentations he had given at her church were well received, but he did not feel comfortable about becoming more involved in her church, or any church.

They passed a sidewalk vendor, selling assorted fruit and nuts. "The dates look good," said the preacher, "would you like some?"

Tamara shook her head, no, with a smile.

"How about some walnuts?" he chuckled, "My mechanic back home says they're good for your brain."

"Maybe, on the way back," she said, as a gust of wind blew her wavy blond hair to the side.

They walked in silence for a while.

"You've been awful quiet lately," said the preacher.

"I know. I have some things on my mind... and I'm a little nervous about seeing Mother Eva."

"But you've met her once before, right?"

"Yes, but I was a seventeen-year-old. Mother Eva was a guest speaker at our church. I was nervous then about meeting her because I still felt guilty about leaving the Catholic Church. But she said it was totally okay. That's when I really made peace with my Catholic upbringing. Ever since I became an associate minister, I've been writing to her. She puts things into clear perspective for me. In case you haven't figured it out, my ulterior motive for going on this cultural exchange tour was to see Mother Eva again."

The preacher fished for something else to say. "Did you say that Mother Eva was the one who told you about that book on brain exercises?"

Tamara nodded.

"I've been doin' the exercises," said the preacher, "just like you told me to."

"Oh, good," said Tamara with a nod and a little smile. "Be careful though. Those exercises are surprisingly potent."

"Seems strange that a Catholic nun would tell you to read a book like that."

"Mother Eva is unique," said Tamara. "As I said, I *am* a little nervous about seeing her again after all these years."

The preacher tried to gently draw the conversation back to the subject of Tamara's moodiness. "So, that's why you've been so quiet?"

"I *am* nervous about seeing her."

The preacher felt that Tamara was telling the truth. Yet, he also sensed that she was concealing the truth. She could walk that tightrope quite well when she needed to."

"Have you ever been to a Catholic church?" Tamara asked quickly.

"Yeah, I once went to a Mass with Vera." The preacher inwardly kicked himself for mentioning Vera. "The folks there seemed nice enough. But I have to admit, their ceremonies seemed a little spooky to me."

"Oh, I think it's grand. As much as I love our church, there's something about those old orthodox religions that's really deep and mystical, like Catholicism and Orthodox Judaism."

Tamara seemed to relax a bit as they walked through a quieter suburban street lined with tall shade trees and paddle-cactus dotted with yellow blossoms. They turned the corner and approached the ivy-covered stone wall that surrounded the church and adjoining buildings.

"I haven't been a practicing Catholic since I was fourteen," Tamara continued, "but I still love all that pomp and circumstance," continued Tamara, "the singing priests, the incense, the candles, the hooded robes; it's so wonderfully…"

"Pagan?"

Tamara giggled and pushed the preacher away, as they walked through the gate. He was relieved to see her cheer up a little.

Tamara seemed to relax even more as they walked along the cobblestone path that led to several large stone buildings. The grounds were immaculate, and the grass and bushes neatly trimmed, but the preacher could feel the warm, inviting atmosphere that beckoned the visitor to remove shoes and socks, walk on the soft grass, and caress the fragrant flowers.

Tamara grabbed the preacher's arm. "There she is," she whispered.

A group of little girls sat in a loose circle on the grass, shaded by a huge and richly foliated tree that could have been a thousand years old. Seated among them were two nuns. One of them was a young lady. The other, who was speaking softly to the children, was a petite woman with wire-rim glasses, who looked like she was in her late sixties.

They discreetly approached the circle and stopped. Mother Eva looked up, smiled, and beckoned the two to come closer.

Tamara and the preacher sat at a respectful distance outside the circle, as Mother Eva continued to address the children in Spanish. The preacher understood some of it. He was surprised how much Spanish he had picked up from Vera.

Mother Eva directed the children's attention to the visitors and spoke some words that the preacher was able to translate into, "Honored visitors from the United States." The children waved and voiced a greeting.

As Mother Eva turned her attention back to the topic of the day, Tamara leaned toward the preacher and spoke softly. "You, know, when she visited our church years ago, she ate very little."

"So?"

"I mean very, very little. I was with her almost continuously for three days. She would sit down with us and nibble here and there just to be polite, but that was it."

"So what are you sayin'?"

"Maybe she doesn't have to eat. Maybe she gets all her nourishment directly from God. I've read about that sort of thing."

"Oh." After a moment of thought, the preacher decided not to disturb Tamara's fantasy; she might get offended and withdraw again.

They watched in silence as the group engaged in what appeared to be pleasant conversation with a scattering of questions and answers. Then, the children and two nuns closed their eyes and made the sign of the cross as they recited a brief prayer and sang a melodious tune that ended with "Amen." When they opened their eyes, Mother Eva smiled and said a few more words, after which, the children applauded and cheered, stood up and scampered off. All but one. She stood up slowly and remained standing, even after the other children had left. She looked apprehensively at the Reverend Mother.

Mother Eva tilted her head to one side and spoke to her. The child responded with a brief statement and a shrug.

After some gentle prodding from the Reverend Mother, the child spoke again, apparently asking a question, slowly and earnestly.

As the child completed her question, Tamara's eyes popped wide open. The young nun who stood close by gasped.

Seeing the young nun's reaction, the child lowered her head and contracted her chest.

The Reverend Mother's face took on a look of quiet amusement. The preacher had seen that same look on Mrs. Bailey's face a number of times, when a child in Sunday school would ask for a 'yes' or 'no' answer to a question which could not be answered with a yes or a no. The Reverend Mother motioned the child to come closer and then she put her hand on the child's shoulder. The old woman's eyes smiled through the wire rim glasses. She didn't seem to be particularly concerned about the reactions of the young nun or the two visitors. She spoke some words to the child, who then responded with a nod and a look of satisfaction.

"Amazing," Tamara said softly.

The young nun who stood by seemed to relax a bit. However, as the little girl made another lengthy statement, the nun became agitated again. Mother Eva smiled and responded.

The young nun tried to maintain a serene appearance, occasionally glancing at the two guests. When Mother Eva was finished talking, the little girl nodded. She said "Gracias, Madre Eva," and scampered away to join the other children.

The Reverend Mother stood up and looked at the two guests. "Please relax here a few more minutes," she said in fluent English, "while I attend to some business inside."

The two nuns conversed in Spanish as they walked along the cobblestone path toward the school building.

"What was that all about?" asked the preacher.

"That little girl was troubled by certain facets of scripture," said Tamara. "Apparently, she is at that tender age when she is still young enough to take things quite literally and old enough to know some of the facts of life," she laughed.

They continued watching as the two nuns walked on, their black and white robes waving gently in the breeze.

"Well, tell me, for Christ's sake!" said the preacher.

"She had two issues. The first one had to do with the birth of Jesus. The children were told that Mary was visited by the spirit of God and thus became pregnant with Jesus."

"So?"

"So, this not quite pubescent child wanted to know if the spirit of God is a penis."

The preacher whistled. He glanced at Mother Eva and the young nun, who were entering the school building.

"So how did the old gal respond?"

"She said, in so many words, 'It is true they both have to do with creation', meaning the spirit of God and the penis, 'but the male organ of reproduction has its limits, whereas the spirit of God has no limits.'"

The preacher nodded. "That was slick."

"Wait, it gets better," said Tamara excitedly, as she put her hand on the preacher's shoulder. "...You know about the communion ritual, don't you?"

"Yeah," said the preacher, happy to see Tamara being playful again.

"Well, the kids were told that when they take communion wafer, they are receiving a part of Jesus."

"So?"

"So, the question that was burning in the mind of this little girl was, 'Which part am I getting?'"

"Oh, God," the preacher groaned.

"She wanted to know if she always gets the same part, or if it changes from one Sunday to the next. And most importantly, she wanted to know if her conduct determined the quality of the part she received. She wanted to make sure she wasn't getting any yucky parts."

"Oh, mercy," said the preacher, shaking his head slowly. "How did the Reverend Mother handle that one?"

"She just pointed out that the wafer contains Jesus Christ's spirit, his love. And, she assured the child that every wafer is equally blessed."

"Simple answer to an impossible question."

"That kid is lucky," said Tamara. "If this had been in a different time and a different place, such questions would have earned corporal punishment and several hours of forced Rosaries."

"I'm surprised Mother Eva stayed so calm and pulled out such slick answers so quick. As I understand it, these nuns don't get a whole lot of sex education in their basic training."

"I think there's a logical explanation for that." Tamara looked around to make sure no one was close enough to hear. "The Reverend Mother," she whispered, "used to be a hooker."

The preacher looked left and right and then leaned toward Tamara. "A hooker?"

Tamara nodded. "That was when she was in her teens!"

The preacher looked at the school building. Through the window, he saw the Reverend Mother having a leisurely conversation with the young nun.

"So, is this one of those long epic stories?"

"No, actually, it's pretty simple. Her parents were immigrants from Italy. Very strict Catholics. But she was quite rebellious. As a teenager, when she lost both of her parents, she supported herself by doing what comes natural. Then she started doing brain exercises. Shortly after that, while she was... rendering service, the sexual sensation suddenly went beyond sex and, as far as she could tell, time and space fell away, and she went to heaven."

The preacher nodded. "I reckon that could change things a mite."

"When it was over, she returned her fee to her customer, and basically said, 'Sir, this one is on the house.'"

"And then?"

"Well, that was the last time she had sex, and the rest is history."

"I guess I can understand how a person can have a life changin' experience," said the preacher. "But how did she manage to rise so high in the church with a past like that?"

"Beats me. But the doors just opened for her, one after the other. She told me that she was secretive about her past for many years. Then she woke up one morning and sort of remembered something. Since then, she doesn't care who knows about her previous profession.

"I'll bet she has shocked a few folks."

"That she has. But she's not into shocking people. She *did* cause a ruckus about ten years ago. She was being interviewed on TV. Not only did she speak freely about her former profession, she also never bothered to condemn it."

"You mean she condoned it?"

"Oh, no. She just never actually said, 'I did a bad thing.' Some influential people in the parish wanted her to be discreetly transferred to some out-of-the-way convent—preferably, an order of silence. But it wasn't that easy. She was doing some amazing work with inner city kids. And, maybe it's a coincidence, but ever since she joined this parish, attendance has increased substantially. All this came out during the TV interview. We have the video in our library."

"So, how did the church resolve it?"

"Apparently, with great difficulty. The monsignor of the church didn't know what to do. So, he went to the bishop. And the bishop basically threw his hands in the air and called the cardinal. And the cardinal wrote a letter to the pope."

"And the big guy responded?"

"Yes. As the story goes, the pope carefully reviewed the matter and promptly settled it. He said, "Let her do whatever she wants.""

The preacher burst out laughing. "Come to think of it," he said, "I thought I saw somethin' wild and sensuous behind those granny glasses."

"Oh, stop. Don't be disrespectful."

"I'm just kiddin'. She's obviously a wise and kindly old woman. How old is she, anyhow?"

"I don't know. But from her letters, I've gathered that she was working the streets around 1930."

The preacher did some rough arithmetic in his head. "No way! She don't look a day over—"

He stopped talking when a little girl, of about ten years, ran over to them. She had long black hair down to her waist, and big dark eyes bursting with enthusiasm. Breathlessly and in broken English, she said, "Mother Eva ready. I carry you."

Tamara and the preacher looked at each other to make sure they understood the same thing. They stood simultaneously and followed the child, who talked almost continuously, explaining that she was learning how to speak English, and that the Reverend Mother let her practice on Americans who came to visit.

When they entered the little office, they were greeted by Mother Eva.

She walked from behind the desk and approached them with her arms stretched out. "Tamara, it is such a joy to see you again," she said as she gave Tamara a warm embrace.

"Mother Eva," said Tamara, "thank you for seeing us."

The preacher saw a bit of moisture on the corners of Tamara's eyes.

"Dear Tamara. I think of you and your wonderful church quite often." She stepped back. Holding both of Tamara's hands, she sighed. "My, you have grown into a beautiful and elegant young lady."

She let go of Tamara's hands and took hold of the preacher's. "And you are Reverend Roy Dobbs. I have been looking forward to meeting you."

"It's an honor to meet you, Ma'am," said the preacher, with a slight bow. For the first time, he noticed that Mother Eva bore a striking resemblance to Mrs. Bailey. Their eyes were virtually identical.

After a brief tour of the facility, they had lunch at an outdoor table with some of the children. Tamara and the Reverend Mother carried on a quiet conversation while the preacher attempted to comprehend the chatter of several little girls who crowded around him, speaking to him, for the most part simultaneously, in Spanish and very broken English.

Even as he spoke with the children, he became more and more preoccupied with the Reverend Mother's resemblance to Mrs. Bailey. He also noticed that she ate very little, giving most of the food on her plate to a couple of kittens and a puppy that stood next to her on the grass.

When lunch was over, Mother Eva suggested that the preacher relax and stroll around, while she and Tamara went inside and talked.

202 | *The Edge of Time*

The preacher walked around the courtyard, still engrossed by Mother Eva's resemblance to Mrs. Bailey. He was frequently interrupted by children who walked by and started a conversation to make him feel welcome and to practice their English.

When the two women emerged from the office, Tamara's face looked lighter. The preacher and Tamara said goodbye to the Reverend Mother. She apologized for not being able to visit with them longer, but she was expecting two other visitors from the United States soon, and had to attend to other matters first.

After they left through the gate, they walked several steps and then Tamara stopped and grabbed the preacher's arm.

"Roy," she said, "I want to get this over with right now. It's time for us to go our separate ways. For a while, I fell into the trap of trying to make you march to the beat of my drum. I should have told you that I felt we were just incompatible. Instead, I kept putting it off, hoping that things would just take care of themselves. Because of my fear of being straight with you, I made things more complicated for everyone. The truth is, I am very much attracted to our new board member, Ron Russell, and he is attracted to me. Yet, I have put him on hold, because I was afraid of having this conversation with you. In my cowardice, I have been unfair to him and to you. Roy, I hope we can still be friends. You have helped me grow so much as a minister and a person. You have generously shared your wisdom and know-how, while respecting my right to follow my own instincts..."

—21—

As Tamara and the preacher resumed walking away from the gate, they heard two women chatting in English around the corner of the stone wall. They were talking about Mother Eva, apparently.

If Tamara and the preacher had not been so preoccupied in a tense conversation, they would have paused to see who would emerge from around the corner, and perhaps converse with these two fellow U.S. tourists, who apparently were fans of Mother Eva, as well.

However, by the time Sarah Chazinov and Betty Gonzales appeared from around the corner of the stone wall and approached the gate, Tamara and the preacher had already crossed the street and disappeared behind a cluster of palm trees.

"I am so nervous," said Sarah, as the two of them walked through the gate. "I feel like I'm about to meet the Dalai Lama. Are you sure I'm not imposing on her?"

"Believe me," said Betty, "if you made it this far, she *wants* to see you."

–22–

Reverend Mathew McCann sat at his desk, leafing through attendance figures, bank statements, and bills. He felt heaviness in his chest and a constriction in his throat. To his relief, there was a knock at the door.

"Come in," he said, clearing his throat and sitting up straight.

A smiling face with long blond hair poked through the doorway. "Hey, Mat."

"Oh, hi, Jane," he said, slumping back in his chair.

"Is this a good time to talk?"

"Talk? Oh, yeah," He said rubbing his face, "I forgot."

"I have some time right now, but I'm actually pretty busy today," she said, walking in and closing the door. "And this afternoon, I have an interview at a big law firm downtown."

"Great! They would have to be crazy not to hire you."

"That depends on whether or not I pass the bar exam next week," she said, as she stepped around the desk and kissed him on the lips.

"Pass? Of course you'll pass."

"Thank you for your affirming words," she said, pulling up a chair and sitting next to him.

He looked at her in silence and then turned his eyes to the papers on his desk. "Okay, let's do this efficiently since you have a busy day. " Things have obviously changed a lot in the last couple of years."

She nodded.

"And you actually believe it's for the better?"

"Definitely." she smiled.

"Even though attendance has dropped, and the Inner Sanctuary has been disbanded?"

"Yes."

"Can you please explain it to me," he said, his hands in prayer position. "Among other things, I have been very confused lately. Answers no longer roll off my tongue. It's very humbling." He swiveled his chair and looked out the window into the back parking lot of the church; it was empty except for the dumpster and recycling bins. "You are probably the only person I would say this to…"

After staring in silence for a while at the parking lot, he turned and looked at her with his bloodshot eyes. "My faith has vanished."

Jane smiled. "I don't think so," she said, casually. "I suspect that what has really vanished is your illusion of certainty. Now that you don't have *that* as a crutch, you can start exercising genuine faith again."

"Lately, I've been wishing the church will hurry up and go bankrupt so I would have an excuse to leave San Francisco and just travel around with no responsibilities."

"And what about me?" asked Jane, placing her hands on her hips.

He swiveled his chair back around and faced her. "I guess you are the one attraction that would keep me here," he said, taking her hand and kissing it. "So, you still like it here, even though the ship is sinking and the captain is becoming unglued?"

"Absolutely. And, if the captain had not become unglued, we would not be engaged right now and I wouldn't be a member of this church. Like many others, I was becoming increasingly uneasy with the direction the church was taking."

"And I was totally blind to it."

"That's understandable. Your success caused you to lose sight of yourself. You weren't all that concerned about the members that left, because your recruiting program was keeping the church comfortably full. And like so many successful charismatic ministers, you became more and more narcissistic."

Reverend Mathew grimaced.

"The Gospel of Love," Jane continued, "gradually gave way to your version of hellfire and damnation. The Inner Sanctuary started as a gathering where people could unburden themselves, reach out to each other, and pray together. It gradually changed into a factory for turning our more impressionable members into glassy-eyed church robots who would go out and recruit new members."

Reverend Mathew rubbed his eyes with his fingertips. "Was I that bad?" he said in low hoarse voice.

Jane nodded. "We were becoming a cult, Mat."

Reverend Mathew chin dropped down to his chest as his fingers plowed through his hair. "You're not pulling any punches are you?"

"Is that what you want me to do?"

He paused. "No. I want you say what's on your mind."

"That's good," she said, smiling compassionately, "because there is something else that you need to hear."

Reverend Mathew rested his interlocked fingers across his belly. "Go on."

"Through all this, you have always been a big promoter of prayer power."

He smiled weakly, relaxing a bit.

"You have developed a reputation," she continued, "for helping people get their prayers answered."

"Yeah," he said, grinning sarcastically, but I think I'm slipping in that department too."

"The point is, you have a powerful mind. In the early days, I believe that you used your mind to call down the Holy Spirit and bring blessings and healing grace into people's lives. Later on, I think you used it unintentionally to mentally mess with people."

"What do you mean?"

"Over the years, I've noticed a pattern, of sorts. The members that you liked seemed to receive blessings, and those that you disapproved of experienced bizarre setbacks. They seemed to stumble over themselves. I know it doesn't sound rational, but it happened too many times for me to attribute it to coincidence."

Turning his chair, Reverend Mathew leaned forward and rested his arms on the papers scattered on his desk. "That phenomenon has crossed my mind," he nodded. "I thought it was just my morbid imagination."

"In one sense, it was. Imagination, morbid or otherwise, is a potent creative force—according to your own teachings."

Reverend Mathew stared at the desktop.

"Granted, we are all free individuals," continued Jane. But, you have convinced me—you have *demonstrated* to me—that we do influence one another with our minds, intentionally or not. And you, Mat, have a talent for harnessing the collective minds of the congregation."

He closed his eyes, "Correction. I *had* said talent. A powerful mind does not remain powerful for very long if it's not also a clear mind."

"Sounds like a nice topic for a future sermon," Jane smiled.

Leaning forward, he rested his forehead on his forearms. "How could I have remained so blind to myself for so long?"

"That's an easy one. You had created a nice little loop for yourself. You drew members who, like yourself, were drifting into a pattern of using the Bible to hide their pain and insecurity. You shielded them and they shielded you. In biology, that's called symbiosis."

Reverend Mathew straightened up and looked at her, feeling a lump his throat.

"You were fooled by your apparent success in uplifting people," she continued. "In the early days, that success was legitimate. Your sermons and classes touched people's hearts and changed their lives. But that same success camouflaged your gradual deviation from your original course. More and more, you fell into a pattern. You were either scaring them or drugging them with the belief that they were somehow better than the church next door."

Raising his head, he looked sadly at her for long while. "You are going to be one great attorney."

"I say yes to that prophecy," she smiled.

He looked down at the papers on his desk. "I guess I'm just reaping what I sowed. If things continue like this, we may not have a church in several months."

"Maybe. Maybe not. Either way, you will have gotten your soul back. All else will be provided." Standing up, she kissed him and walked toward the door.

"Are you sure? What if I have to go back to selling cars—"

"I said," Jane declared, turning quickly, "all else will be provided!"

"Yes, Ma'am."

After Jane closed the door behind her, Reverend Mathew sat in silence for a while. The heaviness in his chest gradually subsided. It was replaced, to his surprise, by the memory of his mother. For the first time in his adult life, he felt her presence strongly. Taking a deep breath, he bowed his head. And he wept.

–23–

The preacher sat staring at the clouds below him through the window of the jumbo-jet. He was hoping that the muffled roar of the engines would lull him to sleep. All day long, he had been doing his best to be sociable and cheerful. It was very tiring. He glanced at Tamara in the next seat, as she conversed quietly with the two young women across the aisle.

His eyelids lowered and the sky above took on a funny shade of blue, almost violet. The noises around him gave way to a deep silence. His eyes were still half open. Everything disappeared except the almost-violet sky. His sense of time dissolved.

"There's something about her that's just timeless," said Tamara. "She's practically a saint."

"Gosh," said Jill, who was closest to the aisle, "I wish I had gone with you instead of going to the beach."

"Same here," said Ruth who was sitting in the window seat across the aisle. "Has she performed miracles?"

"That's not the point," said Tamara with a touch of exasperation. "She works very discreetly. She has absolutely no need for recognition. She is just total grace."

"I think I know what you mean," said Jill, leaning toward Tamara. "When you showed me her picture, my heart just melted."

"Bingo!" said Tamara, leaning over the armrest. "That's the sort of effect she has on people. She doesn't do obvious things like make lame people walk on TV. But, I think when she prays, she very quietly melts into the infinite. I think she is the rare soul who can consciously transcend time and space and not go crazy." She poked the preacher lightly on the ribs with her elbow. "Tell them, Roy."

"Huh?"

"Oh, I'm sorry," said Tamara, placing a hand on his shoulder. "Were you sleeping?"

"Oh, no. I was just… relaxin'. What did you say?"

"Didn't Mother Eva strike you as being somewhat cosmic?"

The preacher rubbed the back of his neck. "Well… I don't know. She did seem like a kindly old woman."

The three women gave him a look that he did not quite know how to interpret, but suddenly he felt like somewhat of a Neanderthal. "What I mean is," he added, "she may very well be… cosmic. I just don't have much experience with that sort of thing."

"You don't?" asked Jill. "What about Reverend Mathew? Weren't you involved with his church?"

"Uh… yeah… for a short spell."

"He's sort of a cosmic dude himself, isn't he? I've heard he can read minds. He supposedly has the gift of prophecy."

"Yeah, I'll give him that," the preacher nodded. "And he's still an asshole."

Again, they looked at him sort of funny. "What I mean is, he has his peculiar side. And, of course, that was over two years ago. Folks do change."

After a moment of awkward silence, Tamara, turned to the other women, "Did I tell you," she said, "even though I have sat at a table with Mother Eva for breakfast, lunch, and dinner on several occasions, I have never actually seen her eat—I mean really eat…"

The preacher politely listened for a while and then turned his head toward the window and stared at the sky through half-closed eyes. When he finally managed to doze off, he dreamed that he was floating on a small violet lake. Mrs. Bailey drifted by on a wooden raft. He asked her how much longer his brain needed to be cooked. She responded, "Until cooking time is irrelevant." As she drifted on, he told her that he had just met a nun who looked just like her. "She isn't *like* me," Mrs. Bailey responded, "She *is* me."

The preacher opened his eyes. The dream made no sense at all, like everything else that was happening to him.

—24—

Back in San Francisco, the familiar sights were like a scene from another world. He felt isolated from everyone. The sounds around him were echoey and muffled.

The feeling was reminiscent of the time that Charlotte left. He felt the same empty, aching sensation in his chest and stomach and same loss of interest in just about everything. Every time the phone rang at work, he expected to hear Tamara's voice. Every time a blue Toyota drove by, he looked up to see if Tamara was driving it. Just as with Charlotte, he lost his appetite, except this time, for some reason, he had a craving for walnuts.

He was baffled by his severe emotional reaction. He and Tamara had been together only seven months, and there had been no formal commitment between them. With Charlotte, his feelings of distress were reasonable. With Tamara, however, he could not justify that sort of turmoil!

He was too embarrassed to mention it to anyone. So, he kept quiet about it and tried to shake it off, which seemed to make matters worse.

For a while, his mind returned again and again to the little quirks in his behavior that may have caused Tamara to pull away. Maybe he should have tried harder to refine himself. She had mentioned that his speech was a bit too crude for a minister. She frequently hinted that he should improve his wardrobe and keep his hair trimmed. Maybe he should have paid closer attention to little things, like not eating salads with his fingers. Maybe he should have talked about his feelings more. Maybe he shouldn't have made fun of her belief in reincarnation.

While drifting through a bookstore, he picked up Webster's unabridged dictionary and finally looked up the definition of troglodyte: "Primitive cave dweller."

He quickly lost interest in analyzing what went wrong. Instead, he just fantasized and wallowed in his pain. For days, he walked through parks and shopping malls, wandering aimlessly though China Town, and staring at the buffalo in Golden Gate Park.

While walking through Muir Woods, he wandered into Tall Tree Grove and stumbled upon a tree that was 368 feet tall, and just about 2400 years old. Surprisingly, he temporarily stopped moping and became mesmerized by it. He stared at it for a long time, until suddenly that immense span of time became real to him. He was thinking, "When Jesus Christ walked the earth, that tree was already four hundred years old." For some reason, he started to get the notion that reincarnation might have some truth in it after all.

One afternoon, while walking through a museum, his sense of time became totally scrambled. At around 3 PM, he started feeling very fatigued and had a throbbing headache, so he sat down on a bench in front of some dinosaur bones. The next thing he remembered was the PA system announcing that the museum would close in ten minutes. An hour had simply vanished in a matter of minutes.

It happened again later that same evening, when he stopped by a pub. He was there half an hour before he realized he was in one of those gay bars. It was an honest mistake; the place was filled with both men and women customers, who were just talking quietly, for the most part. There was some laughter, but it was very tame compared to Esqualita. After he noticed where he was, he became oblivious to it, just as he was oblivious to the passage of time. He just continued sitting at the end of the bar, forearms resting on the counter, staring at his glass. Eventually, he struck up a conversation with a man who had recently been dumped by his partner. They shared their respective stories over a few beers and the preacher offered some insights that the man found useful.

After the preacher left the bar and boarded a streetcar, he noticed he was feeling a little better. He figured it was the beer.

For several nights—he wasn't sure how many—he slept in motels because he did not want to return to Jake's farm. His apartment in the converted hayloft of the barn was part of the lifestyle that Tamara found objectionable, though at first she found it charming.

Furthermore, if he returned to the farm in his current state, Jake might say, "I told you so!" The preacher remembered when he had first told Jake that Tamara was the most wonderful woman he had ever met. To which the old man responded, "You're asking for trouble, Roy."

When he wasn't wandering the streets or walking through the woods, he sat in his motel room, channel surfing, and eating walnuts. He wasn't used to watching so much television. He decided it was less pleasurable than being drunk, but apparently, more effective at rendering his brain useless.

As he half-watched a nature program in which a scientist explained that certain dinosaurs did not become extinct but evolved into birds, he thought about Jake. Tossing the remote control aside, he told himself to quit being silly. Jake would not be so insensitive as to say, "I told you so," at a time like this! After all, Jake used to be a Jungian analyst.

–25–

The familiar landscape around Jake's farm seemed foreign and surreal. Walking slowly along the split-rail fence that enclosed the barnyard, he saw an older woman brushing a horse just outside the open gate.

"Hello Beth," he said in a subdued voice.

The woman turned. "Roy! Welcome home," she said, giving him a hug. "We thought that maybe you decided to stay in Venezuela. Did you just get back?"

"No, I've been back about a week... I think."

"We were becoming concerned."

"Oh, sorry." He patted the horse on the neck. "How's this young feller doin'?"

"Doing great. Hamstring is about healed. He did get a bit of thrush on his hooves from standing around in the mud so long. I've been treating it with peroxide and a little bleach. Pretty soon he'll be his old temperamental self again."

"A thoroughbred, through and through."

"You look frazzled," she said, putting her hand on his forehead. "Do you feel all right?"

"Yeah, I'm fine. Uh, is Jake around?"

"Yes. He's in the house."

"Is he busy?"

"I'm not sure. Just go on in."

Beth resumed brushing the horse, but continued looking at the preacher until he stepped through the front door of the house.

The preacher walked slowly through the corridor, stopping by the closed door of Jake's office. He was about to knock, but when he heard voices coming from inside the office, he sat on the chair next to the door and waited.

Looking around the rustic living room, he felt like he was starting to come down to Earth. He figured that talking to Jake would be helpful, even if he did say, "I told you so."

Eventually, he began catching a few words of the conversation inside the office. "...So, that's the story, Grandpa." The preacher recognized the voice of Julie's twin brother, Justin. "Whenever I think about Barbara, I feel so depressed I want to quit grad school. It's not like I'm so in love with her. I just feel confused, betrayed, and I don't know what else. What do you recommend?"

"Go to San Francisco," said Jake without hesitation, "and thoroughly explore the red-light district."

"Huh?"

"Let your imagination run wild. Check out every pleasure house and strip joint that catches your eye..."

For the first time in seven days, the preacher stopped thinking about Tamara. He leaned a bit closer toward the door.

"Go into those exotic stores and explore every nook and cranny," continued Jake. "Buy all the props, sex toys, erotic magazines, and videos that look interesting to you. Get yourself one of those blow-up dolls, if that strikes your fancy. Then, check into a motel and have at it. Touch yourself all over and stimulate yourself in whatever way you feel like. If you feel so inclined, call one of those exotic escort services and have one or more of their agents come to your room and perform any act that you're curious about. You don't have to be embarrassed, that's what they're paid for."

The preacher wondered if this was the sort of advice that was generally given by a Jungian analyst.

"Grandpa," said Justin in a well-controlled tone, "are you serious?"

There was no response, so the preacher assumed that Jake was nodding silently.

"And eat lots of ice cream," said Jake. "You like ice cream, don't you?"

"I love it. But it gives me mucus."

"Screw the mucus. Eat all the ice cream you want."

"I guess I should also smoke some weed, right."

"That's up to you. Personally, I don't think much of psychotropics. But, if you decide to go that route, let me know, and I will send you to a grower of pure and potent stuff."

"When did you decide to ascribe to the hedonistic formula?"

"I don't have any formulas," said Jake. "If another person walks through that door with a similar problem, I'm just as likely to tell him to go into a cave, pray, fast, read the Bible, and practice celibacy."

Silence.

"So, you're pretty sure this is what I need to do?" asked Justin.

"No, I'm not sure. You asked me for my recommendation. Now your job is to use it or not use it as you see fit."

Justin gave an insane little laugh. "So, let's say I do this thing. Then what?"

"Again, I don't know. But I suspect that such an experience will blow away enough cobwebs from your brain to allow you to see things from a fresh perspective. Breaking through restrictions in one area can inspire you to see new possibilities in other areas."

Justin gave another insane little laugh. "So, let me understand this. You're telling me to do every nutty and exotic thing I feel like doing? No limits?"

"Son, we are on planet Earth. Of course there are limits; and every limit you exceed has consequences. Take reasonable precautions and use common sense. And don't hurt anyone. If you can't experience freedom within those limits, then go find yourself a cave."

"What is Mom going to say?"

"Leave your mom out of this. She's already done her job."

"But if I do this, I may have to dip into my tuition money, which ultimately comes out of her pocket."

No comment from Jake.

"I am still totally shocked," continued Justin. "I mean, I'm shocked that Barbara just dumped me for that slime-ball in the research department. I was clueless."

Jake remained silent.

"I have been trying and trying to figure this out," continued Justin. "Did *you* have any idea this was going to happen?"

"It was plain as day," said Jake softly.

"So why didn't you warn me?"

"I would have, if I thought it might do some good. But you would have just gotten angry with me. And besides, sometimes, if you know what's coming, you don't learn what you're supposed to learn, and you end up repeating the lesson."

"I definitely do not want to repeat this lesson," Justin laughed sarcastically.

"In that case, you might want to know that there are two main reasons people repeat their mistakes."

Jake paused, apparently to make sure he had his grandson's full attention.

"Well, tell me, tell me!"

"Firstly, they overanalyze and browbeat themselves and get all twisted inside. They lose perspective."

"You mean, if I overanalyze and browbeat myself, I'll just make the same mistake again?"

"More than likely. And actually, in this particular case, I wouldn't even call it a mistake. This thing happened simply because it's part of the education you need. Eventually, you'll see that."

"Okay. So, how do I stop over analyzing and browbeating myself?"

"The red light district," responded Jake.

They both laughed.

"You said there were *two* reasons people repeat their mistakes," said Justin. "What's the second reason?"

"It's essentially the opposite of the first reason. That's when people simply don't take the time to honestly look at what they did. They just sort of wallow in their misery and space out..."

As Jake and his grandson continued to converse quietly, the preacher's mind drifted back to Tamara and the events of the previous week. Half closing his eyes, his mind was filled with images of Tamara's church, Venezuela, and Mother Eva. Then, his mind drifted to Hickory Ridge, his failed ministry, and failed marriage.

Hearing footsteps inside the office, he realized that he was still leaning toward the door. He quickly straightened up just as the doorknob started turning.

When Justin stepped out, the preacher was looking out the window at the huge vegetable garden, where three students from the university were taking their autumn soil samples.

"Hi, Roy!"

The preacher turned his head toward the tall skinny young man. "Hi, Justin."

"You're finally back from South America."

"Yeah." said the preacher standing with a groan. "For the most part. How's your thesis coming along?"

"Not too good." He shook his head and looked down at his shoes. His sunken cheeks looked more sunken than usual.

"A smart feller like you? Why?"

"Relationship crap, for one thing. And maybe I skipped too many grades for my own good." He scratched the side of his head and walked on. "I'll talk to you later."

The preacher walked into the office as Jake called out to someone outside the window. "No, no, the herb walk is next Wednesday. Eight A.M., sharp."

"Hello, Jake."

The old man turned. His face was weather-beaten, but virtually free of wrinkles. His long salt-and-pepper hair was tied back in a ponytail.

"Roy," he chuckled. "Where the hell have you been?"

"I think 'hell' describes it pretty well."

"Oh?"

"I think it's time for me to head back home."

The old man studied the preacher's face. "Tamara?" he said softly.

The preacher nodded, as he braced himself for the "I told you so."

Jake put his hands in the pockets of his denim overalls. "Let's go for a walk."

—26—

They strolled along the river, the brisk autumn wind swirling about. The preacher sighed. "How are Julie and Kevin doin'?"

"Happy as can be. You really straightened those kids out. I'm grateful."

The preacher shrugged. "It was nothin'."

"False modesty. Arrogance in disguise."

"Oh. Sorry." His mind drifted back to Tamara. "Jake, I just don't care about anything anymore."

"A broken relationship can do that to you."

"It's not just Tamara. It's everything. It seems like ages ago that I started out like a tornado, ready to conquer the world. Now, I feel like an old ship that's been battered by a thousand storms. I feel beat up and worn out and I just want to go home."

"You're way too young to be old and worn out. It'll pass."

"I don't think so. Nothin' interests me anymore. I have no ambition. I don't even want to get up in the mornin'.' I think I'll just live out the rest of my days in my cabin in the hollers. I'll go fishin', tend my garden, and set on the front porch in the rockin' chair, thinkin' about all the things I wanted to do that I didn't do."

"As I said, a broken relationship can make you feel that way."

The preacher shrugged. "Well, maybe I'm just not fit to be in a relationship."

"No man is. That's why women like us so much."

The preacher forced a smile. He sighed and looked up at the clouds. "I just don't understand what's happenin'."

"What's happening is that you're in love and it hurts like hell."

"But she doesn't want me. And she's already hooked up with another feller."

"That's why it hurts like hell."

"But, it's not like we were married or engaged or anything. We were just hangin' out together. I don't understand why I'm takin' it so hard."

"Well… I told you so."

The preacher shot a quick sideways glance at Jake.

"How did you two happen to meet, anyway?" asked Jake.

"You mean I never told you?"

"I don't think so."

"Well, it was the durndest thing. It was about a month after I got back from New York. I was drivin' on the interstate and I saw her standin' next to an old Toyota on the side of the road. I stopped to give her a hand. The clutch was limp, so I looked under the hood, and sure enough, the clutch reservoir was bone-dry. So, I replenished it with a little fluid from the master cylinder and told her to get herself some DOT-three brake fluid when she got the chance. That would have been the end of it, except that I ran into her again a half-hour later at a rest stop. I noticed her hood was up, so I walked over. Bad solenoid this time. I started her car by hot-wirin' it, but the engine light stayed on, so I followed her to her mechanic to make sure she got there all right. It's a good thing I did. That bozo wanted to replace the carburetor! I had a strong hunch there was nothin' wrong with the carburetor. So, I told her to follow me to Wesley Cobb Toyota, and I took care of it myself in the service department. Sure enough, the plugs were shot and the car was overdue for a tune-up. And, both the oxygen sensor and the throttle position sensor needed to be replaced; that's why the engine light stayed on." The preacher sighed. "By the time I was done, it was dinner time, so she took me out to eat. At first, she just seemed like your typical attractive lady. But as I got to know her, God!"

"She's a fine woman, but you two were just wrong for each other. A blind man could have seen it."

The preacher shot another quick glance at Jake.

"It's not that she's a snob or anything," continued Jake. "But she's obviously not the sort of woman who would be happy with a man who lives in a barn."

The preacher stared at the ground as they walked on. Slowly lifting his eyes, he looked at Jake. "I don't live in a barn!"

He waited for Jake to respond, but the old man remained silent.

"Well," the preacher continued, "I guess, technically, I do. But it's a clean and cozy apartment. It just happens to be a converted hayloft of a barn. You make it sound like I live in one of the stalls with the horses."

"That's probably what it sounds like when she talks about you to her friends."

The preacher scratched his unshaven jaw. They walked in silence.

"I feel like I've been bewitched. Do you think such a thing is possible?"

"That's not for me to say. But in order for a man to fall under someone else's spell, he must first fall under the spell of his own self-deception."

The preacher tightened his jaw, feeling another surge of anger. He tried to shrug it off. "Yeah, maybe you're right. It just seemed like there was somethin' special about her. Seemed like she had a beauty that was timeless."

"You once said the same thing about Mrs. Bailey. I don't see you moaning over her."

The preacher flinched inwardly, irritated that Jake was being so abrasive, making light of his problem.

"The difference," continued Jake, "is that Tamara has a pretty face and nicely shaped body. With that sort of packaging, timeless beauty can be a real pain in the butt."

The preacher's irritation gave way to a soft chuckle. "Tamara says that we were drawn to each other because we were married in a past life."

"Would that make any difference?"

"I guess not. But it does give me a good excuse for makin' such a durn fool of myself."

"True. Past lives are useful that way."

As they walked in silence, the preacher felt himself sinking back into despair.

"You know," said Jake, "many years ago, I had romantic feelings toward Mona."

The preacher lifted his head. "I've been meanin' to ask you about that. Did you two ever…"

Jake smiled. "I was greatly tempted and she was definitely willing. At the time, I had been divorced for about a year, and she was recently divorced, herself. However, she was my client—had been for several years. And, experience had taught me to abide by a strict policy."

"What's that?"

"Keep your dick out of your cash register."

The preacher nodded.

"I figured I would just refer her to one of my colleagues. But after Mona and I both put our cards on the table, I discovered that I was attracted to her because she reminded me of my mother. And she discovered that she was attracted to me because I reminded her of her husband."

The preacher nodded pensively. He waited for Jake to continue, but the old man remained silent.

"So what happened?" asked the preacher, with a bit of urgency in his voice. "Well, she came to the realization that she loved her husband after all. So, they worked things out and got together again. And, of course, I eventually met Beth."

The preacher nodded and smiled, feeling a wave of satisfaction, as they continued walking in silence.

"Seems like women have always been my downfall," the preacher sighed.

"Women will always be your downfall as long as you behave like an immature teenager. When you act like a grown man, the woman will no longer be your downfall. She'll be your partner and friend."

"Thanks, I feel better now," the preacher said sarcastically.

Jake laughed. "You best get off your high horse, or you're just going to get thrown again."

The preacher reached for a branch.

"Don't touch those leaves, Roy."

"Isn't this edible staghorn sumac?"

"No, it's inedible poison sumac."

They slowed their pace as they approached a section of the river that contained rapidly flowing whitewater.

"Damn it, you're right, Jake. Tamara and me just weren't right for each other. I was tryin' to put a square peg in a round hole."

"Worse. Putting a square peg in a round hole is merely difficult. What you tried to do was more like putting a square peg through solid rock."

The preacher tightened his jaw. He didn't think that he and Tamara were *that* mismatched. He sighed and tried to shake it off as he looked at the rushing water.

"Relationships are just too damned complicated."

"No they're not," said Jake casually. "Roy, you simply have to face up to the fact that when it comes to handling yourself in a relationship, you're a bumbling fool without a shred of common sense."

The preacher glared at Jake, too flustered to talk. They walked in silence. "I'll tell you one thing, though," said the preacher, trying to redirect his irritation. "I will never make a fool of myself over a woman again."

Jake laughed out loud.

"What I mean is," the preacher snapped out, "next time I'll show better judgment in pickin' my woman."

Jake laughed even louder.

They stopped walking. The preacher waited for Jake to stop laughing. But the old man didn't let up.

"What's so funny, dag nabbit?"

The old man laughed louder still.

The preacher put his hands on his hips. "What the hell are you—"

Before the preacher could finish, Jake pushed him over the steep bank of the river.

As the preacher hit the water, Jake fell to the ground, holding his belly, still laughing.

The preacher stood up, waist high in swirling whitewater. It was intensely cold. Every thought that weighed him down instantly dispersed in the excruciating experience of pure cold. He was amazed that water could be so cold without turning to ice. He quickly climbed out and was greeted by a blast of cold wind against his wet clothes.

His jaw clenched, he walked over to Jake who was getting up from the ground, still laughing.

"So, you think this is funny, huh?" He picked up the old man, carried him a few paces to the bank of the river and threw him in. Jake yelled like a boy on a roller coaster.

The preacher leaned over the edge. "NOW WE'RE EVEN," he yelled. Then he lost his footing, and fell in again.

When the preacher stood up, he noticed that the water wasn't as cold this time, though it was still plenty cold. He wiped his eyes and saw Jake standing in front of him, still laughing. As they stood facing each other, cold water flowing swiftly around them, the preacher began laughing too.

–27–

As they walked slowly past the barnyard, dripping wet, they met Beth who was putting a saddle on a horse.

"My goodness," she said, touching their cheeks, "you two must be chilled to the bone."

"We were walking by the river," said Jake, "and—"

"Never mind," said Beth with a chuckle. "Go on in the house. Your lips are turning blue, for God's sake!"

The preacher and Jake looked at each other and then silently walked to the house.

"After you take off those clothes and dry off," said Beth, "get yourselves a couple of bathrobes and sit by the fireplace. I'll brew up some herbal tonic."

Fifteen minutes later, they were sitting on the large throw rug that covered the hardwood floor of the living room in front of a roaring fire, their shoes hanging over the fireplace and their clothes tumbling in the dryer, which they could hear humming quietly in the next room.

The preacher mumbled about his plans to go home, as Jake thumbed through a newspaper.

Justin walked in with two mugs of steaming herbal tonic. He placed one next to Jake and one next to the preacher. After turning the logs in the fireplace, he sat on the floor.

Jake passingly mentioned a classified ad calling for men to work on fishing ships.

"Who cares about that?" said the preacher.

Jake continued staring at the paper. "Wow, look at the salary! If I were a younger man, I'd sign up right now."

The preacher turned his head toward the window. He watched Beth on horseback, cantering across the pasture, followed by three dogs. The sun was setting behind the tall trees at the edge of the pasture, creating numerous beams of light radiating through the branches and down to the ground.

The preacher turned back to Jake. "Let me see that," he said.

Jake tossed him the paper. Then he stretched and picked up his mug of herbal tonic.

The preacher looked at the paper and whistled. "That is a good bit of change." He continued reading. "Ah-ha, I knew there had to be a catch. It's in Alaska!"

"Alaska!" exclaimed Justin. "Why are they advertising here?"

"Shorthanded, I guess," said Jake, taking a sip of herbal tonic.

"The Bering Sea," said the preacher. "That's practically the North Pole." He looked at the newspaper a while longer and then tossed it aside. He sighed and took a sip from his cup. "Just as well," he said. "I do need to get on home."

–28–

Three months later

The preacher threw a handful of salted peanuts in his mouth as he half-watched a football game on the TV set across the room directly over the bartender.

A waitress wearing a low-cut white T-shirt and short black skirt, walked toward the preacher's table carrying a tray. She placed a tall glass of beer on the table.

"Here you are, Sir. Shall I put this on the credit card, too?" she smiled.

"Yes, thank you," said the preacher, as he scratched his short stubbly beard.

"Do your friends want a refill too?"

"Probably. There they are at the pool table."

The waitress leaned over the table to pick up empty glasses and dishes, revealing substantial cleavage. As she stood back up, she flashed a smile at the preacher and walked away. The preacher took a sip of beer and resumed watching the football game on television.

He turned his head when the stage at the front of the room became illuminated with a pink spotlight. Artificial mist began rising out of the floor of the stage. "And now," said the D.J., "here is the one you've been waiting for! The Steam Room is proud to present the hottest dancer this side of Anchorage. Let's have a big hand for our own blond beauty, PHOENIX!"

The preacher looked up as a young lady in a ruffled red dress, ruffled sleeves, and a large Mexican hat walked on stage and began dancing to the beat of Latin music.

As Phoenix proceeded through her routine, making eye contact with whomever seemed most interested, the preacher became more and more captivated by her. With her silky skin and soft blond hair that reached down to her mid back, she looked so sweet and innocent that he couldn't take his eyes off her, especially after he started his third beer. The music was soothing and enchanting and maybe a little intoxicating. His main areas of interest, to his surprise, were her big aqueous eyes. When she began taking off her clothes, he barely noticed. A tiny corner of his mind went on the alert. "Uh-oh, timeless beauty again. You better get your ass out of here!"

Justin, who had just returned from the pool table, pulled up a chair and sat down as he stared at Phoenix. "Jesus," he said in a hushed voice. "What a fox!"

"Watch your tongue, youngster. One does not refer to an angel as a 'fox'."

"Pardon me, I meant no disrespect," said Justin, taking a sip of bear. "I'd love to get lost in all that hair."

As the preacher finished his second beer, his head became a little swimmy. Phoenix finished her performance and disappeared back stage. About three minutes later, she came out again semi-dressed and sat with them. Justin just listened for the most part and stared, while the preacher and Phoenix chatted. The preacher discovered that she had just turned twenty and was interested in acting and writing plays.

After her second turn on the steam-covered stage, Phoenix walked to the dressing room and returned ten minutes later, all freshened up, fully dressed, and hair neatly tied back in a ponytail. Justin and the preacher followed her with their eyes. As she walked by, Justin waved shyly to her. As she walked over, they stood up and the preacher held a chair out for her, which she happily accepted.

Sipping slowly on his fourth beer, the preacher talked about the gospel, and Phoenix asked many questions on morality and religion. They also talked about trout fishing, Shakespeare, and the brain-boosting properties of walnuts. When Phoenix said she wanted to learn how to meditate, the preacher told her about the brain exercise with the three laser beams that he had learned from Tamara. Phoenix was very impressed.

Justin didn't say much. For the most part, he just nodded and laughed at the jokes, except for one time when he interjected that Buddhism has some interesting parallels with primitive Christianity. He pointed out that both had a strong emphasis on non-violence and kindness, as he sited reliable evidence that the early Christians, like the Buddhists, were vegetarians. However, when Phoenix leaned toward him and looked right into his eyes to engage in conversation, he got flustered by her beauty and started stumbling over his words, so he backed off and let the preacher carry the ball.

Phoenix was elated when the preacher mentioned that he had seen *A Midsummer Night's Dream*… in New York City, no less! "That is so cool!" she said, leaning toward him, placing her hands on top of his. "I performed in *A Midsummer Night's Dream* when I was in high school. I played the part of Hermia. I loved it." The preacher was impressed, though he could not remember who Hermia was.

The preacher's interest in her accomplishments in theater really got her talking. She revealed that, after a serious fight with her mother, she dropped out of college, where she had been studying dancing, acting, and writing for theater and screen.

As the preacher started his fifth beer, the events became quite fuzzy. When he woke up the following morning with a headache, he didn't remember much, but had a vague recollection of having almost started a fight with one of the other customers who was saying improper things to Phoenix during one of her subsequent performances. He also remembered how he reprimanded the management for not taking better care of their women, as he was being helped out of the bar by his shipmates, who later threw him into the bay, because he wanted to go back to The Steam Room and apologize to Phoenix for ruining her act.

–29–

The front of the ship heaved up as another huge wave rolled by.

"You have to look under the surface," said Justin, taking a bite of his apple, as he stared at the watery horizon.

The preacher felt a bit queasy. He grabbed the railing to steady himself. Considering how rough the water was, he was handling it quite well. He was glad that he no longer needed to take those seasick pills.

"Take, for instance, Christianity and Buddhism," continued Justin. "On the surface, they are as different as night and day. But if you look deep enough, there are some really interesting parallels between primitive Christianity and Buddhism."

"Yeah, I know, I know," said the preacher. "You mentioned that last Saturday night as part of your feeble attempt to impress Phoenix. You've been carrying on about that Buddha feller for the past two months. Because of you, I've had dreams where I keep runnin' into this bald-headed fat feller with a dopey grin on his face."

"Really? That is so auspicious! The Buddha was the master of detachment. He knew how to see the truth hidden by Maya."

"Who is Maya?"

Justin laughed. "Maya isn't a who. Maya is illusion. We see through it by becoming detached. Detachment is how we overcome suffering."

"Detachment, you say?" The preacher stared at Justin. "I've been around you long enough to know that when you carry on about detachment, it means you're sittin' on a pile of fertilizer."

Justin looked down at the water. He tossed his apple core overboard. "You're a perceptive fellow."

"Nah. You're just easy to read."

"I'll get over it. It's just that I thought Barbara and I would one day get married and live happily ever after."

"I know how you feel," said the preacher.

"I guess I was in a hurry. I figured since Julie got married, I should get married, too. After all, we *are* twins."

"That's an unfair comparison. Julie is a woman, which makes her more emotionally mature than you."

"Thanks for the encouraging words."

The preacher slapped Justin on the shoulder and chuckled. "To paraphrase your grandfather, you best get off that high horse, or you're just goin' to get thrown again."

Justin nodded. "You're right. Truth is I just wasn't happy with myself. I thought getting married would change that."

"Well, first off, if you're unhappy and get married to become happy, you'll probably end up even more unhappy."

Justin looked down at the foamy water flowing past the side of the ship. "That actually makes sense to me. I think the sea is making me demented."

"Relax. Marriage will just happen. Right now, just do what you feel like doin'."

"I was in the midst of doing that, as per my grandfather's suggestion, when I got this crazy idea to join you on your journey to the frozen north."

"Do you regret endin' your exploration of the red light district?"

"No. I was getting tired of looking at all those shelves filled with erotic magazines, videos, battery-powered vaginas, giant dildos, and other such novelties. It was all becoming rather mundane and monotonous. Though, I must say, the anatomically correct inflatable sheep was definitely over the edge."

"So you gave up feasting on smut and started reading about Buddhism. You call that an improvement?"

"No, certainly not," said Justin. "The Buddha would agree on that one."

"That Buddha sounds like he might be an agreeable feller."

They stared across the water. Through the corner of his eye, the preacher watched as Justin's expression become progressively more somber.

Justin slowly shook his head. "I don't know what the heck I'm doing with my life, Roy."

"Do you regret comin' up here?"

"No. It's just that I'm still angry with Barbara. I'm even angrier at that slime ball who seduced her. Maybe I should have stayed in San Francisco and confronted them. The more I think about it, the more I realize they had planned this whole thing out. I was such a sap! She used my knowledge and resources to make contacts inside the psychology department. I'm almost certain that she gave him my research material, which he's probably using for his thesis. She used me and then discarded me. I just didn't know her."

The preacher's mind wandered back to Tamara. He was tempted to identify with Justin. It would have been nice if he could blame his misfortune on the evil doings of unscrupulous people. However, he realized that Tamara and Ron Russell had both conducted themselves honorably. Any lingering anger he had toward them seemed to dissolve into the ocean as he continued listening to Justin's horror story. For the first time, he felt genuinely thankful that Tamara called it off. Remembering that Tamara's birthday was coming up, he made a mental note to send her a card and thank her for doing the right thing.

"She used to tell me that I was so sensitive and sweet," said Justin. "I was spineless and gullible; that's what I was. I was used!" He kicked the railing. "It's taken me four whole months to really feel that. Son of a bitch, I was used!" He folded his arms and spat over the side. "I hope they live happily ever after in hell."

The preacher whistled and shook his head slowly. "Mercy!" He had never seen Justin spit and swear before. For the first time, he noticed that Justin had put on some weight since they had been in Alaska.

"Now you're going to tell me that I should try harder to be forgiving, right?"

"No," said the preacher casually, as he leaned his forearms on the railing. "In fact, I think a big part of the problem was that you tried *too* hard to forgive and act noble. Any attempt to display forgiveness from where you were standin' is just a sneaky form of attack."

"What do you mean?"

"You were tellin' the world, 'Look how bad they are and look how good I am'."

Justin looked out across the rough waters of the Bering Sea. "Damn!" he said, leaning his forearms on the railing, next to the preacher. "I didn't realize I was capable of being so slimy."

"Well, I wouldn't say you were bein' slimy," said the preacher. "But your strategy was off. As a method of attack, forgiveness is not particularly effective. You think you're gettin' back at them by actin' noble, but the anger just continues to seethe and it tears you up from your inside."

"Maybe that's why I was getting so apathetic and depressed."

"That's the price one pays for bein' a spiritual jackass." The preacher was surprised by his own words. He didn't know where they came from, but he thought he detected Jake's influence. "You see, Justin, what you wanted to do was punch him out and expose him for the thief that he was. Meanwhile, you were tellin' yourself that you should forgive both of them. So, your twisted mind combined the two by usin' forgiveness as a way of punishin' them. You would have been better off if you had dragged him out into the street and punched him out. Instead, you acted sensitive and sweet, tryin' to punish them by your display of forgiveness. And that's why you're still sufferin'."

They were silent for a while. Justin rubbed his chin and looked out across the water. "What a concept!" he exclaimed.

"Don't tell me," said the preacher. "You just got a great idea for your new thesis."

Justin nodded. "Thanks to you, Reverend."

They looked out across the water.

"Roy, I don't understand why you quit your job as Pastor. Seems to me that with your keen insights and gift of oratory, you could have been quite successful and maybe even graduated to a bigger church."

The preacher shrugged. "That's life."

"I guess it's true what they say. A prophet is never recognized in his own land."

"Yeah," the preacher nodded. "Especially when he's an asshole."

They looked toward the stern of the ship as several ropes guided by a winch pulled in the huge net. "You know, Roy, now that we've had this conversation, I realize that I'm glad I'm here. Alaska, I mean."

"I guess I am, too."

"But once in a while, I get this funny feeling. Obviously, I came up here of my own free will."

"Yeah, as far as I can tell."

"You didn't talk me into it."

"No. I was a mite surprised when you told me that you had applied too."

They stared silently at the water.

"It sure wasn't my mom," said Justin. "She was flat against it. And Grandpa certainly didn't talk me into it. He was rather quiet about it."

"So?"

"It was my decision all the way."

"So?"

Justin removed his elbows from the railing and folded his arms. "So, why do I feel like I've been shanghaied?"

The preacher rubbed his jaw through his short stubbly beard. "I don't know," he said, glancing at the net as it slowly emerged from the water with a load of Alaskan Pollock. "But, now that you mention it, sometimes I feel that way, too."

They silently looked at each other. Then, they burst out laughing, as they put on their work gloves and walked toward the net.

–30–

Two months later

The preacher strained to see through the fog. He kept his eyes down for the most part, so as to avoid any possible hazards such as rocks or deep ravines. He extended his left arm from under the rain poncho and looked at his wristwatch, 7:15 PM. He had to stop and rest more frequently, which meant that he was either getting very tired from his long climb, or the air was getting thin.

The fog was now so thick he couldn't see five feet in front of him, but he was sure he was approaching the top. Though the terrain was still rather steep, he expected it to level off soon. Either that or it would become too steep to walk. He certainly wasn't going to climb on all fours with visibility near zero.

When darkness started setting in, he thought about stopping, but decided to push on when he noticed that the slope appeared to be leveling out.

By the time the ground was completely level, it was so dark and foggy, he could barely see his hand in front of his face. He removed his backpack and took the big flashlight out of the side pocket. It came on dimly and then faded away. All he had now was a small penlight. The ground was too wet to start a campfire, even if he could scrounge enough wood, which was unlikely; he had not encountered a tree in over half an hour. He was not concerned, however. He had assembled his tent in total darkness before.

As soon as he was tucked inside his sleeping bag, he heard raindrops striking the roof of the tent. It was soft and soothing. He felt himself dozing.

From the depths of sleep, his eyes snapped open when he heard booming thunder accompanied by a flash of light. The rain was beating furiously on the tent and the wind was howling.

It was completely dark inside the tent except for the occasional flash of the lightning. He picked up the penlight that was on the floor next to his pillow. Clicking it on, he pointed it at his wristwatch that was lying face up next to his sleeping bag. It was a few minutes past eleven o'clock. He had been asleep about an hour.

He tried to go back to sleep, but found it difficult. He could make himself ignore the howling wind and the tent flapping around him, but the lightning bolts were relentless. They seemed to be occurring more frequently and closer to the tent. One of them couldn't have been more than sixty feet away. He thought he detected the smell of ozone and smoldering grass.

The top of a mountain, which was where he figured he was, was the last place he should be during a storm like this.

He tried closing his eyes, but thunder shook the ground, accompanied by a flash of light that illuminated the inside of the tent. He estimated that the lightning bolt was about thirty feet away, maybe closer.

He sat up quickly and smelled the air. To his relief, he did not smell burning vinyl, just the strong odor of ozone and smoldering grass.

The storm didn't seem to let up. As he extended his arm and touched the floor of the tent, he felt moisture seeping through the corners. One thing he disliked more than anything else was water on the floor of the tent. Now, that was the least of his worries. The tent was flapping so furiously, he felt it would collapse or tear any moment. But even that wasn't his major concern. He didn't care about getting wet and cold and being exposed to gale-force winds. He was more concerned about getting fried.

His apprehension grew when he remembered that the poles of his tent had metal tips. Through the thin fabric of the tent, he could see the lightning bolts flashing on like fiery whips.

He lay back down and covered himself, curling up into a fetal position to provide as small a target as possible. He tried to close his eyes, only to have them snap open automatically every time a lightning bolt struck close by.

What if he got badly hurt? No one knew where he was. He had been out only one week, and Justin would not expect him to return to Anchorage for at least another two weeks.

Behind closed eyelids, he saw images of Jake, Mona, Ann, Amos, Mahmoud, Bailey, his mother, and his father. As the years of his life scrolled through his mind, he thought of things he wished he had done and things he wished he had not done.

As he pulled the cover more snugly over his head and thought of Mrs. Bailey, he realized that he hadn't prayed in quite a while. This seemed like a good time to start again.

His outburst startled him. To his surprise, his rage blew away as quickly as it came and took all fear with it. The storm seemed to let up a bit, but he wasn't sure; it could have been his imagination.

Lying back down in his sleeping bag, he closed his eyes. He thought he heard Mrs. Bailey's soft voice in his head. *Lighten up a little.*

He was not startled. He figured that he was just delirious from extreme fatigue, lack of sleep, and continuous bombardment. He drifted into a restful sleep, even as the storm continued.

He awakened to total silence. To his surprise, his first thought was a prayer of thanks, unforced and unstrained. As he recited it silently, he remembered the days past when he routinely awakened in the morning and spontaneously gave a prayer of thanks as the first thought of the day.

Unzipping his sleeping bag, he walked out into the morning air and stood up. He was in the middle of a broad, rounded summit, surrounded by a carpet of grass, dotted with a few stubby bushes and rocky outcroppings that ranged from basketball-size to bathtub-size.

The sky was a cloudless bright blue, and the sun was peeking over the mountains in the horizon. The air was as clean and crisp as he had ever seen it. For miles in all directions, he saw only an uninterrupted panorama of forest, river valleys, and snow-covered peaks.

Gazing at the landscape, he felt himself enveloped by a stillness that was so thick he could almost feel it. The silence was so deep he could almost hear it.

He expected to eventually hear something, like the distant hum of an airplane, a gust of wind, or some birds. But the silence remained. He stood motionless, barely breathing, barely thinking, as he gradually became oblivious to the passage of time.

Suddenly, he had the notion that something was emerging from inside him. It was a wave of sorts. It was like a sound, except it was silent. It was like a thought, except he could not put words to it. It was like an emotion, though he could not really describe which one. It was like a sensation, except he couldn't sense it in any particular area of his body. He had the impression that some forgotten part of him, something deep and visceral, was spontaneously praying, praising, and singing without bothering to let his logical mind in on it. And, that was okay because the communion that seemed to be going on at the moment was beyond his comprehension. As he relaxed more into it, he imagined the prayer was like a musical tone that was caressing the grass, the rocks, the bushes, the forest below, and the distant mountains, all of which, apparently, were also musical tones.

The throbbing tones coming from inside him and around him all seemed to be saying, "Thank you."

—31—

Six weeks later

The preacher walked leisurely through the forest, chewing on a blade of grass that hung down from the side of his mouth. His face was covered with a dense rusty-red beard that extended down almost to the base of his throat. His hands were inside the pockets of his cut-off shorts. He ran his fingers through his thick, shoulder-length hair.

Realizing that he had lost track of time again, he stopped walking. This sort of thing seemed to be happening more frequently lately. He wasn't sure if he had been walking fifteen minutes or two hours. Couldn't be two hours, the valley wasn't that big, unless maybe he had been walking around in a circle. He wished he hadn't lost his watch. Judging by the position of the sun, he figured the time was about 2:00 P.M. The amount of sweat on his T-shirt suggested he had been walking about one hour.

As he walked on, he remembered that he had also lost track of the days of the week. Neither did he know which day of the month it was.

He forgot why he went for a walk. Then he remembered: he had set out looking for edible plants for lunch and then sort of walked on just for the heck of it. He really wasn't hungry anyway. He was unable to recall if he had eaten breakfast that morning.

A voice in his head told him he should be more responsible about keeping track of the schedule. Justin was waiting for him back in Alaska. However, no matter how much he tried, he found it virtually impossible to be concerned with anything involving the passage of time… which pretty much included everything. He no longer felt guilty about leaving Justin in Alaska, when he realized that it would do the youngster some good to fend for himself for a while.

He wondered if his altered sense of priorities was due to the silence and stillness of the place, or the fact that the valley was completely enclosed on all sides by steep mountains. Except for its one small lake, the valley floor was densely forested with massive pine trees and hardwoods, which added to his sense of seclusion. He had the impression he was enclosed in a huge cocoon that excluded all thoughts from the outside world.

The presence of so many big hardwoods so far north also seemed strange. The only explanation had to be the steep walls around the valley, blocking the harsh winter wind and trapping enough heat to allow the hardwoods to survive the cold. The temperature in the valley did seem a bit warmer than the surrounding areas. Maybe the entire valley was really the crater of a huge extinct volcano. Maybe there was still lava far below radiating heat to the surface. That would explain why the lake was so nice and warm.

As he walked among the hardwoods and pines, He contemplated the funny hiccups in his time-sense. He still wasn't sure when it all started. The first time he really noticed it was in Muir Woods, just outside San Francisco, shortly after he broke up with Tamara. The main difference was that now it wasn't at all unpleasant or disorienting. In fact, he rather liked it.

Nonetheless, he had to know what day it was—eventually. He looked up at the sun again. Judging by the way it had been arching across the sky lately, he figured it was early August, which meant he had been in the valley about one month.

He couldn't believe he was the only person who had ventured upon that spot in 30 days. But then again, the valley was rather difficult to reach, as he had discovered. The steep slopes on either side of the valley were covered with a thick growth of thorn bushes, briars, and stubby shrubs that looked like hollies. Not very inviting, except perhaps to small mountain goats and foolish hikers who were lost or had a lot of time on their hands. It took an entire day to climb and weave his way from one side to the other. If there were a passage into the valley, he certainly did not find it. He was glad that he stumbled across this little paradise, but he was not looking forward to the return trip.

The ground was beginning to slope gently upward, so he figured he was approaching the far end of the valley. When he saw a spring, he was reminded that his mouth was dry. The water emerged from a crack in a rock formation, and collected into a circular pool about five-feet wide, before it continued on as a small creek that he assumed meandered its way to the lake.

The water in the pool was clear, and the sunlight penetrated all the way to the sandy bottom. Getting down on his knees, he noticed his clear reflection. He barely recognized himself; the ruddy complexion, sunburned nose, long hair, and dense red beard spreading out from his massive jaw.

Reaching down with his hand, he scooped up some water. It was amazingly flavorful—even more so than the water from the spring back at camp.

He put his lips directly on the surface of the pool, like a horse and took several long draws. He felt like something exceedingly pure was flowing through his body.

He raised himself upright to catch his breath as water cascaded through his beard and dripped profusely on his T-shirt. Then he resumed drinking. He didn't realize he was so thirsty.

After splashing water on his face, head, and neck, he stood up and shook his head vigorously side to side as beads of water flew from his beard and hair. Taking a deep breath, he let out a groan of satisfaction.

After he resumed walking along the gentle incline, the ground abruptly dipped down again, the trees thinned out, and he found himself in a bowl-shaped clearing about two hundred feet in diameter. It was filled with abundant grass, large rocks, and one very large oak tree.

"God!" he whispered.

Without hurrying, he walked around the tree. It was so big that four people standing hand-in-hand could just about encircle the tree. Sitting on the grass with a grunt, he leaned back against a rock and rested for a while.

He could not determine what variety it was. Gazing at the spiraling texture of the bark, he tried to make a human face out of the many lines and holes. Then, he got the eerie notion that the tree was staring back at him. He chewed on some blades of grass that he found surprisingly appetizing; they tasted kind of bitter and kind of sweet. As he swallowed some of the juice, he became even more relaxed and carefree than before. Looking down at the grass, he plucked a few more blades and smelled them. Looked like regular Kentucky fescue, like the kind horses ate.

He started dozing; except that it wasn't like regular dozing, because he could still see the tree, even through closed eyes. As he dozed even deeper, he heard himself silently ask as question. "What's your secret?"

He didn't know exactly what he was asking or why he was asking it. If that wasn't strange enough, the tree responded. "My secret is that I'm no greater than those blades of grass." The voice was soft and lyrical. "Now, go on home."

–32–

"Come on, Nina," said Justin, holding open the glass door of the convenience store, "move your buns!"

The young lady with short brown hair put the magazine back on the stand and walked toward the door.

"What's your hurry," she said, "you said we don't have to be home 'til noon."

"I know, but you'll probably take a good long time saying goodbye to your friends, and we still have to pass by the auto parts store. Roy wants to spend the afternoon getting the car ready for the trip."

They walked briskly along the sidewalk, holding hands. "Six weeks all by himself in the wilderness," said Nina. "Wow. I would go crazy. He must be so glad to be back in civilization."

"More like seven weeks," said Justin. "And, yeah, he's sort of glad. You would think so, anyway."

"What do you mean?"

"I get the impression that if he hadn't agreed to meet me back here, he could have just as easily stayed in the forest. After seven weeks in the woods, guess what he did yesterday?"

"He went hiking," said Nina.

"He went hi—" Justin stopped abruptly and looked at her. "How did you know?"

"I didn't. You told me to guess, so I guessed."

Justin chuckled and kissed her. "You see; that's why I like you so much. You're just full of surprises."

"Oh, so that's why you like me?"

Well, no. I like you for a lot of reasons. The main reason, of course, is that you have a great tush."

"My tush? Not my mind?"

"No, your tush wins hands down."

"Justin!" Nina exclaimed with an exaggerated look of anger and hurt on her face.

"No, no, please understand,' Justin said quickly, shielding himself against her potential blows, "this is not a commentary on your mind, which is excellent in its own right. It's not your mind's fault that you have super-exceptional buns that, that…"

"Never mind. Just get back to what you were saying about Roy before you sink any deeper in your pool of self-created quicksand."

"Good idea. Yes, I *am* a little worried about Roy. I mean, he looks good. In fact, he looks great. He's calm and his eyes are real clear. Looks like he's lost about fifteen pounds. But, he's so detached and unconcerned. He just sits around with this serene little smile on his face. It sort of…"

"What?"

"Spooky."

She giggled. "Do you think he'll still have that serene little smile when you finally introduce me to him?"

Justin burst out laughing.

–33–

The preacher sat in the easy chair, eating an apple and looking out the window at the traffic and buildings, as the morning sun shone on his face. He glanced at the clock on the wall, 11:00 AM. Justin said he would bring his girlfriend home at about noon.

The preacher was happy to have the time alone. He had been back a week, and the main thing that he wanted, to his surprise, was solitude. Remembering yesterday's hike along Nancy Lake, he smiled as he recalled the drive home, when a bull moose deliberately rammed into his headlight, while he was stopped at an intersection.

He sank a little deeper into the easy chair. Even with the window closed, he heard the street noises three stories below. Raising his eyes, he gazed at the developing suburbs along the hillsides, outside the city proper. In the distance, beyond the hills, he could see the peaks of the Chugach Mountains.

His mind drifted to his time in the wilderness of Canada. Before he knew it, his eyelids closed halfway, his eyes rolled up in his head, feeling like he was back in the woods, walking through the valley, swimming in the lake, and sitting by the huge oak tree. Gradually, he became oblivious of the room and chair he was sitting on. The sights and sounds of the city drifted from his conscious mind as the forest became more and more real to his senses, feeling the earth under his feet, smelling the pines, and drinking deeply from the spring.

The images quickly disappeared, and his head jerked up when he heard an automobile honking outside. For a moment, he did not know where he was. He quickly recovered and realized he was in Justin's apartment in Anchorage. It was Tuesday morning, and he was waiting for Justin to return with his girlfriend.

He looked out the window and saw the cause of the traffic commotion. Justin had just run across the intersection, holding a young lady's hand.

They weren't supposed to be home until noon. Glancing at the clock on the wall, the preacher was surprised to see that it was 12:15. He had been daydreaming for an hour! He shook his head slowly and sighed, wondering when his mind would get back to normal time. Getting up from the chair, he walked leisurely to the kitchen.

As he opened two cans of chili and poured the contents into a pot, he thought of the upcoming trip back to San Francisco. He didn't particularly care for having another passenger in the car, but at least Justin was socializing and acting normal again. He must have hit it off really well with this young lady if she was willing to drive back with him.

When he heard voices and footsteps coming up the stairwell, he walked slowly back to the living room, drying his hands on a kitchen towel. Justin stepped inside and closed the door behind him. He stood in front of the door with his hands on his hips, smiling broadly behind his thick reddish beard, looking confident and almost menacing in his sleeveless down jacket, black denim trousers, and heavy work boots. His muscular forearms bulged through the sleeves of his plaid flannel shirt.

"Well," smiled the preacher, "where is she?"

Justin placed his palms together. "I wish to give this fine lady a proper introduction." He cleared his throat. "Reverend Roy Dobbs, it is my honor to introduce," he turned the doorknob and slowly pulled the door open, "Miss Nina Nesbit."

A slender young lady wearing blue jeans and an army surplus jacket was standing in the doorway.

"Hello, Nina," said the preacher with a slight bow of the head. "Happy to make your acquaintance."

The young lady walked up to the preacher. "Hello again, Reverend Dobbs."

The preacher's eyebrows shot straight up. "Phoenix?"

"Yes, it is I. Except that Phoenix is officially retired."

"Well, I'll be a babblin' baboon!"

Nina and Justin laughed as the preacher stood silently with his mouth opened.

"I didn't recognize you with…"

Fortunately, Nina noticed his mortified state. She gave him a warm embrace and then started chattering. "I know. You didn't recognize me with short brown hair. I just cut it. And this is my normal color," she said, running her fingers through her hair. "Anyway, I am so happy to see you. I didn't think I'd ever see you two guys again. But after you took off for the woods, Justin came back to the club, and we became friends. As a policy, I don't date customers, but in this case, I decided to risk it."

"And I'm so glad she did," Justin interjected.

"I wasn't sure if I should trust him at first," she said, poking Justin's ribs. "But I figured, since he's your friend, he's probably okay; you being a preacher and all. Anyway, Roy, I want to say thank you, thank you, thank you. You gave me encouragement and kindness when I really needed it. And your little talk really helped me get clear on what I really want to do. I've decided to go back to Oakland and enroll at the College of Performing Arts. I want to study acting and screen writing. And our conversation at the club reminded me that I really do have a passion for Shakespeare…"

–34–

Six weeks later

Justin tossed a crumpled piece of paper into the dormant fireplace as he walked across the hardwood floor of the living room. He stopped at the open doorway that led into a screened-in porch. Leaning over so that his eyes just barely passed the door frame, he peeked at Nina, who sat cross-legged on the porch swing. She seemed oblivious to the morning sun bathing her face, her eyes focused intensely on her lap, where a thick book supported a large yellow pad on which she was furiously writing.

Retreating away from the door frame, Justin looked out into the pasture beyond the porch, where he could see the preacher wandering about.

Peeking in on Nina, again, Justin saw that she was no longer writing, but reading, though the look of intensity was undiminished. "Hi, Sweetie," he said cautiously. "Is it okay to approach yet?"

Nina picked up her head, slightly startled. "Oh, yes," she said with a chuckle, waving him in.

"If you're still in your flow," he said, holding his ground, "don't let me interrupt you."

"No, your timing is perfect," she said, flipping back to the first page. "Sit. I've been itching to tell you about this since I woke up, but I wanted to get it all down on paper before I forgot anything." She held up the writing pad.

"'The Merchant's Daughter,'" said Justin, reading the title at the top of the page.

"It's a play."

"So this is why you jumped out of bed at 5:00 AM?"

"Yes," she said, sitting up proudly. "This is just the basic outline. Now, I have to fill in the details. Anyway, what did you want to talk about?"

"It's about Roy." Justin looked out into the pasture, where the preacher was walking slowly toward a tree at the top of small knobby hill. "But first, tell me about your play."

"Funny that you mention Roy. The play sort of has to do with *him*. You see I had this real vivid dream this morning, and—oh, just read it," she said, pushing the writing-pad in front of his face.

As Justin took the pad, Nina stood up and pranced away. "My bladder is *really* full."

–35–

The preacher meandered around the red-oak tree at the summit of the grassy knob. The brightly colored autumn leaves scattered on the grass crunched under his feet. His shoulder-length hair was tied back in a ponytail.

Finally, he sat at the base of the tree and leaned back against the trunk, gazing at the surrounding rolling pasture, where several horses and goats were grazing. The sun was shining brightly, and the air was crisp. He looked straight up at the tree, its multicolored leaves shimmering like jewels in the sun.

Not too far from the barnyard, Jacob Clear-Water and three students were taking down some of the posts that surrounded the garden, in preparation for expanding it the following year.

The preacher looked down at the dry leaves at his feet. His dense beard touched his upper chest. . Leaning his head back against the trunk, he closed his eyes.

When he finally opened them, he realized that he had lost track of time again. It seemed to be happening less since he got back from Alaska, but he still had to remind himself to stay focused if he was going to close his eyes.

The sun hadn't moved much. And the activity in the pasture indicated that no more than 30 minutes or so had elapsed. Beth and the kids were now picking apples in the small orchard, and Jake and the students looked like they had nearly completed taking down the rest of the fence from around the garden. Justin had just walked out of the tool shed.

The preacher removed a pen and writing pad from the bag and started writing.

Dear Amos,

He looked up, tapping the pen on the pad.

Sorry, for not staying in touch the past year. I've been preoccupied. And frankly, I just got tired hearing you tell me to stop acting crazy.

He tore the sheet off and crumbled it.

Dear Amos,

When I sent you the last postcard, I was living at a farm. But for several months, I was working on a fishing boat in Alaska. You would not believe how good the pay was. Sorry for not staying in touch, but I was sort of preoccupied.

Staring at the words, he tore off the sheet and crumbled it.

Dear Amos,

For the past several months, I was in Alaska working on a fishing boat. You would not believe how good the pay was. Sorry for not staying in touch but I just didn't feel like arguing anymore.

He tore off the sheet, crumbled it, and tossed it aside.

Dear Amos,

How are you? Long time no hear!

He tore off the sheet, crumbled it, flung it away, and folded his arms.

The ground was well littered with balls of paper when Justin came walking briskly up the hill.

"Greetings, Reverend."

"Greetings to you, Young Hooligan."

Justin pointed to the writing pad. "Writing your memoirs?"

"Not hardly."

The preacher didn't offer any additional information, so, Justin pointed to the chicken house. "I'm about to rearrange the roosting place, as you suggested, so we can clean their droppings more easily. I want to get that done now, because later I want to help Grandpa with the new fence."

The preacher laughed. "Looks like all those months on the ship have caused you to become addicted to manual labor."

"Nah. I know when to quit. Anyway, this is just a warm-up for when Nina and I get our own place. She likes country living."

"You're really serious about her, ain't you?"

"Hell, yes! We'd like to be married right now. However, we're going to take your advice and just get to know each other better. In the meantime, I can complete my thesis and procure gainful employment. And, of course, she wants to go to school."

"A wise move all around," the preacher nodded.

"She's basically a very practical and level-headed girl. But there's this whole other side of her. This morning, she woke up at five o'clock, jumped out of bed, and started writing. She had a dream that you were her father a couple of thousand years ago. It gave her an idea. She's been writing like a madwoman all morning. It's a play—in which she will eventually star, of course. It's about a little girl named Gandhari who grows up to be an innovative dancer. She is also very outspoken about religion and politics, which was not proper for women in that time and place. The only person who doesn't disapprove of her is her father, Macunda—that's you."

"Macunda?" the preacher chuckled. "What is that, African?"

"No, it all takes place in ancient India, at the height of Hindu culture. And you'll be happy to know that Macunda is one cool dad. He is uncommonly liberal with his kids, which irritates the crap out of his wife. The play has a lot of good drama. It's mostly about Gandhari's struggles for self-expression. Eventually, a dashing young Brahmin sweeps her off her feet."

The preacher nodded and glanced down at his writing pad.

"Well, comrade," said Justin, "you look like you're deep in thought, so I will leave you to your musings. Nina has announced that lunch will be served at 12:30 sharp. Your presence is requested."

"Okay," smiled the preacher.

As Justin turned to leave, he hesitated and then turned back to the preacher. "Uh, Roy, is something bothering you?"

"You must be psychic."

"No, you're just easy to read."

The preacher tossed the pen and pad on the ground. "I've been tryin' to compose a letter to my brother. I haven't communicated with him in over a year."

"If I may ask, what is it exactly that you want to communicate to him?"

"I'm not sure. In the last phone conversation, he was really nasty. I got so disgusted, I said, 'don't bother me anymore. I'll come home when I'm good and ready.' I didn't give him a forwarding address. They don't even know I live here."

"Sounds like you have some cleaning up to do. Under the circumstances, I would suggest that you not say a whole lot in your letter. My limited experience in these matters tells me that family issues are best addressed face-to-face. If you say anything provocative in your letter, he'll have to mull it over until he sees you again. It can complicate things. If I were you, I would just write, 'I'm coming home,' and leave it at that."

The preacher nodded.

"Lunch, 12:30 sharp," said Justin as he walked away.

The preacher looked at the rolling pasture and his friends milling around the farmhouse. He picked up the pen and pad.

Dear Amos,

I'm coming home. I figure I'll reach Kentucky by mid-December. If you're still speaking to me, I'd like to get together.

Your Brother,

Roy

–36–

The thin layer of hardened snow crunched under the tires, as the preacher drove his car up through the long driveway that led to the old Bailey place.

He didn't notice the absence of the sign that read, *Mahmoud's Auto Repair.*

The smile on his face vanished when he rolled to a stop under the oak tree and noticed that the clearing was empty. The shutters on the windows of the barn were closed.

The sheet of snow that covered the barnyard was undisturbed. He glanced at the house. There were no lights on.

As he stepped out of the car, he was greeted by a blast of cold air against his face and chest. Zipping up his jacket, he jammed his hands into his pockets. The wind blew his shoulder-length hair behind his head, exposing his ears and neck to the cold air.

Walking to the barn door, he stepped around a low-hanging branch that had been pressed down by the weight of the snow. Several icy twigs reached out to him like the bony fingers of a crone.

Throwing back the bolt, he opened the barn door. The shelves that used to contain tools and auto parts were now empty, and the hydraulic lift had been removed. There wasn't even an oil stain on the floor. Only one table remained. It was empty except for one old cordless phone. Next to the table was the chair in which he used to sit while exchanging stories with Mahmoud.

In the darkened far corner of the barn, Mr. Bailey's old plow was leaning against the wall. He was about to leave, when a gust of wind blew past him, followed by the sound of paper flapping. Looking more closely at the far end of barn, he saw a sheet of paper taped to the handle of the plow.

Walking slowly toward the plow, he saw writing on it. He removed the sheet, carried it to the doorway, and held it up to the light.

Dear Mr. Dobbs,

I don't know if you get this note. It seem silly to put it here. Makes more sense to leave message with Mrs. Bailey. But Mrs. Bailey say leave it here.

Thank you for sending postcards from Redwood Forest and Yellowstone. Is wonderful you can visit all these places. I wish I could visit these places. America is a beautiful country.

I try to find out where you are, but nobody know where you are.

Business here was okay. Because of you, I met many customers. You warned me about the people in the Hollows. But they are nice people. Some are a little funny, but that's okay. I met your neighbor, Mr. Floyd, when I went to your cabin to mow grass. He had a shotgun and was not smiling, but I fix his truck while I was there, and he send me his relatives. Mr. Floyd tried to give me a jug of special whisky called white lightning.

We move back to my country. I have a most excellent business opportunity there. I will be selling and servicing farm and garden vehicles for an Italian company called Lombardini. It is funny. When I came to this country, I had never seen a tractor. Now I will be selling them and fixing them.

Farm belongs to Mrs. Bailey again. If you need car fixed, go to Timmy, he has become most excellent mechanic. He buy Leroy's garage in town.

I guess we not see you again. I am sad. Goodbye, Mr. Dobbs. You are a most excellent man of God.

Mahmoud Mossavi

Placing the letter in his pocket, he left the barn and walked up the hill to the house. The dry grass was rather tall. It had not been cut since the summer. The shed that used to house the chickens and goats looked like it had been enlarged.

Standing on the porch, he gazed at the rolling hills and mountain peaks in the distance. Next to the house stood the bare fruit trees and snow-covered garden. With his elbow, he nudged the porch swing. It squeaked as it swung gently back and forth.

He looked down the hill at the rich growth of pine trees that filled the one-time cultivated field. Beyond the field, he could see the switchback trail on the mountainside, leading to Possum Lake. The old coal-bank along the trail was no longer visible. The entrance was filled in with rocks and dirt, and covered with dry grass and shrubs, blending in with the rest of the landscape, like a wound that had gradually healed.

–37–

The preacher stepped onto the small wooden dock of Possum Lake. Walking to the edge, he scraped off the hardened snow and sat with a grunt.

The surface of the water was motionless. The trees surrounding the lake were covered with an icy glaze. The barren branches were dotted with empty nests.

The stillness of the forest was broken only by an occasional sliver of ice that fell from the treetops and shattered on the frozen ground. The only other movement was the cloudy vapor of his own breath.

Glancing down, he noticed a pile of golf ball-sized stones on the dock. It looked like a child had been playing there recently. Picking up a flat one, he skimmed it across the water, watching the tiny ripples expand outward until they nudged against the thin sheet of ice at the shore.

Placing his hands in his coat pockets, he stared down at his dark reflection beneath his boots. Next to the dock he noticed the partially submerged log where the frog had been sitting the last time he was at the lake—over four years ago. Seemed more like a *thousand* years. As he looked up at the naked trees, the icy branches glistened in the late afternoon sun. He watched a few water droplets fall to the ground as the sun melted the ice in the uppermost branches.

He figured he would contact Mrs. Bailey first. Then he would get in touch with Amos. He should have called ahead, but he just didn't feel like talking to anyone. He figured he would spend the night in his cabin, or maybe a motel closer to town, and then leisurely make contact the next day.

The motel seemed like the more sensible thing to do in such cold weather. But then again, the cabin was more private and there was no danger of meeting anyone before he was ready to do so. And besides, the potbelly stove would get the cabin toasty warm in no time.

Then again, if he stayed in a motel, he could take a proper shower with hot water. And he could shave his beard and get a haircut, maybe.

Skimming another stone on the water, he placed his feet upon the dock, and wrapped his arms around his knees. He gazed at the rocks and trees surrounding the lake, smelling the air, staring at the ripples in the water created by his skimmed stone, letting time pass.

He was feeling rather peaceful and wasn't thinking about anything in particular, when he closed his eyes and starting dozing. Four stars appeared over the lake. They formed a three-sided pyramid, which descended slowly until it was right at the surface of the lake, converging with its own reflection.

Waking up, he realized he had been sitting there for quite some time. The sun had descended behind the bare trees, leaving a trail of fiery clouds. The air was getting colder. He decided that he better get to his cabin while he still had some daylight to gather firewood.

−38−

The stereo played "Silent Night," barely audible above the steady roar of 60 people talking and laughing. The walls were decorated with holly leaves, a cardboard Santa Claus, reindeer, and rows of multicolored lights blinking on and off. In one corner of the room, several children bounced up and down on a sturdy old couch.

The preacher took a sip of eggnog as he stood with a group of five men who talked football. He was clean-shaven and his hair was cut above his collar and neatly combed.

He noticed that football had become more popular among the men in Hickory Ridge. He assumed that was because more families had gotten cable and satellite service to improve TV reception. He was amazed at the number of satellite dishes he had seen since his return.

The preacher laughed with the other men as he strained his peripheral vision to watch his brother conversing with Reverend Powers on the other side of the room. Eventually, they walked to the Christmas tree, where Candra Winfield was doing some last minute trimming. She put her arm around Reverend Powers' waist.

"The Broncos still have a chance," said the preacher, loudly.

Conrad Simmons, who stood next to the preacher, commented on the preacher's assessment of the Broncos. The men in the group laughed. The preacher laughed, too. He slapped Simmons on the back and watched Amos leave the room, as Reverend Powers and Candra moved toward the punch bowl on the long table.

The preacher drank the rest of the eggnog, excused himself, and walked toward the door where Joe Potter had just walked in.

"Hello, Joe."

"Well, if it isn't Preacher Roy," said Joe Potter, grabbing the preacher's hand. "I heard you was back. I called your brother's house tryin' to find you. I thought you'd be stayin' there."

"No. He's got a house full of in-laws."

"You're not stayin' in that cold cabin of yours, are you?"

"I did for a spell. And it ain't that cold. It's right cozy. But I did check in at the Dixie Motel, so I could clean up proper. I sort of wish I hadn't sold my farm."

You've been doin' a heap of travelin', I hear. Alaska, Canada, California."

"Yeah. Other places too."

"Did you finally get to see the Redwoods?"

"That I did, Joe. Just north of San Francisco, there's a place called Tall Tree Grove. It has the biggest trees on the face of the earth. Tallest one is 368 feet."

"Conrad says you been livin' out in the woods in a cave."

"No, not hardly," said the preacher, forcing a laugh. "In fact, I've been around big cities for the most part."

"I'm lookin' forward to hearing all about it."

"Well, I'll tell ya,' San Francisco alone can keep me talkin' for weeks.

"Is that where you was workin' on a fishin' boat?"

"No, that was in Alaska. Bering Sea. It was a lot of grunt work mostly. But, I'll tell you, it was like bein' at the U.N. I met fellers from Australia, Russia, Norway, China. We even had a real Eskimo on board."

"So, how long did you do that?"

"About four months. Long enough to put some money away. Then, one day, I was standing on deck, drinking coffee with this Canadian feller, and he tells me how he used to take off for weeks at a time to the Canadian Rockies. The more I listened, the more appealing it sounded. So, after I gave the fishing company proper notice, I was off to the woods."

"And you did that for how long?"

"About seven weeks. Once, I ran out of provisions. I went three days without eating, except for a few wild herbs here and there. My trail map had a mistake in it. I thought I was headed for a little settlement to get supplies; instead I was out in the middle of nowhere. That's when I came across an isolated valley with a lake loaded with fish. While I was there, I found me this rock formation with a nice little cave in it. It was only about eight feet high and maybe six feet deep.

I enlarged it some and enclosed it with a few logs and stones, and used my tent as a door. I was even able to rig up a little fireplace in it, which was good because it got chilly at night. So, even when it rained and the wind blew, I stayed toasty warm and dry while I cooked my supper and read the Bible by firelight. And that's where I lived for about a month. I was as happy as a pig in a mud hole."

"Lordy, how did you manage to tear yourself away from there?" The preacher decided not to tell Joe about the talking oak tree "Well," he laughed, glancing briefly at Candra Winfield, "you have to remember, I was there during the summer. I reckon it's a mite nippy there right now."

As they continued conversing, the preacher casually steered them toward the long table, where Candra Winfield and Reverend Powers were talking.

"How is your son, Timmy, doin'? Is he comin' here tonight?"

"I suspect not. He's workin' late. Real busy he is."

The preacher watched as Candra brushed some lint from Reverend Power's shoulder. Reverend Powers responded by playfully kissing her hand.

The preacher yawned forcefully, covering his mouth with the back of his hand.

"Tired?" said Joe Potter.

"Yeah. I'll probably turn in early tonight. I guess I still haven't recovered from bein' on the road."

"Well, when you get settled in, you'll have to come over for supper and tell us more about your travels. You're a man of the world now."

"Nah, I'm still plain old Roy. But, I've had a few experiences, that's for sure, including an education on different religions," the preacher said, glancing at Candra again. "I couldn't tell you how many books I've read on various religions and philosophies," he said raising his voice.

Candra reached over to refill her cup while the preacher reached over to do the same.

"Good evening, Candra."

"Good evening, Roy. I'm glad you could join us tonight."

"Glad to be here." He noticed Candra's hazel eyes and full lips, reminding him of Tamara.

"Have you met our pastor?"

"No, I don't believe I've had the pleasure." The preacher put down his cup.

"Reverend George Powers, this is Roy Dobbs, our former pastor."

They shook hands. "So, you are Roy Dobbs. Pleasure to meet you." Reverend Powers' hand was smooth and soft, no calluses. His grip was overly firm, and had a slight tremor to it. He had a congenial smile, a bit strained at the corners of the mouth.

The preacher took him to be about thirty-eight years old, six-foot-two. He had a full head of wavy black hair, with a few streaks of gray, giving him an older and more distinguished appearance.

"Nice party," said Reverend Powers.

"Yes, very nice," said the preacher, straightening his back so he didn't have to raise his head too much to look Reverend Powers in the eyes.

They both picked up their respective cups of eggnog and took a sip.

The preacher waved his cup toward the crowd. "It's been a Hickory Ridge tradition even before I was born. I missed it the last three years, of course."

"Well, it's good to have you here," said Reverend Powers.

"George didn't make it to last year's party, either," said Candra, as she put her hand on Reverend Powers' shoulder. "He was right in the middle of getting his doctoral thesis on comparative religion, doing field work in Europe."

"Oh," said the preacher, "that's interesting."

"Naturally," said Reverend Powers, "my sermons have very little comparative religion. My focus is, and ever will be, the King James Bible. I think you would agree, that we should respect the sensibilities of the people in the community."

"Absolutely," said the preacher.

"He made some wonderful contacts while in Europe," said Candra. "Unfortunately, that means he will soon outgrow our little community here. He's been invited to a huge multi-faith conference at the Vatican."

"That's right nice," said the preacher raising his cup at Reverend Powers. "When you see the Pope, kiss his ring for me."

"Oh, before I forget," said Joe Potter, quickly putting his hand on Reverend Powers' shoulder, "Timmy asked me to tell you that your car is ready and you can pick it up tonight, if you like."

"Wonderful. Your son is a fine young man, Mr. Potter. Steady and soft spoken. I like that in a man."

"Well, sir," chuckled Joe Potter, "it wasn't any of my doin'. Years back, Timmy looked like he was headin' straight for the gutter. But he changed all of a sudden. Real miracle, it was. And, I think the preacher here had a hand in it."

The preacher stopped in the middle of a sip.

"Yes, sir," continued Joe as he turned toward the preacher. "My wife asked you what she should do about Timmy. And you told her to pray for him, every day. You said that you would pray for him too. Remember?"

"I sort of vaguely remember," said the preacher trying to restrain a smile, as he glanced at Reverend Powers."

"My wife did what you said," said Joe Potter. "She just prayed for Timmy. And sure enough, he started changin' after that."

"Well," said the preacher, "I'm sure other folks had a hand in it, too."

"In the final analysis, of course," said Reverend Powers, "all glory and credit belong to God."

"Amen to that," said the preacher, raising his cup toward Reverend Powers.

"I think the Lord may have other plans for Timmy, besides fixing cars," said Reverend Powers. "I've had some fascinating discussions with him. He seems to have an intuitive grasp of the deeper mysteries of Christianity. His ideas are consistent with my studies of comparative religion."

"Well," said the preacher, "In the Koran, it says, 'God gave humanity 400 prophets, among whom there is no cause for conflict.' Maybe Timmy is one of them."

Reverend Powers paused. "You have read the Koran, Mr. Dobbs?"

"Oh, here and there. Buddhism has some points of interests as well."

"Buddhism, you say? You have studied Buddhism?"

"Well, I realize that Buddhism appears to be far removed from the Christian world," he said glancing at Candra, "but there are some really interesting parallels between primitive Christianity and Buddhism."

"Really!" said Reverend Powers. "I have not run across that in my studies. Perhaps after the holidays, we can sit down and swap notes."

"I'd be delighted."

"Well, I'd best be movin' on," said Joe Potter. "The missus is waitin' for me to bring home the rest of the decorations. I just dropped in to say Merry Christmas to everybody."

The preacher, Candra Winfield, and Reverend Powers said good night simultaneously, as Joe Potter walked away.

Several seconds of silence elapsed. They sipped eggnog.

"So, how do you like Hickory Ridge?" asked the preacher.

"Wonderful town. The horrible drug problem and apathy that seem to be overtaking surrounding communities have miraculously bypassed Hickory Ridge. It's almost like there is a protective cocoon around this community."

They were silent again.

"I understand that you performed the memorial service for Mrs. Bailey."

"Yes. But, of course, if we had been able to reach you, I would have been more than happy to turn it over to you."

"No, I wouldn't think of it. You're the skipper of the ship now. Anyway, I couldn't have done Mrs. Bailey's service. She was like the grandma I never had."

"I assume that your brother Amos told you about her note."

"No. Amos and me haven't had time to really sit down and talk yet, because the holidays and such. What note?"

"She was found in her house, with a note next to her bed. It said, 'Well folks, looks like I'll be leaving tonight. I'm not sick or anything. It's just my time.'"

The preacher smiled and nodded. He assumed that Reverend Powers was waiting for him to be amazed.

"Yep," the preacher nodded, "that's the Mrs. Bailey I know."

"Oh, and another thing," said Reverend Powers, "she mentioned you in her note."

The preacher glanced at Candra. "What did she say?"

"She said, 'P.S. Tell Roy to lighten up a bit'."

Candra and Reverend Powers laughed. The preacher joined in. He suddenly felt hot and a little sweaty. He assumed it was the eggnog; he hadn't touched alcohol since his night out at The Steam Room, in Anchorage.

"We better get going, George," said Candra. "Timmy is probably waiting for you to pick up your car."

As the preacher shook hands with Candra, he noticed a diamond ring on her finger.

He watched them walk out the door, refilled his cup, and then wove his way through the crowded room, stopping by the window. Pushing the curtain aside with the back of his fingers, he leaned against the window frame. The dark silhouette of the mountain peaks was barely visible beyond the buildings that lined Main Street. He thought about the Canadian Rockies and how beautiful they looked in the waning light of dusk.

As he watched the frosted pine trees illuminated by the streetlights, he became aware that just about everyone he had encountered in town in the past five days had been polite to him, but not very friendly. Joe Potter was the first to ask him about his travels.

He took a sip of eggnog and watched Candra Winfield and Reverend Powers walking briskly hand in hand along the inclined sidewalk. Through the closed window, he heard the muffled sound of their laughter. The voices in the room became echoey. From the corner of his eye, he saw Amos and his wife who had just come back into the room. He turned his head to make eye contact with them, but they had already turned to walk to the other side of the room.

Above the talking, laughter, and music, he heard Conrad Simmons say, "Like father, like son."

The preacher's hand gripped the cup more tightly, warping it slightly, as he stared out the window. He was about to discreetly walk out of the room and go back to the motel, when Conrad Simmons, who had also drunk a goodly amount of eggnog, approached him and spoke some words that the preacher didn't quite understand over the noise and music—something about holiday cheer, family atmosphere, and closely knit community. The preacher responded politely with a nod and a smile without turning his head. Then, Simmons casually said something about how the early death of the preacher's parents meant that they were spared the shame of their black sheep son.

The preacher remained silent without nodding politely. As he continued staring out the window, the frosted pine trees went out of focus and took on a dull red hue, as did the stars, the streetlights, and Christmas decorations on the houses.

He put his cup down on the window ledge and faced Conrad Simmons. And for the second time in twenty-five years, he delivered a terrific uppercut to Conrad Simmons' jaw. Simmons spun around and fell to the floor.

Four men escorted the preacher out of the room. By then, the blind rage was replaced by sort of a surreal detachment. Obviously, it was fitting for Conrad Simmons to get what he deserved, but punching him out at a party attended by women and children was definitely not proper. He was puzzled as to why he had totally forgotten where he was. His last thought before going to sleep that night was another line from the Koran: "Allah loves not the aggressors."

Part Four
Rendezvous at the Edge of Time

–1–

"Maybe it's nothing," said Mona, looking out the window at the Manhattan skyline.

Vera adjusted the wedding veil on her head as she looked in the mirror. "'Maybe it's nothing,' you say," she giggled. "That means you're picking up something really important but you're being cautious."

Mona walked to the edge of the bed and sat down, folding her arms. "Well, I just don't know. I'm not getting any visuals. I just have this vague gut feeling."

"What sort of vague gut feeling?"

"It's... vague." She rubbed her eyes with her fingertips.

"But you obviously think it has to do with me."

"I'm not sure."

"It must be about me otherwise you wouldn't have asked me how I'm feeling."

Mona folded her arms again. "But, maybe my filter is clogged with my own subconscious debris. When that happens, I project like crazy."

"Oh, Auntie," said Vera, as she leaned over and kissed her on the forehead. "I don't think you have any subconscious debris."

"Of course I do. Everyone does."

"Okay," said Vera, placing the palms of her hands together. "If you let that very subjective and imperfect gut feeling speak, what would it say?"

Mona sighed and shook her head. "When my impressions are this vague and this emotional... I don't know."

"Could it be about Marcus?"

"I don't know. Do you have any fears about marrying him?"

"Not really. I'm as happy as a pig in a mud-hole."

Mona stared at her niece.

"What?" Vera inquired. "What are you thinking?"

"Pig in a mud-hole?" Mona mused. "That's a rather odd metaphor coming from you."

"Yeah." Vera cocked her to the side. "I don't know why I said it. Most peculiar!"

"'Most peculiar,' hey?" Mona nodded slowly.

"Anyway," said Vera, eyeing her wedding dress on the bed, "the point is, all systems are go as far as my wedding is concerned. Heck, I haven't felt this good about a man since—" Suddenly, she grabbed her temples. Groping for the chair behind her, she sat down.

"What's the matter," said Mona, as she stood and put a hand on Vera's shoulder.

"Strong apprehension... and a little dizzy." She started to fall over and Mona caught her.

"Honey, are you alright?"

Vera opened her eyes and picked up her head. "I'm here... I mean... I'm fine." Vera took a deep breath. "Whatever that was, it's passed. I would like some fresh air, though."

The glass door slid open and she stepped onto the terrace, walking to the four-foot high wall at the edge of the terrace. Vera hooked her fingers through the chain link fence on top of the wall, gazing at the Manhattan skyline.

Mona suddenly looked over Vera's head.

"What are you seeing?" asked Vera, still looking into the distance.

"I just got a visual. There's a heavy dark green and gray pattern around you. I didn't see it before, probably because it's also around me. Do you see anything around me?"

Vera turned her head toward Mona. "No. But I'm not good at visuals. I don't see things, I feel things."

"Are you certain it isn't Marcus?"

"I'm not certain of anything right now—" Vera gasped. "Are you getting what I'm getting?"

"I'm afraid so," Mona nodded.

"My God," said Vera, "I knew I was connected to him, but not *this* strong." She closed her eyes, as if going deeply into prayer. Then her eyes snapped open, and she looked in horror at her aunt. "No, that's wrong!"

Mona sighed. "We don't know that."

"No, no," said Vera, grabbing her head. "It's like ... the fabric of his life got torn... accidentally or maliciously, I don't know! But this is not right!"

Mona closed her eyes. "I get the impression, he might want to go."

"No! He just thinks he does!" Her voice broke. "He has too much to live for."

"That is not for us to decide."

Vera sat down with her back on the brick wall of the terrace and covered her face with her hands.

"Vera, you're being bombarded with a lot of conflicting thought forms. The bottom line is, if he doesn't know what he wants, we certainly cannot assume to know. The fabric of his life is more intricate than either of us can comprehend. Maybe that rip is supposed to be there. It might be part of a deeper order. Your emotional attachment might disrupt that deeper order."

"Well, maybe my 'emotional attachment,'" Vera snapped out, "is part of the deeper order too?" She wiped the moisture from her eyes as Mona sat down next to her.

They were silent for a while.

"You might have a point there," said Mona. "The fact that both of us have been alerted suggests that some input from us might be appropriate. However, I have blindly interfered too many times to assume I know what's best for another human being."

Vera slapped the slate surface of the roof with both hands and stood up. "Well, whatever we do, we have to do it now. I want to do the invocation."

"Oh, God," Mona sighed. "I knew it was coming to this. In a situation such as this, more often than not, the kindest and most helpful thing to do is leave the involved parties alone and let them work out their own problems."

"So, are you saying you won't do the invocation with me?"

Mona paused. "The invocation is not something I would do on impulse. If it is not done with clarity and precision, we might simply be pushing him from the frying pan into the fire... and us too, obviously. We must meditate on the situation and examine our motives."

"Damn it." Vera yelled, "We don't have time to that. We have to do it right now."

Mona looked up silently at Vera.

Vera relaxed a little. "Alright, I *do* realize I'm not stable enough to project that much power responsibly." Tears welled up in her eyes. "Will you help me, please?"

Mona stood up and took her hands, nodding her head.

"Thank you," said Vera. She took a deep breath and composed herself.

"We must be clear with our intent," Mona said, calmly. "We are not trying to save his life. We are offering help in mending that tear in the fabric of his life. He can accept it or not. The physical outcome is not for us to decide."

"Understood," said Vera.

"We better sit for this," said Mona.

They sat cross-legged and took hold of each other's hands again. Closing their eyes, they breathed slowly and deeply. After about ten minutes, they simultaneously intoned a Haitian chant and ended with the Lord's Prayer.

–2–

Jacob Clear-Water sat in the sweat lodge with a group of men. "Does anyone have any personal stories to tell?" he asked.

No one responded.

Suddenly, Jake remembered when he had asked that same question at a sweat lodge where he met Preacher Roy. Back then, no one had responded to Jake's invitation to tell a personal story, which prompted the preacher to say, "Well, does anyone know any good jokes?"

The memory brought a smile to Jake's face. And then, Mona popped into his mind. She had a worried look on her face. Her image quickly faded away, but the preacher lingered, and that's when Jake became deeply concerned.

Instinctively, he threw some sage upon the hot rocks and silently recited a healing prayer that he had learned from his grandfather.

In the women's sweat lodge on the other side of the bushes, Nina was getting a similar notion.

–3–

Tamara sat at her desk working on a sermon. Feeling some stiffness in her neck, she rolled her head around, turning it all the way to the right and then all the way to the left. Keeping her head turned to the left, she massaged up and down the right side of her neck. As she did so, her eyes caught sight of a large pinecone that she had picked up while she was walking through Muir Woods with Preacher Roy.

Staring at the pinecone, she thought of the preacher and smiled. She looked down at the notes she was writing. Her sermons had not been the same after she got to know Roy Dobbs. In fact, she realized that the preacher had provided her with the guidance and inspiration that ultimately allowed her to mature as a minister, so that by the time the board was ready to appoint a new senior minister, she found herself on the top of the list.

Looking at the pinecone, she felt her heart overflowing with gratitude. Closing her teary eyes, she thanked the Holy Spirit for bringing the preacher into her life, as she spontaneously envisioned him enveloped in a dome of golden light.

–4–

Mahmoud Mossavi woke up suddenly from a deep sleep, not knowing where he was. Opening his eyes, he looked around at the hotel room and remembered that he was in Istanbul, where he was going to meet with a big tractor dealer.

A feeling of foreboding gripped his chest, as disturbing images floated though his mind. Rubbing his eyes, he sat up, remembering the words of an old cleric he had met in a mosque just outside of Athens, last week. The old man said that if you are angry at someone or worried about their wellbeing, pray for them, before do you do anything else, because this will ultimately accomplish the greatest good.

Pulling off the bed cover, Mahmoud rolled out of bed and got down on his knees.

–5–

The thirty or so people stood in a loose circle, singing, praising, and clapping more or less in rhythm with the guitar and two drums that added to the joyful noises in the room. When the song was over, everyone sat down in their chairs.

Reverend Mathew threw his hands in the air. "Whew, I just love that song." Sitting back in his chair, he rolled up the sleeves of his light blue sport shirt and fanned himself with an old church program.

The Inner Sanctuary had been resurrected, and was now open to all church members and guests. It had also been restored to its original format: informal sharing, followed by praise and prayer.

The sharing and praising were complete. Time for prayer. Reverend Mathew turned to his six-months pregnant wife who sat next to him. "Jane, the basket please," he said a deep mock-serious tone.

She handed him a small wicker basket filled with scraps of paper with names of individuals requesting prayer support. He was about to stand up to place the basket on the small table in the middle of the circle. He paused, and then looked at his wife.

"Hon," he said, "do you have a pen and piece of paper?"

Originally, there was a strict policy regarding the prayer basket: it was to include only the names of individuals who specifically requested prayer support. Later, an exception was made for one's own children who were too young to speak for themselves. For the same reason, dogs, cats, and other beloved pets were also allowed. Later, the circle of eligible candidates was expanded to encompass individuals who "more than likely would have requested prayer support if they could have, but were not immediately available to do so." And, very recently, a consensus was reached that it was perfectly acceptable to include any person or persons, provided that you receive a really, REALLY strong (and hopefully, divinely inspired) urge to do so.

It was on the basis of that latest amendment, that Reverend Mathew justified the inclusion of one more entry into the prayer basket.

—6—

Preacher Roy was curled up in a fetal position, with his eyes closed, on a secluded park bench, at the edge of Forrest Park. The top of his head was touching a small white igloo cooler. The bench was nestled within a semicircle of rhododendron bushes. Several feet in front of the bench were a row of juniper hedges that separated the edge of the park from the sidewalk.

He didn't remember lying down, or even getting sleepy. He figured that he was just exhausted from not getting any sleep the night before. And, the can of beer probably helped.

He could still hear the revving of an automobile engine that was being repaired at Forrest Park Auto Service, across the street. A large ginkgo tree allowed in enough sunlight to warm his face, while the breeze evaporated the beads of perspiration on his forehead. He heard the laughter of young children playing in the distance, as an ice-cream truck played a happy tune.

The street noises faded. His mind recalled leaving Hickory Ridge without saying goodbye to anyone. His lips parted and he emitted a soft infant-like cry.

He woke up suddenly when someone yelled close by. "HEY, BRO, WHAT ARE YOU DOING HERE?"

"Just hanging out." came the quiet reply

"I MEAN, WHAT ARE YOU DOING IN TOWN?"

"I have a—" The voice was drowned out by a honking car.

"I'LL CATCH YOU LATER. I'M IN A HURRY"

The preacher didn't know where he was, until he felt the hard bench under him, and his hand gripping the writing pad on which he was trying to compose a letter to Amos.

Suddenly, writing the letter seemed pointless. As he drifted back to a dreamy state, the last eleven years of his life flashed through his mind as if it had all happened yesterday. He saw four stars configured into a three-sided pyramid. No big surprise. The pyramid had become a frequent visitor in his dreams. He had stopped wondering about it and simply wished that it would go away.

Everything was blurring together. He was unable to distinguish distant memories from recent memories. His chest and abdomen moved less and less. His heart did not want to beat anymore.

He found himself walking along a trail that cut through a sun-drenched rolling meadow covered with violet flowers. Eventually, he passed by a burlap bag, hanging from a tree. The bag was torn and golden liquid light was pouring down and disappearing into the violet soil. Several people tried to sew it up. The preacher told them not to bother and walked on.

–7–

Smiley sat up in his seat and continued watching the screen, as the preacher faded away as he walked along the violet trail.

Folding his arms, Smiley looked at Brother G in the next seat. "I'm concerned," he said. "If things continue to unfold this way, the preacher dies."

"Yes?"

"Which means that Jason also dies."

"That is a reasonable assumption," Brother G nodded.

"And that means I will have to grow myself another body and another personality, so I can tend to Jason's unfulfilled business."

"Probably."

"So things are sort of going astray."

"Things are unfolding beautifully."

"Of course, you *would* say that. For you and your three friends, everything is beautiful and perfect."

"Yes," Brother G nodded. "We *are* quite limited in that regard."

"Well, I don't have your limitation. But, I hope to. Is there anything that *I* can do to help this drama unfold more to Jason's liking?"

"You're already doing it."

"I am? What am I doing?"

"You're watching. You're watching the drama of death, which ushers in rebirth. One way or another, this is what is transpiring. By watching it from this particular frame of reference, you also participate. The manner in which you watch influences the outcome."

"So, I guess, for best results, I should watch the preacher's drama calmly. I should watch it in a detached manner. I should watch it without—"

"Just watch," said brother G.

The screen now showed an old man and a young man in eighteenth century clothes, the kind that well-to-do merchants or gentlemen farmers might wear. They were both sitting on an outdoor table, with their arms folded, while a huge mansion was being built in front of them.

"Does this ring any bells?" asked Brother G.

"Sort of," said Smiley. "I'm the young guy. His name is Flynn. Used to be a monk. And the old guy is… Preacher Roy?"

"In that movie, he is known as the architect."

—8—

"Her eyes captivated me," said the architect, as he stared at the huge house.

Flynn looked down at the blueprint of house on the table, wondering if he should inform the architect of the flaw.

"Of course," continued the architect, "I knew full well that to openly give any attention to the Raja's young wife was to risk death, not to mention losing the contract to the palace." He chuckled, slowly shaking his head. "But I didn't care. I would have risked everything to hold her in my arms just once—" Looking down at the blueprint, the architect suddenly became quiet. He ran his finger along the diagram of the house.

Meanwhile, Flynn quietly reached down and to his left, fished out a straight-edge from a small canvas bag next to his chair. Transferring the straightedge to his right hand, he held it just above the surface of the table.

"Hmmm," nodded the Architect, as he inched his face a little closer to the paper. "Flynn," he said without averting his eyes from the paper, please hand me the—"

Before he could finish, Flynn offered him the straightedge.

The architect smiled, as he took it. "You saw the error too?"

"I saw it a few minutes ago."

"Why did you not speak?"

"Well," Flynn smiled, "I figured you'd see the error once you completed your story."

"Young man, please do not patronize me. If you see or even suspect a flaw in my design, speak freely. You cannot learn to trust your judgment or develop your creative ability if you get in the habit of deferring to me."

"Yes sir," said Flynn. "My apologies."

"I certainly did not choose you because you're a good little boy who speaks only when spoken to," said the architect. "I know you better than that." He looked down at the paper. "I chose you because you have a gift for innovative design." He fell silent and momentarily disappeared into his work, as Flynn picked up the canvas bag from the ground and started digging through it, eventually pulling out an ancient wooden compass.

The architect was about to open his mouth, but stopped when he saw the compass in Flynn's right hand. Taking it with a hardy laugh, he resumed his close work.

When he finished, the architect folded his arms again, and stared at the house. "Fortunately, the old Raja saw how smitten I was, and was tactful enough to make sure that I and his young wife did not get into a compromising situation.

He was also wise enough to keep me very busy from sun up to sun down."

"So, nothing ever happened."

"No. But some unexpected gifts came out of that experience. The romantic feelings triggered wave after wave of creative inspiration. And I also started to suspect that perhaps the Hindu belief in reincarnation might have some truth in it."

Flynn smiled. "My brother, Donwald, also believes in it, even though it is not sanctioned by the Church."

The architect scoffed, shaking his head. "Another side benefit of my experience in India was that it set me free from the tyranny of the Church. I sometimes think that the words, 'evil' and 'stupid' were invented specifically to describe that vile beast in the Vatican."

Flynn was so shocked he made himself laugh to blow off the energy.

"In India," continued the architect, "they do not seek to shackle the soul by scaring people with eternal damnation and imposing ridiculous sexual taboos. It's only here in the West that the religious authorities seek to chain us though fear, while denying us our natural desires. The Church be damned! Their most despicable act is to make us forget that all of life is a sacred journey. Every bit of it."

Though Flynn was never fully devoted to the Church, he still did not feel comfortable with such blasphemy. "Does that mean," he said cautiously, "that the despicable acts of the Church are also part of the sacred journey?"

The architect looked at his young apprentice, at first confused. And then, suddenly, he burst out laughing, as he patted Flynn on the shoulder. "Touché, young friend! You see—that is why you are my apprentice."

"So," said Flynn wanting to change the subject, "you have no regrets about leaving her?"

"Heavens no. I'm deeply grateful that I met her. Yes, for a while, I did burn for her. But, I was young, the feelings passed, and eventually I met Elizabeth's Mum."

"For which I am eternally grateful," smiled Flynn. "Elizabeth is amazing. She brings to me clarity of mind, even without speaking. Now that I am with her, I can say, life is as good as is can possibly be. Perhaps this is just my youthful naiveté talking."

"Youthful naiveté," the architect laughed. "Young man, don't be so sacrilegious. What you are experiencing is divinity itself. It is eternal truth blossoming for you personally as ephemeral beauty."

"I will not argue with that, sir," Flynn laughed. "Anyway, you left India and that was the end of it?"

"Yes. But, just before I left Kashmir, I had an encounter with an old *yogini* who was also adept at Indian astrology. Somehow, she managed to coax me into revealing my drama with the Raja's wife."

"You went to a fortune teller?"

"Yes," the architect laughed. "Young people who are hopelessly in love have a tendency to do that sort of thing. She informed me that the Raja's wife and I had many lifetimes together, hence the immediate attraction. In one of those lifetimes, I was a wealthy merchant, name Macunda, and she was my wife. She was killed, partially due to my negligence and arrogance. Therefore, every time our souls encounter each other, it's difficult for me. In two of those lifetimes, we supposedly took turns raping each other."

"And you believe all that?"

"I don't know," he laughed. "But it certainly gave me a good excuse for making such a bloody fool of myself."

The scene faded. "So," Smiley nodded, "Macunda became the architect, who later became Roy Dobbs."

–9–

The ball of vibrating intelligence, once known as Preacher Roy, no longer had any specific memories of who he had been and where he had been. There was just a vague lingering unpleasantness, which was rapidly fading away too. He was perfectly content to just dissolve into the violet sea and never come back. Wherever he had come from was another place and another time. He had no notion of how to get back, or if it was possible to get back, or even if that place and time existed at all. Maybe none of it was ever real.

The last vestige of any inkling of a prior existence was about to dissolve into forever, when suddenly, something started pulling at him. It was like a magnetic force reaching out to him through space and time.

He was contracting, becoming denser and denser, as he was pulled into a funnel-like vortex. The magnetic force took the form of a pair of beautiful soulful eyes, smiling at him like an old friend.

And then, his ears were accosted by a screaming ambulance. He sat up on the bench, as if stung by a bee. His eyes squinted as the flashing light from the roof of the ambulance shown directly at him.

Judging from the crowd close by, the vehicle had just pulled out from the driveway of the big house at the edge of Forrest Park. As the ambulance wove its way through the traffic, the preacher felt restless, almost frenzied.

He was still staring down the street, his hand on top of the cooler next to him, when a woman quickly emerged quickly from the edge of the rhododendrons.

They both made a startled noise. The preacher jerked to his feet, knocking the cooler to the ground, where it flew open and released its contents of water, ice, two empty coca-cola cans, one empty beer can, and an empty plastic jar that had the words, "Fresh Walnuts," printed on it.

"Excuse me," he said as he got down on his knees. When he finished cleaning up, he stood up and faced her.

"I'm sorry," she chuckled. "I didn't mean to ambush you like that. I was at Forrest Park Auto Service," she pointed across the street. "I didn't see anyone sitting on the bench, so when I came over I didn't expect to see anyone here."

"I was lying down," said the preacher. The ambulance woke me up."

"Oh, yes, the ambu—" Suddenly, her face became serious, and she looked up and to the left. "I don't mean to appear forward," she said apologetically, "but would you mind if I sit with you?"

"Uh…" he waved at the bench.

"Thank you."

She sat at one end. The preacher followed on the other end.

"My name is Sarah. Sarah Chazinov."

–10–

"Roy Dobbs, Ma'am."

The woman smiled at the preacher. Her long auburn hair glistened in the sun. She had sparkling eyes and a playful smile that reminded him of a bright sunny day at Possum Lake. With her bright pink, floral shirt and flowing green dress, she looked like a flower in bloom. Her body was curvaceous and well proportioned, but he felt most drawn to her eyes.

Sitting next to her, he became keenly aware that he hadn't shaved in four days, or gotten a haircut in five months, nor had he showered that morning.

She looked pensive again. "Mr. Dobbs, this may sound like a strange que—" She stopped when a young lady with strawberry blond hair walked quickly past them on the sidewalk, just beyond the juniper hedges. She seemed deeply distressed.

"Are you," she said, with a probing look on her face, "a minister, or something like that?"

The preacher stared at her. Though he was intrigued that she could pull a question like that out of thin air, he didn't feel inclined go down that road. "No," he said, justifying his answer by the fact that he was no longer a practicing minister and had no intension of ever doing it again. However, when Sarah's facial expression changed from expectancy to one of a disappointed little girl, he decided to qualify his answer. "But, I used to be."

Sarah beamed. "Okay, I'm not crazy."

The preacher folded his arms. His eyes narrowed, as he scrutinized her.

"Sorry," said Sarah. "I'll try to explain. When the ambulance came by, I got a powerful urge to say a prayer for that young man. Hopefully, as a minister, you can relate to that. So, I came over here to get some privacy, thinking the bench was vacant, but of course, it wasn't. And then, I got this voice in my head that said, "He's a man of God; ask him to join you.""

The preacher continued looking at her, arms folded.

"I hope this doesn't weird you out," said Sarah.

"No, ma'am, I think I'm beyond that." He paused. "Uh, is he a friend of yours?"

"No. From what I hear, he got conked on the head by a two-by-four while working on the house just beyond the edge of the park."

The preacher studied Sarah to make sure the sincere look in her eyes was real.

"Anyway, I think we need to get going, Reverend. This particular task is apparently very time-sensitive."

The preacher sighed. For a moment, he strongly considered standing up, bowing politely, and walking away. Beside the fact that the situation was a bit strange, he just wasn't in a praying mood, and didn't think that he would ever be in a praying mood ever again.

He sighed and looked into her eyes. "Look, Seva—"

"No, not Seva. Sarah."

"I could have sworn you said your name was Seva."

"I'm fairly certain I said Sarah."

"Oh. Sorry. Anyway, uh..." The preacher fell silent. "I've lost my train of thought." He glanced at Forrest Park Auto Service, across the street. Finally, he took a deep breath. "Anyway," he said, "I hope you don't mind hearin' my confession, but a few years back, it dawned on me that every time I opened my mouth to pray, I was doin' it to look good in front of folks. If I prayed for someone who was sick and they had a quick recovery, heaven help us, I made sure the whole town knew about it. I was real good at braggin' while making it look like I was bein' humble." He sat up straight, waving his arm for theatrical effect. ""Oh no, Mrs. Jones, I didn't perform any miracle, I didn't do a thing; God did it all. Even when I was asked to pray for someone deceased, I wasn't thinking about the departed soul, I was thinkin' about scorin' points with the next of kin. I was no better than a vulture feedin' on the misfortune of others." He kicked the cooler further under the bench with his heel. "And lately, I just about sold my soul to the devil."

"That's impossible. At worst, you just leased it out for a while. Everyone does that now and then."

The preacher stared at the melting ice scattered in front of his feet. "All those years I thought I was honoring the name of Jesus Christ. I was just usin' his name to put myself on a pedestal. With each passing year, I corrupted his gospels more and more, like maggots putrefy food."

"Reverend, it sounds like you're being way too melodramatic. Anyway, we can discuss your lamentations later, if you want. Right now, we have a job to do."

"This is too strange," said the preacher, shaking his head.

"What's so strange about it? Is it strange to think that your prayers might make a difference in someone's life?"

"That's not the point." The preacher found it difficult to argue while looking into her eyes.

"What *is* the point?"

"If any of this made any sense, which it don't, I still wouldn't feel right about this." With his foot, he gently caressed a single blade of grass that grew between two pieces of tree bark. "I'd feel like a damn hypocrite. Pardon my language, Ma'am." He looked down at the ground again. "There was just one time that I can say I really helped save a soul. And that was in a strip-joint in Alaska. While I was drunk."

Sarah discreetly pressed her lips together to keep herself from laughing out loud. She looked away and composed herself, grateful that the preacher was looking down at the ground and not at her.

"Okay, I understand," said Sarah, fighting hard to be serious. "You're concerned about those days gone by when you used to say, 'God bless you', and it was just self-glorification. But again, I really feel that your harsh perception of your own past is entirely overdone. And whatever mistakes you made, it sounds like you know better, now."

The preacher found himself drawn into her eyes. Suddenly, he was flooded with an irrational desire to cry. He looked down at the ground again and thought about his father in the mental hospital.

"So, are you ready to carry out the task in question?"

The preacher did not respond.

"Suit yourself." said Sarah. "I guess I'll leave and do it myself."

The preacher's belly contracted. It got worse when Sarah started getting up.

"I didn't say that I wouldn't do it."

"You also haven't said that you *will* do it."

Now he was cornered. "Alright, let's get it over with."

To the preacher's surprise, without another word from either of them, they both closed their eyes and became very still. That's when he became strongly aware of her presence. It was almost like there was subtle current of electricity flowing between them. The current had a sweet and familiar feel to it.

He had totally forgotten about praying for the young man, so he was surprised when he spontaneously opened his mouth and uttered a prayer that he often used as pastor. "Heavenly Father, we call forth thy Holy Spirit to surround and enfold our brother in his hour of need. We release him into thy loving hands. For this we give thanks. Amen."

After about a minute of silence, the preacher opened his eyes and waited for Sarah to do the same. When she did, she looked at him and smiled. "That felt so nice," she said. "But, apparently, that was only part one." She stood up. "Part two you're supposed to do solo."

"Huh?"

Sarah shrugged. "This is as strange to me as it is to you, Reverend Dobbs."

As they looked into each other's eyes, that same strawberry blond young lady walked quickly in the opposite direction. This time, she looked calmer.

The preacher glanced at Forrest Park Auto Service, where a red pickup truck had been hoisted up on the hydraulic lift. He turned and looked into Sarah's eyes. There was no way he could say no.

"Well," he said, "I guess this won't be the first time that I've made a jackass of myself."

Sarah giggled, stood up, and walked away.

—11—

Taking a deep breath, the preacher closed his eyes. With the palms of his hands together in front of his chest, he forced himself to think about the young man again. He was feeling self-conscious and wondering if anyone was looking, when another wave of peace swept over him, followed by a stream of words. "Hear me, Lord God, creator of the universe. By your presence, all things exist. You are all there is and the source of all there is. You, who exalt the valley and cause the mountain to bow low —"

His eyes snapped open. Where did that come from? He looked around to see if anyone was looking at him. Scratching his chest, he closed his eyes. After pausing for a few seconds, he discreetly put his hands together in front of his abdomen. And it happened again. "Hear me, Lord God, creator of the universe. By your presence, all things exist. You are all there is and the source of all there is. You exalt the valley and cause the mountain to bow low, causing all flesh to be united…"

Eventually, he found himself reciting the psalms. Somehow, the sequence seemed significant. The words seemed to emanate from deeper and deeper inside him, becoming more and more lyrical and rhythmic. He was a bit disturbed by the strangeness of it. Then, he realized that it felt similar to the spontaneous prayer that emerged from him while he was on the summit of the mountain in the Canadian Rockies, so he relaxed and continued.

As he continued reciting the psalms, his eyes began rolling up into his head, and his arms ascended into the air. Behind closed eyelids, he saw four stars coming together, forming a three-sided pyramid, which was hovering over its reflection in the water. The apex was formed by a bright silver star that seemed to grow brighter as he continued his prayer. As the silver star reached a certain size, it seemed to come to life, becoming more and more human. Suddenly, he felt like a hobo who was being visited by a graceful queen.

He struggled to maintain his concentration. The temptation to open his eyes was great, but he pushed on, even as the presence loomed brighter in his mind, revealing to him a beauty that overwhelmed his understanding.

As the presence became more human in his mind, he was feeling sensations that were just too close to sexual. Suddenly, he was paralyzed with shame. The warmth in his back became like a fiery knife, his throat constricted, and he choked on his words.

"It's okay, Roy," said the Presence. "Lighten up a little," in Mrs. Bailey's voice. It had a quality that seemed be the very essence of benevolence and grace. He relaxed.

Resuming his prayer, he remembered Mother Eva's exotic past. He remembered Jake's grandfatherly advice to Justin. He thought of Phoenix/Nina, who managed to bring sexual exhibitionism to a state of angelic innocence. He remembered when he made love to Vera in New York; it was a weird combination of erotic and holy.

The communion with the angelic Presence became deeper still, until the whole experience became something far removed from sex. The sexual stirrings in his pelvis seemed to transform into a warm tingling sensation rising up his spine.

As he settled back down into reciting the psalms, his own voice seemed distant and echoey. He was in the middle of Psalm 23, when he realized that the words he was speaking were no longer English. It seemed like gibberish, until he heard himself say "Elohim," which he was sure he had heard before, but at that point, his rational mind was too far in the background to make sense of anything. Then his speech changed again, until the sounds coming out of his mouth were more like musical tones that seemed to vibrate every nerve in his body.

Suddenly, his head felt pleasantly empty and his chest pleasantly full. In the stillness and silence, he saw the three-sided pyramid again, hovering over its inverted reflection in the water. Then, he imagined that the pyramid was over his head and its inverted reflection was below his feet. Then, the two pyramids rotated about ninety degrees in opposite directions and started moving toward each other, the upper pyramid lowering and the upper pyramid rising, until the two became overlapped and perfectly centered in his chest. The musical tone became stronger; it seemed to touch everyone whom he had ever wronged or who had wronged him. His eyes began welling up. "What's happening?" he asked silently. The answer was immediate: "Your heart is singing."

His mind became quiet again. The tone expanded some more, touching places in this mind that he did not know existed. He saw an image of a dark-skinned man with long black hair tied back in a ponytail, who proclaimed, "I forgive the Brahmin. Their ignorance is my ignorance."

Finally, the tone surrounded a young man in a hospital bed. After that, all thoughts and images dissolved. The musical tone ushered in a stillness so deep it seemed to extend forever. The preacher sensed that he was poised between time and timelessness. It would have been frightening, but since he had experienced this sort of thing before, he just relaxed and enjoyed it.

—12—

Dr. Hauser sat next to Jason's lifeless body, her hands enfolding his left hand.

"Well, that's it," she sighed. Once again, she questioned why she was given the built-in alarm that allowed her to be at the patient's side so quickly, though she was helpless to do anything, except hold the patient's lifeless hand.

The cold feeling in her chest diminished and became replaced by a warm glow. She looked at his face and suddenly felt the serenity and freedom of simply allowing him to be as he was. For the first time in her professional career, she realized that holding the patient's hand in that manner was every bit as important as any life saving treatment, whether or not the patient recovered.

Her eyes welled up just a bit. Blinking back the tears, she smiled imperceptibly, feeling thankful for her built-in alarm. She almost chuckled when she imagined holding a child's hand and walking him across the street.

The cold feeling in her chest had become a warm glow. Taking a deep breath, she straightened her spine and started to let go of Jason's hand. But, her fingers wouldn't move.

She raised her head quickly and looked at the TV monitor over the bed. Nothing but horizontal lines. She calmly turned to the two attendants, who were removing the tubes and wires from Jason's body. "I'll take it from here, guys," she said. As the two men walked out, she quietly added, "Draw the curtain, please."

She tried to let go of Jason's hand again, but her fingers still did not want to move. She sensed that she could pry her hands away if she wanted to, but elected to hold her position. After about a minute, she thought she felt a mild tingling in her hands that seemed to originate from the warm glow she still felt in her chest. At first, she thought it was her imagination. When it became stronger, she instinctively closed her eyes.

Once again, she got the impression that she was holding a child's hand and walking him across the street. Only this time, they were walking in the other direction. Suddenly, Jason's hand felt like a flattened garden hose that had just filled with water. When she saw Jason's chest start to move, she willed herself to remain calm. When the EEG and EKG came to life and started making sounds, she still remained calm. When a nurse drew the curtain quickly to investigate, the doctor looked at her calmly. "He's fine," she whispered with a smile, politely signaling her to leave.

As the patient's eyelids started fluttering, Dr. Hauser's fingers spontaneously let go. Jason opened his eyes and saw the petite figure of Dr. Hauser, smiling at him through cheerful blue eyes.

"Well, hello, Jason. Had a nice nap?"

Jason looked around and then glanced at Dr. Hauser's name-badge. "I'm in a hospital."

"Correct. How are you feeling?"

"Fine."

She checked the monitor above the bed. The brain waves appeared to be within normal limits, though the delta wave activity seemed rather high for a wide-awake adult.

"What's all this stuff for?" asked Jason pointing to the tubes and wires attached to his body.

"We're just monitoring you. You were unconscious for over an hour. You were struck on the head by a two-by-four that fell from the roof of a two story building."

"Oh yeah, the Johnson house. I don't remember being hit on the head. The last thing I remember is that I was sitting on a crate. And suddenly, I got dizzy and the lights went out. But I feel good now."

Dr. Hauser felt his pulse and took note of the warmth of his skin and color around his fingernails.

"I had a bunch of weird dreams, though."

Experience had taught Dr. Hauser to pay attention when patients talked about their dreams. They often gave useful information about their condition. "Do you remember any of them?" she asked as she shined a penlight into Jason's eyes.

"Not really. Actually, I sort of remember one."

"Do you remember any details?"

"Well, I was living in some strange land. I was talking to this old man with a goofy smile. And I was married to a lady who sort of looked like my fiancée, Katie, except that she had dark skin."

"What do you suppose it means?" she asked, as she raised Jason's arm from the elbow to check his triceps reflex.

"Beats me."

"How's your head feeling?"

"Feels okay. I got this funny little pressure between my eyebrows, but otherwise, it doesn't hurt at all. My stomach is a little queasy, probably from those stale candy bars I ate. I need to stop eating so much junk. That's what Katie keeps telling me. She wants to go to medical school. Katie and my buddy, Sam, are stuck in traffic, but they'll be here soon…"

As Dr. Hauser listened to Jason's heart, she considered asking him how he knew that his two friends were stuck in traffic. However, Jason didn't seem to think anything of it, so she decided to just leave it alone for now. Putting her stethoscope in her pocket, she moved her fingertips lightly across Jason's head. She noticed that his scalp was emitting heat and an erratic field of energy. The last patient who showed such an eccentric pattern was getting ready to go psychotic. But this one was even more intense!

"Well," she said, "no bruising, no swelling, no sign of trauma at all. And all your vital signs are good." She glanced at the EEG again, which still showed unusual delta wave activity. "So, you feel nothing out of the ordinary?"

"Nothing. I guess I do feel a little spacey. Otherwise, I'm fine."

–13–

The preacher became aware that he was sitting on a park bench. He opened his eyes and noticed that his arms were spread out over his head, like two antennae. He pulled them down quickly. Looking around, he saw a few adults and small children watching him from across the street. He lowered his head and started playing with his fingernails.

He felt relieved when Sarah returned and sat next to him. She was holding two cups of ice cream.

"Raffi still hasn't figured out what's wrong with my car." She sat next to the preacher and gave him one of the cups.

"Thanks," he smiled.

They ate in silence for a while, just watching the traffic, like a couple of old friends.

"Well, Ma'am, now are you goin' to fill me in on what's really goin' on here?"

"No.'

"That's what I like, a straight answer."

"What I mean is, I don't understand this either. But, it's kind of fun, though obviously quite strange. And it helps to pass the time while my car is being fixed…hopefully being fixed."

They smiled into each other's eyes and then looked at the scenery.

"So," said Sarah, "tell me about yourself?"

"Well, I wouldn't know where to start," said the preacher. "Right now, I'm workin' at Mama Tang's Chinese Restaurant."

"You're kidding! You work at Mama Tang's?"

The preacher suddenly wished that he had a more important job.

"That is one of my favorite restaurants," said Sarah, almost placing her hand on his knee. "What days do you work there?"

"Tuesday through Saturday, noon to eleven. But, I've been a little out of sorts lately, so Mrs. Tang told me to take a few days off. Hardly a proper job for a preacher," he said, tugging at his jacket.

Sarah looked into his eyes. "I love the food at Mama Tang's. And Mrs. Tang is such a sweetie. Anyway, next time I'm there—" she stopped and looked across the street. "Raffi's waving to me. He's also throwing his arms in the air and shaking his head side to side. Darn," she grimaced. "He still doesn't know what's wrong. Anyway, I have to go and deal with this automotive mystery." She stood up. The preacher did likewise.

Suddenly Sarah stood very still, as if trying to hear something. She smiled, picked up the pen and writing pad from the bench, and quickly scribbled something. The preacher's heart began pounding.

"Here," she said, tearing out the paper.

He looked at it and was disappointed to see the word, *Bonnie,* and a phone number.

"What's this?"

"Bonnie is a nice old lady trying to hold a church together. I spoke to her a few days ago. They're having problems and I think you can help them."

"What sort of problems?"

"Just call her. If things work out, it's quite possible that Mrs. Tang will need new kitchen help."

The preacher frowned. A church job? No way! However, out of politeness to Sarah, he made a mental note to call Bonnie. "Thanks," he said, "I'll check it out."

She looked into the preacher's eyes and then quickly looked at her car across the street. "Well, I guess, I'll have to take my car to a transmission place for serious diagnosis."

"What's wrong with it?"

"The gears aren't shifting right. I have to really push the clutch hard to make it catch. And sometimes it doesn't catch at all and I can hear the gears grinding. Even I know that's not good."

They were silent for several seconds. Finally, she sighed and held out her hand. "Well, it's been a pleasure, Reverend."

"The pleasure was mine, Ma'am."

He watched as Sarah walked away. "Uh, Ma'am?"

Sarah turned quickly. "Yes?"

The preacher looked into her eyes. "Did you check the rug?"

"The rug?"

"The rug on the driver's side. It may have slid under the clutch. That would prevent the clutch from goin' all the way to the floor and keep the transmission from engagin'."

"Oh! But, I don't think that's it. I don't even think my car *has* a rug."

"Well… just a thought."

"Thanks, anyway." They stared at each other for two very long seconds, before Sarah smiled and waved goodbye.

Taking a deep breath, he sat down, looked at the piece of paper, and slipped it into his shirt pocket.

Placing his hands behind his head, he stretched out his legs and took in the scenery. Then he glanced down at the writing pad on the bench. He grimaced and closed his eyes. Picking up the pad and pen, he tightened his jaw and quickly began writing.

Dear Amos,

Again, I'm very sorry for the way I acted at the Christmas party. If I have to apologize another hundred times, I will. And now you hear this. You did not respond to my letter, and last week I called to make sure you got it, and your wife indicated that you no longer consider yourself to be my brother.

Amos, if you're still mad at me, I understand. What I did was disgraceful. But I will not listen to any foolishness about us not being brothers. We were both yanked out of the same belly, and that's all there is to it. Truth is I was mad at you, too. If you didn't want me there at Christmas, you should have said so instead of treating me like a stranger. Yes, I know that doesn't excuse my behavior, so, you can ignore me for as long as you like. I won't bother you anymore. You can contact me if and when you're ready.

Your Brother

Roy

Tearing the sheet from the pad, he reached in the bag and pulled out an envelope that was already addressed and stamped. Sealing it, he stood up, walked through a narrow gap in the juniper hedges, and dropped the letter in a mailbox.

On the way back, he noticed a young bearded monk sitting with his eyes closed under a tree, not too far from the bench. Had he been there all along? The preacher did a slight double take.

Back on the bench, he sat back and closed his eyes, interlocking his fingers around the back of his head. Hearing muffled footsteps on the grass, he opened his eyes just in time to see Sarah come into view from beyond the rhododendrons.

His heart started racing. She sat next to him, looking rather astonished. "How did you know?" she asked.

"Just a hunch."

"There I was, getting ready to have the transmission replaced, and it was just the rug. Raffi is still laughing his head off. Look at him." They looked across the street where Raffi was laughingly conversing with another mechanic.

"Thank you so much, Roy."

"You're quite welcome, Seva - I mean, Sarah!"

Sarah laughed. "Maybe that name has special significance for you." Sarah looked at her watch. "It's one thirty already. I'm starved. Have you had lunch yet?"

"No, just ice cream," the preacher smiled casually, as fireworks went off inside his chest.

"May I buy you lunch? It'll be my way of thanking for my car."

He wasn't hungry, but that was irrelevant. "Sure. Thank you."

"How about Mama Tang's?"

"Sounds good to me."

They stood and walked away, talking about Mama Tang's excellent sesame noodles. The preacher did another double take as they walked by the young monk, who was still sitting under the tree, with his eyes closed.

—14—

Smiley popped the last kernel of popcorn his mouth. Chewing on it thoughtfully, he watched the screen, as Sarah and the preacher walked past Brother Jerry. The scene faded.

"Now I get it! I think." He pointed at the screen, which lit up again and now showed the pyramid of four stars hovering over its own reflection on a still body of water.

"Yes?"

"The pyramid on top of the water is obviously you four guys."

"Yes."

"And the pyramid's reflection in the water is…"

"Brother Jerry, Katie, Sarah, and the preacher."

Smiley nodded. "Symmetry, again!"

"Yes. In this case, it means that the activity in the heavenly realm is reflected in the material world."

"Obviously, Brother Jerry and company were doing some high powered reflecting," said Smiley.

Brother Jerry appeared on the screen, again. Smiley waved to him. "Good job, Bro. Thanks a lot."

Brother Jerry remained motionless with his eyes closed, except for a fleeting whisper of a smile.

"There's one more thing I'm curious about," said Smiley. I understand the connection between me and my friends," he said, pointing to the screen. "But, what about you four guys…"

"You mean, what's in it for us?"

"Yes."

"Well, quite simply, you are helping us in the same manner that we are helping you. You see, my companions and I reside in a realm comparable to this theater. In other words, the edge of time. However, it is what we might call the 'outer edge.' We have been waiting for an appropriate signal to initiate our full transition into the next realm. You provided us with that signal."

Smiley nodded. "More symmetry!" He looked at the screen, which now showed Sam walking quickly through a hospital corridor.

Smiley felt his thoughts starting to melt. "You know, in just a little while," he beamed to Brother G, without bothering to use the formality of speech, "all this information is going to be irrelevant. Why am I learning all this."

"For Jason's benefit," said brother G, silently. "He will eventually remember this in a way that is meaningful to him."

Smiley smiled inwardly. Of course. Everything he was experiencing was actually happening inside Jason's head… for a little while longer, anyway.

They looked up at the screen as Sam rushed into the ICU, where Jason was standing next to the bed, chatting happily with the doctor. Sam ran into Jason, and both of them fell on the bed.

–15–

"Whoa mule!" Jason cried. "What is wrong with you? Get off me."

They stood up, as Dr. Hauser chuckled.

"You're alive!" said Sam, grabbing his shoulders and shaking him.

"Yeah, I'm alive," said Jason. "Now calm down. The doctor will think we're a couple of homos."

"God," said Sam, "the way you looked when the ambulance took you away, I thought for sure that you were dead. I swear you looked like a corpse. And now you're standing here like nothing happened."

"Well, sorry for sending you on a wild goose case."

"Yeah," Sam laughed, giving Jason a shove, "don't let it happen again."

"Oh," said Jason, "Doctor Hauser, this is Sam. Sam, Dr. Hauser."

"Hello, Doctor. I apologize for barging in here and tackling your patient. So, what happened to him?"

"At this point, your guess is as good as mine."

"So, you have no idea why—" Sam stopped abruptly, as Katie flew into the cubical and grabbed Jason's arms.

"Jason, honey, you're okay?"

"Yeah. Totally."

She turned frantically to the doctor. "He's okay?"

"Apparently."

Katie embraced Jason, spun him around, and they both fell on the bed.

"Yes, I'm really, really, okay," said Jason in a muffled voice, as Katie continued to hug and kiss him.

Dr. Hauser laughed quietly.

"Hey, you two," said Sam, "get a room."

Finally, Katie let go of Jason and they stood up. "Are you going to take x-rays or a CT scan?" she asked Dr. Hauser, catching her breath.

The doctor watched as the energy field around Jason's head continued to settle. "Maybe. Maybe not. We'll see."

"Yeah, I feel fine. I feel really, really fine. So, let's just calm down. Katie, didn't you say you had a big test this afternoon?"

"It was postponed till Monday. One of my classmates called me at Mama Tang's and said there was a flood in the lab. So now I have all weekend to study."

"Lucky you," Jason nodded. "Oh, and that reminds me. I was telling Dr.. Hauser here just before you two roared in here and attacked me, when I first woke up, I had the strangest urge. And the more I think about it, the more appealing it is. In fact, I think I've pretty much made up my mind. I'm going to college!"

"My God," said Katie. "A miracle!"

"Doctor," Sam laughed, "are you sure he's okay?"

"Why is that so strange?" Dr.. Hauser smiled.

"Well, it was never something that ever appealed to me before," said Jason, "even though you two guys have been nagging me about it." He turned to the doctor. "Anyway, can I go home now?"

"Well," said Dr.. Hauser, as she watched the energy field around Jason's head, "you did get conked on the head, and you *were* unconscious for about an hour. I suggest you move to one of the rooms and rest for a few hours. I'll be back around five. If nothing shows up, you can go on home."

"Good. I don't want to miss the softball tournaments tomorrow."

<h1 style="text-align:center">–16–</h1>

In the darkened theater, Smiley glowed with contentment. No longer feeling the need to see the rest of the movie in a linear fashion, he savored the wholeness of Jason's life, cherishing it as a precious and complete experience.

The screen faded to violet. Then, it became totally white.

The popcorn bucket was empty. His body was becoming increasingly translucent and luminescent, transforming into one continuous seamless garment that looked less and less like Jason Mazarosky. The theater was gradually dissolving around him.

The beginning and end of Smiley's existence slowly merged, like a great serpent reaching for its own tail. All his thoughts and memories continued melting and fusing, gathered into a tiny sphere, which he fancied to be a seed, because it immediately began germinating into a lotus of a thousand petals. His perception of the physical beings on Earth morphed into a multidimensional awareness that vibrated with deep reverence. As he savored the sacredness of linear time, his sense of time became progressively more non-linear.

As the new awareness continued blossoming, he became dimly aware that 'Smiley' was nested within a larger presence. Slowly and gently, that larger presence became more tangible. And, more familiar.

He turned to Brother G, who was becoming more luminous, as well. He also looked more feminine. Smiley felt the need to say goodbye to him/her. However, as Smiley's body continued to become more luminous, saying goodbye seemed less relevant. Nonetheless, as long as time had any meaning to him, completion was appropriate.

He savored the sweet dance between the part of him that needed to say good-bye and the emerging presence that had no such need. Gradually, his awareness of himself as 'Smiley' became a precious and complete experience.

Smiley silently said goodbye; just as the emerging presence said hello.

–17–

Jason sat on the bed, now in a regular hospital room, chatting with the nurse who was taking his blood pressure.

"Yeah," said Jason, "the pressure between my eyebrows is totally gone now."

Around the bed was a small crowd, including Aunt Maureen, Uncle Max, and Rusty. Lisa, the cashier at the lumberyard was talking to Sam, next to the window.

"Yes, actually, I do like softball," said Lisa.

"Well, if you're not doing anything tomorrow, come watch us play."

"Sure, that sounds like fun."

There was a quiet knock on the partially opened door. They all looked up and saw Brother Jerry's smiling face peeking in from the other side.

"Is it okay to come in?" he asked.

"Sure," said Jason. "Join the party. Just don't grab me, okay?"

The group laughed.

"I promise," said Brother Jerry, as he walked in.